JUDITH LINDBERGH's work has appeared in *Archaeology* magazine and in connection with the Smithsonian exhibition *Vikings: The North Atlantic Saga*. *The Thrall's Tale* is her first novel.

Chosen as a Book Sense Pick
Selected for Borders Original Voices

"Every once in a while, a writer creates a novel that opens our eyes to a lost world. Arthur Golden achieved this with *Memoirs of a Geisha*, and now Judith Lindbergh has performed a similar feat in her re-creation of the risky, arduous Viking settlement of Greenland. Gripping and wholly original, in *The Thrall's Tale* Lindbergh places her prodigious research in the service of a story that transports through time and place, but always remains anchored in the unchanging territory of the human heart."

—Geraldine Brooks, author of *Year of Wonders* and *March*

"*The Thrall's Tale* is an epic of the first degree. Historical fiction at its best not only evokes and enlightens a time long-lost but engages the reader via a flesh-and-blood story. Lindbergh has done that and more. With a mother vs. daughter theme, murder, revenge, a heartbreaking love affair, and a heroine reminiscent of Celie from *The Color Purple* but singularly her author's own creation, *The Thrall's Tale* defines the genre."

—*The Philadelphia Inquirer*

"*The Thrall's Tale* is not only a wonderfully rich historical novel, it resonates strongly in our current age with its exploration of religion-driven cultures in collision. The voices of the story are pitch-perfectly convincing, and tenth-century Greenland is evoked with absorbing vividness. Judith Lindbergh is a greatly gifted novelist and she has created an enchanted and provocative reading experience."

—Robert Olen Butler, winner of the 1993 Pulitzer Prize for Fiction

"Lindbergh has done something bold. She has co-opted the archetypal 'male' tale—the story of a warrior—and made it feminine . . . A portrait of the whole human race in adolescence. On these desolate plains, surrounded by cruelty, humans somehow learned to embrace forgiveness."

—*San Francisco Chronicle*

"Lindbergh is a master storyteller, deftly weaving meticulously re-searched detail with unforgettable characters. This novel satisfies on every level—an escape to a faraway time when the Vikings settled in Greenland and the gods still walked the earth—and a gripping tale of magic, lust, deception, retribution, and love. . . . The plot unfolds with the suspense of a thriller, and you'll stay up all night to follow the many transformations of Katla's life. With *The Thrall's Tale*, Judith Lindbergh emerges as one of the finest historical novelists in recent years."

—Jonis Agee, author of *The Weight of Dreams*

"[An] epic debut . . . Well-researched and emotional evocations of characters in a time of religious and social upheaval are dramatic and entertaining."

—*Publishers Weekly*

"A deeply imaginative and moving tale of a young slave who fights for her life and freedom while voyaging to, and settling on, the south-western shores of Greenland."

—Gretel Ehrlich, author of
This Cold Heaven: Seven Seasons in Greenland

"Thoroughly researched and beautifully executed. Highly recom-mended."

—*Library Journal*

JUDITH LINDBERGH

The Thrall's Tale

A PLUME BOOK

PLUME
Published by Penguin Group
Penguin Group (USA) Inc., 375 Hudson Street, New York, New York 10014, U.S.A. • Penguin
Group (Canada), 90 Eglinton Avenue East, Suite 700, Toronto, Ontario, Canada M4P 2Y3
(a division of Pearson Penguin Canada Inc.) • Penguin Books Ltd., 80 Strand, London
WC2R 0RL, England • Penguin Ireland, 25 St. Stephen's Green, Dublin 2, Ireland (a division
of Penguin Books Ltd.) • Penguin Group (Australia), 250 Camberwell Road, Camberwell,
Victoria 3124, Australia (a division of Pearson Australia Group Pty. Ltd.) • Penguin Books
India Pvt. Ltd., 11 Community Centre, Panchsheel Park, New Delhi – 110 017, India •
Penguin Books (NZ), cnr Airborne and Rosedale Roads, Albany, Auckland 1310, New Zealand
(a division of Pearson New Zealand Ltd.) • Penguin Books (South Africa) (Pty.) Ltd.,
24 Sturdee Avenue, Rosebank, Johannesburg 2196, South Africa

Penguin Books Ltd., Registered Offices: 80 Strand, London WC2R 0RL, England

Published by Plume, a member of Penguin Group (USA) Inc. Previously published in a Viking
edition.

First Plume Printing, January 2007
10 9 8 7 6 5 4 3

Urnes-style brooch and runes illustration by Laura Hartman Maestro
Map by Jeffrey L. Ward

ⓟ REGISTERED TRADEMARK—MARCA REGISTRADA

The Library of Congress has catalogued the Viking edition as follows:

Lindbergh, Judith.
The Thrall's Tale/Judith Lindbergh.
p. cm.
ISBN 0-670-03464-9 (hc.)
ISBN 978-0-452-28817-1 (pbk.)
1. Greenland—Fiction. 2. Middle Ages—Fiction. 3. Women slaves—Fiction. I. Title
PS3612.I5327T48 2006
813'.6—dc22   2005042410

Printed in the United States of America
Set in Aldus
Original hardcover design by Francesca Belanger

To Chip,
for the courage to take the first step
and every one since.

CONTENTS

AUTHOR'S NOTE

The reader will notice that many character names in *The Thrall's Tale* begin with a similar prefix, "Thor-" or "Tor-." This core prefix, denoting kinship with the thunder-god of the Old Norse pantheon, was so common during the Viking Age, it sometimes began every name in a single family. I have retained this confusing element, wishing to remain true to those figures I have borrowed from the original sagas. In order to differentiate them to some extent, I have alternated the spellings between the historically accurate "Thor-" and the more modern "Tor-."

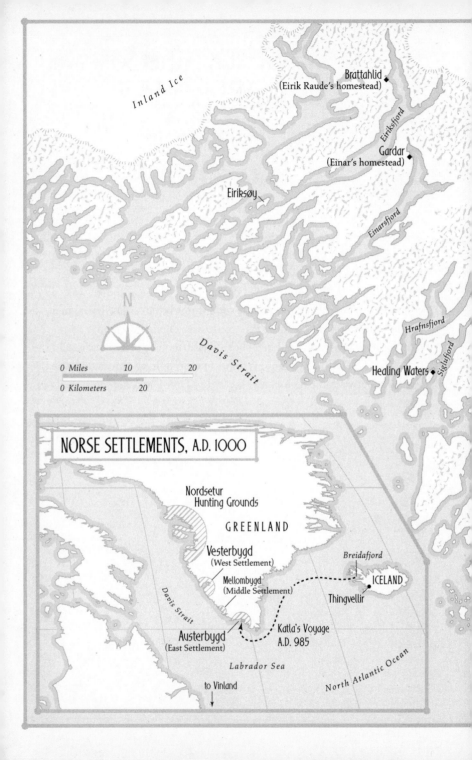

Inland Ice

Brattahlid
(Eirik Raude's homestead)

Eiriksfjord

Gardar
(Einar's homestead)

Eiriksøy

Einarsfjord

N

Davis Strait

Hrafnsfjord

Siglufjord

Healing Waters

0 Miles   10   20

0 Kilometers   20

NORSE SETTLEMENTS, A.D. 1000

Nordsetur
Hunting Grounds

GREENLAND

Vesterbygd
(West Settlement)

Breidafjord

Mellombygd
(Middle Settlement)

ICELAND

Thingvellir

Davis Strait

Austerbygd
(East Settlement)

Katla's Voyage
A.D. 985

Labrador Sea

North Atlantic Ocean

to Vinland

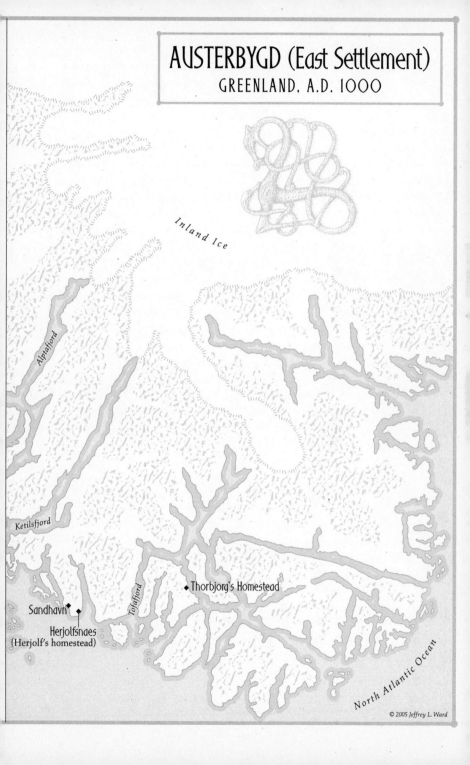

AUSTERBYGD (East Settlement)
GREENLAND, A.D. 1000

Inland Ice

Alptafjord

Ketilsfjord

Tofafjord

◆ Thorbjorg's Homestead

Sandhavn◆ ◆

Herjolfsnaes
(Herjolf's homestead)

North Atlantic Ocean

© 2005 Jeffrey L. Ward

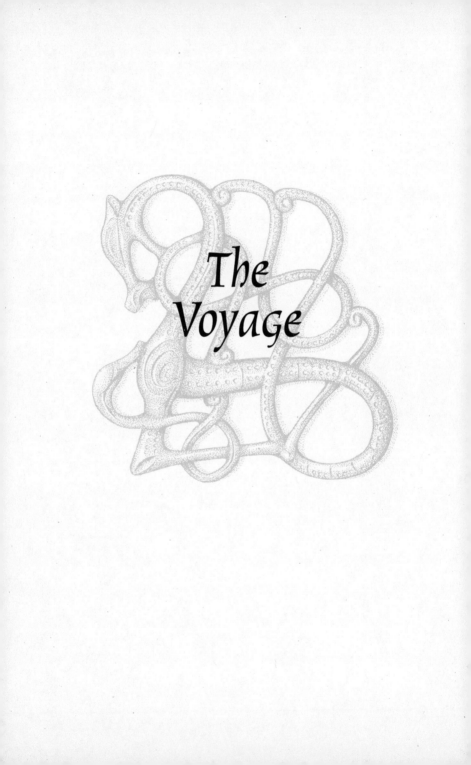

The
Voyage

KATLA

EINAR OWNS ME, the runes at my collarbone speak from the carved stone, smooth with wear. The amulet belonged to another before me, another thrall whose name is lost. They don't remember even how she died, only that she did about the time that I was born.

At my birth I was named for the fire burning beneath the mountain's ice, "Katla," and the string was tied, and so I have ever worn it. I have always been a slave.

Then why the unfamiliar sorrow that I am leaving the only land I've ever known, this land of my bondage? Yet I gaze about me almost mournfully as my master, Einar, stands upon the shore, tall among the circle of chieftains, setting the last of the plans before we see this place no more. The only one taller is Eirik Raude himself, his flaming head bright beside the others' mostly gray. It is he who planned this voyage to the great land to the west, beyond the open sea.

Serving at my master's banquet table two years ago at Yule, I heard Eirik tell of its lush pastures and its deep fjords brimming with walrus, seals, and birds. "So broad and vast and rich, friend Einar," he said. "Think on it! Think, if you dare, to come. Already there's a fjord named for you. I've set it so myself—Einarsfjord!—all flush and green, the fairest farm save perhaps my own—and set beside mine, with naught between our mighty homesteads but a pasture thick with grass and moss so fresh, sprouting up to make your cows' milk sweet and your sheep fat enough to slaughter even before the springtime's melted snows."

"You say 'tis such . . . ?" I saw my master raise a grizzled brow.

"Well, to think on it. There's naught so fine about this Iceland now. Thick it is with homesteads, and only the lowliest grounds left upon the ashen hills—barely enough to feed our sheep, yet quick run thick with blood and feud if others have first claimed it. Your talk is tempting, Eirik, almost too fair to be believed."

"Yet you know me well, Einar."

"That, old friend, I do. I would not cross you in a fight, or when you're hard at drinking. Yet I'll tell you, you are mostly honest, if hard-tempered. For this, I'll think upon your offer and speak of it with my mistress, Grima. Yet what shall I tell her is the name of this new place?"

"Ah . . ." Eirik Raude full-smiled then, his teeth rough-chipped, yellowish some, and broken in his ruddy beard. "Greenland," slowly Eirik Raude did muse.

"Greenland." And the sound of it, so thick and fresh and hopeful on my master's tongue. So, and now, many months long past, we are set about to go.

I wait with the other thralls in a line before the plank. Einar's hefty trader's ship keens chorus with the other knarrs: twenty-five in all, each with bright-painted shields of wood and clanking metal hung upon their low-slung rails, and outstretched, dripping oars. Each is set to be captained by another master: Hafgrim, Herjolf, Ketil, Hrafn, even Helgi Thorbrandsson among their lot, all powerful here in Iceland once, but pushed out by hunger, vengeance, greed. They and all their households, their wives and sons, daughters and married kindred, and all their thralls, like me, packed to go to sea.

Such a crowd. All about are bondsmen's scalps—bald pates, shaved and shining as this morning's springish dew—while we bonded women wear our best and only sheath of wadmal cloth, gray and drab and of a sweaty woolen, with a flaxen kerchief tied around our brows and braids. Nay, we look yet all the same, all dull and soiled, reeking, worn threadbare upon our elbows, while the freemen and their ladies nearly dance upon the Breidafjord rocks, flaunting all their finest, thickest woolens, their boots of fur and leather, their cloaks of seal, reindeer skins, and sometimes even bear with claws, all cheered and tucked and warm, set about to face the sea's fierce chill.

The knarrs rock to and fro, jolted by each foot stepping cautiously from plank to deck. Beneath, the fjord's waters brew up darkly. Barely I raise my chin above my bundle—small and coarse, it holds all that I possess. I clutch it tightly to my bosom. My heart pounds against it. Already, my skin is cold.

We crowd of thralls are thrust about. Upon a shouting, "Off!" we are pressed to let a horse, heavy-laid with bundles, pass. It steps upon the planking board, which sags, groaning loudly.

"Oh, 'twill break!" sudden the other thralls quick-whisper. "Or sink the ship!" "Nay, I'll not ride upon it." "Nor step—not another foot aboard."

The master's thrall's-watch hears us. He comes, heavy with his step, a seal's-gut cord twined about his fingers. "Hush you—all of you! Or upon your backs will fall our fate, as swift and ill as the whim of the weaving Norns."

The fateful Norns—three weaving ladies. So we're told they weave even upon the Norse gods' fate. Old One-Eyed Odin, Frey and Freya, Frigga, Thor, and even Loki fear them! I like it not to think upon them now, upon this coast, before this swaying board.

Yet the foreman's words hush up the rest. The horse passes from the planking, settling in the hull of our master's ship. More they load the knarrs, ever tighter with cattle, boxes, trunks, bags of meal and seed, packets of skin, and coiled rope. Around me, braying goats and sheep soil bundles we packed just last night or many weeks before, while the sea laps still and hungrily upon our clamor.

From the first, there had been talk of dread upon this trip— thralls' talk, mostly—all fired up and wary. Grumbles, grunts, and reluctant groans from those who feared to stay or those to go. Well we knew Einar could not take us all. He would choose, and many terrored they'd be sold away. They trembled at their fate, looked about askance, plotted some, and planned and fretted mostly. I think I alone did not wonder much, for I knew where my mother went I would surely be.

And she would be with Einar. She had been his favorite—even until the day she died.

So, last spring, as I chored upon the hill watching old ships in the fjord raised up and repaired and fresh logs hewn to build new knarrs, I began with some excitement—and much unexpected dread—to realize we would truly leave this Iceland. Some say life is always better far away, where a slave might be freed if he proved his worth, or at least free to do somewhat more as he pleased; but I say life here is all I know. What lies ahead I cannot see.

With last autumn, the real preparations began, the storing and packing of grain, and drying of fish, and brewing mead, and catching fresh water from rains and streams in barrels lined with tar, and weaning lambs, and slaughtering sheep too old or sick to cross the ocean with us. And the selling of goods. I held the rag to catch my mistress' tears over her chest of heavy oak with its sturdy iron lock, from which she removed her fine-wrought linens and gauzy silks brought from afar, and tapestries stitched by her grandmother's hands, and other such treasures from her folk all long past, to be sorted, and many forsaken.

For me, there was cloth, too, to be woven for the sails. Had I known how hard and long and tedious the task, I might have thought to run away, but by the time I knew it, we were well into winter. There was nowhere to stray. Through the long nights and the cold, short days, we worked before the standing looms, weaving, ever weaving, until our arms ached, and our feet and our backs, and we could barely lift the threads. But at last the sails grew wide and strong. Just with springtime they were completed. We did not dye them as we might a Viking's sails, for these were not for raiding or battles, unless to win this foreign shore. But it is said there will be no one to conquer. Where we go there are no people, only ruins of campfires and strange tooled bones. Still, some speak of draugs in the night, dead walkers who would lure us to the mountain and madness or worse. So much I fear I will be dragged away that once, in a fit of terror, I begged my master if it were true. But Einar promised, upon his soul, Eirik Raude had seen none.

As the ship's builders set the mast secure and strung the rigging aloft, to the harbor we went, me, Inga, and Groa, with the tight-bound roll of cloth resting on our hips. There the strongest men set the sheet upon the yard and raised it up—"Pull! And pull!"—blinding white in the noonday sun. It rippled until they rigged it sharp, then flooded full with the wind's breath. We watched the new ship bound from the harbor toward the fjord's mouth. In a moment it was out of sight. From where we stood, we could see no farther than the hill where the homestead lay.

Now I stand before that very ship, with only the narrow plank to tie it still to shore, foreign though it is, as my mother always told me, though now she's gone, buried beneath a shallow mound of earth, with a stone upon her feet to hold her still, and I am alone, with before me only the great black water and what lies unseen beyond.

On such a trip my mother once sailed, though with even less hope than I, for it was then she was enslaved. So she'd told me many times at night, whispering while the others about the slaves' hall slept, and she beside me in the straw, her warm, soft body pressing close to ease the cold, the painful tale of the place from which I'd come, a place I've never seen, a land whose air I will likely never breathe, yet of which she told me ever and again, until my thoughts and my heart call that place home.

They came along the Irish shore with the dawn, stealthy and silent in the mist. Only the smell of smoke through the house's thatching warned of them, and then the sound of clanking metal as the raiders took the town, hut by hut, farm by farm. My mother told how my father hid her in the filth of a pit beside their byre, from which she watched him bravely fight against these enemies with only his sharpened ax, and then, when they'd cut it quick, only with its broken stem. He was bold but could do nothing against their heavy Viking swords. They were so many, so large and cold and fierce, and he was alone.

When they split my father's skull, my mother said the Vikings laughed, spattering the grass with his honest blood, kicking his writhing body with their hard, thick boots. Her cries she could not quiet, and for this she blamed herself, for then they found her and wrenched her from the hole where she'd been safe. She showed with pride the scars from where she fought their rough hands as they dragged her through her own husband's blood, blood which stained her dress, a dress she kept even to her death, in which I saw her buried. From a molting satchel hidden in the corner of the servants' straw, I took the rag and dressed her in it myself, and my tears through my hands brought up my father's blood as if it ran anew.

That day the raiders bound my mother and all the others up in chains, but buried deep beneath her dress was her beloved's final gift. And so I came with her to slavery and to this land unborn.

They'd come then and taken us in a mist of silence, secret as death. But this day there is no need for stealth. This day we stand waiting to depart in a spray of these freemen's Viking songs.

Well, through the jostle, tone, and bustle, I look about for Inga, my one true friend, like a sister to me really, though somewhat older and of a different sort, all round and red, short and stout and quick to laughter, while I am mostly of a straight and somber sort, and sometimes, though I do not mean it wrongly, sour. Still, she is the dearest to me since a child, who has known my every secret and kept them ever still. Even now, though I am fully grown, I long to feel her somewhat safe beside me. Yet she is none about me now—only some way off— yes, there!—I see her—attending to our mistress Grima's youngest children. Torunn—she's the girl—and the boy, Torgrim—both sweet enough, and most well used to Inga's constant heeding. Yet now they are off, and Inga running in a flail of skirt and pebbles flying, hailing them with exasperated shouts, "Yea, Torgrim, get back! Torunn, you stay here. Torgrim, come ye back here!"

I would go myself to find him, for I run so much faster than Inga can. Yet I am barely from our line when I hear behind me, "Katla, think you 'tis your concern? Stay back where you belong." Nay, I know 'tis Hallgerd. Hallgerd, who finds her chore most fit to tell us all our rightful cares, though she is but a bonded slave herself. "He is Inga's charge," she jeers, "and well she knows just what to do. She'll do without you even better, for you know our mistress wants you not too close about her kin."

It is true, my mistress does not like me. Perhaps 'tis on my mother's 'count, yet I do not ask and dare not wonder. Instead, I stay within our line, for now it is moving slowly closer toward the shore. First we cross the last of moss and grasses, then upon the gravel's clack, then to stand before the creaking board—nay, it does but sway! And the waves leap up, sudden ranging higher from the deep, menacing there before my bundled feet as I take my final step from this Iceland shore. *A Dillard*

I am pressed ahead, first by Hallgerd, then by others. It is but quick across, then I stumble on the wide-berth knarr. Trembling still, I catch myself. Each body's weight tips the vessel ever deeper. The fjord's waters rise, hugging close the wooden boards as I try to sit where I am bidden, between the bundles, crates, the bags and chests, upon the rough and rocking floor. *Cumulative sent!*

Barely have I settled on a place when, down the beach, I sense a stranger watching. I know at once he is no slave. His stance wears a self-conscious grace, though his cloak is cloth, not leather, his cap soft wool, not pounded bronze. His look is fair and lean—a freeman, though a poor one, if I am any judge. Yet at me, his mouth is set agape, on his lips an almost speaking. His fingers reach as if to catch my own, sudden pressing through the throng. I draw back sharply, calling quick for Inga. Almost he is at our ship, but she is nowhere by. Yet, when he hears my voice, he bows his head and murmurs, "I am sorry," turning, shrinking fast away.

Strange, for he turns again several times, even as he tends his burdens, loaded up with sheep and goats and other goods in a wind-washed chest. Twice he has to thwart his goats upon the rut, and nearly loses a lamb with no one else close watching. He turns and smiles softly as I try to hide my laugh. Then he is gone, lost among the crowd.

Now, at last, comes Inga, breathless, up the plank. Her skirt is soiled and she is bent, fretting over poor Torunn. "Katla, take this Torgrim from me!" she begs, as Torunn retches over the side. "Nay," Inga coos, "Torunn, already? Even in this little waft of sea?"

Torgrim squirms within my grasp. "Katla, think you my father— will he send us off upon the deep alone?"

Einar still stands on the shore with the other chieftains, setting fires and sacrifices up to Odin and to Thor. "Nay," I hush him, "of course he'll not. He but prays to have us make the safest journey."

I press Torgrim close against my bosom, patting gently across his narrow back. Yet, after not too long, he wriggles quick away.

Escaping fast, he tries to climb the railing. "Father!" he shouts, setting out to leap just as the sacrificial flames set up to roar.

"Stay back!" I grasp him, falling hard across a pile of boxes. But Torgrim's close to me now, clinging, pulling some, yet starting up to shout, "Father, do not leave me!"

"Nay." I stroke his sun-bright crown, enduring the soggy damp of his tears soaking through my wadmal dress, and the breeze as it shifts and cuts now harsh across the shallow rail.

Another heavy step sets the vessel jostling: Einar himself, his broad shadow blocking the sun until he sees us, comes, bends, and pats his child's brow. "There, Torgrim, be proud and bold as a proper Viking. Now Thor's eye will watch our ship with favor. Hush you, so, and clutch upon our Katla. There, I know you like her well."

To me, he cups my chin within his hand. Then, at last, he turns upon the risen deck where his high-seat stands. The helmsman Audun waits, his hands clutched on the steering oar. Einar sets to wave and gives the master's call. Then the walking planks are swept swiftly up. With their sturdy oars, the rowing men push the ships from shore. The gravel scrapes. The water slogs. Stroke by stroke, the pyre's flames recede.

Slowly the shoreline empties of all who've come to wish our masters well. Around me, cries burst from freeborn women, mostly matrons pressing sodden rags against their softly shriveled jowls. Too, even whimpers slip out from the thralls. Yet my eyes are dry. I cannot cry for loss of what I leave or in terror of where I'll go. It is all the same to me, for I am slave to them in either. My life will be no different, only the dirt that will be my grave.

We push down the harbor, the ships cutting the fjord with lines of foam like a loom's taut webbing, the rowers' arms gleaming soon with sweat, slowly reddening in the sun. My mistress, Grima, standing lean and haughty on the deck, notices me at last and beckons to bring her Torgrim. With a foul look on me, Grima takes him back and props him on her lap, proud beneath the shade of the risen deck where her husband conducts the progress of the ship. Then she sends me off. I must stand now, for there is no place left to sit. All the thralls huddle where they may, in empty spots along the ship's cramped sides, or by the mast and yard, lying long and low within the hull beside the thick-furled sail. They are like a hefty pair of spindles, one twined around with threads, waiting only for the first brisk gust and the master's call to be raised up high. Yet for now we must bide with them as well.

A brace of wind cuts across the hull. Just beyond a mounded isle—there, behold the open sea! Though it is still far, the other ships fall into line beside us, and all let Eirik Raude's knarr take the lead.

There he stands upon his high deck, gesturing, calling orders we cannot hear. Eirik's figure's grand and fierce, his head and beard afire. They say he was always much the same—boisterous, unruly, outlawed in his younger days, first from Norway for killing in a temper, and then again from Iceland for doing much the same, which sent him adventuring to this place, this "Greenland," to which we all now follow, blind but for his flaming lead.

I look behind as each ship falls in line. Yet, as I do, feeling some and musing, I am caught again by that same freeman's watching. The ship—I think 'tis of Hafgrim's house—and there he sits upon the oars. His shirt's pressed back around his waist as he strokes in rhythm with the call. His is a bare, fine shape, and his deep-blue eyes are locked with mine—ah, they spark a frightening fire! Hot, I turn away and try to hide my burning cheeks. But when I look again, Hafgrim's ship is pulled upon the waves, tangled somewhere among the others, like small whorls dropped to weave the sea. assonance

Swift, we cross the fjord heading toward the open water. Soon the lift-and-falling makes me sudden ill. With each stretch we put between us and land, with each heaving of the men's great arms, my stomach quakes, jolting back while I am thrust forward. I put my hand upon my neck and lay my brow just upon the railing. The cool of the shield helps calm a bit, but, almost as the sickness fades, my mistress tumbles forward, thrusting Torgrim into my arms. Then we three together vomit into the waves.

I offer the child back as soon as she is recovered. Torgrim's weight is heavy, and my own arms, sudden weak. Yet the mistress simply stares at me with an edge of condemnation. I am a slave and so, I suppose, not allowed to sicken. Yet, Inga comes to me. "Here, poor dear!" she says as she takes Torgrim to her arms, wiping off the spittle from his lips. "There, I'll have him, mistress. You should go and rest, if it should please you."

Then Inga eyes me, "Hush!" and bids me, "Come."

"If only I might sit," I beg, "lay my head across my knees, or simply rest my limbs upon the deck."

Inga takes my hand and, with Torgrim in her arm, guides me gently to a place beneath the bow she's guarded quietly for me.

"Here." She holds a well-soaked rag. I squeeze what I can and drink, then Inga presses the dampness to my brow, all the while blocking the mistress' view with her own son's drowsing body. "If Mistress Grima knew, she would lash us thrice apiece that we should take their precious water before we've even left the home fjord," Inga hisses in a whisper, but with her touch she helps me calm.

Beyond the harbor rocks, Einar calls to raise the mast and then the sail. With its steady pull, at last I grow used to the rolling waves. The open water takes us. Inga helps me stand to see beyond the deck. There, the ocean, thick and black as an endless slab of obsidian, but fluid, cresting white to the very seam of the sky. I squeeze her hand and meet her emerald eyes perched above her freckled cheeks, but we hear again the mistress calling, "Inga!"

"Likely Torunn has to piss over the side." Inga rolls her eyes as she runs away to the mistress' shout. Yet I am almost well now, beginning to enjoy the waves. I thrust my face into the wind, so hard and fast my ears ache from it, but I do not care. I feel almost that I am flying.

Then a hand falls on my arm. I do not turn. I hear his voice. "So— is this lovely Freya standing here?"

I keep my eyes toward the sea. "You think it wise to match the goddess with a slave?"

With his thick, coarse hand, Einar's eldest son, Torvard, turns me roughly. "Katla, with name so hot, why are you so cold?"

He grips my chin with such a force I have to look at him: at his slack, grizzled cheeks and his weak, small mouth with its breath smelling thick and putrid. Torvard holds me, smiling. I am not sure what he wants, if he might bite my face or try to kiss me. He works his fleshy fingers harder and harder into my jaw.

"Torvard, come!" Einar shouts from the high-seat plank. "Leave the girl alone!"

My heart is pounding. Torvard glances toward his father, then groans and lets me go. But before he leaves, he raises up my amulet. " 'Einar owns me,' " he reads the runes with a vicious lilt. Then he whispers, "Remember, one day it will be me."

My face throbs in all the places he's touched me. I bend to the rail, feeling the cord choking at my neck. Against the metal of the closest shield I press my cheeks. Still I know they watch me, these others, as they always do: the thralls in condemnation, the young freemen with their blood between their legs, and the freeborn women in jealous rage at Torvard's lust for me. Every farmer's daughter to the very highest rank seems to strive to steal his attentions away; while I would gladly give them, gladly be rid of Torvard, with his foul breath and his rime of sweat and his stench of urine and mead. But he is the master's son. For a freewoman with ambitions, there could hardly be made a finer match. All the families know it. Yet what have they to fear from me? I am but a thrall, a reluctant toy for a man who is but a boy, filled with his new-grown strength and all too eager to shrug his father's binding fingers from his thickened neck.

He is but nineteen. He will not marry till he's twenty. In another year. How I wait for that day! Though I know well enough it will not save me. If Torvard willed, he could take me to his loins right here and now, and ever after, whether I wished to linger there or not. Only his father contends to protect me while he can, for my mother's sake; I know she begged it of him often. She knew, as Einar does too well, that Torvard is neither wise nor gentle nor loving, as he himself was to my mother.

With our lot it is all the worse to be pretty, and I am fair, fairer than I would choose. I am tall like my mother, and shapely, with her long copper hair that curls with the damp. Some have said I might rival even the fairest maids of the finest houses, if it weren't that I'm a thrall. But I do not know, having never really seen myself save in the mistress' own silver bowl, which, when I rub it hard until it shines, still shows me but a strange, distorted vision.

Just once, when we were sent to the water to help clean some fresh-caught fish—it was a clear, calm day then, with the sunlight bounding off the fjord's water. The stench was up to my elbows and down about my knees, and globs of pink flesh stuck to my dress when Inga laughed and bid me follow her to wash in a shallow pool. There I bent and would have dropped my hands in fast if Inga had not caught my wrist and held me, saying, "Look. That's why the others stare so cruelly when Torvard comes."

And I saw, only for an instant before the wind stirred the image, a face like those I thought only goddesses wore. Inga touched my cheek, and I knew she wiped away a tear, but then I smelled the fishy stench, and both of us laughed, thinking how silly such passion could be roused for a stinking fish-girl.

But since that time, I have tried to see that vision again clearly and for longer than before. Some have called me vain, but it is not so much that as curiosity, especially as the time has passed and daily Torvard troubles me more and more, until it seems even his father, Einar himself, is hard-pressed to keep him back. Torvard listens with far less care than Einar is due, simply because he was fostered by Eirik Raude.

Now there is none to Torvard so great as that man. Since his return to his father's stead three years ago, there has been no peace. Constantly they are fighting over how a man should be: Einar is moderate and calm in all his dealings, while his son seems to mimic his foster-father's airs, being wild and bawdy and headstrong, affecting whims in manner and dress. If he could dye his blond hair red he would, but happily he cannot. He is no Eirik Raude. Eirik, despite his wild temper, has wisdom, too, and a sense of righteous justice. The crimes of Eirik's youth were made to protect what was his, while Torvard's crimes, Einar fears, when they come, will be random and raging as the winds.

For that reason most, my mother tried to keep me safe, for it is not strange for a man to take a concubine. My mother was for Einar since the day he bought her at the Althing market; and well he treated her, as well as he might a slave; and even shed a tear when he learned last winter she was gone: dead with his child. Yet he knew she was never happy here. He'd always known, for my mother made no secret that she was not willingly a slave. Even in his arms, she said she never would allow him to forget she had once been free and always would be in her heart.

For her stubborn, still resolve, I think Einar most admired her. Often he told over the drinking horn the story of my birth, how proudly my mother dared defy him, giving me suck at her breast just at the moment he'd prepared to see me killed. If not for my mother's courage, I'd have lain exposed before the winds, to fend until death took me to Thor's palace, Bilskirnir, where all thralls of the Norsemen go, or to the gentle arms of the White Christ, of whom secretly my mother whispered. But my mother would not have it so. I was her husband's child, the last she would ever have of him. She would not live to see me slain by the same cruel fate as he. This last she told me many times late at night, and then would kiss my forehead and say her Christian prayer, "Kyrie Eleison. Christe Eleison." By the Al- thing's law, once I was given suck, Einar could not expose me. For that courage, he put me in her arms and said she could keep me. Mother always laughed in her telling then, saying that I howled out my lungs, which is why he named me Katla, for the mouth of the Norse's cold Hel.

Up till the day she died, he'd kept me safe and close, yet I can feel my mother's power waning. Her memory fades from Einar's thoughts like a shield that's begun to rust and crumble. Torvard's attempts since her death have grown bolder, while my master, consumed with plans for these new lands, pays less and less heed.

Now it seems only Inga stands by me. All the other thralls sit in wait and judge. I feel their eyes even now, as I sink down to the deck to rest my head against the planking of the bow. I gaze straight into their condemning looks. On this long trip, there will be no place to hide, so I will face them. We all do what we must. My mother did, and for me also. She gave her body so I might not give mine. For her I will protect what she has saved, even if it means they hate me and say I gad about as if a chieftain's daughter. How can they understand? They don't even remember from which land they came.

I am glad there are some new faces aboard: men mostly, broad-backed, with thick woolly beards and eyes as sharp as the sky, clear in their faces which are ruddy as if burned by the sun's distant fire. Some of their women already have cracked their chests' heavy locks to fetch a blanket or toy to keep a child from climbing the rail or up the mast. My master, Einar, is unused to such traveling companions, though in these past years he has traveled less about. Of late, he's been more farmer and husbandman of sheep than a Viking doing battle on foreign shores. Yet I've heard prideful talk at table of those days of raids and plunder and conquest and brave men now all gone to Valhalla. Often I would see my mother wince at his honor in such tales. Still, I know he does not fancy these softer days.

Nor does Torvard, who has yet to see such fight. Even now he anxiously flings his knife into the thick mast-pole. Forthwith, my master scolds him, "Beside this mast, only Odin's humor and Thor's strength will carry us again to land," and sharply withdraws the blade, angrily dulling it with his whetstone. Then he hands both back. "Here. Hone this, and keep your ire at bay."

I want to laugh, for Torvard is an angry fool, but, fearing he might see me, I bite my cheeks.

The ship bobs in the current as wind fills up the sail and sweeps us farther and farther from the home fjord. Audun, at the steering oar, charges the men still to work the oars to breach the rocks beneath the keel. Their stroking slaps barely sound in the heavy surf. Far in the distance, the land we leave is but a thinning line of gray.

There is one other on this ship, one I dare not cross or catch with an eye or even pass. From where I sit, she is far across the deck, but still I draw back in fear, and I see the others do so also. Even on this crowded boat we leave a wide circle of air around her, for it is said she knows the gods, that they twist her tongue and make her speak and whatever words she tells always come true. They call her Thorbjorg the Seeress, and say she comes alone, with no husband, no children, and none she leaves behind, with only her sheep and cattle and a handful of thralls and a chest full of gold got from the invisible ones she caters in their earthen mounds.

For some long while, she has lived upon a distant spit, far, but not yet far enough, from Einar's homestead. Well I've known but, grateful, never ventured, hearing oft of her evil eye, her evil hand, her evil foot. It is said that wherever she steps trips death, that her nights are filled with shrieking, that, where'er she goes, she mutters softly on the shadows' murk and sometimes spits and seethes upon her seeing.

'Twas one such sight, all weird about, on which she called a plague to sweep nearly all the farms at Arnarstapi. And the people there—those few who lived—in a rising rage burned Thorbjorg's household to the ground. It is said her stead was razed before, in Norway long ago, upon a famine's fate. Hard, she fled from there to Iceland—first to Herjolf Bardsson's farm, then, after this last plague's burning, to my master Einar's place. Though my master never speaks such things; and sometimes Mistress Grima feeds her, sending provisions from our own short stocks. 'Twas ever other thralls who bore them, trudging up the fell-slopes and across the glacier's ashen fields, then returning, breathing hot with running terror, bearing back in shaking hands stinking, greenish ointments the seeress said would heal.

From the first, when it was rumored she would come aboard this ship, all the thralls in the house and in the fields clutched hard their amulets, put fresh herbs in their hair and pockets, spat in their shoes as they put them off for bed; but these things did not keep the woman from our deck. Our only comfort is that the others of her household do not sail with us. They are broken up among the other knarrs, for it was thought unwise to shelter all beneath one sail, dangerous all together on the same thin boards. Better to spread such dubious power about and lessen its potent for harm. Yet now their mistress sits far at the rear, beside Audun, and I swear her lips are sparked with cants, and I see that her hands are moving—perhaps over a stick of secret runes.

At last, Einar calls the oars withdrawn. They set the sail at its tautest rig. The other ships pull close or pass us by, filling the sea as a sailing crowd. Great white billows puff up full and catch the wind. In the distance, I watch until the last of the land is gone, and only water, sky, and cloud and our ships fill my vision.

And then I breathe, not "I am leaving," but "I have gone."

THORBJORG

THERE ARE WORDS for what I am—for what, Odin, you have made me. Seeress, yes, but something other. One day, in another speech, another time, they would call me "witch." Yet they would not understand the subtle nature of this thing I am, or the difference between grace and malice, between words for harm and words for good.

I am the voice of a thousand, thousand seasons. I am Odin's tongue. When he grasps me up, then thrusts me down, I must submit. I must comply.

Such words as I utter forth are not my own.

Twice they burned my household for it. Once in the mountain house in Norway, where I and my nine sisters shared one board. So many years ago. All were seeresses. All but I consumed by flames. And I was, nearly. See, Old One-Eye? Upon my legs, the scars remain.

Then a second night, more nearly dear. My husband and all our children burned. Our homestead in Iceland's just a char. Their graves I will never witness. I have shed my tears. They are long since wasted. Yet I go on, as e'er I must. The sores upon my legs well sealed, but the fire within them lingers.

'Twas thanks to my servant Kol and his Finn's magic. Thanks, if thanks be given to live one more day with so much pain. Yet he pulled me from the flames, hid me well beneath a bull's-skin blanket, fed me meat and mead, and now, here, I am. Upon this ship. These rocking boards.

Silence, still. The sound of my own thoughts. Wafts enough to calm the winds which blow across these beams and rigging.

This ship will go where none can reach me. At least, not for a breath. For a time. Yet it will not last. Ever it will start again: they will come, ever with their fawn and pleading. Pleasant for a little, they will bend before me. And I will speak. I am ever meant to serve. But then, when such words I am forced to form turn against their wanting, they will come with fire or with sword, or perhaps some other cutting thing.

KATLA

AT DUSK, while we set the night tents, I see the man again. As I turn from unrolling the tarps, he is standing just near the railing on Hafgrim's ship. The knarr passes slowly. His eyes are soft and somehow hold me. . . . Even now there's gentleness in his stare.

Inga touches my arm. "What's wrong?" she begs me.

I tell her, "Nothing. It is the wind."

As we lie down to sleep, again I look, but the man is gone. Some others, though, are still about: sailors, their shouts muffled beside the ocean's washing as they pull the rig to true the knarr, always beneath the swath of stars which shines with a milky glow. My master calls it Bifröst and says its light makes ever clear the footpath of the gods and that, just beyond it, One-Eyed Odin watches from his throne, Hlidskjalf. Yet I sense only our navigator, Halldor, lifting up his bearing dial to mark the bright polestar. And below him, the seeress Thorbjorg— for it seems she does not sleep—still sitting in her vacant niche, her eyes wide and fingers moving while her lips shape endless words without a sound.

I am restless, yet in time a kind of sleep does conquer, till suddenly a raindrop falls, startling me awake. Forgetting where I am, I nearly topple toward the railing, then catch myself and see dawn's come, ill with ominous clouds.

Suddenly there's a frightful rippling. The men about the deck strain hard upon the rig, holding taut the billowed sail, while my master calls, "Oarsmen, add your stroke!" Even Torvard lends his hand, bearing muscles sharp to drag on ropes. They bark commands, sending us to lash the sleeping tent. We must run about, pressing children and freewomen deep beneath, then cattle close, and finally all the goods tightly inside. We thralls are left to find whatever place we can. Some cling to the sea-dashed sides of the slivered rail. I huddle in a corner, barely beneath the cloth, but it matters little. In a moment, none are dry and none are safe. The gods tear back the heavens and pour their wrath upon the sea.

Great bolts of lightning break and fall as sharp-honed spears, hurling hailstones down to tear at the tenting cloth. They clatter on the shields we hold high to protect our skulls. The sailors dash about, wearing battle helmets as they man the rig or bend their backs to bail the knarr.

The hull fills quick and the waves crash high. Soon we all are bailing—freemen, women, even children with their fathers' drinking horns or their mothers' cooking bowls. Torunn beside me wails woefully that we'll all be drowned, but her mother slaps her, sharp, upon the mouth. "And where would you run from such a fate? Don't add your feeble water to what already falls." Torunn picks up her cup and continues meekly, though I see the slap does not much to quell her tears.

Then, almost as quick as it began, the storm abates. For a time, there is but gray and murk, then the heavy mists are sudden cleaved. Great, glowing beams of light pierce like the daggers of the Valkyries, Odin's war-maids. High above, they parade in brilliant regalia, glee'd upon the mock of us they've made, while our men shed their helmets and shake their storm-tossed beards, leaning, weary, on the sodden rails.

All that day grows calm and fine. The winds blow light, so light we seem to sail upon great Odin's murmur. With the late-come dusk, hopeful mounds appear at the west sky. I nudge Inga—"Look!"—but Torvard's near and hears us. Laughing, he wraps us about with his meaty arms.

"Can you say you were afraid this dawn? Ah, that was but a squall! And those peaks there? They're not land at all but ice."

Ice. Ice like mountains. Even the great ones I'd seen from Breidafjord far off were never so many, so close, so huge, rising out of the water like great giants' backs. Hunched and laboring, they loom ever nearer through the night, and with the dawn, all the water around us is cluttered with them. Thick and small, some white, dull green, or brilliant, glowing blue. With each hour's distance they seem to grow as children before our eyes, playing against the hull, ever learning meaner tricks, until we crackle our way through a solid film.

Torvard leans over the rail with the other men, trammeling the brittle crust beyond the prow with oars. They can barely cut a path while, in the distance, a great blue whale blithely slaps its tail at the rigid sea.

Audun says we are not halfway there.

This morning two ships turn their paths. One's hull is cut so thin by sea-ice, it dares not weather another slice; and sudden winds have breached the other's sail.

Einar draws our ship close to Eirik's to share this news. Just so, we receive word that the squall, as Torvard calls it, has wasted our water barrels. There's little left to drink. We are sent to gather water from the night-drawn awning, but the morning's dew's already dry. Then, these several hours, there is no rain.

The sun beats chill but brightly, though the wind is weak and does not move. Soon Eirik orders all the ships to put out oars and row.

I think, for an instant as the oarsmen bare their backs, of my stranger-man, the one whose gentle looking I have tried hard to brush aside, though still he holds my thoughts oftener than he ought. Nay, I am in no place to begin to dream. Dream of what? I am a fool! What would he want of me—a thrall? That I can answer without doubt: well, but that he'd use me for what I'm worth and hate me for it and hurl me off when he was finished. Never would he think to love me as my mother said my father had loved her. I have seen it so with others. It is said that for a thrall to dream of love is to dream of pain. Still, I cannot keep my eyes from drifting when another knarr draws near.

For several hours, I see naught of Hafgrim's vessel. Sudden I am gripped with wonder—his might be one that's turned about. I think to go to Einar. Surely he will know. Without a breath, I set to ask, but I see Einar's just gone off in a smaller skiff to Eirik's ship, leaving Torvard at the helm. At once I turn away, for I loathe him more than ever with this secret in my heart. Yet already Torvard's seen me, smiling roguishly from the high-seat. His gloat, as if a hand, commands me near.

"Katla?" he cajoles. "Katla, yes. You want something of me? Never have you wanted such before. Ah, but your face is fretful. You wear a bitter frown. On such a lovely, wind-calm day? Perhaps you fear you'll have to row? Ah, fear not, unless my men grow weary—and then I'm still unsure which woman I am fondest to see bare-breasted at the oars."

"I would not row, even if you asked." I've seen this mood before and know he means to tease me.

"What? You are too fine?"

"Nay! Too weak and would set the knarr in circles."

"All by yourself?" Torvard laughs. Today he seems grand-hearted, so I dare to speak, lightly as I may, "Which of the other masters' ships have turned home?"

"Why?" he asks. "Have you some friend upon their decks?"

Startled, I feel my cheeks aglow. "Torvard," I try, "how might I have a friend? I know no one except the thralls who labor under Einar's watching."

"And me? Say you, am I not your friend?" His hand reaches out and catches me about my waist.

I slap him back, then realize what I've done. Einar is nowhere near.

The others, both settler and slave, have seen the slap and now gape crudely. Even Torvard's mother: Grima's face is stern, expectant, as if she would be pleased to see me turned upon in ire.

Torvard's big, hard hand rises to his cheek. My heart is pounding in my ears. But then he laughs. "The girl is quick, that's for certain! And weak, she says? As weak as the giantess Skadi! You could whip Odin's very steed into action with your palm!"

Then he pulls me down upon his knee and bounces me as if I would ride him. I scramble from his grasp, but he holds me fast to force a kiss. His coarse whiskers burn my lips and scratch my cheeks. At last he lets me go. The whole ship is laughing. I turn, wipe his spittle from my mouth, and rub it hard upon the cloth about my knees.

"A proud one!" taunts Torvard's bosom friend and foster-brother, Lodin. "Too good for Torvard's kisses! And this one's but a slave!"

"She'll take what she can get from me and find herself wanting more one day!" Torvard reaches again, but I escape him, dashing through bundles, animals, and men. Though nowhere can I hide from their mocking glances. I find myself at the very prow, where none do stand for fear of the witch Thorbjorg.

With a start, I edge from her, too, but her eyes are upon me. I dare a moment's look. No ridicule mars her lucid gaze. Her hands still move as they always do, but, for the first, I see she is merely sewing—a fine white embroidery stitch on a field of red. Behind me, I hear them still, but their mirth is settling slowly, so I take a place—close, but not beside her—and watch her make the tiny stitches with her aging hands.

THORBJORG

THEIR LAUGHTER. It is a strange, distant recoil, yet it draws me back, brings me from my musing. There, to the bright, hard light, the rocking chaos of this ship. Its crew. These men and women. Thralls.

Thralls. This one. I had not seen her. So young and fair. She ventures close, seeming ill with fear, but not from me. The others eye her, almost with a sneering. She sits. I would not stop her. I set upon my stitch and sense she watches close my hands.

Too well I know what is said of me. Too well, but what is told is merely what can be perceived. Truth needs no words to speak. So I let her watch and wonder. Hard to believe I am a woman, too? Crooked, yes, but not so unlike the rest?

Her eyes are calmer now, almost grateful, as I twine my stitch. Simple thoughts, simple deeds, a thread upon a needle. Not the Norns' thick bind with its ever-brittle muster, but a strand of flax I had spun into a coil myself.

Myself, long ago. I was young and simple, knitted fair, yet fragile for a fall, having ne'er yet felt the waft of Odin's breathing or tripped upon Yggdrasil's roots. So very long ago, yet still I can remember when first I stood beneath that tree, three streams beside me, ever flowing, ever whispering, one for strength, one for wisdom, one for fate. Upon this young girl's eyes, the same rough passion: that callow, certain boldness which knows not what the future holds.

Strange, for a thrall. From her look, not yet dull or beaten. But frightened. About the decking: Einar's son Torvard—his cheek is hot. No good will come of it. I need no special vision; I see it clearly written in her eyes.

What would I tell her? That we are all but bits of flesh, insubstantial as the glaciers? Though they tower up and ever seem to groan, still they move and stretch and melt and crack and die. But I will not speak it. She would not know how to understand. So I let her sit and watch, asking of me nothing. My presence is enough to fright' away the rest. I will lend it. What little that I can.

Shrieking fulmars flit about the rigging in the blinding glare of sail before the sun. But the din about has quieted some. Those others have gone on to other dealings. At last the girl rises, takes a step, then flees across the deck, looking not at me. I do not blame her. I turn my eyes and gaze again at the subtle turnings of the sea.

KATLA

MORE DAYS PASS of this calm, almost balmy weather. While the row-ing men burn their backs before wind and sun, we women bend to milk the goats or spin up wool or other chores. I set about and soon have spun some fine, thick, sturdy skeins, though the other bonded women eye me ruefully. Seems they'd planned a scheme to dodge their chores, and now bemoan, soft-breathed aloud, upon my industry.

So the mornings go. Then, of a sudden, we wake to see the sky bleeds red. Strange it is and horrid. Waves froth up, hurling chunks of biting ice against the knarr's frail sides. We cling to the rails, weak and fumbling with bare shook sleep, sick with rocking decks, empty with unsated hunger, battered and blurry-eyed with salt and spray.

'Tis a storm far worse, 'tis true, than the meager first. Babies scream for their mothers, and I long to join their strident wails. With a crack, Thor heaves his thunderbolts, striking fine and surely the mast of a near-borne ship. It bursts aflame. In the torrent we cannot see at first who burns, only that they fell the timber quick and douse it, leav-ing them without hope for wind.

Across the clashing waves, I look with pity and see, clear as a sign, the figure of my young man with the gentle heart. Nay, he's there, and on the forlorn vessel. My voice sticks in my throat, though still some sound searches for my tongue—a helpless whimper, not for my life but his, unknown though it is. 'Tis foolish, wanting so. Yet I am reaching across the rail for his hand, which I have never touched. I stretch to dive into the waves, but Inga grabs me. She slaps me hard and puts a bucket in my clutch.

"Katla, come! Grasp your wits about and help to bail!"

Heartsick, I begin. The sea is to our knees and rising faster than we can toss it back. Each wave crashes with ease above the bulwarks. Then a slow yawn—a crack! The posts which hold our sleeping tent collapse. Screams come shrilly from beneath. Hands press against the cloth. We dive and tear it open where we can, using knives and spears and sticks and tips of horns. Through the riven sheath, those caught beneath emerge bloodied, scrambling. But two are caught, too long tangled in the sea goddess Ran's thick net: a little boy born of a free-woman, and the daughter of a slave—both drowned or trampled, huddled still within each other's arms.

Shivering from terror, we turn again to bail. The other knarrs spike and dive. Ofttimes we feel we sail alone. Or have we ourselves already sunk beneath the water's surface, but not yet reached cruel Ran's abode? Some men squeeze small bits of gold to bribe the greedy ocean mistress—but none reaches the hands of any thralls.

Then I notice, all at once, Thorbjorg.

For the first time she is standing, still and tall even against the rolling deck. Her arms outstretch. Her eyes are wide. Water strikes, yet she remains unyielding. With one hand, she clings to the shaking mast with its tattered sail, while the other bears a bit of twig—a mere limb of rowan wood torn from a broken bough. 'Tis such stuff as never grows in Iceland, and somehow precious. So it must be, for, as she bears it out, at its tip a crystal flashes tiny shards of great Thor's mighty flame.

It is then I clutch my mother's well-worn beads—such wooden things she called a rosary. I know not what they mean or do, only that in times of fright she prayed upon them fretful, whispering words to her strange god Christ, "*Spiritui Sancto. . . . Sancte Domine.*" Nay, never once would she even tell what these should mean, for she said, in this foreign land, such words were better lost. Yet now, as I think upon their phrases—strange—the sea does calm.

A sudden stillness fills the air, and with it a heavy mist falls down like a thick hung shroud. We look about us, wary, for we cannot see beyond the watery circle round our knarr. Only Einar dares to call, "Hafgrim! Herjolf! Eirik!" Of the others, we hear naught and dare not ask, for the sounds along the edges of the hull might be scraping ice or broken boards of a ruined ship, but seem most like the rough-ripped nails of the wretched, fate-bound Norns.

Within this spate of calm, we give cruel Ran her due: our lost souls' bodies over the rail and, with each, praises sung out loudly for the goddess who will greet them. But our hands are quick, our homage hasty. It is unwise to sail long among the dead.

Still the old seeress stands, her arms outstretched though shaking slightly with the weight of them. Her runestick with its crystal drinks the last of light. So she stays until the dawn, which comes up with bare shadows. The mist some clears, and we see at last where we have lain: within a field of bergs, sharpened teeth in a craggy mouth, with no stretch of passage anywhere about. How many of our number still remain we cannot count for the bedraggle and the dim. Einar orders the oarsmen, "Work the craft now, gentle, steady. . . ." We move ahead, creeping about the icy bounds.

Of a sudden, there's a shout—"An open strait!"—from the mast-man.

"Heigh-ho!" And we lurch forward. I grab the rail, peering once behind at the lair we have near escaped. 'Tis like an ice-giant's palace, all blue and dripping, towering up and cold. Then I see, half sunk in nipping mist, another knarr trapped about the ice-hall's corner, there, and its company stranded on a frigid slab.

I cry out, but my master does not hear above the sucking oars, the creaking mast, the flapping sail. Stroke by stroke, we gallop farther. I know I must stop them. I must save them or be cursed and blamed and banished for the sinking wreck.

Above me, Lodin dangles among the rigging strands. Farther back, beneath the sail, Torvard chimes his father's commands from bow to stern. Trembling, I reach for Lodin's hand. He glares as if to strike me, but I stand firmly, pointing back. Then Lodin sees, drops his binds and shouts to Torvard, who bellows to catch my master's ear.

So swiftly the ship turns round, I lose my grip and nearly fall. The others are stunned and fright'ed all about that Einar's turning proves some madness. Yet, as we race closer, even the cringing freewomen begin to see. Mistress Grima sends us scrambling about the deck, making room where'er we can, loading already tight-pressed crates higher, one upon the next. With a splash, two skiffs are launched, and jolt about through the cluttered sea. Then we pause to gaze upon this shelf of sea-ice. Standing there are only twelve, mostly men but some seem women. One holds the body of a child in her arms.

They come aboard, tendering shivering hands from dripping, ice-torn sleeves. Their looks are chilled, weary-eyed beneath wet wool. Their captain's last to set his foot upon our anxious boards, and I see the long, bedraggled face of Hafgrim.

It is Hafgrim! I search the stares but cannot see beyond these ice-caked hoods. We are sent for clothing. Sodden mops are all we find, but they're better than what little remains of theirs.

I bend among the strangers, offering blankets, bread, and what calming words I can, when one hand grips me, wan and white and shaking slightly on my wrist. I know it is my gentle man. He holds me for an instant, his grip too weak, his face contorted, almost fright-ful with its need. When I meet his eye, it is as if the ice itself has been ignited. Yet he draws back. I must pass again among the stranger crowd.

The oarsmen row us free. Beyond our icy haven, we find more ships which have withstood the storm. But six are gone. Missing. Sunk. We do not know. Of them, we never do hear more.

Through the dank dawn, the strangers tell their tale: all their goods, all their provisions lost, all they've packed, all their livestock drowned, but this is not the worst. One woman breaks, "My chil-dren!" in a horrid wail, "Oh, my sweet children!" Mistress Grima, standing near, holds the woman to her heart, and while she sobs, all are quiet, watching and afraid.

"By Thor's good," Hafgrim breathes after a time, "you saw us, Einar, and saved us."

Lodin says, "It was Katla. Katla saw you on the berg."

"Katla?" Einar smiles and comes to me. He hugs me heartily. "You serve your master well. To Katla!" he toasts. "And to Thor! May he make for you a fine place in Bilskirnir!"

Bilskirnir—Thor's hall for honored slaves.

Einar pours the mead to warm away the edge of death. I take my sip, for to me the horn is given first. Then the hunched figure at my side takes up the drink.

"Katla," he whispers, staring now with some new pain. He sips and passes the horn along.

THORBJORG

MY ARMS are weak, Odin. How long must I bear them up? Yet I can bear them long enough, for their strength does come from you.

From you to me, Old One-Eye. To pass among these others. Drip' and crying, still so little calm, even as the waters spread into a smoother surface. I walk among them, saying nothing. I would lend a hand, but most shrink back and look away. So I withdraw; I would not act cruelly. Already I have given what I can.

I take my place just beyond their shivered circle, feeling the twig you made me cut so long ago. Scarred with runes upon the rowan wood. Knife lines drawn as if in blood. At each fair stroke, I fumble and I whisper. The words I speak, my little, helpless whimpers—what might are these before the strength of chaos, tossing us about as if some driftwood on the shoals?

Chaos. Nay, the giants of the frost, the gods' most ancient rivals. Even you yourself, Old Graybeard, are bent to heave with them and die. On the battleground at Ragnarok, where the drool of Fenris-Wolf is loosed to drink in your own blood, and Jormungand, the Midgard serpent, wraps around your son's great muscled arms three times. Nay, pinned down, even Thor cannot fight forever, nor for very long before the final darkness falls.

Why, then, should any mortal life be different? Why, though we may cry and scream and grip these rails? We all will die. Even now the Midgard serpent writhes beneath us. Circling the whole wide world in patient wait. In stealth he's silent, certain when to strike and how.

There's the fear in it. There's the terror. Oh, such a need—to live—and such a fragile prospect! All the same, I cannot bear to bide in wait, but twist my breath to try to calm.

I spell my little chants. My hands do shake. They are grown feeble, gnarled in their infirmity, made to suffer such mighty burdens, such cruelties, all such godly whims. All about are dark and shadows, the just-made dead rising up or sinking down. Beneath the surface: it is a cold, dark place to perish. Still I will not yield, not till death itself does stop my fingers' quake. So, to render order in the world.

KATLA

ALL THE DAY and night, as we lope under the power of the oars, he sleeps. I tend him as I'm told, with blankets and, when he wakes, with mead. But otherwise I keep away. I am a thrall. He knows it now and comes not near and says no words, even when I press some porridge to his lips. His eyes at once warm and condemn me. My dreams, which had seemed almost real, are dashed as if in this cruel, grinding sea.

Soon Hafgrim and some others of his crew stumble about. Their legs are weak, but their spirits, rousing quickly. My master guides Hafgrim to the captain's deck, bragging of Audun's skill to outwit the storm. But I know, as well as any, it is Thorbjorg who has seen us through—Thorbjorg, with her arms outstretched like a winged Valkyrie. Now she stitches on a corner of the tattered sail, heeded by none but—I tender—watching all.

By next evening's fall, there is singing on the deck. Some of Hafgrim's household know their music well. I am sent to fetch the lyre from my master's chest. Its wood and strings are damp, but we cut fresh strands from a horse's mane to repair it, and then we do our best. The tunes are rough, the singing buoyant. My gentle man—I must not call him that anymore—still, as I pass about the mead, he leans against the angled railing, huddled beneath his cloak and heeding not the drinking or the song. As I make my way, once or twice he shivers. His breath comes hard and sometimes quite rattles, even above the clamor of the crowd.

Against my own heart's wisdom, I find myself before him. I hand him down the full mead-horn. He reaches up, but his arm drops sharply, spilling the precious drink. Before my master sees, I bend to mop it up. The man's lips tremble, as blue as they were when first he stepped aboard.

Shy, I feel his brow, and there is fever. He closes his eyes and takes my hand to pleasure in its sudden cold. Then I know I must go away at once, running through the crowd in search of Hallgerd, for she is somewhat wise with herbs and healing. I find her stumbling, drunk already. Yet, with a huff and a crooked look, she deigns to follow.

Shaking away her stupor, she glares into the stranger's eyes, then opens his mouth with a force to smell his breath.

"Ah, 'tis foul! And his hands are icy. His forehead burns. Look, see how his eyes are glassy and weak." All this she tells me word by word, as she is wont to do every time I've ever seen her treat the ill. She'll speak her observations to any who are near, as if she wished them noted down in runes. But she knows not runes or special chants or many prayers. She knows but little, yet more than all the rest.

"What is wrong?" I ask.

"He has drunk far too much mead."

"He's had none! I passed the mead myself."

"Well, then, he's caught the evil eye." And once around him she trips a circle, then twice, times three, finally spewing a gob of spit behind his back.

"Now rest. He'll sleep." She gives me a soaking mat of muddled herbs from her storm-drenched pouch. "Go, make the man a drink. The bitterer the better. The more the bite, the more it will do good."

I do as she orders, bringing him some water to wash it down, then make him a pallet of soft, damp clothes and cloaks, and even a sack of seed to rest his head.

All that night I sit and watch him. I doze in spurts, waked often by his groans. Once or twice, he cries aloud, "Rannveig!" My heart beats hard, for Rannveig is a woman's name, yet, when I lean, he mumbles, senseless in his sleep. I try to feed him drink and meal. He takes it calmly, falling asleep against my breast. I mop his brow and rock him as a baby, but with morning he's grown only still more pale.

"I said to feed him the drink by the quarters of the moon's pass," Hallgerd comes at once and begins to shout.

"I did just as you said."

"I saw you sleeping! You did leave the man to die."

"I tended him properly. I barely closed my eyes."

"Then why does he tremble so? His skin's grown damp and colder. See how blankly he looks? He doesn't even know our words. Nay, now look, he strips off his cloak. Will you let him raise it? Go now, fetch it, Katla, before he throws it overboard!"

I reach for the mantle and gather it back around his neck, but then he laces off his shirt and jerkin. It is brisk about; I am shivering myself. His eyes, 'tis true, are glazed and distant, and his lips murmur words none of us can tell.

"If he dies, Katla, it will be your fault."

"If you saw me sleep, Hallgerd, then why not come and wake me, or feed the drink yourself?"

In fury, Hallgerd shouts full breath to Einar's ear, "Master, your woman Katla kills this man!"

"Master, I do not!" I cry. "What was I to do, Hallgerd? I have not your wisdom. . . ."

"Hallgerd's wisdom's false." It is Thorbjorg's voice, the first any here has heard her speak. "Is this how you always shield your fault?" Her voice is rich and porous; I had thought it would be raw. She rises, holding tautly to the rail. No wind or wave could still her step, yet as she nears, she masks a limp with her cautious pacing.

"Your potion is too potent, Hallgerd. It caused the stupor but did no good to heal. Just as well the girl did not feed him more. If she had, he might have died."

Thorbjorg proffers up a pot of steaming herbs. She pushes past Hallgerd and begs me kneel beside her. All grow still about the deck as she begins to work her skill. Soon come words, slight chants, which, in time, rise and chime aloud. She begs the Norse gods, each and all, for healing hands, raising her own high to the clouded sky so her sleeves slip back, showing ancient, rippled arms. Nay, she drops them down, laying one slim finger, wretched, sharp as a wind-raw bone, and scrapes upon the sick man's brow a single rune.

"Now," Thorbjorg cries, "Alfather, see! And, Redbeard, look! Come! Part the clouds and blow a breeze!" Then she reaches for the brew which is in my hands. I pass it, shaking, daring not to spill. In her eyes, her look is almost pleased.

Other prayers come after, ones I fathom even less, though I sit many hours as I'm bidden, aiding as the seeress needs. She bows and chants, fingering her runestick now and ever with its tiny crystal. When the man stirs, she motions me to bring him food and water and a sip of mead. I place the bowl of moist meal into her hoary fingers, then the ladle, then the horn. She takes them each and feeds him with surprising ease, lifting his whole back against the rail, where I had struggled just to raise his crown.

When night returns, he sleeps between us—for warmth, Thorbjorg says, lying at his back and setting me before his heaving chest. I sleep but little, for his breath is in my hair and he whispers once or twice again the woman's name, "Rannveig."

Yet, as morning dawns, the man beside me wakes. He mumbles, "Katla . . ."

"Yes?" My heart is pounding as I feel his brow.

"Ossur," he says. His voice is low and full of breath.

"Ossur?"

"Ossur"—he takes my hand—"is . . . my name."

I smile at him. I cannot help myself and brush his cold palm lightly. "Ossur." It seems again, perhaps, he has been saved for me.

Just past the noon, far to the west, a jagged line breaks above the waves. Little more than a rigid spine, but it is earth enough to prompt great cheers. The low boat rocks with sudden, wild celebration. Ossur

and I watch from our perch, a corner high away from the rowdy crowd
and shielded from the wind, and warm as the sunlight leans toward
the distant shore.

Inga comes and sees him better. Snaebjorn, her somewhat sweet-
heart, is standing at her side. As they bound off to dance, Inga's rusty
braid bouncing round the ring, Ossur asks me softly if I would join
them. I shake my head and touch his hand.

Yet, when I lift my eyes again, Torvard stands above us. His thick
form throws a veil before the sun. "Your charge seems stronger, Katla.
Perhaps you have some healing skill?"

"Torvard, you know as well as I who has done this work."

"Still, you seem to like the chore. Better even than to dance?"

At once I shake my head at his outstretched offer.

"But you are so fine a dancer," Torvard coaxes, "and I know you
like it well. Come, you must show our guest."

"Torvard, I . . ."

Ossur murmurs, "Go. I will be fine here," smiling slightly as he
releases me. I look for pity but he does not seem to understand.

Torvard raises me to my feet, and I clatter down the deck, for his
footsteps do not wait for mine. In the dancing circle, Inga is laughing
with Snaebjorn and holding tightly little Torunn's hand, and my master and his mistress dangle Torgrim between them, and even the chieftain Hafgrim dances, breathing hard and quickly heated from death's
chill, while Torvard's meaty fingers crush my hand.

He drags me round the romping. At the knarr's center are heaped
high goods and goats and meal and sheep, and atop the pile the sailors
sing with what instruments they find. Even those who have none
bang the rail or their fists against rough boxes, or whip lengths of rope
to make a terrifying whir. I try as I can to catch Ossur's glance, but
each way I turn, Torvard yanks me back, smiling with his crooked
teeth while anger burns behind his eyes.

Such anger I've seen in him before—well I remember some years
ago, when he returned from his fostering—only for a visit, yet he'd
come to catch a pauper's hand upon his father's calf, and in a rage
killed both man and beast. How he seethed and spat, savagely hurling

bits of the calf's flesh while the poor man's hungry frame writhed and bloodied the nearby stones.

The memory strikes me cold.

Einar paid the wergeld—blood price—for Torvard was thought then just a boy, though his boy's rage was worse by far than any full-grown man's. And now his fingers wrap about my own.

I dance as light a step as I may. The jig is quick. The singers' pitches crack the icy air. When, at last, the music quiets, the dancers fall. A sunlit mist of pant and perspiration drifts away. Still I stand, because Torvard's hand is all about mine and squeezing hard.

With his free palm, he wipes some sweat from beside my eye.

"Don't forget," he whispers, "who you are and what will be." He takes me by the chin and kisses me so hard I pull back and touch my lips to see if they do bleed.

Laughing, Torvard strides away toward the captain's deck. I watch him mount the angled stair. He keeps me always in his sight, even as he reaches for the bearing dial from Halldor's hand. Against the sun he sets it roughly, as if this act would make him chief. Yet, when Halldor gently offers to set it well, Torvard boasts out loudly, "I know the way!" Then he looks down at Ossur, then at me. His glare beats as if angled sharply at my cheek.

By the next dawn, we are rounding cliffs, high, steep, and thick with ice, stone-studded like fingers through a tattered glove. Sullen glaciers reach our way. What land we see is anything but green. Yet Eirik Raude leads us forward with aplomb, his own ship first, we after with patched sails aloft, some others under oar. Fifteen ships remain of the twenty-five that left from Iceland's coast. So many lost along the way, their spirits hang in the dew that chills our waking lids. I lean against the rail, grateful for the crowded ship and light of day. Alone or in the dark, one cannot guess what the dead might do.

Around this blue tip of ice, they say, a greener land must lie. Eirik Raude would not dare deceive his chieftains. I press my nose to the wind, sniffing for a whiff of freshness. I open my mouth. Sudden someone stands beside.

It is Ossur. I shut my lips. "If you could," he laughs, "you would eat the land, if only to stay upon it. I think you do not like the sea."

"I like it better when it does not wash on all sides."

"And I prefer a fjord to the sea. Deep and narrow and thick with fish and seals. I was a hunter and herder in our homeland, though now I pray for game alone, since all my stock is drowned."

"I'm sure someone will lend some calves and lambs for you to start again. Perhaps Einar—my master is a generous man—"

"Hafgrim and some others have already taken what there is to spare. I heard their talk. Their bond is deeper than my own."

"Surely he will find you one or two. Ossur, you need only a healthy ewe to breed."

He smiles wryly. "Katla, for a slave your talk is bold."

"You must go to ask him, or I could for you—"

"No!" He grasps my arm.

With a sudden, foolish breath, I have stepped beyond my bounds. I bend my glance toward the rocking deck, examining Ossur's feet in their rough calfskin sheathing, stained with salt and damp with spray.

"Your boots," I plead, "they're so worn. Let me mend them. Their seams are split, and the laces rotted from the deep." I take him by the arm. "It's a wonder you are well at all with your feet so damp and cold."

I press him to sit while I rummage through a chest of our mistress' leathers. Finding a fine, thin length of sinew, I begin to strip new lacings with a knife. All the while, Ossur watches, his glance like hearth fire, so hot my cheeks flame rosy. At last I take from Ossur's foot a wasted shoe. Then I notice Hallgerd's bended glare.

"Those are the mistress' skins!" she says. "Did she give her leave? They are the last we have. Dare you take them without permission?"

"Hallgerd," I try to calm her, "there are plenty in the chest."

"But see you any green upon those hills? Is there anything but ice and rock? Do you see a single beast on those cliffs to skin? Perhaps a bird's pelt will suit to shield your back, but not mine. If we reach this shore at all—the seas so thick with ice, we could wreck and need those very laces to secure the mast."

"Hallgerd, hush! It's unwise to say such things. The sea-grim spirits will hear you." I scold her harshly, but then speak calm: "Yet, if in the meantime these strands keep this man from ill and cold, won't they be better used than lying in this chest?"

Hallgerd seethes. "Just because you are your mother's child . . . Your mother was the master's favorite, true, but you do not serve him as she did, and seem too proud to do such bidding for his son. Perhaps you have an eye to choose your men. . . ."

Her daggers sting my heart and taint sweet Ossur's ear. I clench my fists around my work to keep from tearing at Hallgerd's eyeballs. I search for some retort but can only find, "Woman, say not another word—"

Then my master, Einar, calls, "Katla? Hallgerd, what is this?" His steps are heavy down the creaking stair. "Come, now, both of you, what fuss? What can be worth tarnishing this hour? Come and look."

He takes us both about the waist and leads us up the master's stair to the very high-seat's arm. From there, indeed, we see fjords cut deep and, in the distance, a verdant coast above the brighter sea. Islands and shores ripple thick with seals set to breeding, and overhead birds squawk and dive among the shoals for fish swimming beneath the jade-green waters in great schools.

Eirik Raude had not misled us. The truth is all he'd promised— this land, fair and greener even than the one we'd known. Hallgerd at last is silent with the sight, and, below us, the other thralls and freemen stare. Ossur, too, presses his bare palms to the rail. Torvard is not far, but his father's arm about my side is strong, safe as a father's grasp.

If only my mother could have lived to see this land.

Hope

p1,
Women's
uncanny
6 sense?

THORBJORG

SUCH A PLACE! I scan about the hollow distance, the ice-scraped flesh
bleeding frozen tears. These about me do not see it. They shout or
stare; yet, in all their hopeful noise or silence, they do not know
what lies there, hidden. The skull wears but a fragile skin, and beneath
is something other, something dearer, something older than the gods
themselves.

It is said that this earth is made of the giant Ymir's corpse, that,
when he fell at the Norse gods' hands, his spine decayed to mountain
ranges. Stones and pebbles once had been his toes. The other giants
fled defeat unto the farthest reaches, yet, within the crags and shadows, still the invisibles remain. Shakespeare's Tempest?

Older than the tree Yggdrasil, beyond rock and ice and soil and
mound, beneath, within, these spirits lie and wait. Is it these I seek,
Alfather? These whose pleasure I must make, whom I must trick with
humble thoughts and bare a tinge of fear, to bargain and appease if we
should tarry in this land?

Great One-Eyed Odin, guide me, for I know these dark ones'
thoughts and they are not kind. Long have they suffered here alone,
with the winds biting cold, beating on their bosoms. And now I feel
they watch us. Their breaths, heavy, slowed from endless sleep—watch
us as we come on blithely, as if boldness itself could claim this place,
with our strong gods at our helm and mighty oaths and plans and
dragon ships blazing shields, reflecting fire.

Mere hollow reflection. And our gods, weak gods of our own weak fate. Immortal? No. Not even you, Alfather. Transient, ephemeral. Even as the wind that blows our hair.

They listen now to our oars' slaps splashing. They watch their trespassed waters washing back. Trickling in. And wait, as they have waited throughout time, for the present to meet the past. And what will happen then has yet to bear a name.

KATLA

WE SKIRT so many islands, then rush into the mouth of a wide fjord. Ahead, Eirik Raude leans over his knarr's rough railing. With a grunt, he hurls the heavy posts of his high-seat overboard—wooden beams carved with shapes of Thor subduing the Midgard serpent. They are fierce when flying, even as they spin and fall. First they splash, then bob upon the waves beyond us, as all our host raise up one voice, "Lead us onward, Thor! To our new home, and ever in your sight!" Where these shafts should beach, Eirik will make his homestead, someplace along this wide and sloping stretch—Eiriksfjord—already it bears his name.

"No greener place in all this Greenland!" He shouts it loudly, and well, it is his right. 'Twas he who'd come, exiled and alone, to sight and set his claim upon these coasts. Yet, to quell a tide of the other chieftains' grumblings, Eirik, boasting, reassures, "Within three days' stretch from here, there are near as splendid lands all up and down this shore!"

"There had best be," calls Hafgrim from my master's ship, "for all I've lost upon this venture!" From the other knarrs more chieftains answer also.

"Trust me! Trust! I swear upon great Odin's boundless wisdom. From here you'll take your ships to race away and hurl your own seat posts to search for where they'll fall! Yet, for now, all our company is sea-weary. We'll make a camp at an island I know not far from here."

"Called Eiriksøy?" quips Herjolf.

"Aye!" Eirik laughs. "Of course, and well it should be named for me!"

We follow. Come the chieftains' shouts to banish quick the knarrs' sharp dragons' beaks. Such savage visages about our prows were fine for wielding fury on the waves, but now 'tis best to show a meeker face, lest we fright' the fickle invisibles who guard this shore. My master lifts a mead-horn high upon the wind, plying toasts to the One-Eyed god and Old Redbeard Thor, who have guided us here safely. About our ship, jugs are poured and drink is passed among the freemen while our men-thralls work the oars. We lurch against the flooding current as Eirik sends a six-oared skiff to follow his bobbing posts along the wide fjord.

Finally above us rises a rocky bluff and, far beneath, a stand of trees. Still this place seems barely lush. Tales of thick groves, forests even, I had heard; yet these trees are spindly as ever I have seen.

Soon enough come the sounds of gravel. Our shallow hull bucks and shudders. The men leap out to pull us to the beach.

Ah, we are here! At last—alive! All the gods must see me joyous—the Norse gods themselves, and perhaps even my own mother's dear White Christ. And, if he would turn his glance, the gentle eyes of this man Ossur.

We scramble about the deck, setting the plank and leading off the braying goats and bleating sheep. All that day and well until dusk, I have no time for more than to scent the grassy air. The earth is dizzying; my first steps wobbling on the fresh new ground, damp and cold with sharp shore rocks all sullied with seabirds' goo. But it is green beyond, indeed. Now I see 'tis but a subtle compass, bound with willow boughs and alder growing in fragile clots, wind-twisted limbs bearing crow- and whortleberries, thick, fat stalks of angelica along the creeks, bluish juniper, mosses of several colors, heather growing in reddish flushes, and everywhere, small but bright beneath my feet, flowers of every kind and stretch and fashion.

Oh, how I long to run and fall and stretch my arms and bury my face within this new, green freshness! But by night's dim fall, my back

and legs do ache; my fingers are raw and cut with sea-struck iron and
slivers of splintering wood. Still they work us—all us thralls—having
already raised their tents and set their livestock out to grazing. Now
the men roll out the heavy cauldrons so we women can but cook the
meal. I myself am sent to collect wind-dried wood from beside the
pelting sea.

I bend for my first stick. The sound of ocean rises and falls like
breath upon the breeze. I look up and raise my arms out to my sides
and think perhaps to twirl—to dare half a spin in praise of this new
ocean and this new shore—yet I do not, for others near would see me.
Instead, I bear my load up in a rough-sewn wadmal sling, laying those
twigs still somewhat damp in rows above the tide's high-line, facing
east, to dry in the morning sun.

On the wind drift some bondmen's conversations, snatches of gossip about which chief will seize the finer lands, rumors of trysts and
deaths aboard, and of which ships were lost or turned away.

"Note you well," one says, "with all that was fully wasted, still the
witch Thorbjorg and all her household have survived."

"Aye, so I had heard," notes another, "not a one among her lot is
lost, though each was borne upon a different knarr. . . ."

A third man mocks, "Well we'd thought to fear sailing off with
them aboard. Yet now it seems 'twas the safest plan of all."

They laugh upon it, but their mirth is strained—these stranger
thrall-men with their shaved bald heads now showing shades of hair
from these days of travel. They dig about the beach's stones for clawing crabs and mussels from the sand. Their fingers are thick and
meaty from the pinching. As they pass, they jeer crudely at me beneath their phlegmy breaths. I hide my face and wish I could hide my
body. Yet what would they dare if they should know I spent the journey working at the witch's hand?

There, beyond the ridge's crest, is the object of those wary ministrations. Ossur sits upon the ledge, gazing toward some lands beyond
my vision. Since we set aground, we've had but time for fleeting looks
between, and even times I've tried to catch his eye and he would not

see. Always seems Ossur is up to some small favor for a freeman. Now
he must know he needs but live on what generosity he can muster,
that and what he can earn from the might of his back, which is growing again strong. I have seen him helping lift some heavy log up from
the beach, bending his back, taking an ax to do the work as might any
bonded thrall. Nay, but he is gentle—suited for better work than this!
He is no fool. He will find his way. Yet I fear, in all his sudden hunger,
he will see me no more. In truth, of what use can I be to him?

As I sit with Einar's thralls before the heat of the crackling fire,
warming the ache from us, wet and cold, I think, well, how I might
help this man. Taking my place among the bondwomen, passing bowls
of broth made from fresh seal meat and shucked shellfish and meal
ground from sandwort found along the dunes, I watch for my chance
to catch my master Einar's eye. Most he is brooding or, when he's
not, he's fit with grave attentions—choosing oarsmen, master sailors,
navigators from among our crew—bearing all the cares which must be
tended. Not until the platters are gathered up and I have been with
Inga and Groa to wash them in the sand do I find him, soft and stepped
away into the dark.

The stranger beach is dotted with yellow fires and laughing, music, up and down the shore. I go to him, quiet, waiting where he is
contemplating. Then music comes, a bright old song about one master
and his favorite slave.

"The song has always spoken to me of your mother, Katla," my
master says. "I wish not to think it now, to mar this bold new soil with
such weakness as to long to weep. Yet I think of her too often. Even
here I feel her hand's touch in the wind and hear her laughter in the
waves." He beckons me closer. "What is it, child?"

"Naught, good master, but that I thought to ask—"

"Ask anything of me this night and you are like to have it. Anything, that is, but your freedom, for I cannot bear to part my vision
from your sweet face. 'Tis there I see your mother's eyes."

I take a breath, remembering the man's broad back turned brown
from weeks of rowing out at sea—Ossur's back, which I have rubbed

with salves as Thorbjorg showed me to ease his breathing. "Master, do you recall the young freeman who was shipwrecked in the storm? The one who grew sick and Thorbjorg tended and . . ."

"Katla, I remember."

"Then you remember how he rowed on Hafgrim's ship before it faltered? Now he has regained his strength. His arms are thick again from lifting goods and raising tents. His legs are strong from herding cattle when they panicked just today upon the shore—"

"Katla," Einar stops me, smiling, "what is your cause?"

"Naught, my master—only surely he can row a knarr as well as any man. And for this he might be paid with a sheep or a breeding ewe?"

Einar blinks at me with a sidelong gazing. For a moment I fear I have asked too much, but Einar smiles and pats my hand. "So much like your mother, Katla! So bold, but loyal, good, and strong." Einar laughs and sends me off, though he does not say if he will give Ossur an oar.

With the morning I go, as seems to be my chore, to gather more wood from among the rocks along the beach. Far above me, trees are felled with heavy iron axes. Grunting groans burst from chopping men as they strip the trunks to boards to reinforce the knarrs' hulls. When I have piled logs enough to dry for a sunset fire, I gather up what last night I'd laid aside. My load is sagging in my sling, and I am about to start back, when I see Ossur coming.

How can I help but watch his gait? His feet kicking sand, each heel pressing firmly to the ground, each leg in its tattered legging—how good to stitch him some of better cloth, like my master's soft and well-spun wool. And he, reaching out with a strength that says he does not care if someone sees him greet a slave, his face looking pleased and happy as he meets my gaze. I place my bundle on the beach. He takes my hands, both of them, in his.

"I'm leaving," he says. My eyes water with the wind. "I will row on Einar's ship and earn my way."

"Yes." I nod, holding my breath. "My master is a good man."

"You are lucky to be his."

"No slave is lucky."

"No." He gently drops my hands and touches the amulet at my neck.

Through the silence I ask, "Who is Rannveig?"

Almost with a look of pain, Ossur turns away.

"I'm sorry," I say. "I should not—"

"How did you come to hear of her?"

"While you slept, when you were ill . . . you spoke her name out several times."

Ossur covers his eyes with both his hands. Sighing, he brushes the hair from his brow. Then he speaks so softly I must listen hard to hear. "She was my wife."

"Your wife?" My heart skitters slightly. "On Hafgrim's ship?"

"No. No, she died three years ago. Of plague."

"Yes." I chew my lip. "Many were killed when the plague twins took up their rake and broom. In some households, they swept the place quite clean. I'm sorry."

"No. She is gone, yet she is always here beside me. Even you—" He stops.

"What?"

"No. It is too strange. . . . When first I saw you—in Breidafjord, as we packed the knarrs—you don't remember—"

"Yes." I bow my head. "I saw you stare at me across the sea. Three ships passed, and still you stared as if you stood before me."

"You looked like her then. Yet now I think you don't."

"That must be why your stare did not hurt as other men's do."

"Katla—you speak such things. I don't know what to say."

"Say nothing. There is nothing anyone can do."

"Nothing?" he asks, and touches where the amulet grazes my chest, and takes it hard into his fist, and squeezes as if to break it. I hold his hand to stop him, but I don't want him to stop, and he takes my fingers between his own and holds them for some moments and kisses them there and there, where they are rough from bark and raw from salt. And he reaches for my hair, and his fingers trace my scalp and bring my head nearer and nearer his own.

His lips are sweet and tingle as the orange fruit I tasted only once, that came on a ship from very far away, ripe and dripping. I suck the nectar from them. Then I fear and think to stop, but his hands are close about my back and warm where my neck was chilled, and I would not pull myself away.

I don't know how long we stand where the waves shift and pound. The arctic terns above our heads squawk as if to tell our tale, but no one comes; only voices, at last, calling for the wood, "Katla!"

I move to leave.

"Please—" he whispers.

"You know I must."

Reluctantly, he releases me. I long to return to him, but instead I gather up the sling.

"Let me help." He reaches. I stop his hand.

"You must not help a slave with her burden. You are a freeman."

"I don't care."

I smile at him. "Yes, I believe that's true." Still I take the sling and start off toward the camp. When he follows I urge him back, yet still he comes and walks beside me, in silence but for the clacking of beach stones.

At the tents, Inga comes from out the throng of animals, thralls, and squalling children. "Katla," she says, yet looks at Ossur as if she speaks to him, "you must be seen no more together. There is talk, and Torvard has heard too much of it. He's heard how you asked of Einar for this man's sake, and now he's raging to know what care it is of yours."

But even as she speaks her words, Ossur's face changes to ruin.

"What is this?" he whispers as Inga presses my other wrist. "You spoke to your master for me? I told you I need no help!" His words are hoarse and dry and strained.

"I only thought to show what perhaps Einar did not know of you. I'm certain he did not notice you as I did before the storm. . . ."

"I could well have proved my strength and earned the oar without you. You've made of me a fool! As if I need a bondgirl's aid."

"Ossur, I only thought . . ."

"Katla, you are too bold—too bold for a woman, far too bold for a slave."

His harsh words strike as hail from a storm. I can see nothing save his reddened face and his fists clenched hard as if to hurt me, but instead he reels away across the sand and climbs the rocks and disappears along the shore.

I stand amidst the bustle of brooding horses, cows, and soot, and smelly children with snotty fists. All of it whirls in the storm of Ossur's leaving, and I stand in its eye, having endured the blow and yet knowing well that worse is still to come. Ossur has left me. He will not come again, for he hates me, as well he should. He is right, then, for I think I am more than I am and want more than I will ever know. I am nothing and matter not to anyone. Yet I cannot bear this truth. I bend at my waist and hold my belly tight in anguish, but the pain only grows with each breath I take to calm myself.

Inga hushes me eternally: "I had only meant to warn you both. I am sorry!" A trickle of words, but no sense seeps to my ears. Still, her patient tone and gentle fingers firmly guide me as they always have— as they always will. Yet now I know I am nothing but a heap of flesh in a tangle of string, masquerading as a woman in a wadmal dress. No woman held in bondage is a woman after all; no woman who is a thrall should dare to dream.

Two days pass, then the knarrs pull out their sails and split the sea. Three go north and two go south. I do not try to see which one holds him, only I know it is not Einar's. I do not go to see my master off, but step toward the hills where there are herbs and berries to be gathered. It is my duty. I am a beast and do my chore without a soul. Yet I cannot keep my eyes from peering as the ships pass beyond the shoals.

The days come and then they go. I stumble through them with no hearing and no touch. The others around me surely know, for they turn and snicker as I near them. I feel it not; there is no feeling left. I could mew or bray and would hurt much the same and feel no more the candor of their words.

Torvard comes and barks at me. He is captain now of our camp. He sets our tasks and we carry them out. His voice is harsh and yet dull as I listen and do his bidding, and even if he pulls me down upon his lap, I let him touch me as he will, but I feel nothing and do not answer, not even as I used to with bile and displeasure. So he throws me off, and I fall but do not yelp at any sting of pain. I simply stand and go on walking to my next chore. Whether it is to milk the cow or start the fire or stoke the ashes or wash the clothes of the old thralls' sweat, I cannot care, for I am nothing and ever will be.

THORBJORG

I BOW BEFORE this fire and watch the flames eat up my sacrifice. This fine horse heart, first death upon this land. So we taint this first stone beach with blood, and the blood burns and rises up as a graying smoke toward you, Alfather. You like it well, Old Graybeard, this taste of meat? I savor it but little, for the dead eyes haunt me. Yet I will eat—as I must. We all must eat. Or die.

The blaze ripples with this new-blown wind, mocking the brittle chill which bears upon it. The spirits in this place—I sense them high up in these glaciers—crawling now, creeping from their shadows, watching our pitiable flames with devious, calculating eyes. These trolls and elves, these grims and nøkks, these haugbo and these fylgie. Ne'er like the draugs—all dead—and never like the living, but set between and angry for it. Mound folk, hill people, water sprites, and such spirits of the woods—beyond breath, beyond snow and ice, beyond all wind and spray. Here they watch and listen, waiting, bearing every shred of our laughter, savoring every sort of lingered pain. For, with these invisibles' favor, men do well upon their soil; and with their ire, all men's hopes but wither and fail.

KATLA

Two weeks are gone. Only once and again do I search the shadows at dusk for a rippling sail; and even when I think I see one through the constant haze, I begin to run farther into this island's crags, deeper into the thin, misted stand of birches that grows along its rise.

At dusk, too, each day I collect the wood I laid to dry the night before, and lay again another armload of driftwood twigs and logs, dragging them up through the sand, snagging them among the stones. They bump and catch, but I jiggle them or lift the stones, leaving none behind, for there's but greenwood from above, and that they dry and cherish to make ships and carts and homes.

Each night, too, as I load the wood into my sling, comes the pounding stomp of Torvard on his horse. Fierce and wild is the beast, but brighter than his master, though gnashing just as hungrily at his bit. Now Torvard daily explores these new grounds, surveying each dune, taking several strong thralls with him. They ply the heights and then report what little they have found. Mostly it is rock and weed, some little shrub beneath a sheltering mound, but not much land for grazing. Still we must feed the cattle grain from our lowering stores, and are sent every morning to gather sandwort for their meal and our own. The beasts eat even seaweed, which is slippery, salty stuff. I pick it from my bowl every time it's used to salt the soup; but Inga likes it fine and takes what I leave aside, so no one chides us that we waste our little food.

Torvard protests there's rich land to come, for his foster-father said it so and it must be. Every day he says they travel farther, but I hear among the thralls they've thrashed the same path twice already and now they're on their way to pound it yet a third.

I stand alone in the growing dark beneath the glowing on the cliffs and lay my wood in pleasant, time-consuming rows. At camp now there's no peace for me with Ossur gone. The others smirk as if they know and mock my pain, their lips glaring with gossip, their smiles quick-turned when I am near enough to catch their words. But here, along the empty beach, with just my footsteps and the birds, no one mocks me. No one smiles. Only the lowly mourning of the hungry child-gulls squawk, as I would to my own mother if she were here. Even the heavy sighing of the surf against the rocky shore reminds me well I am alone within my grief. Yet is it ever so? Is ever there a grief that can be shared?

Then hoofbeats. Torvard and his men racing with my heart: each night their shadows break the dusklight's peace on the high, cold stone. I stand, though in all defiance I long to sit. Let them pass a bondwoman at her ease, mocking their hungry, breathless return, their foolish, futile prancing! But such display would do me no good. It would only set Torvard, in his master's mock, to send another thrall, saying loudly I could not manage all my chores; yet I know well he'd only send that one to stare and goad me as I labored.

Their sounds descend the rocky crag and cover quickly the shallow slope to the sea. Really it is but a tiny spit of land from an angry tongue. They leave their trail like warm breath rising from its grassy tufts. Soon the horses snort in anticipation of their food. Then come the voices as the men dismount to tell their tales, and the hearty, thrallish laughter in response.

When I no longer care to sift their sounds out from the others, I bend to gather up my sling. Suddenly, at the end of my arm's reach, four hooves stand. My eyes follow up to Torvard's boots. For a moment, my heart's in panic, then anger sears my fear. I want to glare, but instead I turn as if I do not see and start taking up the rough driftwood.

Torvard drops from his horse. His steps slightly kick the earth. From my downturned view, I see the beast adjust his weight. A stone tumbles to the sea.

"Girl," Torvard says, knowing the term raises my ire. "Girl, when your master stands, do not go about your work."

I respond in my calmest tone. "The wood is for the fire, for the hot food your men will want to end their day."

"My men are thralls. They will wait."

"We work hard here, Torvard, and put up with much." I mean more than my words dare and would love to roll my eyes in exasperation.

"Thralls should be made used to suffering. You are all too well treated in this soft camp."

"You are bold to criticize your father's hearth."

"It may be his now, but it will not be forever."

"Yes, so you've told me, often and again."

"You don't long for the day, Katla? Ah, but I plan to make you."

At that, I turn and see him. It's not like him to threaten so openly. Yet Torvard stands, oddly patient, almost waiting, almost calm. He smiles at me. I clutch my wood. It is hard and heavy. Whatever it is, he will surely have what he wants of me.

I begin to go as I was bidden, seeing the first early bristle of the evening's fires. I am a donkey at its chores as I start down the beach with my sack of boughs.

"Where are you going?" Torvard demands. "I did not give you leave." He steps out quick to block my way.

"To the cook fire"—I toss almost a playful laugh—"where do you think?" But my heart is beating.

"No." He stops me with his arms. "Not yet." He takes my sling from my shoulder and flings it hard into the rocks.

"Torvard!" I start, but when I stir to fetch it, he sets his lips upon my neck and sucks the flesh hard into his mouth.

"Stop! That hurts!" I try to escape, but he holds me harder, his fingers gripping about my chin.

"It didn't hurt when your lover held you so." He thrusts his head again toward my lips.

My shriek comes as a whisper: "I have no lover."

He pulls away, surprised. "Dare you say it? They all saw you here, then came and showed me. Do you think you can hide what your master sees with his own eyes?"

"You are not my master!"

"Perhaps not yet, but my father is not here. You have nowhere to run, no one to protect you now."

I laugh. "Protect me? From you?" For a moment, he is too startled to speak. I take my chance, shake his arms away, and run.

I kick sand hard to blind him, for I know he will follow fast behind. He is arrogant and stupid, but not so slow that I can stun him long with a haughty laugh.

For a moment I hear nothing and think perhaps he will not come again. He can dare little more than to scare me, with his father's return so close. Yet the horse's hooves sudden break down the beach at such a gallop the stones beneath them crack and shatter. I dare not turn, but hear Torvard driving his knees into the beast, grunting and pressing. I can feel them near. I think I smell their breaths.

He grabs and pulls me hard across his horse.

I shout, "Leave me alone!"

"I have left you alone long enough!"

His grip is so strong I am barely breathing—the shock, the pain as he thrusts me hard over the rigid saddle and holds me there. Its wood and the pounding pace cut off my breath. Still I struggle, trying to slip off as he turns the horse, but he wrenches me up and gallops back toward my row of logs, and there, at last, he hurls me down.

I am falling. I hear a crack. My skull hits hard against the soggy wood. The world is dim and I am dizzy, watching him towering there.

"Here is where you met him! Here is where he had you, in this sand!"

"Torvard, no, it was not . . . He is gone."

"Gone? But with him what you gave so freely—what you have always refused to me. What do you think, that you are free to choose your mate like some daughter of a chief who can tell her master-father yea or nay?"

He descends to where I lie; my arms are tangled in my hair; it has fallen from its braid and chokes around my neck.

"Torvard . . . ," I crawl back, groping to be quick, but my limbs catch clumsily on logs and stones. There's a tremble in my voice I can't control. No hint of laughter now will set him back, and there is none in me. "Torvard," I beg. I can barely breathe. He steps nearer. It all seems slow.

"Please," Torvard mocks me. "Ask me, Please!"

I dig my feet in hard, but the ground just falls away.

"Katla, Katla, so pretty. It did not have to be this way. I could have had you gently, but you're too proud. Now I must make you humble; I will make you so ill and rude that no one will want you, as hideous as the first thrall in Bilskirnir. And then you will be grateful when Thor opens that gate, for the pain I will give will only be forgotten there."

He strikes me. The first blow is the quickest, and after that all is dull as he beats me down among the logs. I taste my own blood. It is warm and salty. With his fists he beats me hard about my head. For a moment, I cannot see and am terrified I am blind, but then I think, Let me be blind so I'll not care.

I know now his threat is no folly. My eyes clear and I see him. He's ripped at his clothes and stands exposed, hanging wretched, his demand rising, red and pointed, thick and cruel and lurid, as his fury is toward me. I can barely feel as he strips my dress and separates the tatters. I hear a scream from somewhere and think that someone comes and screams in response, but then I know. The scream is mine.

He bends to me, rends me—how long, how many times I cannot say. Just the rhythm of the waves washing over and over. Never will I hear them well again. Never will I know their sound without the need to scream, but my screams are hushed by the weight of his hand across my face, so hard my tooth is in my throat and I swallow it and it cuts and then is gone and the blood of it streams like the water from my eyes; and blood is on my thighs and on my chest where he bites me hard and wrenches the nipple away.

It is no more. I know. I feel it missing.

Through it all, I long to lose my thoughts, to lose my mind, but my mind stays with him and smells his filthy clothes and feels his sweat trickling in my ears and hears his breath. His breath and his groans, and mine. I curse my body for what it feels, unwilling, unable to decline, over and over as he breaks upon me and I fight him but can no longer resist, for my body will not serve my mind.

He takes me. And he owns me. All of me. I am his. Forever. I will never be for anyone. Not even for myself.

* * *

In darkness, for six days, I am told I lie. I do not know; only that, when
I wake, my wish is to go away again into the darkness of my shadow,
my mind awash in dream with no dreams, no thoughts, no fear, no
feeling. No feeling, most of all.

Still my eyes are swollen shut, but in time I know I see: the splin-
ters of light are driving through me, as if made not of ether but of
glass. If only my body were of ether, but it is solid and racked with
pains. Even when the tender hands do touch me, I hear my screams.

I know those hands—Thorbjorg's hands—know them and I fear
them, but then I remember what good they'd done before. The memory
brings another right behind it—Ossur—straight as a blade and slashing clear the finer one away. So I think only of those hands, sharp they
should be from the way I know they look, and yet they are gentle, patient, light, so infinitely kind.

At first I think the smell is poultice, but then I know it is my
blood. My blood, rotten and solid, still upon my breast. I dare to touch
it—to know—but my listless arm itself prevents me. Saves me, or tor-
tures me. I cannot ask. I cannot speak. And there are other things, too,
I long to answer but cannot—will not. My face. What is a face after it
has been taught that it can bleed?

But, then, a slaughtered animal has less to fear than I—sent
quickly to its death, not left to live within the horror. Its horror is
done once, and then, not e'er again. But mine, I see, will live forever,
on and on.

On and on. So he had said to me. Whispered he would do as he
liked. Promised he would take me so, when and how he would, whenever he pleased, as often as he pleased, for as long as he pleased. Forever. I would know my place. Dug in the dirt, two steps from death,
but ever living. As I am now. I am a slave.

So how can I long to live as the witch's hands . . . they try to cure
me? I know they do and strive to let them, but I do not want—no
more, yet they bid me linger. Linger here? Why? Must I ever and
again? What good is life when so much is hatred, pain, cruelty, evil?

What have I done but to be born where I'm not wanted except for the labor of my back and the use of the hole between my legs?

And then I think . . . The horror of the thought, I cannot think it, but instinctively grope my stomach and feel the mound. Even in the pain, I know that mound is growing with all the hatred, filth, the evil that was thrust in me. He is in me. He! How can it be? And yet it is in me, as the most terrible creature the foul god Loki could have ever made.

Now I know no other thing but that I must perish. I cannot live. I cannot drink the brews Thorbjorg holds to my lips. I tear the wraps she binds so carefully. I do not care but that I do not see this life. I do not want but that this new life and mine should end.

A Freewoman's Claim

THORBJORG

"WHAT BEAST IS THIS some call a man?"

My words. In whispers. They come over, over, tripping on my lips as I mend the girl. Yet none do hear me, none do care.

"Just a slave girl," they say, "and lazy!" Though I say not so. No. I remember her patient hands.

I mend her as best I can, with poultices and bandages and soothing words when she will hear. Yet she wants it not, this healing, and I don't fault her. What course has it except to let her live again with all this memory of pain?

Einar comes and looks from time to time. With his glance, he bears this trouble, then turns away. On his lips, "Cliona . . ." The name means nothing to me.

"No one deserves such cruelty," I mention. "Not even a thrall."

Einar bends upon his knees, near to weeping for a man whose pride is wrapped in strength. He lays a hand on her. "All sorrow cannot repair this work."

The girl shudders at his touch, shrinks back.

"Too soon," I say. "She still fears the touch of men." Then I think, She always will.

Yet I let him look at her, quiet for a time, at the lips sucked in where her teeth had been, and the face swollen red and black with lines of scabs.

"These will fade," I utter when he does not speak. Yet it is not enough for him, so I must pull the bandage from where the breast is torn.

"What," he cries, "what is this? No—he is my son!"

I press the wrapping back in place as Einar quivers.

Out, beyond, upon the beach, the son stands somewhere between strut and stumble, feigning pride in such a deed, yet I see in his shadow a mask of things to come.

"He will pay, in time, in some subtle way."

"Speak it not, woman!" Still Einar will not bear this cause, so I prod no more, washing a bandage in the blood-pinked brine brought up from the sea.

"She can be of little use to you now," I state offhandedly. "Let me take her and make of her what good I can."

"Yes." Einar turns, relieved to hear it. "Yes, woman. Of course. It is best."

So her master goes away. Goes and takes his son roughly by the shoulders, and late into that night their voices come from a distant tent, and even Eirik Raude's, hard and cold against the leathern dark. But little more.

Little more, for now.

Late into the darkness, I watch her. The slightly amber stone on her collarbone glows just above her heaving breath. I reach and take it up. Oh, Great One, Odin! Hold it, feel its weight. Its nearly fatal rune-marks cut. Alfather, I hold it, hot within my hand.

KATLA

IT IS DAWN. Inga stands above me.

"Katla, we are heading out this day. You must dress." She reaches out her hand.

Hardly can I think of it—of even moving. I had never thought but to lie upon this straw until it withered, dried, and wasted, then to sink myself into this sand, this grave, cold comfort, and never rise again. Yet the sounds beyond this shelter's cloak break: a clamor of cows' bells and donkeys' brays, a parade of thralls, voices rattling, scoffing men and mocking girls. They shuffle past, daring to laugh aloud.

The seeress, beside the heavy sealskin curtain, parts it slowly. The sounds drift off. Her look alone must have frightened them away.

"Katla, come now." Inga's arms are round and soft before me. Her touch is thick though trying to be kind, yet too strong, biting, wrenching, as she lifts me up. The wadmal scratches, rough at my bruised shoulders. Wrapped in trusses, my arm tangles in the slave dress' sleeve.

"Sth-op!" I cry.

The sound slathers. In a sudden shock, my tongue gropes for some barrier to sound. Once my words had seemed so pretty, but now they come out ragged, tattered. A twist of spittle, a senseless slop falls upon my rag-wrapped breast. Inga steps away, her eyes shot pink with horror.

"Inga"—the witch sweeps near—"burn the sickbed straw. It is thick with lice."

"No!" I beg, but Inga turns upon the order. There's a rustle of the matting. Then Inga is gone.

Thorbjorg does not speak, but leans so close I dare to watch the lines upon her face. Lines like runes. She takes away the cursed wadmal, brings for me a freewoman's sheath and a pair of rugged iron brooches in her long, cracked fingers. With these, she pins the gown, one cold, rusting metal ring at each of my sullied shoulders. I dare not cry, yet there is no pain. With the same calm grasp, she knits my hair and wraps it in a sheath of linen. Then she turns me back, gazing hard now, reaching of a sudden toward my eye. Her nails are dark and dirty, fingers withered to the bone. Long, dark veins dance upon their spray of spots. I draw back, but she only strokes aside a strand of hair.

"Come now," she orders.

"No"—but Thorbjorg wraps her arm about my waist, presses me forward. "I cannot"—I begging, but she knows no mercy. The witch is strong. Her grip is hard and I must walk. I can. . . . I remember how.

I stumble now only from weakness. She lets me rest against the tentpole, panting there for breath. The witch waits, patient for a time, bringing me the ladle from the bucket, "Here," pressing it to my lips, so I must sip cool water through my toothless hollow.

"Now." She grasps again the curtain. I catch the pole, but she grips my shaking head. "You must," she says. "This is how you must face them for the rest of your days."

Thorbjorg's hand is at my back as the curtain flies apart. All of them are there before us, all who have ridden on those ships, all who have survived. They mill about, making show of how they work to load the vessels, but the corners of their gazes are black and sharp, tripping across the beach to catch a glimpse of me. Their lips, cracked to show their teeth, and jowls, sucked to hold back their horrid jeers. I wait for laughter! Laughter! Most like, too, they will whisp' under their breaths that I deserve this shame.

Yet from them comes only slowly silence. What chatter had been before is gasped away. Not a snicker. Not a sound, as if some terror stills their souls.

I step.

One woman—she does not know me, yet her hand goes to her lips.

"Don't stare!" another hisses, pressing a pair of ragged children to her breast.

Farther off, Audun stoops with Eirik Raude and some other men, drawing a line in the dirt with stones and sticks to mark our soon-come passage. Audun looks up. His eye catches mine. He turns as if he does not see me, then looks again and tries to smile. He raises his hand, then swallows hard and lets it fall.

One step more. Each footfall draws me farther. I see little Torunn. Her eyes are two wells of tears. She stands so still, as if to move would spill them out, gripping hard upon her mother Grima's hand.

But Grima—she does not turn her eyes. She seems almost glad at what she sees. So I know—I must be hideous. I must be a beast. My face, reflected in their eyes, frozen with Torvard's cold hatred—Grima's foul son, Einar's tainted child.

Yet I do not see him. Not among them. Nowhere. Can he not face the harm he's done?

Thorbjorg leads on, beyond their gaping gazes, past those ships and bundles, herds of cattle, and baleful, whimpering dogs. Then up a ragged path. Soon only the wind whispers, soft and chilly. A cliff rises before us. Is this, then, to be my fate? To plunge into the deep, a poor slave's death at this woman's hand? I would fight her off, but then I think to be glad of it. The way is steep and cobbled. Barely can I lift my feet, grasping at stones with my one good arm. At last, the path is nearly level. The Norns' frail net cannot catch me here. I laugh, stepping forward now, as fast as I can stumble toward the empty air. But Thorbjorg grasps me back.

"No," she says. "It will not be so easy for you as that."

Her eyes are weary, small, and gray, with pupils shining back the sun's hard glare. She reaches, taking the pendant from my neck, and tugs it sharply so the string does break.

The runestone dangles in her hand. With a thrust, it is this she hurls into the sea.

I look at her, too stunned to ask.

"Go, then," she says. "Fetch your things to Herjolf's ship. Stay and wait among my thralls."

She presses me back again, down the same path we have just traveled. My head is spinning, filled with a fresh terror. I am hers, then: I am the witch's thrall.

I fetch my bundle and make my way as I am told. So I see Thorbjorg's hands bore no true mercy. They had their price—to save me for herself. A cheap-bought body, not to save my life.

Herjolf's knarr lolls against its mooring, anchored by thin-stretched cords and thralls' hard hands and feet dug among the beach stones. The planking rattles along the railing as limbs clamber up and tumble down. Yet I see just bodies moving, not names for faces, but flesh and empty eyes. Only thus can I go upon the stranger's ship when all these strangers know too well my shame.

"Katla." It is my master, Einar, waiting. He stretches out his arms as I shuffle past. He says, coming nearer, "Go gladly, Katla." I clutch my bundle against my damaged breast. "Obey her well and be obliged. She has done you better good than you can know."

Yet I cannot hear him, his voice bearing heavy with the same thick slab of sorrow I have heard but once, upon my mother's death. But now I see his sorrow's false, as is all kindness from a freeman to a thrall.

I turn from him quickly. Inga now is waiting. Upon his nod, she comes and hugs me gently.

"Be well," she says. "In time, you will remember only the happy things." She brushes her hand across my battered cheek, but I cannot raise my eyes to meet her own.

My head's borne down to keep my feet from tripping as I turn at last toward Herjolf's plank. Almost I am glad to go, to hear no more of their loathsome pities. My steps shy back from the frothing spittle of the sea. Not much farther. I press myself along.

But before I step, a hand stretches out and sudden holds me. That hand—my heart thrashes within my wounded chest—a man's. It must be Torvard. I raise my eyes to behold my terror. Yet worse—far worse—before me, Ossur stands. He stares. Across his face is a pity worse than any mock. A pity like a poison. I want to hate him for it— yet I see he tries his lips. No words come. Then, after a moment, Ossur turns like all the rest and lets me pass.

Not long before the ships push off. I take my place. I know precisely where to sit, for it's well rumored which are the witch's thralls. One I know is a Finn called Kol. There he carries on his back his mistress' trunks, all on his own. He's crooked and stooped, his legs are badly bowed, yet he is strong and wiry, with face and lips pursed and drooping like a goat's, with massive arms and muscles thick about his thighs. They say he bears such strength with magic, and upon his neck his powers dangle from a strip of hide—bears' teeth and twigs and bits of fur and jagged stones and beads and shells. They say, too, he and the witch make pacts and dance with the invisibles upon moonless nights.

I place my bundle and then myself. There is little talk upon this ship. The thralls of Herjolf's house avoid us. And the witch's thralls are a wary lot, their eyes bent down as if hard-beaten.

Only once Thorbjorg comes to check but scantily my wounds. As she does, I note the strangest happening. It is not the witch whose presence makes her thralls quick-wince, but the passing of a stranger-thrall or a freeman from Herjolf's household. When the witch comes close, there is soft exchange, some subtle whispers. Thorbjorg leaves with but a weighty glance at a graying, hefty woman whose name I find, after some time, is Gyde. Sitting beside me, Gyde wraps me in some blankets as the winds quick-rise beyond the shelter of Eiriks-fjord's cliffs. She brings me, too, some salted fish she's softened for my missing teeth with a bit of drink. But most, she sits beside me, letting me lean against her bulk, her warmth seeping to my skin, her thick hands on mine.

I sleep for a time, and when I wake, another thrall rests on Gyde's far shoulder, a youngish girl whose face is much like Gyde's. I think at once she is her daughter, and when I ask, Gyde nods. "Her name is Arngunn," pressing gently both our hands. This brings but the sharpest remembering of my own dead mother. I turn away and quickly close my eyes.

'Tis but a dawn and dusk we sail before we reach the point named this very day Herjolfsnaes, a rocky strand beside the sea and well ex-posed to all kinds of weather. Here they land the craft and load out Master Herjolf's things, all his thralls, the women of his household, and his tall sons. All but some few men who will stay to guide the knarr and Thorbjorg's household yet farther on with the morrow.

"Seems a troubled spot to make a homestead." Thorbjorg leans against the rail, peering out with Herjolf at the bulky crag jutting up beyond this narrow plain.

"Yes, but I am pleased with it. It is farthest to the coast and will make first port for all the ships come traveling. Even Eirik Raude and his mighty sons will rely on it and me."

"Wise, then." Thorbjorg nods. "A blessing on it from Odin, Thor, and Frey."

"Prophetess, to hear you say it I am full pleased."

I watch their eyes, for I stand quite near, helping Herjolf's thralls by passing down lighter bundles as I can manage. To Thorbjorg, Herjolf is kind, solicitous. He does not seem to fear as much as hold her dear. Like a sister, for they seem close in age and, from their manner, have known each other long.

"One day this land will fall to Torkel's shoulders." Herjolf looks toward a fine, tall boy with his hands upon his hips, still beside the steering oar. "He's well born to the task and will protect you, just as I do, if only to have you near to call great Odin's eye."

Thorbjorg sighs, "For what little help it does us." Her words bear up foreboding. My new mistress seems sudden very slight as Herjolf wraps a heavy arm about. Yet I wonder, what cause has Thorbjorg to ever fear or need protection?

That night we rest upon the anchored deck beneath the bare-dipped dusk of nearing summer. The sky burns with an orange glow while Herjolf's household's fires warm this Greenland beach. I lie away from all the rest, pretending I am sleeping, looking out beyond the rail toward another rough-hung shelter where someday will stand, I suppose, a mighty Viking longhouse. Now it seems but frail and bare beneath this black and towering cliff and this feeble glimmer of uncertain stars. Oh, in times like these I feel the darkness! Those sparks like little flames as my mother used to hide in Einar's byre, lighting them to pray as she had long ago beside my father. How they had begged, she said, for their Lord called Jesus to let them have a child! And at last a child came.

Such a child's growing in me. Yet nothing like. Would that it could be but a horrid dream! That one morning I will wake. Yet I do not wake; and with each morning now comes a sudden wash of sickness, worse than any I ever felt at sea, for I know 'tis not the wafting now, but this bit of him, this horrid beast in me! So I pray in secret. I beg the gods—all gods, any god of any place or name—only that I hate this child, that it should never come, that it should never live to breathe.

I shift my sight, trying to find some ease in lulling sounds: the crackling fires, some insects' creak, dull whispers of the other thralls. Beyond, all about are shadows, shapes cast by the moving fire-light. Then I see: my new mistress walks up a bluff upon this foreign soil, then slowly, alone, down.

THORBJORG

ODIN. You call upon me like a chill. You seize me, crawling slowly, your cold fingers on my arms. I go alone to you, for you do not linger long before such others. I climb these foreign grasses for you, to huddle among the knolls, my body pressed between the frost-formed heaves.

There, in time, you come again to do your work and leave me ravaged. When you're through, I stand and wipe the spittle from my lips and gather my limbs in pieces to set them right again.

Not unlike the girl there, Katla. Not much unlike her.

Yet your pain brings pleasure. That is the beast of it, though perhaps it is just that I am old and familiar with such work. Long ago, in those earliest of passions, you left me longing, torn and wracked yet aching to have you back again.

When first you came—not just to me, but to my sisters—together we bent our heads and learned to mend the pieces of your pillaging. Such cogent wisdoms which our bodies bare recalled—fragments, at first—one single strand of your fine hair, but enough to begin to weave our strength. So we together, my sisters and I, went about among the towns and farms, giving great performances in your name, using sticks and stones, quick-scratching runes and whatever we'd gained of the healing balm of herbs. These were our faulty gleanings, yet enough. And so our reputations grew.

We had learned the god's game and could play it well enough for others. But you, once tricked, would not have it so again. Indeed, my love—you did grow fickle. You would not come—except only when least expected, and then but wily, wary. Never more in kindness, and never when we called! I think, perhaps in time, even for this you did your vengeance—let us play just long enough before my sisters burned.

Yet you come upon me again this night. I languish in your chilling grip, feel you take my body, taste you on my tongue. Nay, these god-let moments! These of speaking tongues which are not my own, which froth upon my lips, clamping until my tongue does bleed! Nay, such are the mightiest, the rarest, most wanton, and most cruel. Quick-struck and left alone I'll be, but I'll cling to you and lie down for you, willing, aching for your use.

And now you tell me in your passion, *Child.*

Child? I think I hear you speak. But madness. Whispers. Child?

The child of this thrall, you say again, *will be mine, and yours.*

KATLA

WITH THE DAWN, we sail. Few are left upon this ship now. Only Herjolf, returning with his son Torkel from the comfort of the beach-tent fires, and some thrall-bound men to bear the sheet and oars. Of Thorbjorg's household: nine thralls and she. Among them, me. That's all.

Ahead, this place they have named Tofafjord gapes, a narrow cut like a wound in this so-called Greenland's side. We enter slowly, probing. Deep and harsh are these cliffs' crags, scattered with falling heaps of ashen scree, pinkish quartz, and bits of feldspar, slightly green—the sort of green which speaks of sickness, moldy bones, and, ever, death. Not the green of life, not a bit of moss, not a scraggly bush nor hint of tree. Still, above, in a cloud, ivory gulls and guillemots squawk and swarm their nests, cached up in the speckled peaks. I cannot help but raise my eyes. Their shrill echoes like a screaming. Yet 'tis drowned again by a greater noise: between the hoary pinnacles, glaciers spouting melted sprays, waters clatter-falling, rash and harsh and willful, wild as if to break this broken land's already wasted frame.

We sail ahead, plunging straight and long, though my stomach's weak and twice already I have retched over the railing. Seems no one thinks on me much, and I am glad to hide my misery when it comes. Yet, with the third wash of sickness, Gyde's daughter, Arngunn, brings me warm, fresh-uddered milk.

"Here," she says. "I was bent before the goat already. I thought 'twould soothe your ill." Though she's young, perhaps she's somewhat wise, for she does not question, as I drink, why after so many days at sail the sea should pain me still.

All morning, my new mistress leans across the bow; yet now, toward noon, she draws Kol by her. "There?"

He nods and points. "Follow east till the land sweeps low."

"Fair," she answers, sending Kol off toward the steersman to give these new directions.

I dare ask Gyde, "Was Kol ever in this Greenland? Perhaps with Eirik Raude—"

"Kol's been in Iceland since a young man."

"Yet he's told the mistress where to turn the ship—"

"Yes," says Gyde, but answers nothing.

The ship wends with Kol's strange vision, heading toward a breezy junction of emerald waters laced about with peaks. Here five fjords bend and join into a cluster. "As a star," Kol whispers to the mistress.

The knarr turns again and comes before a stretch of rolling hills, some lushly green with streams catching the sunlight like embroidered threads of gold or silver.

"Here," says Kol.

My mistress calls out then to Herjolf, casting her eyes first upon her thralls, then toward the heavens' cloud wisps. So she closes her lids, raises up an arm, and flings her tiny rowan twig with its fine-carved runes and its crystal stone. It barely splashes as it strikes the sea. Yet her slaves and she all bend over the railing. They watch it bob. So do I, hearing Herjolf's laugh, "Thorbjorg, we can bare find your rune-twig dancing on these waves! How are we to follow it to shore?"

Yet Kol calls to Torkel, "Turn the ship about!"

For some long hours, we follow the fickle current tickling at the bough, till sudden we hear Kol shouting, "Mistress! The runes have found their mark!"

prophecy

Everyone aboard is hugging close. I look but do not see it. Gyde guides me with an arm, and, indeed, the twig is caught upon the beach stones. Its crystal glints as if a beacon.

There before us is a rise of land, ripe and green, and a rolling heath well met for grazing. "Seems almost amiss that there're no sheep or goats yet pastured here," Herjolf jests as he calls the sail lowered, and we row ashore.

He and his men do not linger long, just enough to see us settled. Then they turn their sheet into the wind. It ripples full and pulls them, almost racing back to their new home port. And then only Thorbjorg's household stands on the empty bank with a clutter of bundles and bleating goats and sheep and Thorbjorg's aging bull and two small cows.

We set about to heaving. There is not much, yet we are so few: a thickish man called Teit who seems a yardman and a stabler; a woman, Nattfari, calling to him "Husband!" every time she drags another bundle up the hill. Strange, the sound of it as she giddies about with a girlish lilt, for it is well known slaves are not allowed to wed. There is Vidur, but an awkward boy, yet he sets about the sheep and goats as sure as any able shepherd. Another man, Alof, seems likely a hunter, for it is to him Kol turns to tend the arrows, clubs, and spears. There are also tools to form a smithy; yet these, weighty though they are and massive, Kol insists are his, and surely manages himself. Then there's Gizur, most strange of all, old and hobbled and somewhat prone to endless grinning. Little can he do to help—less even than I—yet none do scold. Nay, the very mistress sets him to rest upon a rock, where he lays aside his crooked cane and takes up a bit of broken willow. In some short while, after I barely slog three times up the slope with smallish bags in my one good arm, I see Gizur has carved of the skimpy branch a fine and sturdy sort of hoe.

As soon as we have distanced all the mistress' goods from the lapping tide, Alof sets along the beach with spears and netting. Kol, young Vidur, and the husband-man called Teit bend their backs to cut sod clots into a hovel. Gyde and Nattfari raise flat stones to build a hearth. I help as I can, wedging smaller chips to hold it steady for the cooking pots to come. The work is slow, and as I wait, I notice Arngunn walking on the shore, stooping, picking twigs and boughs to burn as I'd often laid along the beach at Eiriksøy. The sight brings brutal memory. My eyes turn quickly toward the rise. There the thrall-men's arms beat, fierce: Kol hurling the ax and Teit thrusting hard the spade.

Behind me comes a sudden breathing. I shiver, startled, turn about. Nattfari's standing, asking of me kindly, "You are tired, Katla?"

"I am fine," I say, taking up another fist of stones.

"Yet rest." She tries to guide me from the work.

"The mistress—"

Nattfari almost warns, "The mistress begged us watch you closely."

She sets me far away, on the very slope where Gizur whittles—jolly with his clubfoot dangling—saying not one word yet ever with his guileless smile. Something in him pleases me, for he is old and sweet and toothless. He catches up my eye and waves, pressing his knife fondly in his wrinkled fist. As I glance, his wizened cheeks wash with fluster and he raises up what now he works: a simple stone he has shaped into a raven, Odin's messenger.

Soon the hearth is roughly finished, but the shelter only halfway raised, a sheet of wadmal barely clinging at its top, when a gust brings clouds and a sudden, frigid hail.

Thorbjorg rushes out and calls into the wind, "Come back!" louder than I've ever heard her, with a voice like a shepherdess' that I'd known of Einar's house, a woman with a bellowed chest who'd tried once to teach me how to sing with such a sound. I'd been young and even slimmer than I am, and could not learn it. Yet Thorbjorg stands now, craggy though she is, raising arms as if the gods would see her, and calls again, "Come back!"—seeming not to care as she is whipped and pelted by the hail. There she waits till all her thralls have rushed up from the shore—even Alof, though he was well beyond this cove.

A fine, thick skin Gyde bears to warm Thorbjorg as she comes in. Damp and shivering, she sits, saying nothing, scolding not at all. We serve up broth Gyde's made of seaweed brine. As she takes the bowl I offer, Thorbjorg's face is flushed, her hand still shaking from the chill. Strange, that she should pain herself to wait for thralls.

We all eat, sipping softly, soon tasting the white-fleshed meat of the fishes Alof's netted and Nattfari's cleaned. None speak for some long time, till, finally, Alof offers, "There are seals about. I've seen their leavings. They mark the shore, but I've not yet found their harbor."

"Tomorrow," Thorbjorg says, "after the boundary's drawn."

"Boundary?" Vidur asks. "Why, when this land is empty?"

"One day it will not be so." Thorbjorg recites, "By the Althing law, a freewoman's claim is the distance she may walk with a heifer in the length of a new spring day." She tells the law out boldly, as might the Lawspeaker at Thingvellir, the wide plain where every year Iceland holds its parliament.

"Mistress, you'll not mark the round yourself?" Gyde begs.

"No," Thorbjorg answers. I think of Thorbjorg's limp. I see now her leg is thick with scars, as from a fire. "Yet the boundary must be drawn or disputes will come when Greenland has an Althing of its own. 'Twill be done from dawn to dusk," she commands, "tomorrow, if this storm subsides."

"Let me mark it, mistress." Nattfari turns.

Thorbjorg holds her gaze, then refuses. "Katla will draw the bound."

"Katla?" Nattfari breathes upon a huff.

I stammer, longing yet to question, daring not to try.

"Katla will bear the torch and scorch the marks to claim this province. Katla, you are well enough now." She eyes me keenly. "You will go."

Nattfari's color rises, though her ire's not for Thorbjorg. It moves toward me, but she is silenced with a hush and gentle stroking touch from Teit. She whispers out, "My husband-man . . ."

The storm subsides with the fall of darkness. I lie awake, bearing with the chill, listening to their snores and speaking out in dreaming. Once even I hear Thorbjorg wake to lull some other's terrors back to peace. I cannot help but wonder, thinking it strange, this tenderness, such comfortable talk among them; yet, from the mistress, ever a wary, strained reserve. And now Nattfari's rancor—I cannot think but why, until, late that night, I hear her rouse and press her Teit to join in grope and groaning. Ah, such memory comes upon their sounds—I cannot bear to hear them! I tuck my head beneath my arm, waiting through their last, unwieldy gasps, wishing I could close my ears as I close my eyes.

THORBJORG

DRAW THIS FENCE with a fertile belly, twice around with both wombs brim-full: the heifer and this woman. So, this rounding rite, this rough-stitched hem, this subtle noose, I twist upon your wisdoms. Will it be enough, Alfather, to bind us tight or let us bide alone?

I do not know, yet I do as I am told, Alfather. It is no strange recall that this law was struck by men; while they themselves take the greater part—claiming all each captain's crew can cross in a day's time, bearing fire. But they know not much of the subtler art. With my wisdom-ways, I will turn their ploy to serve my purpose.

Still, it is strange to think such bounding can bear the shape of owning. To own a place—so many have I called mine, yet now all gone. All lost, all burned, set to soot and ash and bleeding. Still, today, we draw another round.

Round and round. It is not much to mark this earth for men, but for the gods—to draw such a fecund circle—we beg the gods to see! Frey and Freya—gods of fertile beauty, of spring and rites recalled of such a bloom—I pray to you, like all springs, to linger but a little. A brief gestation. Only for a time, then all too soon will come again the brutal cold. Such warmth will not last long upon this isle.

Yet I prefer it so. Better this one, set about in ice and somehow honest. Yes, I see—there's a glacier high above. Like a brow furrowed low and long over a dark, hard face. Within that face, a glaring eye. It does not hide. There. Strange, it glows peculiar blue. When I close my sight, such chilly vision.

Now my eye's full open to the sun: upon the cliff's cold side, 'tis a fateful mountain just like any other. At the water's edge, clacking shards, ice ne'er melted from the winter's night. Even now, gnashing at the beach as at a bite of hunger's meat dangled from a bone.

When winter comes, these will set their fangs again. Still I send this woman off, ripening with child. Barely now a seedling sprout, yet she grows as in a bit of sod tucked within a shallow. While I stand withered on a crag, battered by the winds—such breezes—"foehn winds" they are called. Blowing from the north, they sweep to turn this edge of green into a desiccated hollow.

No, she does not know the power that she wields.

Protect it, Almighty Asa! I pray, to bring this new-wrought hope. I will treat it kindly. I promise I will tend it well.

KATLA

WITH THE DAWN they rouse me, bringing an oil-soaked torch on fire, and a heifer lashed upon a yoke. This heifer's pregnant, her belly set soon to bear or burst. With this, I must draw the marking bound.

So, I know why I was chosen—for my womb and what already lies within. Thorbjorg strives to conceal it with her gentle touch and her thralls' fair, false concern. Still she is like any other; indeed, the witch would use me well.

For some yards Kol carries the torch, chanting twisted words to the slapping fire. Vidur leads the heifer, checking that her yoke is taut on its sinew rein. At the crest of the hill, Arngunn stuffs my shoes with moss and grasses. "There." The girl brushes clots from her knees as she stands. "You'll be warm enough that way."

The wind blows chill. Nattfari stays apart, her hands upon her belly. The sun has no strength to break through the thick of clouds. Vidur ties the rein about my still-bruised wrist; Thorbjorg takes the torch and passes it to me, placing it in my one strong hand.

"Odin, guide her," she says into the wind, "with your all-seeing eye. Frey and Freya, lay within her path all this household's bounty."

Then to me she says, "Redbeard Thor, who watches all fine, faithful slaves, guard your steps. All our fortunes lie within your circuit."

If I do this job but poorly, will she kill me then, or wait until the child's born? I know this answer, too, for another body cheaply bought is worth the spell of waiting, especially when I see full well there are few riches here. This mistress has not much, despite all faithful rumors.

I set upon my step, yet, before I have gone far, something small and cold is pressed between my fingers. It is Gizur's offering: a small black stone scoured smooth and cut with the shape of Thor's great hammer. "Protection!" His voice is dark and shy, his smile bright as a child's who is simple. I slip the stone into my apron pouch, beside my mother's Christian praying beads.

The torch seems heavy now, ever taller as I lift it. The stem is long, so long I use it as a staff, leading the heifer slowly with my injured arm. The flame dances wild in the frigid wind. The others walk behind me, quiet as I go. At each rock or knoll, I pause to graze the grass with fire. There the others stay behind to see it well put out. Soon I walk alone, leaving a sooty score which will not be erased, at least not until another winter's snow and a spring's new growth, and by then the men will surely mark it with cairns of rock or boundary stones.

Each step becomes a breath, for the breeze is constant, warming with the day's slow rise, softly, gently pushing me along. At last, the sun breaks in brilliant swaths. Draped across the mountains' backs, the silent glaciers, like unsewn panels of a linen cloak, are etched with soot, dripping slowly with the sudden glow. Lower down, some greening reaches ever toward such barren heights. And I think, No one has ever stepped here. No man or woman has ever seen these hills, or smelled this grass, or spied these cliffs which tower over.

I come upon a brook which has never once been crossed and leap beyond it. It babbles in some unknown tongue. I laugh at its futile protest, thinking, Now this land is mine! Yet I curb my thoughts. This land is not my own. It will never be—as nothing ever can be. Now I do but my mistress's bidding. And that mistress—Thorbjorg—none about will shield me from her wants. Nay, come quick upon my mind my mother's tales of the devil's daughters. Then I drop the rein, reach into my pouch to take my mother's praying beads, whisp'ing *"Sancte Christe! Hallelujah!"* and whatever other Christian words I can recall.

The sun dips, dark and strange, behind a cloud. The flame above me seems to flicker. As I listen, a wailing rises just beyond. The sound comes once, then twice, so I know I have not dreamed it.

"Jesu Christe!" I glance behind to see if the others near, though I cannot choose if it is better if they do or no.

I creep across a grassy hollow, holding low the torch to hide me, though the smoke drifts up to give my place away. Through some willow knots and tight, tripping alder branches, I stumble toward a cluster of great boulders, plying with my hands as best I can, until I realize I've somehow let go the cow. Oh, I turn and run aback, struggling not to stumble on the risen bumps of sod which prick this frost-cracked earth, fearing what the witch will do if I have lost her heifer. Oh, I cannot think, but nearly fly until I see the cow, gone nibbling at rough grass, caught in a gray-blotched sea of stones which nearly match her speckled hide.

I tumble toward her, prodding heartily, but she will not go. I tug her yoke, but she tosses back her head, snorts halfhearted threats, then lowers down into the sweetish sod again. About me is naught but a hill rearing up to plunge before the sea; above, a rise of hacked and jagged cliffs; yet, between, this valley flat and these massive boulders. Oh, and my light's gone out; the cow won't move; my path is lost; the boundary ruined. I fall against a stone, turning my fear wet and salty, spreading across my cheeks my tear-soaked palms.

"Katla!" Kol is coming quick beside me, loping down the hill, all bandy canter on his ill-bent legs. Nay, he will be angry, his arms set wide with raging muscles, bare but for a ragged sheath and his amulets of tooth and claw bounding off his chest. Yet he seems not so as he reaches, taking up my soot-soaked torch. With the swiftest flick of stone and bunch of grasses, he lights the flame, then goes to bring the cow again. Nay, he uses no force at all, just a click of tongue on teeth and a simple tug from a gentle hand.

"Why such terror, woman?" he asks at last, barely heedful of my cowering.

I cannot speak. Yet, a moment more, and the sound rises again in a mournful wail. Kol sees my fright, seeming but to laugh. "Woman, it is the song of seals!"

Just as Alof told, Kol is right. I listen to the sound now, feeling foolish. Kol sets himself upon a stone, pulling from his pouch a slab of dryish meat which he presses to my fingers. "Eat." Then he turns and scans about. "Nay," he breathes, " 'tis near a circle!"

Now I see it fairly: the varied, wide circumference. Before us is a whirling out, a nearly perfect round. Each stone is large, nipped by wind and frosts, facing white and glowing in the dancing dews.

Kol whisp's, "As if waiting since the dark ones' time. Formed upon the jaw of the very giant . . ." He pauses, fingering his baubles on their string. Then he hands me back the torch, holds for me a bladder bag with a bit of wet, waiting for me to drink. "There, now, get ye onward." Kol pats me gently on my arm with a coaxing touch, as if I were a child.

I stand, taking up the rein, tearing another chunk of meat carefully with my broken teeth, stepping beyond this almost circle—most unlikely chance—leaving Kol to watch my fire burn.

By the time I reach the hill's crest, Kol is standing in the center of that hollow, singing strangely chants and charms in some unfamiliar tongue. He bends and bows as if offering upon a sacred altar. In some few steps more, I smell again my fire: it rises up instead of smoldering down. Nay, I walk more swiftly till his music slightly quiets. Yet, even beyond the hill's first height, the wind carries up his sounds.

Beyond at last, I mark a lake brimming wide with fish running close upon its clear, blue reaches; and three more streams cutting through the fells high up where soon our sheep will graze; and a flat outcrop where, most like, we'll build a summer hut for the shepherd's keep. Then down again, claiming cliffs that reek with the muck of birds—great auks and murres and, far beneath, diving ducks leaving downy feathers floating on the surface of the sea.

By dusk I have made my circuit: a fine, wide line stretching from fjord to high-fell, from pasture down to shore, encompassing all that lies within, even the seals' rock beach and the strange stone circle. My legs are weary from the walking, but light and spry as if tingling with the fire's dance. My torch has ne'er gone out but that once, and now, in the failing light, it sparks to show my way.

I clamber down the final distance. In the earth below I notice gashes thickly drawn, great ax-lines already marking out where Thorbjorg's house will stand. The smell of fresh-killed seal hangs in the air like a fatty veil, so I know Alof has found the beasts and made quick work of them. The others gather near the smoky hearth, all but Teit, who stays behind me on the hill to guard over the last of my smoldering coals.

"Katla"—Gyde meets me as I tumble down the crest—"you must be tired." Comes the mistress just behind her. Reaching for the torch, Thorbjorg says, "Redbeard greet you." She says no more, only sends me off to where the others huddle before the gurgling cook-pot, with no sign that she is pleased at least to see her boundary drawn.

Through all that night, though we thralls eat well and share some tales and gather close before the meager fire, the wind and dark nip at my neck. The stars spark bright and brittle, cold. Thorbjorg and Kol are not about. When I ask, none are quick to tell. I ask no more. Yet, lying late, wide awake upon that half-froze' earth, I, perhaps more than all the rest, wonder not where they have gone.

THORBJORG

WE CLOSE the circle. We two together, though I limp and cannot lend a hand. Yet Kol's are wide and leathern. His back is bent, but it is sturdy. Kol's arms are thick and stronger than my own. They can do the work to round this hof—this sanctuary hallowed now for you, Alfather—while I recite the words, the kvads, as you have taught me well and long:

*The giants came from Ymir's sweat. So the cow Aud-
humla licked upon the rime.*

The ancient speak-lore, ever told upon such sacred dealings:

*At the first day's dusk, a clump of hair came from the
stones. On the second, rose a head. On the third, came forth
a man.*

E'er from the beginning, as ever they were borne:

*Buri he was called. So Buri sired a son called Bor. Bor
made upon his wife, called Bestla, three great sons: Odin, Vili,
Ve. All these three ruled together for a time. Yet, of them,
Odin rules now over all.*
*Father of the gods, Alfather. Father of the slain, Valfather.
God of the hanged, Hangagod. God of the imprisoned, Hapta-
god. Old Graybeard. One-Eyed god who sits upon your
throne, Hlidskialf, and watches all the goings of this middle
world, the petty works of men and all their woes.*

Your countless names! I sing them out, though my voice is hoarse
and crass and bears a whistle, as Kol wraps the boulders in thick cloth,
ties such ropes and reins about the yoking of the bull. A scent of musk
and shifting mists rise above this shadowed hollow. In the hard glow
of the moon, these other stones stand, silent watchers, as Kol guides
the boulders into place upon my croon.

*Odin's son, called Asa-Thor, whose breath is wind, whose
arms throw heavy thunder. Odin's wife, called Frigga
Fiorgvinsdatter, who knows men's fates but does not prophesy
aloud. The foul one, Loki, who bore upon the giantess Angr-
boda three bastard spawn: the Fenris-Wolf, the Midgard
snake, the cold and hated Hel, his daughter. So, and Frigga's
beloved son, wise, beauteous Baldr, most favored of the gods.*

Yet, on Loki's tricks and cunning craft, the Aesir saw their
Baldr murdered.

On and on, until the final toll. Slowly, slowly, with grunts and
groaning. With sweating as with birth, the figure grows right and
proper. A circle perfect. And then the Vé is cut: the sacrificial center,
the ax blade breaking quick the fragile earth, the skin come black and
rich and oozing. Into this breach I will place my sacrifice, burn my
praises up to you—Alfather, greatest of the Aesir, wisest, wisdom-
truest god—to plead upon your eye, your single-sighted vision, to
guide my path, my stumbled steps, my limping falter.

KATLA

THE WOOLEN WARMTH of sleep still wraps about me, yet Gyde is up,
her shoulders bent and busy as she sets the cauldron on the hearth
fire's heat. She says naught to me as she sends her daughter out to
gather twigs. My aching limbs and my thickening belly rail against
the morning's chill as I go to bear some water for the boil.

Already the men are full upon their digging, setting out the shap-
ing stones which will frame the mistress' household walls. I move
beyond them groggily, my footsteps stumbling, my empty buckets
slapping against my thighs, up toward a creek which I know does run
with freshness.

I move in starts, feeling my mouth gone sour once again, my
stomach, as now seems constant, sudden queasy.

A voice calls, "Fair ye and a-day!" I turn and see there Teit. "You
look a fright, Katla. Did you not sleep?" He stands, quick to his ankles
in frigid water, digging out a channel toward the homestead from the
stream.

"Nay," I say. "It is nothing."

"What?" He takes my buckets. "Are you weak or ill?"

"Neither—naught—" Yet I cannot hold my sickness. Flushed, I bend upon my knees and retch into the sod.

Teit is quick beside me, sloshing mud yet bearing wet, cool comfort in his hands. He stays for some time, despite the filth and fetid smell. Then he helps me stand. I can barely give him thanks when Nattfari comes.

"Husband-man, have you heard the news?" To me she smiles wanly. "So you should, for they've found some sign of haugbo in the homestead's walls."

"Haugbo?"

"Indeed, mound folk—a pile of stone and sticks, some scars of ashes in a pit, and, very near, some well-gnawed bones—"

"Bones?" I stare from her to Teit's impassive visage. I fumble in my apron's pouch for my mother's rosary, finding only Gizur's hammer-stone.

"What kind of bones?" Teit eyes her keenly.

"Broken bits of seal and walrus, or so Kol seemed to say—"

"Nattfari—"

"It is true! This Greenland's full of such—huldre folk who live upon the hills, grims and nøkks which haunt these streams and play such frantic music. All such invisible ones, as was the talk upon the feasts at Eiriksøy."

"Thralls' talk?" Teit says slyly. "Nattfari, hush. You'll frighten off our Katla. Already she's had fears enough."

Yet Nattfari's eyes sparkle. She even giggles, wrapping Teit's shoulders quick around, hanging heavy there as he leans upon his shovel's haft. "Katla, I mean no harm. I'm only saying what I have heard." Her grin turns more a grimace, bearing out her brutal taunt. "There, now, not to worry—our Katla!" Then she kisses Teit hard upon the lips and wafts away with a swing of hips and a foolish, cloying wave.

Teit sighs when she is gone. "Do not worry, Katla. The mistress Thorbjorg says such signs are fair and fortune. If others once have warmed and feasted here, very soon so we shall, too."

Teit's gaze bears honest reassurance. I try to smile, then draw my buckets full. Teit offers me his hand, but I beg him off, saying, "I would rather go myself." So I would, and escape such harmful hearing, yet, all that day and night, I think upon such frights as grims and nøkks and Nattfari's strangeish malice.

"Why?" I ask Gyde later in the eve, as we stack damp moss to dry, then cover such with thick blanket-skins for sleep.

"Nattfari knows little gentleness. Only quip and gripe, but her heart is good despite her bite. She is just jealous because she cannot bear a child."

"Jealous?" I choke upon the word. Even the thought, spoke for the first aloud. It stirs the sickness in my belly, screws it and the healing scar which barely binds my mangled breast, growing now in size and pain.

"Katla," Gyde tries to calm me, "what's done is done. You only harm yourself with anger. Our lot is not to bear in vengeance. That is but a freeman's boon."

Yet I cannot stop, so show my own true heart with all its hatred blooming. "Anger? Never will it go from me! I would not let it, even if I could."

"Say it not, for there is life growing in you. It will sense your hate and grow twisted from within."

"I do not care but that it should never live. Bare two months have passed to prove it. Perhaps 'twill fall away, or die within me, or I die, too!"

"Katla, it is there. It is there and quick. You must not hate it. You will live and bear it out, for the mistress will not let you die."

Gyde says aloud what I have sensed since the beginning: as a pregnant cow bought upon a market's chance, so the mistress made this bargain, too. The seeress will not let me die. Nay, she'll have my back and my body's labor. I bear Gyde's words, then turn and keep apart. That night and through some several days, indeed, I wander, straying as far from the homefield's bustle as I dare. And Gyde, though she is the mistress' woman, does not speak to Thorbjorg or pain me for my sloth, but lets me pass as well I might, to bear with my morning's retch, my aches and wrack and rage alone.

Still, every dawn I awake to sounds of the scraping out of stones, to the slicing of sod and the lashing of driftwood. Every day, Thorbjorg's men mount the casing stones into sturdy walls, then stuff them with sod, thick and wide for warmth, then make a roof of grassy turf laid over driftwood beaming. Once full enclosed, the house is dank, with a meager hearth for warmth set upon the inner row. On either side, dirt-built benches tuck beneath the roof's low eaves. On these we will sit, eat, sew, and sleep—and, fair, most likely die.

When all is set secure, no longer can I rightly keep away when we women are called to build a better cook's hearth, then to set the standing looms against the far walls, leaning. By the dim creeping through this homestead's door, Gizur carves the doorposts thick with twists of dragons' heads and horses entwined, while I fumble with the threads, listening yet again to the sound of grunts, broken earth, and scraping stone as the men set to build a byre for the cows.

Soon outbuildings scatter about the fells, with a summer hut for Vidur on the hillslope and a smithy Kol spends half a moon to build. Now a ring of stones draws clear the homefield's bounding, but this Greenland's season's short and chilly. With what time is left before the autumn frost, little flourishes. Even the barley barely grows.

Still my stomach swells. The dark nights lengthen and the winds begin to howl. Beneath their loudest wails, I reckless whisp' my mother's prayers aloud, until, one night, the others hear and Kol comes, eyes me odd and gives to me a new name: "Katla Christian." So I think perhaps I like it, for all the haugbo, draugs, and grims and brutal men—perchance even the seeress, too—will hear the sound and be afraid.

When winter comes, daylight lasts barely one hour. Not much rises up to stop the snow and ice from cutting hard and drifting before our household's door. Thrice already we are nearly trapped within, but for Kol, who wakens in the middle of such storms to cut a path from the homestead to his smithy.

I have been there only once. The walk is long. The snow and ice and winds are brutal, yet that hour spent was the first ever since in Greenland I was warm. So warm, to see Kol's sagging jowls bent over

the heat and lighted by the flame, and even his shirt set off from his
chest, looking much like Thor, with a twisted, aging grimace at the
quick-lift and his hammer's falling clank. I had brought Kol food as
the mistress bid me, told to come right back when I was done. Yet,
when I stepped into the fire's glow, I bare but begged, "Could I stay for
just a little longer?"

Kol set down his tools and ate with me, talking some of his
thoughts on stoking coals. I hardly listened, feeling the heat at my
back like the melting of my bones, till I noticed, somewhat hidden in
the flames, a blade half made but of handsome form and fashion.

"What is it?" I pointed toward where it lay reddening in the coals.

He hesitated, then stood up, reaching for the blade with his long
black tongs.

"It is beautiful!" The markings fair as any Gizur might strike, yet
here the mode was finer, caught upon with fire. And the runes—
strangeish ones. "A gift for the mistress Thorbjorg?"

"Nay, it is a gift upon your child's birth."

At that I felt a shiver no spark of coals could ease. I stood, quickly
took my cloak and wrapped it round. "It is time I left."

"Indeed." Kol led me out and closed the door behind me. I bore
away from the smoky, fragrant flames, back into the world of gray and
white, of dark and cold confusion.

Am I never to be comforted, as tormented through each day I
wait, tucked within this household's strangeness? Its sodded walls, so
small and dark, narrower than I'm used to, not near so neatly fashioned as Einar's old Iceland stead, and crowded with all us thralls
within, and the cows and calves which must now bear with us against
the winter's chill. For all their lowing, fetid heat, still my fingers
stiffen as I work the spindle's thread, my shoulders cramp as I stand
before the towering wall-bound loom tossing weft threads among the
warp. My only solace is Gizur's cadenced pounding as he carves nearly
every beam and wood exposed. He seems to know it, watching me
with the shyest sort of smile as I sweep away his flicking chips, then
bend to watch them burn, each fleck rising from the hearth fire's heat,
a fleeting crimson-gold.

* * *

Just before the Yule, comes a scrape and the sound of horse's hooves upon the ice, then a shout from beside our frozen harbor's edge: "Up there on the hill, hallo!"

"Who comes?" Kol rises to answer from behind the unopened door.

"I am sent from Eirik Raude to call the seeress Thorbjorg."

"For what cause?"

"By a fortnight's jaunt, to celebrate first Yule. She and her best thralls are to come to my master's homestead, Brattahlid."

Kol turns to the mistress, who sits upon her corner making marks in runes on a bit of twig. "Tell him he is welcome," she says, ever sharpening her blade, never lifting up her eyes.

Kol answers back and swings the doorway open. Soon the bearer sits warming his thick hands beside our fire. " 'Tis cold without. I am grateful for your comfort. A full night's rest and a bite of food is what I need. And you here, ne'er about with many neighbors on a side— indeed, 'tis two days' travel to the nearest farm." Gyde sends Arngunn to gather frozen meat from our deep-dug stores for a meager supper while I speed the others at their chores so they might come and hear this bearer's news.

All that night, the messenger is much content to sit among us, eating from our pot and telling tales of Brattahlid. Too, of the homestead built at Herjolfsnaes, beside the sea, and an even finer farm, Gardar. " 'Tis Einar's place. No grander hereabouts save Brattahlid itself, and these two joined by a narrow isthmus and soon to be full-joined by blood."

"Who's to marry?" Nattfari's quick to beg for gossip.

"Only the Red's own bastard daughter, Freydis Eiriksdatter, and Einar's son Torvard." He tears a shred of boiled meat between his teeth. "They prepare the wedding feast for this very Yule."

There's a hush about the house. I bend to stir the coals to bring the fire's heat.

Alof says, "She's reputed a peevish woman."

"Harder than the winged Valkyries," the runner tells. "Still, they'll send rich praises up to fertile Frey and kill a fatted boar. 'Tis the first proper wedding ever held anywhere in Greenland."

"It is a match made in the frigid halls of Hel!" Kol makes light, and I am grateful for their loudish laughter to mask my shaking hands, clanking at the fire rack. So the beast's to marry. He! Marrying, while I wear the scars of his brutality upon my face and breast and within my belly. Borne his hate, have I; yet, for all my worthless life, he'll wed unto the most powerful house in Greenland.

I move the kettle from the coals, stooping to scour it in the stream Teit has trenched across the hard dirt floor. Truly, he deserves it— married to this Freydis, rumored worse than merely savage-tongued. She's said to be Eirik's daughter by another man's wife, yet bears her paternity defiantly and challenges her brothers boldly to their greater right. She will never suffer even one touch of Torvard's malicious handling. Nay, most like, she'll have him to her bed but once—enough to bear an heir—then throw him out and surely take another man. Oh, and do it laughing and spitting, as I should have done—as I had tried.

So I brood as I slosh stones across the tarnished iron. It muddies underfoot. Barely would I notice but that the mistress sends Nattfari next to me. She hovers like a task-woman. I tremble, fearing what new punishment I have brought upon myself. Yet Nattfari reaches for the pot and scour-stones quite gently, nudging me to mop the mud.

"There, now," she whispers. "Katla, calm, for you know some good may come of this."

"Good?" I turn to her. "What good can ever come for me again?"

Nattfari shakes her head as she spreads dry earth, then some hay upon the floor. "Such good as you have courage for. Katla, surely you can turn this to your favor."

"How?" I sniff.

"Your molester now will be an influential man. Think you not, you are due some little boon for bearing forth his child?"

"A slave? What is due a slave but some mercy to let her child live?" Or, better, I am wont to say, to let it die.

"Yet think again, Katla. Like as not, Torvard will bear some pride for getting you so quickly big with child. He'll boast it, surely, even before his new-come bride at the feast of their very wedding day. Play upon it. Girl, if you call him so out loud—name him for the father that he is—then at least, in the name of fertile Frey, in his freeman's pride he'll throw you some chunk of silver or an ell of cloth or an ivory tooth to make your child's way."

'Tis a strange thought, though I have heard done stranger things when men are drunk and merry feasting. Yet this is little hope and naught to ease my pain. Still, even this comes with a sudden, anguished choking. "I cannot speak it out, not there and boldly before them all—"

"Katla," Nattfari says with some disgust, "you need say little. Just stand before him with your belly rising. Do it, girl, there for all to see, and get of him one-hundredth of what he's had of you, or be wretched all your life for having not the will."

There's a sudden harshness to Nattfari's words. Her face turns bitter. Her lips tighten as she bends, taking again the scour-stones, rattling them with cracked and certain hands. I ask not why, for I know she's had no children. Yet for all that night I think upon her words—on the hate in them—strange hate, like such as got this child into me. And I think on Nattfari's thoughts, spoke' aloud, which my tongue has yet the strength to form. Now I force them out slowly, calm in whispers, till they echo with the wind's chill breath and hiss beneath Eirik's messenger's vociferous snores.

That morning, after the boiling of a seal-bone soup, the mistress gives Eirik's runner half a peg of silver hacked from an ancient chain she keeps in her treasure box under lock and key. With such payment, the man goes quickly toward his driftwood sledge to spread his invitations and ill-wrought news to other farms. When his form is but a shadow in the heaves and dark of this unremitting snow, says the mistress, "Four days hence, we'll ourselves prepare to journey. Nattfari, Teit, Kol, Katla, you will come with me."

Strange, I dare not wonder why the mistress picked me, fearing what Nattfari might have whisp'ed. Yet Thorbjorg mentions nothing, and soon I sit high upon the board beside Kol as we leave our homefield's course, our old mare bumping and gyring over the fjord's icy wrinkles.

My heavy stomach makes our travel harder. Indeed, sometimes, to give the beast a rest, Mistress Thorbjorg bids us forgo the sledge and walk. Yet she says nothing of my pace, herself leaning on her crooked cane of driftwood, her stride falling behind even my own. She seems but tall and taut in the cloak Gyde made of thickest ewe's wool, black with cuffs of white rabbit's fur, and her touchwood waistbelt clanging, heavy with her household's keys. I slow my step to meet hers, listening as our breaths merge and footsteps come in rhythm, gaining strength with each puff we share to buoy our trembled limbs. Thorbjorg never stumbles, complains not once, even with her limp. And to Kol's oft urgings, she frostily refuses to be set upon the sledge and pulled.

We make our way, resting rarely, guided by the stars and the ebbing moon. Little talk's among us, no sounds at all most times but the horse's clop, no singing for fear the brittle ice on the cliffs above will crack and come crashing down upon our heads with a bended note; and only sometimes Nattfari's girlish giggle at how well 'twill be to revel at the thralls' lard-table.

That night, the sky glows grim as unstoked embers. The fjord's black but for the icebergs' crests glittering with a final slice of moon. Far ahead, at last, we sight Brattahlid. Eirik's longhouse is a shadow but for two squarish windows, bright with firelight through their calf's-gut casing, seeming to watch us near like eyes. I try hard to remember now the words Nattfari'd whispered. Yet they do not come. My heart turns a terror-quake. My feet begin to falter.

"The cold upon them?" Mistress Thorbjorg comes. Lending me her arm, she takes me toward the homefield. I know not why, but I calm a bit; the mistress' touch, so strong and certain, reassures.

'Tis such—she rubbing my hand as if I were a timid child—that we two together stand before Eirik's door. It is massive, carved with dragons dark and fierce as any Gizur's knife has yet to yield. To either side, Eirik's roof rolls low, heavy-set with snow-caked sod. The iron-bound planks swing back as four rough, head-shaved thralls emerge to greet us. From behind them, music, dancing, laughter fly across the homefield's hush, bounding off the hefty byre stalls, clattering against the wall stones of the distant, brimming horsefold. My head tips, dizzy but for the mistress' steady-guiding arm.

Within, Greenland's highest master's hall is a-whirr with bodies, smoke, tapestries, voices, hanging lamps from heavy rafters and torches clinging to the beams, and a hearth so long—never have I known before a fire so great and heat so hot after so long in the cold.

"Thorbjorg Seeress, welcome!" Eirik Raude himself claims my mistress' cloak. He takes her from me, guiding through the freeborn crowd. Near' I am adrift as Kol quick-follows behind the mistress, till Eirik's goodwife, Thjoldhilde, quickly calls her kitchen-maid to guide us to the cooking hall.

I am glad for it, for our proper place and chores, for a time apart from that push and noise and bustle. There's a long passage connecting master's hall to cook's. I steady by its end, pressed with thralls and rich foods whisked away on steaming, greasy platters. At least Torvard will never catch me here. It is a cooling thought, the first I've had since setting sight upon the windowed eyes of Eirik's long-hall. Yet, behind me now, Nattfari's griping, "Katla, you are so thick! Move yourself and let me through!" then loudly, waving over my shoulder, "Astrid! Bera! 'Tis Nattfari! I am here!" like a petty, ill-taught girl, nearly shoving me, so I am pressed into the scratching wall stones to let her pass to greet such unknown, thrall-bound women with squeals and screeches.

Teit then quietly eases me into the kitchen light. On the cook's hearth, a carcass is boiling, meat of a tender boar indeed. Its hooves clank in the old bronze kettle blacked and hot from stewing endless long. Near the chill of the doorway are stacked bulks of cheese, salted butter, and in piles fish, mushrooms, herbs, and onions. The kitchen-woman takes one look upon my belly's state and shakes her head. "This one's no good for heavy lifting. Get some roots, woman, to strip and clean, or something for some cutting." Then she says aloud to no one near, "What, there were no better thralls than a fat one, pregnant, to bend and fetch for the old seeress Thorbjorg?"

I set about in silence, my hand upon a pile of hard roots, working fast, for already twice the cook's come shouting, "Work! The food's fast growing scarce. What little beer is running low. Quick! Quick!" then rushing out once more.

My pile is bare begun when a hand rests on my shoulder. I see Inga's ruddy, rosy grin. "Ah!" she cries, holding her palms upon her bosoms. "How I've missed you, Katla!" She leans to hug me heartily. Yet her arms about me—such weight—like heavy memory. I do not drop the root or the scraper from my hands. Instead, I look on her, feeling almost nothing. She sees me clearly then. Slowly her joy turns sober. "I had not thought . . ." She hesitates, then her hand's upon my chin. I let her turn my cheeks from side to side. "It is not so bad, you know," she tries. I press her hand away, but she slips it down until it rests upon the mound beneath my aching breasts. "So that's the work of it."

I bend my head to start at the next knobby root.

"Hush, now," she says.

"I am not crying." Yet she knows my pain. She always has.

Inga sits, taking up a scraper and a root. "He is here," she whispers. "You know it."

"And betrothed to Freydis Eiriksdatter." I nod.

"Yet the witch has made you come this way? Then she is as hard a mistress as they say."

For a breath, I do not speak. Then, "Nay. Thorbjorg is a solemn kindness."

Inga sighs, "Katla, they say Torvard's betrothed to keep him from further trouble, say Eirik's daughter's harsher than any full redress—"

"Who says it so, the masters or the slaves? Inga, do not bundle me as you used to when one of Einar's house-thralls scolded. I am far beyond need of that kind of care."

Her face falls dark. Her puffed hand stiffens around the root.

Over the crowd's rough din comes another voice, familiar: "Katla's come again to celebrate?" Hallgerd cackles. "To toast the happy marriage of Torvard?"

Inga mocks beneath her breath, "Seems she's sneaked some sips of Yule beer early," then quickly stands to block the woman's way.

Hallgerd presses, "Let me greet the girl!" and thrusts her face at mine. "So here's the one who used to press her cheek against Mistress Grima's silver? Not so pretty now, and, ah, big as a well-bred milk-cow—"

"Hallgerd, leave her be," Inga tries, but it makes no difference. I myself rise, drawing back my apron so my stomach stands out proudly.

"I do not care," I say, "if all of you now know my state. If house-thralls hear one word, you quickly breathe out seven others. Go and talk and tell among yourselves. It won't be long before Torvard himself has heard the gossip and comes to gloat over his finest deed!"

I move to another corner, daring not to catch Inga's injured glance. Yet not long—indeed, before half the night has passed—comes again the kitchen-wench, this time shouting, "Katla of Thorbjorg the Seeress' household, you are called!"

I find my way among them sudden cleared, and all their dagger-eyes quick-honed, as I am ushered through the passage, then into the heat and sweat of drunken freemen, torch smoke, and giddy servant girls set on laps and groped and grieving. I am handed now a plate of meat and pressed with it toward the table where my mistress sits beside Thorbjorn Glora, chieftain now of some new place called Siglufjord. Kol stands behind our mistress as a sentry. With her cane pressed against his shoulder, he is fine, imposing, though his stature's twisted and somewhat small. He nods to me as I pass. So odd, though he barely breathes and does not blink an eye, I sense his vigil stands to guard both Thorbjorg and me.

I bow my head to pass the plate before the mistress. She takes a large bone without much note. Yet I see myself she sits precisely far from Torvard. Down the meat-laid board, he is feasting, with his thick, soft arm about his new-come bride in her blood-red gown. Oh, at first, I am loath to move at all! I stand transfixed as a hare before the hunter's bow, but Thorbjorg bids me, "Katla, bring me ale. The horn is dry."

At her command, I slowly straighten. I know any moment Torvard will notice me moving there before them all. Now I fear his eyes, my boldness in the slaves' hall lost. I dare not look in his direction, clinging to the long-hall's walls.

"A horn to fertile Frey, for my pole is long and fat, as bursting-fit as his to have this wife upon our wedding straw!" Torvard's voice is thick with drink. All the freemen toast this vile boasting. I would faint, though there is nowhere here to fall but among their scorn and plates and laughter.

The freemen scoff, though now it seems not at me. Nay, their eyes are on Torvard's bride. Freydis Eiriksdatter finds no humor in her husband's toast. There she sits, twice my girth even with my current measure, her head a height equal to Torvard's own, her hair flaming red as ever Eirik Raude's. She stabs at some thick, brown meat with her carving knife, looking quite vicious with her great amber beads swinging side to side about her breasts and her oval brooches flashing. When her husband reaches his hands to clutch about her neck, she gruffly shoves him off. "Keep your hands away, husband, until I need them."

Torvard quick-barks back, "Lady, you're a bold one, and not yet even bled upon the marriage couch!" He takes another sip of beer. "But I'll teach you there to behave and enjoy it well!"

His words rattle my soul with remembering, as if again such words are hurtled down at me. Still Torvard does not see me, not even as, finally, his father, Einar, catches on my glance. He sits at Eirik's shoulder, pressing now a hand before his lips to whisper into Eirik's ear.

"Torvard." Eirik Raude stands, taking time to lay his knife upon the greasy table-board. "Make no idle threats. This woman's free and is my daughter also."

"How can I forget it, Foster-father?" Torvard sips his horn, too drunk to note good counsel. "Jesting—just—to raise her hopes. She's a wild one, your Freydis, but I will tame her."

"Better, Torvard," Eirik warns, "to keep her wild."

"Father!" Freydis herself now speaks. "I will deal upon you later. Yet, husband, swear! Such men's words as yours are weak and naught compared with action. So I'll tell you—all of you!—I need no man's protections. Sooner, Torvard, you will find yourself hard-pressed to satisfy on me. And quicker still, find yourself without hearth or home, wife or heir, than 'twill take to rise from my disdaining pummel."

The room bursts laughing on her boast, but from the size of her fists, raised high and hard and flashing with the cutting angle of her garnet wedding stone, there is no doubt, her threat is e'er but idle.

"Menace, woman!" Torvard boils.

"Lay one hand amiss upon her cheek," Eirik says, "and after she is through with you, I and your own father here will stand with any divorce plea she makes upon the Althing mound."

"Ha!" Torvard laughs. "Divorce, when we are barely married?"

"Torvard." Now Master Einar stands. "Be wise. You hear your foster-father's words. See now my own hand laid on the sacred oath ring, here before all our fellows and friends." His father grasps a golden circlet from his arm and passes it to Eirik Raude.

Barely do they grasp the round when comes Eirik's mistress, Thjoldhilde crying, "Hush! Enough! All of you, even on the very wedding feast!" She presses her husband back into his high-seat. "Eirik, Einar, Torvard, come and drink! And Freydis, too! Another toast in praise of Goddess Freya for this marriage's fortune! No more talk of divorce, I pray to Thor, at least as long as this Yule log burns."

Then she calls out, "Women, fill the horns around!" I bend before the full ale bucket. My hands are quaking as I lift the ladle up and try to pour, spilling but a drop upon the dirt near some freeman's toe before Thjoldhilde is shouting, "Woman, watch your work!"

Her nettled gaze shows no recognition. She sees only a faceless thrall. Yet, suddenly, though the shadows hide me and the crowd is thick, I know Torvard has seen me. He is standing now, his horn outstretched, waiting as I make my way around the hall.

Just as Nattfari's words foretold, I feel my belly rising. I stand as tall as the very beams, my state exposed before every freeman's eye. I want Torvard to say just then—"Here! A sample of my work! And such fine work! Freydis, see what shape you'll wear upon the springtime?"—just so, to admit his fault, right there and then, before them all.

But no word comes. He lets me fill every horn before his own, then, shaking though the ladle is as I fill his up, he stares right past, as if he does not know me. Stares beyond, as if he never knew my face or any other part of me, though I know every stretch of him, from every vile hair to the savage scratch of his ragged tongue.

"Say you nothing?" I whisper. I cannot help—the words slip out.

"Bondwoman, what?" he demands. "Girl, what did you say?" His play at ignorance is more foolish than any boast. "Say, but, who—is it? No, it could not be! Katla? Is that you? Father, Mother, look. It's your old girl, Katla. Nay, I wouldn't recognize her. She is much changed."

"Changed," I hiss, "much changed by you."

"But, say, I'm glad to see you here to celebrate my wedding."

"Celebrate? I would have once, happily and pleased. But now—"

"What? Oh, you wish only you could have me for yourself. Surely, after our last jauntings! See, Freydis, if you like it not, there are others who would gladly have me—"

"Ah, husband," Freydis cants, "if you prefer a bondwoman's rough, cold moss-bed, then well enough. I can do alone to warm our wedding sheets!"

All the hall breaks then with laughter as Freydis grasps the horn from Torvard's hand and, like any Viking warrior, drinks it swiftly down. "There, girl, come fill up this!" she orders me, slapping the empty horn so it rolls across the board.

Torvard takes it. I fill it, shaking, feeling my tears, blind and nearly falling, but I hold them back and sudden shout, though the shout comes out a whisper, "Torvard, this child in me's yours."

"What?" Torvard giggles now, as any nervous girl, and spits his beer. "What did you say, woman? Say, this thing? This thing that's in your belly is—a child? Thought I you'd grown but thick and ugly while you've been away. Oh, and you claim this thing within your gut is mine?" He struggles hard to strangle back his mirth. "Mine? Not mine! I think you cannot prove it. Prove it, thrall, and even if you could, do you think I owe you something for it? Say, six marks of silver is the proper price? If you were a freewoman, perhaps. But, first, you are a thrall, so I owe you nothing for the pleasure of my use of you. And even if you were somewhat more, you would have to prove no other man had used you first!"

"None has!" I cry, feeling the ladle clank and clatter from my fingers.

Torvard smiles. "As I recall, your lover—your absent freeman—now, what name was his? Ossur Asbjarnarsson, was it? Yes! I've heard he's out on Ketilsfjord, dredging muck to make his way. If 'tis any freeman's seed within your belly, it's his, not mine. You should go and beg his six marks, if you think he has so much!"

Now their laughter's shrieking. Even Freydis mocks above them all. I look across, but find no tender glance, just bemused faces, red with drink and shadowed dark with hairy beards and leering gazes. Only Einar seems unmoved; and, not far back from him, Mistress Thorbjorg.

"Come away." She stands. "Katla, you are in no state—no state to serve. Go and send Nattfari. Kol, go with her."

Thorbjorg's words are cold. She makes her way around the table-board, her hard wood cane thumping on the pounded floor. Yet, when she comes to me, her eyes speak somehow softer. Her hands are gentle as she passes me to Kol.

He leads me out and back into the kitchen, where Nattfari shrills, wild with the other thralls, and Teit's beside her, sitting somber. All look at us as if they know just what has passed. Nattfari turns to me with a scornful glancing.

"Know you nothing better than to cleave upon a freeman? Such revenge is never had and always wanting. You'll bear this child out alone. Indeed, some would enjoy it! Yet you, you'll call it doleful luck if the child survives. Be sure, there is no recompense for all your suffering. Better to love a slave and have some comfort for your woes." Then she takes her own man's mouth and lays her lips down, hard and wet, so all hear their sound as they uncouple. Turning with a lilt, she smiles as she goes with Kol toward the feasting hall.

I feel the slap of Nattfari's turning, her bitter hate, her beguiling heart, this new pain laid hard upon my ever-miserable load. Inga comes to me, reaching with her warming, tender fingers. But Hallgerd is there with her spit and gloat: "Now what say you, Katla? Whose child lies within your womb if the master's son will take no fault?"

I glare at her. "If ever you had a child, Hallgerd, of either hate or love, surely it would choke upon the bile in your breasts."

"But this one, Katla? What of this one? Dare you name its father now?"

She taunts me, and my anger ripens as it could not have done before. "I call this child's father—listen, all of you!—I call it out, and none may deny me now. I call this child's father the Mountain King, crown of the invisibles, the demon lover. From the mountain it was made, and this child will be demon-born. I swear it so. May it live to plague you all!"

THORBJORG

I TURN HER OUT—Katla, shivering, rage unspent. Her elbow rough against my fingers. Her clammy sweat. Beneath: hard bone set and healed by my own hands. But only bone and cuts and bruises: those upon the face and breast. Still the deeper wounds remain.

Odin, that I should feel such kinship with a slave! But the feast goes on and I return to it, to the toasts and laughter, to the sacrificial meat—the dead which makes the living hearty. Their mocks ringing in my ears. The man beside me: "She's a bold one, yours, this Katla!" Thorbjorn Glora gloating. "If she were mine, she'd bear a whipping for such gall."

I cannot speak my feelings. It is not my place. Even I, the mistress, am not free. But I do say, in vain effort of her defense, "You'd shatter, then, a vessel already broken?"

I eye him straight. Glora swallows hard his beer, offering up another sip from the horn we've shared this evening. I refuse him. In time, he leaves me. Quiet upon this bench before this sordid meal.

Strange, in some sense, all that's done is in my favor. The father will not claim the child; thus, the child is my own. There's no satisfaction in it. When has any man seen the value in a child unless an heir, a kin, a piece of property to be bargained with or traded? But a slave girl's misbegotten? Most would set it out upon the fells, exposed to weather and the teeth of wolves.

I suck a boar's bone, listening to the din, until I hear my own Nattfari. "The Mountain King!" she prattles. "Katla says the child's of the Mountain King." Then laughter. Ah, the cleverness, indeed! I feel upon my cheeks a warmth where it rarely dwells. Odin, see how the Norns' threads weave a pattern pretty? Strange, surprising how the dull and docile, set upon their own defense, in the end turn wiser than even they would know.

It is not far from truth, this tale of Katla's. Old Graybeard, so you've told: this child will be mine and yours. Yet now 'tis whispered even here among their hearing.

I shake my head and push the plate away with the last meat uneaten, cold, congealed with grease upon the gristle. That night, and some thereafter, though my heart's aligned with hers, I treat Katla without due courtesy. Cold I am to her. Yet still the talk about is that the seeress gives too much favor to her wayward slave: lets the pregnant thrall sleep beside her in the warmth of Brattahlid's dark hall. I tell them it is only to serve my chilly bones' old misery. Better Katla bear this coddled mark than what torments await in the cold, unfriendly quarters with the other slaves.

Barely does she rest, most nights shaking with her pregnant torments, oft awakened by the child's forceful kicks, though she makes no groans or gasps. Only I can feel the child as I lay my arm for warmth about her waist. I feel it squirming beneath my own decrepit fingers.

Yet there's something else, something worse perhaps than all these pangs. Katla sleeps with one eye open all these three long weeks which last the Yule. She does not rest, and I do not blame her, for Torvard rouses from his wedding bed each night and stays upon the shadows, watching her.

KATLA

Norse origin?

FINALLY THE BOUGHS are burned, the Yule log ashes swept and saved to ignite the next year's fire. Too, the bridal red's well stained and torn from drink and squabble and lust; though Torvard bears no strut or boast, as once he did upon another fouling. Indeed, if any about here struts, 'tis the hip and bosom of Freydis Eiriksdatter.

I try not to hear, not to know or understand. I endure this place because I must, with no eyes or ears but the slightest glance before me on the icy ground. At last, the mistress calls to Kol, "Bear down the sledge upon the fjord's frost. We are heading home."

Such a thought, after so long in my fearing! Such comfort in it, even with the mistress cold and Teit silent, sitting close with Nattfari's grip entangling his fingers, and all the while, that woman smiling at me sweetly.

No longer will I trust her. Still I smile back, to keep her treachery at bay. Only Kol gives me a thoughtful gaze. But I do not care—only that we break from here, slip over the icy crust of Eiriksfjord and roughly toward our home fjord.

That first night's travel, it is like the frigid breath of wind screaming my own anguish, while I sit some silent, bound up in the sledge with blankets and shaggy woolen cloaks around me, bundled close by the mistress' own gnarled hands. This time she will not let me rise, even when she bids the others walk. I plead to stretch my aching limbs, but Thorbjorg tells me, "Katla, you are grown too big to venture out much more."

That night and into the next morning, the wild wind kicks up and rages for me, tearing the drifts to cyclones, whipping clouds of snow about our cheeks and caking the men's rough whiskers hard with frost. Up and up, I revel in its fury. Yet, suddenly, the wind about us dies. The next days pass but chill and rigid, guided by the pinprick stars and the sharpened poker of the moon. Just so, we are all full weary when, at last, the small house far along Tofafjord shows upon that hill, covered with snow and purple in the frigid twilight, tiny and dark, with a stream of fat-smoke rising in the air.

Nattfari nearly cackles, running from the sledge toward the scented warmth, till the mistress calls her back. "Nattfari, help us with our bundles!" The woman glares as Kol frees the mare, then offers his arms to lift me and I'm not let to lend even a hand. He carries me across the homefield, his footsteps steady on slick, patch ice, then sets me down gently before the hearth's fire.

The air smells thick and dark and rampant. Gyde's busy at the pots, her countenance rosy from heat, her arms bared to the elbows, making ready for the mistress some boiled meat and fatty cheese. She smiles lightly over her shoulder at me. Such a look upon Gyde's face. She knows naught of my last days. Then the mistress comes and turns to her with a quick and subtle whisper. Gyde nods, casts again upon my downtrod glance, wiping grease and soot onto her apron, bringing me a bowl of boiling stew.

Those next few days, we return to our household labors: the men to tending sheep despite the dark and stabbing snow, we women most to stirring curds about the hearth or standing at our wall-bound looms. Hours before long lengths of hanging cloth. Even the mistress Thorbjorg weaves. I alone am let a seat and set some smallish work, mostly carding ill-used wool or turning at the spindle. Seems Nattfari would be jealous, yet she's quick to aid me, taking my place when 'tis my turn to help roll the heavy crossbeam woven thick with woolen, or kneeling at my feet untangling the weighted whorls dangling on the warping strings.

I wonder why she seems so kind yet is so foul. I go to Gyde, standing for a time before the hearth to warm my fingers, which are aching from the cold and calloused from the threads. Then I whisp', "Whence did Nattfari come upon this house?"

Gyde smiles. "From a fattish farm in the south of Iceland, from a chief who bought her for a concubine. Yet never did she bear a child, so her master beat her ill and set her to serve upon the whim of every passing chief or mate or freeman. For a time, it drove her mad, till the

mistress Thorbjorg came and paid for her a proper price. He let Nattfari go; and since, she's been some better."

I look on her. I do not want to trust her tale. Gyde stirs the broth
again, then sets the ladle back and touches some the scars which hatch
my cheek. "It is the mistress' way to fix what's broke' and make it
again useful."

I turn. I do not like the temper of Gyde's touch. I do not like to
think we are all so broken here. Yet I look about at Gizur, Kol, at Teit
and Alof, perhaps even Vidur, Arngunn, even Gyde. And Nattfari, too,
perhaps the most like me of all.

The mistress seems not to listen. Her head is stiff. Her hands have
not paused upon their looming's web, marked as it is with signs and
symbols, strange runes over which her fingers trace discreetly even as
they twist their threads.

THORBJORG

I STITCH a child's blanket, taking the threads I have spun myself, not
those of my women, whose strands are finer for their more limber,
practiced fingers. No. I take these knots, these fraying, lumpish coils,
and stitch my marks, still dripping with the dye of blood.

Three sacrifices I have made upon three moons this winter. In the
center of the circle, thrice, when both night and day appeared within
the vault of Ymir's skull. First a fox. Then a raven. Then, when Kol
had caught a falcon, I cut its throat and let the life drain down.

Now that stain is twisted into secret markings, twined with dragons' talons, sharp, and teeth upon hard, spine-flecked tails. Such a gift
I'll give her, for she will come in a woman's form. So, Old One-Eye,
you have told me. Yet told me, too, to give to her another gift. The
knife awaits, the one Kol hammered. Blade grown sharp and black
from the fire's tongues, first forged metal of the smithy he has built
beneath the cliff, where smoke and the sound of the hammer's fall rise
together—up to touch the giant's brooding, icy brow.

KATLA

IN THE WINTER MONTH called Thorri, just some weeks past the Yule, one morning as a thaw's seep drips about the house's roof sod, the pain enters in me slowly. Small and subtle, at first so I barely notice. Yet it grows bit by bit through gritted teeth until I can bear no more. I fall upon the floor and lie, struggling like a sick horse wasted. Now the pain drives like a knife, full sharp, and slices me in two. Gyde and Arngunn drop about me, and Nattfari shrieks so loud, her voice splits me where I've little left that's not already severed.

"Woman, hush!" Gyde says, "Get the mistress. Go!" shoving Nattfari so she scuttles out and over the slushy homefield mud, slipping and sliding, to find where Thorbjorg has gone—most likely off with Kol, as she often does alone for days or hours. All the while, Gyde bends and prods and checks me. "It is not your water yet, but soon. Katla, calm. The baby's coming." She rambles as if her words could soothe, "It is not so bad if you bear without a fight," but no comfort will I have of it. No, even as she hushes and pats my head and lifts me up to lie upon an earthen bench beside the hearth where there's light and the heat is warmest. Instead, I shove her off with what strength I have, now that the pain has left me briefly, and stumble hard across the floor.

"Where are you going?" Gyde shouts, and Arngunn comes to hold me, but I push the slender girl away so she falters and nearly falls.

"I will not have this child! I will not have it out!"

"Woman, it will make its way whether you want it out or not."

"Then I will set it to the winds. I will dash its skull upon the rocks. I will kill it!"

"Nay," Gyde hushes me, and comes to me, her arms outstretched, and suddenly I am withering, bent and crumpled in her arms. Another wrench of pain grabs inside me, worse than the pain before. And soon more, others, worse even than the pains which got it there. So Gyde and Arngunn lift me up and set me down again to bare endure it. Seems but a breath or hours; I cannot speak for the pain that seizes hard and presses down.

In time come the mistress and Nattfari, panting.

"How long have been the pains?" Thorbjorg asks, throwing her cloak aside to kneel and take my hand. Nattfari tears up mattresses, extracting moss to sop up blood, and Arngunn piles snow into the kettle to heat and melt and, soon, to wash the child. Steam rises toward the smoke-hole, dancing above my head. A drinking horn's upon my lips: the draught makes the room's light waver, their figures floating about me in the fog.

But the pain—the pain! I am soaked and stinking, stiff and cloaked with soiling. Thorbjorg bends and tends me, but now my body writhes, doing deeds it does not want, yet I lie enfeebled as it does its work, with the women round me, and the mistress shouting "Push!" and "Breathe . . . ," or silent, rinsing the sweat from my hair.

Somehow I sleep a time, then waken, smelling the mistress' coverlet: a bear's skin soft against my cheek. Her hand's upon my forehead, firm yet gentle. "Here." She presses something in my hand. Cold and hard, they are her very household keys from her goodwife's girdle. "To protect you from the labor." Thorbjorg squeezes my hand tight around them just as another reaming starts. She lets me clench her own hand till it reddens.

So it goes. I know not now if it be day or night. Hours pass, or days, but I am labor. Yet I float above, buoyed by the mistress' magic— potions sipped from a rune-rimmed horn. Magic they must be, for even my hatred's numb and silent, and my thoughts—I feel naught, know not my body or my heart, until, in a sudden rush, the thing is forced from me.

And then the rip and press. All at once, the wild burning. The keys cut into my palm. They cut, and truly I would stab myself to keep this child back, but Gyde holds one limb and Arngunn bears the other, and they are screaming "Push!" as Thorbjorg steals from between my legs something horrible, a bulbous thing, encased in blue, a filmy slime.

She cuts the cord, then cleans it fast and holds it up.

"It is a girl."

"A girl," Nattfari whispers. Gyde and Arngunn hum. But Thorbjorg is gone. The door swings wide. The light of dusk comes blinding. For a moment I hope she will set it on the ice and leave it. E'er to be exposed! Yet Thorbjorg stoops to take a measure of snow in her bare hand.

Her words: "Bibrau . . . Alfather, look! It is Bibrau!"

Strange name. Bibrau. Not any I have ever heard.

With the fresh melt, she anoints the thing, as is any master's task to accept a newborn infant. So it will live. Upon its brow she makes some signs—her movements: small runes whose fate I cannot think, or perhaps just Thor's quick hammer for protection.

Then to my breast she comes, pressing the tiny, horrid beast—so like its father, gripping, groping, its fingers claws, grasping hold, and, toothless, sucking. A force draws hard upon my single nipple. I would throw it off of me in pain. "I will not give it suck. I will not feed it!"

But Thorbjorg, sharp above, her face close and still, says, "Katla, so you will," then leaves me, as do all the others.

This beast and I. We are alone.

Flurry of
Falcons

BIBRAU

FROM THE START my mother hated me. In her bitterness I was born, and from hatred conceived. So they question why I am as they see: if they thought one thought, they would know about it. Ah, what they would know! And then I'd laugh—I can laugh, though few have ever heard me—laugh and dance about until I'm bent in two for the joyous pain. But never will such people know it, for they don't look beyond their own blind sight. So I go about in silence, and know them all so many fools.

My mother hated me for the seed that bore me and the love I stole away. But I was pleased to do it. I will have my way, and it does not matter much which paths and what casualties I leave.

My mother hated me, but Thorbjorg did not. She knew exactly why I'd come, and took me to her breast. If it had borne milk, she would have let me suck it, but as it was, only my mother's weak juices flowed. And so still do they in me.

We all carry weakness. We all carry death. But some may defy death. I will. I will find a way.

Long before she ever thrust me from her womb, my mother hated me. Long before she ever saw me, but the minute I was born, the bitter winter rush from her abused me. Yet then the mistress, who could have had me killed, raised me up to gaze with equal eyes beyond my mother's scorn. Thorbjorg shields me and promises me I will never be like she who sets her head as if she were better than her lot while all that watch her call her "fool."

My mother's songs still ring to me clearly, and her stories—all of them wrong. Born a slave, she believes she ought to be other, but her soul has not the courage to find her way. While I, though born of her, flee from her shackled womb. I was made for freedom, and I will have it mine. Thorbjorg daily gives me the tools and has taught me in my heart that I am free already.

Yet she would have me as her daughter and all that would imply. Even that, even for her, I would not have. I belong to no one but myself and never will. Such is my way.

Though before strangers I must dance the bondwoman's dance and give semblance of nothing strange. These others who are about, how would they understand? What would I tell them? That Odin's wish is that I be what Thorbjorg makes me: a slave girl's child, heir to all the wild wisdom which only Odin's lips are not a-feared to tell.

Even I, as I take the training sip by sip from the great well of Thorbjorg's store, do often choke before I swallow. It has always been that way, for the nectar's thick and the taste is often bitter. Still, in time one can learn to savor a bitter root. And so it is my nature. Now I long for the misty nights when only she and I go out and break over the just-laid dew to reach the stony circle where our chants ring out and twine with the creaking ice, which in the dark sings softly.

"That ice," she tells me, "is the clotted blood of the giants who once ruled this earth. But now their time has passed. Now is the time of the Norse gods, Odin, Frey, and Thor, and the table at Valhalla. Now we will feast at their board." She and I. Not with the Viking warriors nor the slaves at Bilskirnir, but with those few who share the gods' hushed confidences and know their way, who can read the world when the gods will turn it cold, when the light will leave, or when, bright or low, the living wait for death. This meat she has promised me, and I hunger for it. On the lips and on the tongue, I salivate to taste such sweet tidings.

THORBJORG

Bibrau.

Bibrau.

Bibrau.

My own mother-priestess, in days of old, when Vikings battled and death-bound blood was honored. My own mother priestess, standing before such signs of might and glittered hoards. First in Denmark, then in Norway, gold and rubies tumbled at your feet. Offerings. Gifts upon your visions. To each of us was given one—a single treasure, but a gaudy stone. Now lost. All lost now—your nine daughters—stolen from their charred and crumbled bodies. And the slag swept off. Baubles safely prized away by such brutes who had not wit enough to use them—treasured for their magics, when all such good and meaning they'd already razed and vicious-roasted from my sisters' inestimable bones.

Bibrau—my ancient mother. Weep with me! Now again you are here beside me. When I look into this infant's eyes—limpid, reborn beauty—such a startling blue, and her straw-bright hair reflecting in the sun. Though her face is sullen, silent. Flat as the moon and near as pale. Not like yours, which was bright and round and warm.

Still, to her I will return all that was taken. To her I will give back such ancient trade—such wisdoms and such secret skills which are now barely remembered. Upon your soul and all my sisters, perhaps we will yet right all that was wronged.

KATLA

THIS CHILD that's born to me lies wrapped in a sheath of fine white linen. With tiny fists, she grips the blanket the mistress stitched full of

Odin's runes. Beside her, Kol's blade glints in the lamp oil's fire. Perhaps he thinks, or Thorbjorg even, this metal keeps aback the dwarves
who'll quick exchange it for their horrid, twisted offspring. Know
they not, already this child's changeling-formed?

How she lies here in a vile, constant silence—not a gurgle, not a
belch, not even a whispered, stinking fart. Only staring with her hateful moon-eyes, night and day, chilled upon their piercing blue. She
even sleeps with wide-eyed rancor, her face, flat, fringed aglow with
silver slivers of the moon.

The mistress does not notice. Daily she leans over the child, fawning, preening as if it were her offspring, cuddling it close to her wrinkled, flaccid breasts. They sag over her hardened rib cage, while mine
are pained and bloated with such burden that I must suckle it and keep
the beast alive.

Three weeks now my body rests from its bitter straining, but still
I'm weak, as if the infant sucks off all my strength. Just so, the mistress keeps me close, set inside to sweep and weave, to boil bones and
bear Nattfari's flirts and piques upon the baby, to clean the filth from
the infant's waste rags, and to tend the mistress well herself.

Daily now I pin Thorbjorg's thick, black wool about her chest with
her dragon brooches, their stabbing brass tucked into the wadmal shift
I must drape each morning about her bony shoulders. I bend though
my limbs are frail, tacking her sleeves while she holds my child, jaunt-
ing it up and down as I try to stitch the fabric close about her wrists.

"Tighter this day, Katla. I'll bear no cold as I did yesterday upon a
dangling sleeve."

Thrice, for all her moving, I prick her with the thin bone needle.
She begins to scold, but when I say, "Lady, please, you must stay still,"
that little bit she does with no reply.

Then she wraps my baby within her rune-scrawled quilt and sits
beside the hearth fire while I'm spinning. "Child," the mistress coddles, "here—upon this cloth—see the pictures I've embroidered for
you? There—swift, eight-legged Sleipnir, great Odin's steed, bearing
his master high across the bridge Bifröst to his great hall of Valhalla.
See the guardian, Heimdall, there with his watchful eyes? There are

Odin's ravens, Hugin and Munin, their great wings flapping after Al-father's ears. They swoop down and bring their master news. Listen! They make their way to tell him of your birth, and he is pleased."

I wish to know no more of what her symbols say, biting my tongue upon my mother's Christian words. But daily on and on the mistress talks, even late into the evenings, when the embers are cold and all the other thralls struck down with sleep.

" . . . Winds blew, Bibrau, but Odin hung nine days upon the ragged trunk. Just so, at last, the rune-gaze struck his vision! Ah! He drank the draught of mighty poetry. 'Twas worth twice again the giving of his second eye, for half a blindness brings more vision than any globby orb can see!"

Such stories! Talk and talk, under her breath. " . . . And the names of the runes Old Graybeard sought from Mimir's spring? Uruz, strength. Othila, tradition. Ansuz, signals from the gods. Fehu, rich possessions. Inguz, fertility. Eihwaz, defense! And Algiz—ah, yes, Algiz—for protection. . . ."

And my daughter, curled within the mistress' bearskin, listening ever on of Thorbjorg's master's deeds. Seems, though she's too young to know, her eyes grow wider as she hears of Odin's bold son, Thor, of his thunderous hammer clatter-falling on enemies' skulls, tales of battlefields and bloody foe and Valkyries, thick-armed, pouring drinks for Viking warriors in Valhalla's hall. All the while, I watch from the dark of my own hard bench, far away from where the moonlight shines upon the misty chill of the mistress' breathing. My head rings with Thorbjorg's strident kvads—all of giants' fight, foul invisibles, the creation of this wretched world—these songs that haunt my dreams. But most, I am frightened by her stories fraught with a maligned seeress' sight, for, when she tells these tales, she calls that witch "Bibrau."

Some weeks later, I am let again outdoors. Most Thorbjorg sends me about the homefield's tending, or soon to climb the fells, that bitter bundle on my back, to gather up the sheep's shed wool where it catches on the hillocks. This we spin, then weave into wadmal cloth, saved to sell at Herjolfsnaes' Sandhavn market. At the pasture, I am let to sit in the chilly shadow of the shepherd's hut. There I milk a nanny goat's thick teats, even as the changeling beast milks me.

For our meals, Kol and the other men search the cliffs and capes for seals and birds setting up to nest for springtime breeding. Too, the homefield must be broken up and spread about with seed; though for now such work seems nary but indifferent, the earth is still too fixed to yield.

All the while, there is cleaning. Gyde, Arngunn, and I must sweep the muck that's risen in the house's crooks—all the filth from the cows kept within throughout the winter, and from ourselves when 'twas too cold to go outside. It is nasty work, and we are soon thick with it, covered and stinking. Just outside the door, Nattfari and the mistress stir a dye vat, tinting new-spun wool. There the child lies beside, on a bed of mosses, wrapped in tender quilting as the mistress coos.

Comes a call—"A ship! A ship!"—from Vidur high upon the fell-slopes. We turn and, clearly, there among the icebergs, rides a tiny six-oared craft with three men rowing mightily. From the speed, their prow beats up against the waves. As they near, two seem plainly thralls, from the color of their wadmal dress and their shining, fresh-shorn pates, but the third's a great, burly man with a beard the color of darkness and a shaggy cloak made of grayish Iceland wool.

"It is Thorhall, mistress!" Gyde drops her rake and hurries out the door.

The mistress stands holding in her hands a red-dyed cloth. Her wrists upright are stained out to her fingertips, looking as if she has bathed herself in blood. "Make haste, then. Go. I will finish at this work." Of a sudden Thorbjorg drops her cloth on a nearby stone and sets about to sweep away the last of the mucky dung herself.

With her near, Arngunn and I labor with amazing swiftness. When Gyde returns, she hurries us to peel away our sullied shifts, finding for us cleaner clothes from those we'd bound up through the winter's weaving. Then Thorbjorg shoos us off, all together running to wash upon the creek. She sets Nattfari racing to pick a lamb from

Vidur's flock for slaughter, then Teit to call back Kol and Alof, then Arngunn to set in search of weeds, shoots, and sweet sea-meats to simmer in the pot Gyde has already set to boil on the fire. So, yet I am called within to bear my child, aiding as I can with half a hand, turning Gyde's thick ladle, wondering why such fuss, till sudden comes another round of barrel-bellow sounds.

"Hallo there, mistress!" bandying up from the fjord's edge. "Thorbjorg, come and greet Thorhall the Hunter, if ye be happy and alive!"

Gyde snatches the ladle from my fingers and drags me rushing toward the door.

"Thorhall!" Arngunn is nearly squealing as she bounds across the hillside, skipping on the slick beach stones. From all about, nearly everyone is hurrying. Even Kol from out his smithy's smoke. Even Thorbjorg limping quick across the muddy yard with Gizur on his crutch, both their old, gnarled arms entwined. There our men are reaching out to grasp the ropes and ties so this Thorhall's men can haul ashore the craft.

"Thorbjorg!" the great man calls and laughs, bounding through the icy water to grasp the mistress boldly.

"Old friend!" Thorbjorg presses him, smiling broader than I've ever seen.

"You look stronger, woman. This frigid Greenland gives you challenge." Then this Thorhall reaches out—"Ah, Gyde!"—and she, surprising, settles eagerly into his arms. "You look lusty!" he quips, setting a slather of lips upon her bare white neck. Gyde shoves him off with a slap—upon the freeman's cheek! Yet Thorhall laughs and strokes her in a flirting nature.

"Well, Arngunn, come to me!" he shouts as the girl bounds, breathless, hugging him, laying her cheek against his salty, windparched jerkin. "There, my girl. Grown so big! You are looking near a woman. Yet who is this?" Thorhall sees me upon the crowd's rough edge. "Thorbjorg, I had not heard. . . . She's a pretty one, but for this face, all set about with scars." Thorhall reaches toward me, but I draw back in a sudden flush of terror.

Gyde grasps my wrist. "Katla, hush, now. Thorhall is a friend."

"Katla she's called?" Thorhall's hand, sweaty, callused from his rowing, grips upon my cheek. "Well, then, yes. I had heard. Ah . . . yes, indeed."

Thorbjorg takes him from me with a gentle, pressured touch. "There, now. Here's another one to greet, who's even somewhat newer." She takes the baby from my arms.

With his brows some piqued, he leans in close. As he does, the child's eyes grow wide and full of murk. Closer, closer, with his shaggy chest and his hair ragged, till, silent still, with not a sound of fright, the girl reaches up and pulls this Thorhall's beard.

He wrenches her off and bellows loudly. "She's a fine one, Thorbjorg. Fine and full of fire! You've done well—well for yourself, indeed." He laughs until he holds his belly. The rest laugh, too: Arngunn and Gyde; even Gizur, though his chortle's faint and shy. And through this mad guffaw, the mistress cradles my baby.

Thorbjorg guides Thorhall from the fjord's edge up the meadow, letting her waist be wrapped within his arm as she's never done before—not with any other person. Such, into the dark of the house, with its scent of boiling meat and this crowd of thralls and games and fancy-playing.

Yet in their mirth they neglect to note I linger outside, sluggish. In the shadow of the byre I stand, in the stench of the muck heap, empty-armed, watching Kol take up the last of the sheep's blood-butchering. There I am shaking—nay! Must I stand awhile silent before this stranger as Thorbjorg takes from me my child? Like a cow, like a beast, takes from between my limbs and claims it as her own? Without any count of me, without any choosing, and thanks me not, nor gives consideration, but passes it about as if it were her own bit of property. As such it is. As such I am myself. Owned.

Yet, then . . . it matters nothing who he is. Let the witch have the baby. Let her have that blot, if she should like, for it is Torvard's taint and I want no part of it. Let this Thorhall think Thorbjorg bore the child herself!

Still I am quivering when Kol begs me aid him as he sorts the last of the lamb's entrails and stacks its last of bones. I return to the house bloodied, fingers sticky from the flesh; and all that evening, can barely think but to smell the stink of it and taste my rage upon my tongue as I serve the meal.

Thorhall calls, "Katla, my mouth is thirsty." I bring the bladder spigot, and he gulps down our thin beer, spilling all about his whiskers, then laughing, licking liquor off his lips and then his hand. "Thorbjorg, it is good to be here. Too long it's been since last we shared a table or a tale."

"Past a year, Thorhall."

"A year—a year—lady! And you with all your household here, yet me far across the sea, waiting, waiting for Eirik's ships to break and return to Iceland—me with all his riches wasting on the Breidafjord cliffs. Twenty head of cattle, sixty sheep, half again of goats, and flour, seed, such barley, wax, honey, and mead as I could sell for thrice the price at the Althing market at Thingvellir."

"Ah, but you were wise and well to wait. Should you have caught such price, you'd've caught your death from Eirik Raude soon or later."

"Such as it ever was, all these years in Iceland. Ha! I should've slipped away when I had my chance, taken all his goods, then gathered you and Kol and Arngunn, set Gyde upon my lap. . . . Ah! Yet here I am, faithful as a dog! You saw yourself, long ago I stood beside him when the Lawspeaker outlawed him at the Althing trial for his second murder; and now I'll stand at his side again, for soon we'll have an Althing of our own, and he himself will set the law and choose the Speaker for this Greenland. Know well, Eirik Raude's not a law or temper I would cross."

"You say there'll be an Althing here in Greenland?"

"Aye, an assembling at midsummer of all these chiefs from Austerbygd to Vesterbygd—"

"Austerbygd?" the mistress asks.

" 'Tis what this place is called now. And Vesterbygd up the coast, where seems some lesser chiefs thought to make a larger claim. Next you know, this Greenland will teem like the streets of Sweden's Birka

market. Besides"—he leans toward Kol with a wink upon his eye—
"this Vesterbygd is called a finer spot to set off ships toward Nordsetur's
hunting waters. I hear the walruses' teeth there grow thrice long."

They sit late into the eve, talking much of hunting trips and the
price of ivory, while I spin with one hand, the baby on my breast, and
Gizur carves and Arngunn stitches, and Nattfari and Gyde scour
stones in the kettles just beyond the hearth fire's glow. Mixed with
their sounds seep in Vidur's sheep-song falling through the smoke-
hole; he's returned upon the fells, wanting not to leave his charges
to the midnight's sharp-toothed hungers. All about the house seem
pleased, warm, and happy on this evening; all but I.

When time seems ripe, I lift my burden, begging of the mistress,
"May I take my rest?"

"You may." Thorbjorg presses me off with a gentle hand. Yet, as I
turn, she calls me back. "Katla, leave the child."

I lie now far upon a bench in shadows, feeling strangely cold without her in my arms. I do not want her. I am glad she's gone. Yet I cannot sleep, can only lie awake and listen to their whispers. Against the
household's walls I press my head. The cold and sod and scratch bring
me no comfort. In time even their lights grow low as Gyde sweeps the
fire's embers into the cinders' keep. The house grows slowly silent, till
I hear what I feared should come after all Thorhall's flirting gestures:
his thick harumph and Gyde's quick gasps combined with wretched,
muffled laughter. The smells of their meeting linger thick about the
house, hanging rough as Thorhall's contented snores.

Still I do not sleep—not through most the night, until the moon
comes slicing through the smoke-hole, cold like a knife and twining
with the hearth smoke's rise. This light that shines down from the
moon is blue—blue like the iceberg's shadows, blue like the thick, cold
hulks that scab this frigid sea! I shiver from my thoughts and wrap
my blanket-skin around me. Through my own soft rustle, I hear
someone else awake. In the haze and cold is Thorbjorg rousing Thorhall. He wraps Gyde's whistling body in his warm skin-sheet, leaves
her with a peck upon the cheek, then turns from the sleeping bench,
enfolding Thorbjorg in his own thick sheep's-wool cloak. Too, Kol is

bending, taking an oil-soaked brand and lighting it in the last of the fire's coals. These three—Thorhall, Kol, the mistress—slipping from the household's quiet. In Thorbjorg's arms, she takes my child.

Beast! I hate her with all my mangled breast and blood and body—still the infant's mine! Thinking not, I race from the house and round across the footpath. Following their steps, close and silent, I trip into a valley—to that place I've been but once before, that wide-strewn circle of ash-white stones, sharp like a giant's broken bones.

Now they are all made up right, perfect in a circle's form. By whose strength? By whose will? By what wretched force of the invisibles' power?

There Kol bends, digging up a pit in the middle of the stones with but a flat slab and naked fingers till his hands are bloodied. The sod is stripped to a rough, bare ground. Then Kol lights last season's dried-up grasses with the firebrand till they sizzle, crack, and writhe in tempered flame. Meanwhile, the mistress holds my baby close above. I stay upon the hillside, high behind a stiff-stuck rock, daring not to dart forth yet. Just then, from behind a cloud's mask, the moon grows bright and whole and spiteful, lighting up all the world.

"Woman!" Thorhall sees me. "Back! Go back! Do you hear?" His voice is all ruddy gruffness. Thorbjorg turns her head, tells Thorhall hush, and says no word to shoo me off.

Below me, their fire burns amidst the stones. Its warmth flies on the wind as I shiver in my housedress. Sudden, far above, six ravens circle. They wing around and land—all six—upon the stones. Black they are against the ashen whiteness, preening, fixing oily feathers, clamping, clawing blood-sharp feet. They peck upon the stones and squawk and stare and toss up bloody bits of something. My child!

Still, I hear no infant's scream, no baby's bawling. The birds fly up, a cloud, a string, cawing, sudden mad, entrails hanging from their claw tips, bits of meat and broken, marrowed bones.

The mistress' song rings out as the ravens drift away, a sonorous tone as never I have heard before. "Wyrd, mother of the Norns, I give you gifts of meat, sweet-smoldered in the smoke of rowan branches. Here! Do you smell it? Norway's wood, brought just for this sacrifice.

And fresh flesh burned upon this sacred hof. I send them sweeping up into the sky. Pray, take this flesh, this blood, this gift. I pray to you, embrace this child!"

On she chants, such wild things, as she passes the babe to Thorhall, whole and sound and silent, even as he presses her up toward the sky. Now I am frightened more than if she had been killed. I pull my rosary out from my apron, clutch it mightily against my bosom, and would wound myself with holding its cross so tightly as, from my lips, tumble out my mother's Latin prayers, "Sancto Spiritu! Domine Deus! Filius Patris!"

"Hush, girl! Stop!"

I cannot stop. Out they come, those words whose meaning's lost, but power's in them. I see them all below me, shivering. The winds strike up, flaying hard their heathen fire.

"What?" Thorhall balks, "A Christian? Thorbjorg, in your household?" admonishing my terrored sounds.

The mistress' kvads ring higher as she takes up more and more from Kol's blood-butchering—bits of beast—and sets them down upon each stone, a leg apiece, and then the lamb's soft innards, tearing one and winding out another, and stringing them, brutal red upon the ashen boulders. In time, more birds land, raucous, on the heads of the rocks, to pick upon these offerings. As they squawk and feast, Thorhall laughs at me aloud.

At last, the mistress ceases singing. "Katla, come."

I make my way, though my voice is hoarse and I am quaking. When I arrive, the bits are gone, the birds flown off, the fire but a glow to match the dawn.

"Bibrau is hungry," she says, rocking my child.

As I reach to take her, Thorbjorg grasps the lacing of my dress, tears it down, at once both harsh and slowly. The wind bites at my nipple—the twisted one, the one with pain. With no effort, the small thing clamps and starts to drain me. I slip down before a rock, before Kol and Thorhall and the vicious wind and the smoke there twining, to rest in their chilly shadow as they watch the infant feed.

THORBJORG

IN THE ANCIENT DAYS, *the old god Rig stayed one night with Módir and Fadir—Mother and Father. That evening, he took Módir in her bed. Come nine months, Módir bore a boy named Jarl, who was so fine he made others bear his burdens. On another eve, Rig stayed with Afi and Amma, Grandfather and Grandmother, and ravished Amma in the night. Soon she bore another boy, called Karl. He was fair and sturdy, but ne'er so fine, so he bent his back to cut Jarl's soil. But first—this first—Rig slept with Ai and Edda, Great-Grandfather and Great-Grandmother. Upon old Edda, Rig got the child Thrall. He was a dark-skinned boy who was made to bear the lot of slaves.*

Katla, what can I do for this? Who am I to doubt the ways of gods? I, too, am only servant of a master, and though I am some favored, I have but power to serve his call.

Yet I can pity. In Katla is a desperate hunger; in those eyes, the slaking of an empty soul. She will ne'er be filled, not by any other's love, because each drop she drinks is lost by two, and each tender touch she turns to brawling. Yet, even when some love is offered, she bare rejects it: 'tis not fine—not fine enough—

I will take what is not wanted and make it mine.

Call her by her name, Katla, the name that I have given. I am your mistress. It was my right. But that name is never spoke'. Not once. Nor are these words of mine, though I long to shake them from my lips, to hear it once upon her own: "Bibrau."

Instead, I press her harshly toward her duty. She turns her eye on me. I see in her the soul of hatred she bears for me, and half again for the child's father, and half again for the child herself, and half again for the life that is long lost to her, stolen from her, taken as surely as my own life has twice burned.

We must go on, Katla. We must. All this and more—each breath is something, Katla! Take it!

Oh, to be a woman—much more, to be a slave—

We are all slaves, Katla. All of us.

Call her by her name, Katla. Katla, "Bibrau" is your daughter's name.

KATLA

SOME WEEKS this Thorhall stays with us, through the early planting of the hay. His arms grow thicker still with working. Surely, too, he is as he's named—Hunter—for he's wise to seals, and often goes with Kol and Alof, clubbing hefty numbers and dragging them back along our fjord's edges. All the household cherish his aid and make him welcome, all but I, who now hide my place and watch him warily from afar. He calls me "Christian!" and his voice is scornful, yet he dares no harm before the mistress' gaze. Most he just laughs at me and takes such food as I bring with a crooked, vexing greeting, and seems to think I am less foul than just a fool.

One dawn, while Alof and Kol are early off to trapping on the hills, this Thorhall stays behind, as he sometimes does, bearing at the mistress' patience. There he's prancing all about the homefield yard with my daughter on his shoulders, laughing and plying, and she, though somewhat smiling, silent as she ever is. I labor below at Gyde's broad side, stacking sod and driftwood, when Gyde stops and sets her hands upon her hips.

"Such a sight!" she breathes. "Much the same was he with Arngunn when she was but a babe."

"Arngunn?"

"Indeed. Though Arngunn's laughter—such a precious sound—"

"What had he to do with her?"

"Don't you know? Thorhall is her father."

"Father?" I gape.

"Aye, and fair enough, as fine a kin as can be any freeman with no duty, no rightful obligation or means or want to own or keep a slave.

"Katla," Gyde chides, "hush your thoughts. I am full-pleased for it—pleased then and now—and want no more of him than I have already. Thorhall's not a one to sit at home playing husband-man to wife or beasts. Better off I am—and Arngunn, too—to stay about with Thorbjorg's kindness. Yet I miss him much when he is far away." She speaks with an almost wistful musing. Upon her eye I sense some fuss, some fine affection's strain.

I bite my lip. "Ne'er could I be so content."

"No, Katla. You would not be."

Not long till over the hill come Alof and Kol returning. They are early from their traps, but Alof raises his line, already hung full-thick with carcasses of arctic hares.

"Hallo!" he shouts from off the fell-slope. But it is Kol, crooked Kol, who sudden turns our stares. He wobbles on his twisted legs. From his two long arms outstretched come a flutter and an awesome screeching: falcons, great and white against the cloud-bright sky. He carries a pair of them, and their feathers reach, but Kol holds them close upon a tether. Still they fight and struggle, bearing beaks and talons with a slashing strength. Gyde sees and sends me from my chore—"Katla, hurry, fetch a cloth"—and she races, too, for an ointment from the mistress' tinctures. We stumble up the slope, bent to mop Kol's scrapes and bleeding from the birds' quick claws. Yet, when we reach him, Kol seems almost unhurt. But for a tiny drop and a bitty scratch, his face is crinkled up only with triumph.

"Found them on the cliff's hangs!" he utters, breathless. "Far above the sealing grounds. We were climbing toward the nests, hauling eggs at most, but then I saw such birds as these—as never I have seen before—"

"Beauteous, Kol!" Thorhall bellows, handing my daughter to the mistress, strutting quickly from the far hay-yard. "Beauteous beasts!"

The birds shriek loudly. Before long, Thorhall has one and then the other upon the thick of his jerkin's sleeve. With a sudden toss,

he sets one flying. It soars, circles up, almost free, before Thorhall
snatches back the binds. The tug sends the great bird twisting, grappling, trying not to fall. 'Tis an odious exhibit, yet Thorhall laughs,
bounding Kol with his big hand on his crooked shoulder.

"Good work! Good work! Most like, they're worth far more with
feathers on than plucked. You train them well, Kol, as you did with
that surly breed in Iceland, and I'll find a trader at the Althing market
who'll pay good silver for them."

Kol nods, bobbling back and forth on his thick, bowed legs, as at
last the mistress nears. She is smiling, not on the birds or men, but at
my child in her arms. The bitty thing has reached hands out, small and
stretching toward the frantic fowl. The mistress wraps the swaddle
tighter round; then, with long, thin fingers shaking, Thorbjorg lifts up
my girl.

"Mistress—" I stammer, reaching against my heart to keep her from
some wild ripping—yet Thorbjorg warns me back with dagger eyes.

One falcon draws and cocks its beak, but the mistress coos, "Bibrau
has no fear of them. To her, they are just as Odin's ravens." Seems 'tis
true, for, even as the beast grows livid, my daughter touches light to
stroke its plumes.

Some days later, Thorhall Hunter rows off upon his skiff to do for Eirik
Raude his chores. Yet, each afternoon as more weeks pass, Kol sets about
to teach these birds. They go back and forth across the homefield
plain, while the witch bears my child up to watch them, as their wings
are clipped, and thongs bound about to tangle up their feet, and blinds
set before their ebon eyes so none can gaze or move or fly, though
they quiver frantically against their bindings. Soon enough each has
learned its duty: to come to the thrall-man's call, bear up a hare or
grouse upon its spurs, only to lay it down with unnatural disinterest.

Upon a fortnight, Thorhall returns with a frank and greedy eye
toward Kol's new charges. So pleased is he, they go again to lure more
birds—he, Alof, and Kol—from the cliffs' ice-sides. By the month of
seed-time, falcons are roosting at the corner beams, pecking, cawing,
scratching, jostling clumps of turf and turd upon our heads.

Falcons, falcons! From dawn to dusk, all those wings about me. I fear them in the dark. And then, one night, wildly I shoo them, waking from my dreams. One lies upon the earthen floor, wriggling and broken, while I sputter out, "It tore my face! It punctured skin— its beak—" Yet there are no marks on me—none but those which have been there since that long-now hated day. Thorbjorg sends me back to bed with cautious chiding.

Still, with the morning, she sends us off to gather bones and willow strips, which Gizur binds to fashion cages. Now I must watch over them, for it is my chore to set them food—thick bits of seals' coarse innards, over which they scrape and bicker. Like thralls they have become, these birds clipped in their cages, furious and vicious. Yet somehow they are better off than I, for at least they have known freedom for a time.

Comes near two months of Thorhall gone again. A still has set upon the homestead, with its winsome breezes and its endless summer sun. I sit upon the high fells oft—at the dairy hut, churning butter or helping make the cheese. There Gyde and I sing old songs in rhythm with our work. All that's cruel to me is the caged birds' feeding and the child's jaws upon my breast; but even that bite grows somewhat tempered, and afterward the mistress comes and takes her quickly back into her arms.

Such peace lasts not forever. A messenger sails soon close, shouting, "Come! The Althing! Hail! All to Brattahlid upon midsummer's eve!"—this time not even stopping at our shore.

Bare is his ship beyond our sight when we are counting ells of cloth, length upon length gathered round our arms, everything we've stitched and woven since our first days settled here in Tofafjord. We load them in a short-hulled vessel Alof and Teit have fashioned from driftwood logs. They seem too thick to float upon such meager boards, yet they do, and, too, the fine knives and ax heads Kol's tooled upon his smithy fire, and spades of shoulder blade, antler rakes, carved combs of Gizur's pretty craft, and, of course, the birds—seven trained and lost their will. Kol looks upon them proudly, his goat lips pressed before their caging ribs, kissing at their black and beady eyes as if he played a jest with pets; and the mistress, some steps above the beach, looking down upon him near as fondly.

We load our goods and then ourselves—Kol, Alof, Gyde, and me with the child at my breast, and Thorbjorg, of course, for she must see her goods bought for a price that's fair and worthy—till the ship draws low upon the water and Alof plies the oars to set away.

With a rough-patched sail we raise aloft, and the swift, loose, open water, the trip is quick to Brattahlid—far quicker than across the ice in winter's dark. It is strange to see it there again—Eirik's longhouse— broad and greening with flowers growing in its very roof sod; and I now thin, almost as I once had been, my belly light without my child. She travels in the mistress' arms, a small, wrapped bundle, awake but unafraid as the skiff scrapes loudly and is dragged by strangers over rough beach stones. When we are still, I hie the mistress over the skiff's rail, then follow myself, close behind.

The Althing's all excitement, with people bustling on the hills beneath the mountain Burfell's peak. There are meets of horses showing off their skill at fights, sheep and cows and goats for trade, and dances hopped in great, wide rounds. Across the sod come sounds of strings and pipes and drumming, yet my daughter startles not upon the noise. Nay, her eyes, wide ope', unblinking at the wafting tents, the sod-stone booths, the curtains waving with the winds. For the first, I am almost grateful for her silence, fearing such prying looks so often drawn to infant's cries.

I am sent at once with Kol into the fuss and frenzy, laboring among the stalls to bargain for salt, honey, flax, and malt. My arms are full with strips of cloth with which to do the mistress' barter. I stand with Kol at one and then another household's booth, till soon we have learned to bark together for the mistress' price.

"What for that bag of brewing grain?" shouts Kol above the masses.

"Nine ells of cloth," calls a bald-pate thrall.

"Nay," I counter, " 'tis not worth more than four!"

"Then seven," bargains the bondsman.

"Seven?" I turn as if to drag Kol away. "I see a better grade farther down, at Egil Thorsson's booth," I cry out loudly.

"Five, then," the thrall begs, "though my master will beat me for it."

I turn off again.

"Four . . ." He shudders. "Four—and 'twill be your fault if I am bruised!"

"Here." Kol thrusts from my store four wadmal stretches.

"Nay," says the thrall, "give one at least that's got a bit of thread!"

I give him a russet bit Arngunn stitched with her timid, learning fingers.

"It is not as fine as that." He points to a piece I stitched myself.

"It is not for sale." Kol tucks it toward the bottom.

The thrall wipes his brow on his wadmal jerkin, takes the cloth that was offered first, muttering, " 'Tis the best grain you'll have any-where for such a price. You've got a bargain for it, I promise!"

Kol heaves the bundle on his shoulder and we sweep away. Soon we are laughing, our hands all hefted up with goods got in much the same fashion.

"Just one piece left!" I wave my favorite bit of cloth, falling weary on some bundle-hay. "What need have we for any more? Let's rest awhile."

"Nay, I must find Thorhall to sell my birds."

"Why Thorhall?" I ask. "Why not sell them yourself?"

"With him, they'll fetch a higher price to do the mistress justice."

"Do *her* justice? Kol, what of you? What have you, for all your sweat and scars?"

"Thorbjorg does me well for what I profit."

"While she takes your gold and Thorhall takes the grace of all your work?"

"Katla, think on it—Thorhall the Hunter will have a better price than Kol the Slave."

"Yet Thorhall boasts it out even while you stand before him, and Thorbjorg works you as a beaten dog when you could buy your free-dom if you had one-tenth of that bird-silver."

Freedom — problematic?

"Freedom?" He looks at me, shaking his bony jaw, which is hacked with falcons' claw-marks through the scraggled whiskers. "Had it once, and for it was harder beaten and far worse crook'd by as many men as ever menaced you with lustful glances."

I turn my eye from him. "None look on me now with so much menace."

"Aye, and it is the mistress' good that saves you from it. Don't you know, woman, though you're scratched and jagged, you're still well enough to bear a look? But none will dare it, for fear of the mistress' evil gazing. And for me, too. Once, when I was free in Norway, they took me for a sorcerer. Took all my rattles and white-bear's claws brought from my northern home. They bound and gagged me—would've hanged me—said I'd cast down spells I had no wit or any want of, broke these legs three places each. It was the mistress mended me then, just as she did you."

It is not too hard to see him in the tale.

"Katla, I've had my piece of that sort of freedom. Thereafter, I swore to serve the mistress gladly. She owns me less than I owe her. You see it not, but she treats you rightly also. Come, then." He rises up. I take the bundles, and he a thick line of timbers, rough from cutting, bare on his wiry shoulders, brought and bargained well from trader's wood. "To our home-booth, lass, to lay these down. Then we'll get a bird and see what bustle we can make."

I follow him across the Althing plain, and we find Thorhall not far away, dallying some young thrall-girl against a hay bale. Yet when Kol shouts, "Come to sell some birds?" Thorhall gasps as if the word itself has prompted satisfaction.

"Well, then." He trundles back with us, bending as Kol withdraws the whitest, calmest creature caught within those cages. "A fine one—female—pretty as a woman. The best to set them stirring—eh, Kol? Come, come! Katla Christian, too. You'll watch a feat to set even you calling out to Thor!"

I follow this time down to the water's edge. There great, packed knarrs rock and rattle, and captains call their mates—young men who rush about with anxious fury, knowing well they'll be off to the wide seas soon. Thorhall walks, Kol and I beside him, slow with the bird tall and regal on his shoulder. Once or twice, she flutters out her wings as if in show to catch their sight, then returns to her noble calm. Soon there's a sort of hush over the watching crowd. Thorhall turns to the nearest ship—her captain, a man with ruddy beard and a thick, hard belly, taller by a head than even Thorhall himself—and calls, "Eyjolf, look ye! You're a wisdom-market. Come! Come down! Here's the finest bird you'll find this side of the Greenland ice, and none like her anywhere beyond!"

Thorhall holds the falcon out, and she but gentle-creeps to gain her comfort on his sleeve. The captain Eyjolf tromps down the plank, looking Thorhall up and down, saying, "She's pretty, sure, but will she catch?"

Thorhall warms his eye upon the captain, turning to give the bird to Kol. Kol takes and thrusts her up with a squeak of his lips into the sky, and fast the falcon flies. Fast and high, with her white wings soaring, circling above for a breath of freedom. I can but see, for her wings are bright and only barely catch the near-noon rays. She flits among the wisps of cloud and watches down upon us. Then she dives.

There's a gasp of silence, for the bird is gone, high up in the cliffs of Burfell, and bare but nothing comes for seems a long and brutal time. Then a flap of wing and she is rising, rising with a white, fat beast hanging in her talons' grasp.

"A hare!" Thorhall triumphs. "A fine, fat hare for your supper, Eyjolf, if you'll fare the price for her."

"What price?"

"Name it." Then Thorhall shouts, "And, men, there're six more like her besides!"

The bidding flares, none noting when the bird sets down and Kol takes her up, kissing and caressing her. From all corners of the shore, men come running, panting, waving, shouting to get their bid.

"Twenty-five ells!"

"Forty!"

"Forty, plus two ivory combs!"

In the midst of them, there's a flash of lightness—golden hair against the dark of wadmal shirts and woolly tresses—straight and smooth as thread spun on the goddess Frigga's spindle—

"And a pair of silver brooches."

"Two pair, and one with gems encrusted."

"Katla."

It is Ossur. I try to slip away, but somehow he reaches even through the crowd and takes my wrist. "Katla, wait."

"You will lose your bidding," I murmur, pressing him back.

"Sixty ells," he shouts, "four bronze brooches, three pregnant ewes and a ram, and twenty pounds of smelted iron."

"Sold!" Thorhall shouts. "You have the lot, sir, or so has your master. I hope he'll take pleasure from so generous a slave."

"I am no slave, sir. I am Ossur Asbjarnarsson, mate to Thrain Ketilsson, set for Norway's court this very eve. Thrain saw your birds and said to bid at any price, for sure's a bird as that should sit upon the shoulder of a king."

"Sure it should, sir, sure it should. And you'll send the word abroad there're more of them from Thorbjorg Seeress' house at To-fafjord, Greenland. Kol's the master who's trained them well enough for king's gold."

On they talk while I am sent for Alof to fetch the lot back from our booth. We return long past, when the crowd is tapered. One by one Kol checks the cages as Alof sets them on the deck of Thrain Ketilsson's ship. Yet Ossur keeps me on the beach, sending a slave to get the trade goods for exchange.

We stand silent, with the bustling around us.

"You look well," he starts.

"Please do not lie."

"Katla . . ." He bows his head. "You are bold as ever. Are you well recovered, then?"

"Well enough," I say, but feel a strange welling up inside.

"There is—a child, then? I'd heard of it since Yule. How does it?"

"The baby's born," I say, "and lives."

"That's good."

"It is not!" I nearly shout, cover my lips then, heat rushing up from somewhere to my cheeks.

"Hush, now." He reaches for my hand, but I withhold it. "I will see it someday? Is it a boy or girl?"

"I hope you never do—"

"Don't say such things."

"I'll say them as long as that child breathes cold air." Then I calm myself. "Ossur, you are leaving."

"This night." He nods. "It is strange, Katla, to see you here again."

"You'll not return?"

"Not for some several seasons. Thrain's a good mate to me, Katla, as a foster-brother even. Though I'm due to his father, Ketil, for his loans and kindness, this trip should bring in trade enough to set me on my feet again."

"I hope so for you," I say in earnest.

"Then hope so for yourself."

I see some pleading in his eyes, some blind heart-wanting, but I cannot meet them. No. I have forsworn all dreams. "I will be glad for you if it is so, Ossur."

"I never wished to cause you ill—"

"Hush!" I draw back a step. "I will think of you in safety. Odin send fair winds upon your ship, and Thor aim straight his thunder-hammer."

He tilts his head then, stepping closer, cups his hand about my cheek—the very cheek that's mangled. I pull in force away.

"Katla," he whispers, reaching still. "Even cut, it is lovelier than it was."

So he goes, as Kol lays the timbers we had bargained for and, with Alof, sets about to truss them up into a sturdier skiff for our return. That night, by the midsummer's endless daylight, Gyde and I bend over the widest wadmal to sew up sheets for a good, thick sail. I barely raise my head to look as Thrain's ship pulls away from shore, barely listen to its scrape and draw, barely notice Ossur leaning there, watching me, over the rail.

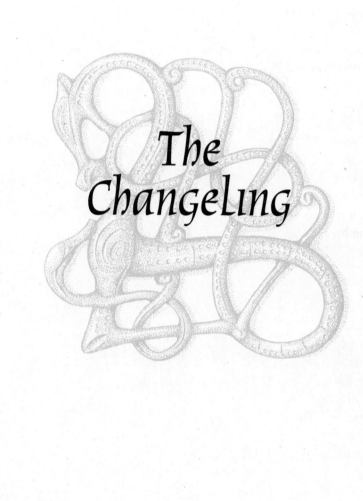

The
Changeling

THORBJORG

HERE, CHILD, press your hands down among these stones. Take this body of a fox and watch me as I split it up. Its meat—you see how I cut it? And these entrails, how I separate them well. Here, child, I give you little pieces. Go, now. Place them, dripping blood, upon the white faces in the boulders.

You see the faces, Bibrau, my tiny foster-daughter? There, though they've ne'er been carved by any human hand. Yet set within, just beneath the rutted surface—offspring of the icy beast—the invisible ones who watch this land and watch us also. Ah, I see you can see them, too!

Here. I give you my rowan twig so you may cut yourself. See your own blood? Blend it now with the wild other. Bibrau, bear the scratch of it. It is little pain. Pain is part, my girl; and you must bear it to get the better. Just as Odin did when he hung upon the tree Yggdrasil nine long days and nights to gain the wisdom of the runes.

I'll teach you all, my foster-daughter, just as my own mother once taught me. Then you'll fly upon Old Graybeard's ravens' wings, Hugin and Munin, thought and memory, to see what only the great god himself sees with his single vision. Then, one day, you will whisper in Alfather's ear as the ancient seeress who sat before Valhalla's board, telling the great god wisdoms and singing to him songs.

BIBRAU

As I GROW WISER, my mother turns more from me, looking at me bitterly when she looks at me at all. Most oft she'd rather please to eye the blank horizon, lazing on the high fell-slopes where she plucks up wool from the shedding sheep. There, as she trips away, mostly missing better clumps and dropping even those she catches, she conjures dreams of the man Ossur, who comes and comes again, yet never stays.

In all my days' remembering, I have heard her whisper some to Gyde, or in her sleep, since she will never speak of such to me, of him of the noble heart and gentle hand and lilting whisper, who cares not if she be a wasted slave whose lip lies hollow against broken teeth, who once took her hand as they sat upon the fell-slope, painting pictures upon the sky of where they'll someday walk together for their length of days. Oh, such tales! Now they grow callus with their wearing. But, fool, my mother believes his talk, though he comes but lightly, then he goes, swift and fickle as the summer's breeze.

Bare, but I remember well when first he came to see her, rowing a rank skiff poorly and alone after three years on the Viking seas. By then, he should have been bound up with riches, captaining a ship! But, nay, he came to her with leggings soaked, his feet bare blue with the chilly iceberged water, as he dragged the fretting boat-boards from our hungry fjord.

She thinks I cannot remember, but I do: how she shunted me quick from out his sight, but this Ossur nagged me back with some peevish coaxings, and gawked and petted me and called me pretty. Me, pretty—ah! With such disgust, I hid away—I was but three years old then, cowering beneath my mistress' sheets, but this Ossur dug me out, so I was put beside them both and made to stay and listen. To their kiss of words, their hiss of whispers, their gritty clasp of hands as this Ossur told his tales of far away: such places as Hedeby in Jutland

and the Swedish Birka market, and of some sea whose waves are
washed with steam, they are so calm and warm; and how this water,
swept, reflected with my mother's visage, how the sun's set rippled
with the length of her bright hair, how the seabirds upon the waves'
crests used her voice for singing. Such loathsome things, yet I endured
them, groaning stilly as he laid his gifts upon her arms. Thick they
were with red and glitter, but the fine chain broke, and the gold scraped
away to useless metal, and the red faded with one washing or two.
Still my mother hid them beneath the byre stones as if they were
some treasures the other thralls would steal away.

At last, he went again, this Ossur, and I was pleased to see him
gone. Yet each day he lingered in her sighs and longing looks, in her
false caresses upon my crown. Then she'd look on me and, scowl-
browed, wipe her hand as if she'd found it fouled. With that I knew
her silent wishes, too. Knew them as I've always known them, even
waiting in the womb.

And to think once she would have had him as my father. A father
to me. Ha! If he were such—so weak and stupid—I would have my
life! For this one thing I am grateful; yet she hates me for it. So oft
she's said in anger what a beast my true blood father was, and why I,
too, am like him in all my ways—in how I look, in the way I walk and
breathe. But she will tell me not, no, never, tell his name.

The others about the household hold their silence also, though
rarely do they side with her in other things. Even my mistress does
not favor me with privilege. Such knowledge, she says, will only do
me harm.

Yet all my life I have watched and wondered, searched out the
faces at the Althing gathering, and from among them all, one day I am
certain I will see him, and I will know. Each season since my first, I
have been and I have looked for him. Yet never have I found a face
which is my own. Perhaps because others always are before me, always with their gawking eyes—until they meet my gaze.

This season is the first of the Althing held on the Gardar plain,
Chieftain Einar's valley, wider than the hills at Brattahlid. And the
crowd, so vast after the dull peace of our fjord, brimming with noise

and color and the stench of animals. Animals, all of them, as they mill about and hock their wares, and I at my mother's hand, reaching up, for I am but a wasteling child, bare six winters old, and it is so far to grasp still. The earth has turned to mud with all the tramping and grappling; booths are set all around; and the harbor's thick with ships, fine square sails hung upon their yards, some furled but others whipping in the wind. From one of these, my mother expects her lover back from the shores of someplace she calls Spain. She's had a scroll of it, a mere patch of parchment entwined, as if by happenstance, in one of Thrain's own missives to his father, telling grander tales.

So we walk among them, searching wearily, my mother's arms growing heavy with goods for our mistress' house. We are rich this season. Kol's hunting has been good, and some two dozen fine white-feathered birds have we for selling. There he works a booth of our own, built of stone and sod and sundry sticks; and the birds flap their feathers but cannot fly, for they've been clipped. They squawk and squeak and lather in furious fleetings, but to no avail, as the ships' captains who've come from afar stand before him and bid one after another, higher and higher, to have the birds.

Till one of them shouts, "I've seen a better breed upon the Orkney Islands. I'll have me one and gain even a prettier price for it!"

Just so he brags, yet he buys one anyway, then struts there bare a distance from our booth with the bird on his collar, its claws wrapped about in burlap and skin. So I, just for meanness, step behind and, reaching for the dangled tying strings, tug so the talons stick out sharp.

The bird whips white fury, cocks its beak, and throws barbs up. They battle, yet the bird is quick, scoring a fine red strike upon his chest and cheek and shoulder, then, aiming, pecks the man's gray eye out. Finally the captain parries, bearing blindly with his blade. So the great bird topples, bloody, in the footfall. But the man is maimed. Ever will he wear the scars.

Yet none do know to be wary of me, for I am but a child walking at my mother's side. Still, not long there till the children begin to stalk me. Their gawks wide-eyed and their fingers pointing, shaking. Then do I make out their words, "Changeling . . . huldre . . . haugbo . . ."

"Have you ever heard her speak?" one hushes.

"I hear she speaks no sound."

"Not even one?"

"I hear she's never cried."

"Never?"

"No."

"Go on and look at her! Would a tear freeze on that icy cheek! Touch it if you can and it will shatter."

"Dare to try."

"No, you try!"

The taunts prate on, all in whispers as they follow, and in their ruddy hands their little swords and daggers of stick and stone. My mother's hand in mine grows wet and cold, and the red that patches on her cheeks glows brighter with each teasing.

"Come, daughter!" She pulls me sharp, away toward another booth, there to stand examining some yellow wool, when, from around the booth's corner, a small towhead appears and, with a tiny blade, he grabs and snips the length of my blond braid.

With a shout, he brandishes it high in the air—"I got it! I got it!"—running fast away, but I am quickly after him, dodging the crowd as I might loose boulders on the hills, following as he skirts beyond the meeting grounds.

There, behind the byre, the other children stand. He whirls around me, dangling and dancing my hair as it falls in a shower from its cloth tie.

"Changeling! Changeling! I will make you cry!"

He is a full head taller and his arm twice as long as he passes my braid off to another boy. I leap to grab it, but he tosses it to another, around and around, while I dodge, attacking first from the left, then the right, while the children's laughter rings and a crowd of thralls gathers to join them with claps to match the rhythm of my strikes. But still I will not stop, and my anger boils for their words—"Go back! Go back, changeling! Back to the hills if you're a huldre, or if you're a haugbo to the dirt! Look! Do you see that bit of filth tucked behind her earlobe? Go back where you came, or we'll brew up beer in eggshells to send you where you belong! Or drag you to the bonfire in turns and bare your soles to the flames, and see those dwarves come running from the hills to spare their changeling bitch from the fire!"

I want to scream. Want to, and to tear this towhead's hair from his scalp as he's torn mine, but my voice stays within me, choked and swallowed, deep and tight, until I see the more I fight the more they torture me.

And then I think, What's a bit of hair? Barely a strand remains of the bunch, tangled now and flying through the mist of gray air and the cloudy light. So I stand and wait until the very last has fallen to the dirt, wait as they laugh and jeer and taunt, until they see at last I have stopped and stooped, picking up a rock to hold it, warming in my hand.

When I see the first glimpse of fear—the first, barely a flicker—I throw the stone and catch the first boy hard about the throat. He gasps. All the mischief drains from his face and the air from his lungs, strangled by the force of my throw. He clutches his neck, and some of the others come running, a thrall-woman and another man, then some of the crowd, but the children all soon scatter with wary glances tossed behind as the boy, my tormentor, crumbles to the mud and falls asleep and turns somewhat blue.

I stand watching, for none then seem to see me, until a big arm sweeps me up and carries me bodily. The ground passes quickly before my eyes, and my legs dangled somewhere above my head. The arm is of a man, not my weak mother's, and his leather jerkin smells of blood and sweat and a bit of sea. When he puts me down, I know him for Thorhall, my mistress' companion of times. I remember his grizzly beard from the touch of it, for he used to let me grip and tear it when I was a baby, and laugh if I pulled out a hair. I remember him well, and turn to see him smiling.

"Ah, a child after my own heart, you are, you are! You did right, girl, to teach that boy a lesson, if you didn't kill him with your mode!

They'll not trouble you again." He picks me up and whirls me, which only he or Kol might dare, and drops me down so he can gloat into my eyes. But even in this shining pride, still I do not laugh. Yet he does, heartily, and bounces with me on his lap like a horse and saddle, and nearly would grasp and hug me, but that Thorbjorg comes sudden to his side.

Thorhall lifts me up and whispers to my mistress, "Thorbjorg, she's a fine lass, a fine one. Did you see the way she—"

"Thorhall, hush. Enough." Her glance is firm and full of warning. Then to me she stretches her hand. It shakes, inching before my lashes, bony and white, with cracking crevices like the nips of wind, until I reach and take it sharp. Then we walk together among the crowd.

Now they look on me, but their boldness is diminished. Their eyes are full of terror and they quickly turn away. With each step, Thorbjorg firmly holds me by the hand. I feel her stretching and so stretch taller, too. When her feet press hard into the earth, I, too, make a mark, step by step across the compound, until we come upon the boy.

There he lies wheezing as the crowd trips back and Thorbjorg leads me through. His eyes grow wide so I think they might pop from his head as she lays my hand across his throat. The thought occurs to me to grip him hard and rip it out, but Thorbjorg's fingers hold my wrist so I feel the power there. I keep still and only touch him gently as she shows.

Thorbjorg reaches down in the mud beside him and picks from the dirt the very stone I hurled. She holds it to me questioningly. I nod, and she shows it to the crowd. Then, with her bony hand around it, she squeezes soft and whispers words.

In a moment's pass, she has crushed the stone. Dust falls between her fingers and into my outstretched palm.

She rises. "The boy will heal in time. No true harm is done either by the girl or boy, but be sure she is not taunted so again."

She leads me away from the hail of protestation, but does not turn until we've passed into the covert comfort of our booth. There she whispers to Kol a silent instruction and leaves me. I do not go from the booth again that day, but watch with amusement the surly children passing from time to time, staring only surreptitiously from behind their nursemaids' skirts, or, if they come, forced at someone's hand to see our goods, they cling most closely to the thick turf wall.

Some days fly, and soon they all do shun me. Just as I like, for now I walk about almost as if I am alone. Almost, but not quite, for there is oft my mistress' welcome guiding; or some my mother's, with whom I play the frail thrall's game. With her I bow and cower, cringing as a wound oft struck, while beneath my brows I keen my eyes on all the slaves and freemen, scanning for some stranger face that I might recognize.

The game grows coarse as, each night, I am made to sleep and eat among them, set apart with the other thralls beside my mother in the stinking byre. The stench is foul, but the board is worse: a rough feast of seal meat porridge and tough bits of caribou hide, while my mistress shares a finer feast in Einar's Gardar hall. Yet before us lies more fresh meat than most these thralls have seen through the winter season. I pick among the vile gruel but cannot eat for listening to them munch and crumbling, taking red seaweed to their lips with such a slobber it paints thick swaths of rouge upon their cheeks, then tossing about narrow ewe's-horns of weak-brewed mead, jolly as if it were the thick nectar of their masters.

In silence I watch them, and am grateful for my peace. They disgust me as they speak with their food gushing out the corners of their lips. My mother's head bows over her own platter as she nibbles some small bites of meat. She pleases me not even with this doing, for I know she eats so neatly only to keep her eye upon the byre's door.

This very day, we have seen Thrain Ketilsson's ship come into Einarsfjord, there with his sail emblazoned red, a dragon painted, breathing fire, and a wily bunch, all a-row on their bandy sea-legs, bobbling up the Gardar slope. Their arms are full of trunks and burlap sea-bags, smelling of salt and sweat. But only the worst trunk and the bag least full are carried by the slimmest, weakest, poorest of their lot. Just so, my mother's Ossur returns to Greenland.

So, as Thrain's crew sits in Einar's hall telling tales of their adventure, Ossur, moonstruck, just as my mother'd hoped, comes to sit among us thralls. Forsaking all the finer fare of the chieftains' board, he sinks down, taking a bowl of meat to eat with his filth-caked fingers as any bonded man might do. Soon the thralls themselves begin to grumble that a freeman takes their food, but Ossur pays no notice. His glance is full of my mother's features.

I can stand no more. I rise and stamp my feet and go from the byre into the day's dull dusk, then through the crack of the door into the Gardar hall. There I sneak among the crowded benches, avoiding the freemen flinging mead-horns and their bold, broad, laughing backs, until I find Thorhall and my mistress beside him, their platters full of roasted horse and tender pig, their hands clasped about the mead running so thick it seems as blood.

I stand behind them, saying nothing. With a simple turn, Thorbjorg glances and sees me there. She takes me to her lap. Then the whole hall hushes. So they sit and watch as, from her plate, Thorbjorg feeds me roasted meat. Their silence grows with each strand I take from between her fingers and slide between my lips. The fat sticks to me, hot and rich and scented with death and life.

Then one man's notice strikes me—a thick, blond man with ruddy beard and a mouth laboring over gummy teeth, stingy at the roots, and a face marred and round as a winter's cratered moon. I've not seen this man before, but something about him irks and turns my stomach rotten as he rises from his bench, two places down from the honor-seat of Eirik Raude, pushing against the board so that it slowly tilts. Plates slide about and almost fall. Others nearby catch the board and set it right as he straddles the bench and steps back firmly.

The chieftain Einar catches this man's arm. "Torvard, sit."

But this Torvard shakes him off. "I'll not have her here." He bites at words through clenched teeth. He steps nearer, his stance threatening enough to spend even my callow bravery.

I put my sucked meat back down on my mistress' plate.

"She will not sit here—she does disgrace me!"

"Torvard, you disgrace yourself." This time a woman speaks, sitting closer still to Eirik Raude. Even bent, this matron stands up tall, head high with all the freemen. Her face is sure, her hair on fire, her eyes cutting-sharp as rough sapphire. She does not turn about, yet Torvard does, clenching his fists and slamming them against the precarious board.

"Enough!" Eirik Raude himself now rises. His high-seat jumps and topples. "Freydis, Torvard, sit and calm or be gone from us. Will you destroy our feasting for the child of a thrall?"

He rights his chair and sits again. All the guests set themselves to give some room for me. Einar signals Mistress Grima to bring another serving. So I begin to eat of my own plate's food as a proper, freeborn maid.

This Torvard, red with bile, sits again, squeezing beside the matron Freydis who has thwarted all his ire, as Einar, with a shove, slides the full-meat platter so it stops just before Torvard's eye.

I finish my plate and, with my stomach warm and full, sleep that evening well, not in the frigid booths nor in the stinking byre with the other thralls, but in the Gardar hall with all the freemen and their wives and daughters, sweet and peaceful by my mistress' side.

KATLA

HE IS THINNER, true, and his muscles sinewed in his arms and legs. The palms of his hands are calloused, hard as stone. When I touch them briefly—while the others eat their meat and chide us cruelly with their laughter—there is little feeling in them. He seems not to know I hold his hand until he looks upon my own rough fingers. Then he closes his around them, soft and tightly.

I turn with my words deep-hushed to slip beneath keen, bonded ears. "I have . . . ," I stumble, "missed you."

"I have longed for you," Ossur whispers back, setting his sour meat aside to twine his other fingers around my hand. From them falls a string of bright-sparked beads.

"Ossur, what—?"

"They are called amber, from near the Baltic Sea. Beautiful, is all I know—yet ne'er so much as the one who'll wear them."

"Ossur, I cannot take them."

"Why?" Though he knows already. "So," he hushes, "you have always been a slave. What is different now?"

I bow my head. "Ossur, you could have had yourself a warmer cloak for such fool things."

"What would a cloak have given that a thought of you could not?" His fingers reach and touch my lips. Soft, their brush is chilling. "Come."

Through the crowd, which watches with its love of rumor, we pass, and slip behind the byre wall. Outside it is cold, with a touch of nip, though the winds smell of sweetest summer. The hayfield grasses up the hill whisper songs as Ossur sets the beads about my neck and fingers them tenderly, then the skin beneath.

"Ossur—please—"

"I have missed you—"

Though he presses still, I push him back and take the beads, hiding them within the curtain of my dress. He, laughing softly, follows until his hand rests upon the pocket.

"What is this?" He jests, "Katla, have you some finer strand you do not wish to show me?" drawing out my mother's rosary. Yet I snatch it up with such a sudden sweep Ossur stuns back, staring. "They are Christian things. Katla, I have seen such strings clutched in the dead hands of English maids."

"So, and very nearly they would have lain within my own mother's. Tell me not you have killed in such hard places, for I've no heart for you if you could do such things."

He says naught but bows his head, so I turn his amber back to him, starting to go, yet he grabs me nearer. "Katla, don't. Stay. I beg you." He cries it in a frantic whisper.

"I cannot bear to hear—"

"I have but dreamt to tell you in all these seasons—"

"I am listening." I slip down upon a night-damp bale, folding my arms across my chest, as Ossur tells me his long, slow tale.

"Know you well, Katla, our first trip—Thrain Ketilsson and me—
it was just for trading. Yet we made acquaintance with a chieftain
named Tryggvason. When we last returned, he came to us, asking
Thrain to join him in a raid. Thrain was fast upon his fleet and pressed
me, too, to come along. In truth, it was the thought of you which
brightly guided, for I'd heard some years ago of another fight rich
enough with gold to make the Danes pull hard upon their dragon
ships' oars. Just so, this Olaf Tryggvason planned to raid the English
coast and make their king, called Ethelred, pay us dearly."

"You blame me for this?"

"It was my thought that, for my might, I'd bring gold to pay back
Ketil's patience, then, with luck, have left enough for land and then,
my love, some bit for you."

I bow my head at this, biting my lip to feel the scar there with my
tip of tongue.

"We set upon it and soon plundered Ipswich, then followed and
defeated them at another place, called Maldon. But, Katla, with such
blood and menace—you cannot know! No thought for maid nor man
nor horse nor rat nor ravenous beast—there, to take even babies from
their mothers' bosoms to cut their heads and make toys of them for
gaming! Such were our men, running thick among them. And in their
midst, to play reluctant was to play the coward or the fool."

"So you cut them down? And have wounded each as if you
wounded me—"

"Katla, don't you see I had no choice? Even there with the battle-
ax upon my hands, I swung but wildly and hollered madly and could
not see or sense to fight, for all my horror. As it was, they found me
madder even than their warriors' raging. Soon I was sent off from the
fight and made to spill the slop and churn the victuals and take whatever tasks were less for ruin. Seems, in my terrored frenzy, I'd cut a
man and fairly lamed him, yet he was not among the English foe but
one of Tryggvason's own."

I look at him. "I know little whether to be glad on it or pity."

"Better this, Katla. Be glad for it—for me. Better that they, who
wish to, live to die upon a battle and fly off at a winged Valkyries'

proud beck. For me, death-straw and your hand upon my brow are sweeter things. I care not for great Valhalla's fires, for they will only part me from you until Ragnarok. Rather I would serve beside the slaves at Bilskirnir till the end of days."

"So you say." I shake my head in bitter meaning. "Yet you are no slave and would not be one."

"Nor am I dead upon the battlefield. Be glad on it! I am here beside you, and with some gold—some little sum for taking place upon the battlefield. And with a fine helmet, too, got from a dead man's skull when the battle bore too near to mine. They are not much, but are worth something—enough to trade for a boat to hie me to the hunting grounds of Nordsetur."

"Nordsetur?"

"Aye, this Greenland's hunting waters. Have you heard what price they pay upon the market here for walrus tusks? Six times the worth of wadmal cloth, twice that of smelted iron, and I will tell you, too, the Christian church about the southern seas pays even more if they are carved in shapes to suit the Christian need."

"So you will go again."

"I must."

"Nay." I feel myself some choking. "Of course, you must."

"But not right now." He lays his hands upon me. His touch, so soft and warm, I grow sudden fearful.

"Ossur, please—don't set such store . . ." I press him back, and as I do, his beads fall from my fingers. "Forgive me. Ossur, oh—forgive . . ." I stoop, groping for them in the dirt. "Give me naught. Ossur, give me nothing. Nothing, for I can give you naught without thinking ever more of *him*!"

"Hush, now. Hush." Ossur scoops me up from where I've crouched against the byre wall and holds me as I barely keep my stumbled stance and choke and, silent, cry. He nuzzles off my tears. They clot upon his beard's light bristles. "Then I'll ask nothing of you, Katla. Nothing more, until you say—and then . . . I will keep these for you, waiting, ever patient, for that precious day." He takes the amber beads, brushes them clean of the dirt that's come upon them, and, before he slips them back within his jerkin, kisses them gently, sweetly, once and then again.

I leave him, rushing, yet with the morning Ossur comes and watches at the mistress' booth, though I am bent with work and cannot bide him but with the slightest guilty glancing. Yet he smiles when I do. My cheeks blush hard with his attentions, till he eases toward the corner where I ply and leans across the tall-stretched loom.

"Katla, come upon the horse games later. I'll be there to stand with my foster-brother Thrain. You must meet him if he's to be one day your foster-brother."

He knows, as I, that both Gyde and Kol are listening. "Do not speak like this!" Yet a sparkling's in his grimace, as though the light of my reflection makes glimmers in his world. I whisper, "I will try," as he stands above me, watching my fingers, agile down the strip of cord turning slowly into a waistbelt for some freeborn mistress.

My dreams come flooding to me: that one day I will wear a belt like this and be his house-woman, his mate, perhaps, too, one day to be free! For this hope alone, I am almost happy. My work grows light, and seems even my daughter, skulking there beside us in the booth, shines with a pleasant sort of glow, so much unlike herself.

Yet comes a shadow quick: the face I am most feared to know. Torvard stands with his large wife, Freydis, bearing in my sun and light and breeze.

"Torvard Einarsson!" Gyde notes and comes out briskly. "And good Freydis Eiriksdatter. Such fine and well-born patrons, the mistress Thorbjorg will be pleased! Come, look among her wares." Gyde scoops her arms full with mats in fine cream wool and woven grayling, as Ossur slips away behind the booth's sod wall. All the while, Torvard stares at me as if his eyes could break what fists have not yet maimed or tainted. He says naught as his goodwife bends upon our wools, spying soon the very band I'm half through weaving.

Freydis spreads hard fingers over its undone knots, saying brightly, as if she knows me not, "Bind this well, woman, and I'll have it when it's finished. Torvard, see? It will look fine about my keys."

She takes the tail of it and wraps it round her widthy waist, but Torvard's noticed then Ossur peering out behind me.

"No!" I hiss, for Ossur's hand is quick upon his knife. Yet the lady Freydis thinks I'm surly.

"No, girl? Would you dare deny me your mistress' wares?" Here starts some haggling as Gyde explains away my shrewish fault, while Torvard bends his neck to find where Ossur's hiding.

As he does, at once he sees the child. His child—the way she looks at him, standing there to meet his eyes but boldly. I cannot say—I cannot help myself—why do I fear for her when she knows no fear herself? Yet my sense, like an animal's, deeper borne than from my heart, shoves her back behind my skirts, though she wants no part of me. She roughly slips away, climbing quick atop the hay bales stacked for Kol's white birds. Whirling, I find her there, standing above us, turning murky eyes on Torvard and watching, watching. He holds her gaze, then turns a-sudden and is gone, pounding out in a spurt of mud into the throng.

His goodwife shouts, "Fool! What do you do? Running from a child . . ." Then she shouts at me: "I'll have that belt, woman, done with a twine of silver—a twine for the same price. Have it for me by the end of day!"

My own arms are shaking, bristling, as she reels away. I reach up for my daughter, but she steps down from the bales without my aid. Her face a-glisten with a scorning triumph, she bends calmly, brushing straw and feathers from her shoes and apron, then dashes off into the crowd.

"Nay!" I try to stop her; and Ossur, too, sets himself to fetch her back. I beg him, "Don't. She has never stopped for me before. Know you well, she will not for you."

By the length of noon, I have seen no more of her, yet I've stitched the silver where Freydis will be praised to wear it, scheming she'll have no choice but to think on me with each compliment she gains. Then I beg my leave. Kol and Gyde are quick to give it, knowing the mistress is upon the Althing councils and would have no cause to keep me back, now my work is through. I hurry toward the gaming fields, across muddied grounds, seeking the green forked flag of Ketil's house—the flag well known as a gift from Thrain to his father from his trading rounds, for here it is rare to find such a peculiar shade.

I see it well. And there beneath is my good Ossur, bearing the flag's own staff above his Viking cap, its rim etched with dragons twisting, shining, spitting fire with the sun's bright blaze. I would laugh aloud in sweet mocking of their fierceness, but think better he should wear this crown than be known for a gentle man and hated.

None take much note of me as I slip in through the crowd of freemen. There are thralls enough about, sharpening weapons, mending wood and leather shields, hammering at bits of sturdy mail. There's much slap and scrape and clanking as men prepare mounts and brandish swords, most bending half an eye on Thrain himself as he winds his horse away, unscathed from his recent match with a Vesterbygd freeman. Ossur, as his second, wipes sweat from Thrain's flushed brow and proudly bails him up a ladle of cooling water.

I rustle closer, passing among Eirik Raude's own sons, Thorstein, Thorvald, and Leif, preparing for the next match on their mounts. And there Snaebjorn, of my once-master Einar's house, standing before one of Einar's horses, and Inga—my dear Inga—beside him, her belly big with child.

She lays hands upon her blooming hips. I reach and nearly wave to call her. Then Snaebjorn heaves a carved wood saddle: Torvard's. Well I know that seat, feeling almost its cutting sides and the pain thereafter—the pain that will not ever die.

My heart's first joy at seeing Inga falters. I duck away behind some tumbled strappings, meaning to escape unseen; yet out of the edges of the milling crowd comes a little shrieking.

"Katla! Katla! Nay, don't you remember me?" A woman shimmies from the arms of a grubber farmer grasping her behind the bales. "I am Yr—little Yr," she says as she neat and quickly rights her lip-slobbered bosom back within its draping. The grubber slinks apart. So she has but used me to escape from him.

"I remember you," I calmly mention, though her exclaim has brought the others' ears.

"Katla," Inga trills, "come! Welcome! It has been too long—"

I eye about, fearing only Torvard; yet I hug her well and kiss her lightly on her freckled cheek.

"And what of me, eh? For I'm fond to say this child in me's got from Snaebjorn's doing! Look at it and guess the master's promised I'm to keep it. He says his Gardar farm grows faster than there're thralls to tend it."

"I'm pleased for you, Inga," I say, but quickly, hoping to race away.

"But let me look at you—not much changed, though somewhat sorrowed." She turns my face then, to this way and that. "Oh, it is not right—I've barely seen you in all these years—ever since your pretty daughter's born—"

"Speak not of her!" I hiss, then soften, "Inga, please—I must go." I kiss her twice again, upon both cheeks, as if such touch could change my perturbation; but even as I lay my lips, Torvard lurks toward his lard-thick roan. His eye's upon me as I step back from his thrall-flesh property. Torvard makes no stride toward me. Instead, he stalks in stewing, measured steps to leap upon his horse and whirl its massive head around. The roan bristles, neighing, while Thorbjorn Glora, chief of Siglufjord and caller of these Althing games, shouts, "Who is next to take up challenge on this Gardar plain?"

Without a blink, Torvard steps his horse up, planting his black spear's point deep into the ground.

"Who will meet Torvard Einarsson upon this field?"

With a hearty laugh, Thorstein Eiriksson prepares to meet his spear, but Torvard pulls his back and swings it till it shudders first and firmly on Ossur's flag.

Glora prods, "Torvard, is this challenge or humble mishap?"—for the touch of spear to flag is not a proper call.

Torvard does not speak, standing on his ground.

"Ossur Asbjarnarsson"—Thorbjorn Glora turns—"you do not even play upon these trials. Do you take this oddish challenge?"

Ossur's look is fear, yet shifts to stillness. For a moment's breath, his eyes rest on me. "I will take it," he says, pounding the flag's stick down firmly, peeling away to prepare a mount for fight.

All the crowd's a-murmur. My heart is tumbling, clinging to my heaving ribs. I push my way across the game field, "Ossur, I beg you," nearly falling before him to block his path. "Please, there is no honor in this strike. Torvard touched no weapon with his spear. . . ." Though he knows full well the rules for gaming, already Ossur is changing out his light wool cloak for Thrain's waistcoat of mail and leather. The metal's rattle smarts my ears. "Ossur, he means to kill you."

Ossur turns to me. "If death is where I'm bound, then meet me there, love. Knock on Old Odin's gate. For your pretty face, he will surely let you in."

But his fingers tremble. His face is pale and shadowed. The chain mail on his figure fits but loosely. "Here." I press away his hands and help him snug it up.

"Foster-brother,"—Thrain comes upon us—"take my russet mare. Know you well she's stood by me through so many battles." Then Thrain looks to me. "You are the woman, then? Katla? Nay—I hope you're worth this fight. Few about do think so, yet my good man, Ossur, likes you well."

Scarce do his words fall off when Ossur sets upon the horse, adjusting the saddle, raising up his Viking helm. Lo, it shines upon the sun and in my eyes! I shrink back from the anxious shouts and rowdy bidding on this ill-thought match. Then I see, at the edge of the fighting grounds, my daughter stands alone and watching.

Torvard's beast breaks with a windy cry. He charges Ossur's mare to begin the bout. Quick, the russet turns upon the sound, raising up and dropping low. For a moment, she burns fire in her bearing. The two men circle, Torvard's roan pawing the dirt like an angry bull. Then he rears to show his horse's hooves: sharp with bladed, iron shoes.

"A maiming horse," I spit, "like his maiming master." Yet Thrain Ketilsson says naught as, fast, Torvard drops his roan's heels into the russet's flanks.

With the spurting up of blood, Torvard pitches farther. Ossur will be crushed beneath the roan's bandy legs! Just as soon, Ossur bends about and fair surprises, raising his horse with a belly jolt to set the savage roan trembling back. Falling off, the roan digs hooves again into the dirt, stamping step by step away, and his master scowling and my own heart pounding praises. Yet now Ossur's quick to brighten with this single wit of triumph. He turns his beast and tosses me an emboldened glance, prancing his horse about in hearty, fool parade.

"Too soon," I shout, "Ossur, too soon!"—then hold my tongue as Torvard's horse catches Ossur's on the thick hindquarter, cleaving a scratch of hide as wide as my quivering, jaw-gripped hand. The mare whinnies, bounding back in anguish. Worse, Torvard rears again and presses the mare's sweet hind legs, grinding down until a snapping sounds.

"The beast is broken!" shouts a freeman giddily.

Comes a plaintive moaning as I've never heard before. The mare's slim limbs slip back and twine about her haunches. The look upon her rheumy eyes is of white, cold shock. Still Torvard's at her, inching his own brute, pressing harder to lift and kick quick forelimbs out while Ossur's tangled now in strap and rein.

Oh! My Ossur's huddled beneath the belly of Torvard's beast—I pray to my mother's Jesus Christ upon it! Yet Ossur sets his eye from fright, reaches back for his slender knife, and stretches up to stab Torvard's roan upon its heart.

Torvard's beast's a-startle—a great dun cloud falling, spilling, tumbling back with a coughing breath, and crashing forward. Torvard scrambles from its wasting form, but the roan falls down and crushes him beneath.

"Foul move! Foul move!" shouts the crowd together as Torvard's mother, Grima, races out with Einar fast behind her. Only Freydis stays, claiming ground with feet set wide; on her lips, I swear I see a smile.

On hers and on my daughter's: my daughter, standing close enough that her apron's spat with blood. Pushed and pestered by the rumble, she steps not back as she eyes Torvard. She stares as they

bend to mend him, listening to his screams—for his limbs lie broke'
just as the tattered mare beside him, and he's quicked with blood as
thick as the hot, dead roan.

She cannot know him. Cannot! She but likes the blood and lingers
for it—it is Thorbjorg's doing. Yet I see she even catches up his eye
as they lift him past upon a litter. With her sight, Torvard's look turns
slowly from anger to a pallid raving. "Changeling," I hear him speak
beneath his breath, "changeling, go," his voice jiggering up and down.
"You demon's daughter," rising to a laugh, "born upon a mountain
troll . . ." This time his words are thick-hindered with a righteous
heaving, his face turning full red. Then, upon a wild breath, nearly rising from his damage, "Bibrau," he shouts. "Bibrau. Bibrau. Bibrau!"

But she does not fly, as legends say changelings must at the speaking of their name. Instead, the girl steps from the crowd and stands
upon the bloodied ground—bare a breadth beside him, as he reaches
out his hands to swipe the air with strangely feeble strokes. To these,
she raises up her arm and holds it close, never even shaking. Sudden
he, too, raises up his arm, his hand held nearly still. Till I can bear no
more. I shriek to part this crowd and, with a harsh and rigid yank,
snatch her back into my apron's folds.

Six days hence Torvard lies, until he has the strength to lay his claims
before the Althing council: "The weak-fart Ossur Asbjarnarsson
cheated—bearing blade upon my beast—a mighty one, worth more
than this flimsy coward!"

So many freemen come to stand beside him, and barely any know
Ossur at all but Thrain, who must argue that his horse was lost upon
this fight, that soon the Lawspeaker, Herjolf himself, is pressed before
the chieftains' council to give decree. Just so, every piece of Ossur's
gold and silver and all his goods got upon the seas, even his fine
dragon helmet and my amber beads, wend their way into Torvard's
keeping.

Through the rest of the Althing gathering, Torvard jaunts on
sticks Hallgerd's fixed for him as crutches, jiggering with Ossur's ill-
won grille too small upon his brow. Yet of Ossur I see little—mostly

from a distance. Even then he catches not my eye, but only bows his head and turns to sulk in shame.

Before the meet is over, I hear he's bound as clubber for the walrus hunts. The talk's that few survive that chore one season. As I listen to this fate, I squeeze hard upon my mother's Christian strand. Yet I know now this Christ cares naught for unhallowed anguish. Nay, he listens not to my pagan prayers or pleas. So, at last, I rush to beg my mistress, "Lady, show me such a rune to speak protection on the seas."

And Thorbjorg does, etching it upon a very small, flat stone. She hands it to me. I run and, finding him, grab on Ossur's wrist and, without a word, press it hard into his palm.

BIBRAU

DON'T CALL ME BY MY NAME, I thought, and think it still, all these months since the Althing season. Day and night since that bloody meet, his voice rings loudly in my ears.

'Tis a haunting, and I would hate this Torvard for it. Yet somehow I cannot, as I recall him lying, crushed and trembling, reaching out toward me. Then drawing back. So proper was his terror, it somewhat pleased me. I cannot help myself and think perhaps to like him well.

Like him, too, because my mother hates him. So I sensed from how she drew me back, the way she gripped and quivered even as I tried to grasp his bloodied fingers. Though I had the will and fought her weak arms keenly, I did not have the strength. Not yet. Someday I will.

Even with our return to Tofafjord, she wakes up striking at this Torvard in her dreams. Each night I wait to watch her fight, and listen till his name comes tumbling from her mumbled lips. Yet sometimes Ossur's dribbles, the petty wasteling, lost of all his dignity—what little bit he'd ever had, tromped upon that pale horse-meet. Nay, after such a flailing, such sordid, pitiful display, still my mother whispers of him. Still my mother dreams of him. Well I pray he'll drown upon the walrus-seas—for that is where I've heard he's gone to ply his useless muscle. Too, I know he's stolen one of the mistress' runestones, for I followed silent at my mother's heels and saw her stick it in his hand. So, every night, I bait upon the cold, hard blood of the mistress' chanting circle that he'll be bit upon a summer frost and, trembling, drop it into the sucking sea.

Yet this Torvard, him I think on fondly, though he called me loudly foul and troll-born. So I think I will seek him at the coming Yuletide, follow on him close and, watching, silent, come to know him well.

From That Smoke Wafts Up a Being

THORBJORG

ALFATHER, see the girl? She is bandy with power, moving through the subtle rings which glide across the surface of the still. Her first lessons are well learned. In these midnights she picks among the weeds, choosing rightly, making cures, sensing well their strengths and humors. Of the runes, upon the nights we sit before your rock-bound fire tearing scratches into bits of stone. 'Tis true, her cuts are crude, for all Kol's tender labor on her dragoned silver birth-blade. She carves them best when I pass my ancient walrus-handled point—the one round which, upon the first, you wrapped my callow hand.

Too, among the mounds and boulders, she senses the hiding places. Sees, lying in the shadows clearly as if they stood upon the open fields, the secret, dark ones who live within this frozen ground. Hears, too, when the winds fly back and breathe their secret songs.

So much so, I must turn her head away, for the dark ones tempt her. Sometimes in the nights I watch her before the circle stones: her face bears an old, cragged visage with a wrinkled twinkle-eye filled with wiles. So much she seems as one of them that all this talk she is a changeling seems nearly true. Yet then the image passes. I take her to me and she follows, sure and faithfully. She is a good child, though none about do understand but me. And you. And perhaps Thorhall, though his admiration's bent on fondness more than any proof. He sees her only as a sprightly filly and heeds not the signs.

It is not his task. It is mine. And I will teach her. I promise that. Strange, to hold such power in my hand. Was I such? An unformed piece? A wild fury? For the girl is wild, with a vicious streak that speaks of her conception. Speaks it loudly. Sometimes, even with her silence, I think I hear the screams.

Yet she is gentle. To the animals, she plies her touch, light and certain—even more than mine when I was such a child. She would rather have her hands upon a beast than on any other being, and fares it well, sitting close beside me in the byre, reaching out to catch the lamb upon its birthing dawn.

Yet, Alfather, strange, when first she held one—so tiny even in her tiny hands. Oh, and calmly! She kept it some fine minutes, bearing it, studying it with a desperate keenness, until I turned from the ewe I tended to see the caul upon the four-legged foetus' form. I took it up, and just then knew, the beast had been brought stillborn. Yet Bibrau would not let it go. Twice she picked it up from deep within the midden heap where it lay wasting. So I had Kol bury the foetus here among these very circle stones. Even now, I find her sometimes kneeling at its grave.

BIBRAU

I WAITED for that Yuletide season. Yet it did not come, at least not for me. Nay, for my mother begged the mistress, "Let me not go, and the girl stay here beside me!" And the mistress, though she loves me well, granted I must stay behind. I know not why—'tis not worth to break my peace to question.

So this Torvard will yet wait. Cold and stilly, I bear my fury, choring in the dank, dark house with my mother, Teit, and dull Nattfari. Dull, and the work still duller—to card and spin as my mother presses out wool. I sit upon the labor, bare but a pity-strand of ashen thread rising from my spindle, until, at last, in her ire at my uselessness, my mother teaches me somewhat how to weave.

Ah! To weave—that I favor well to learn. Not such weaving, plain as my mother makes it, all practical and sturdy, but another kind of twisting twine which the Norns do know, as my mistress oft has told.

I think, as I ply the chore: Like they, I am twisting fate, and I like the pleasure.

So for my first piece I strive to make a caul. A caul. That is what I call it, though the others think it a queer sort of blanket for the doll Gizur carved me of a scrap of wood. Such a tiny doll, with so little wood about to spare, I've long thought it a foetus as the one I saw still-born among the ewes. So small and purple in its bloody sack, I thought it pretty and tried to keep it. But the mistress would not let me. Still, in time, I've come to like the doll nearly as well.

I used to carry my little charm among the herds, pushing it against a pregnant nanny or a ewe while she was heaving, hoping to help the birth come well. When first my mother saw me at it, she went running, shrieking, dragging Gyde from the cooking pot to keep me from it. But then my mistress came and, slow, contented, she drew me off. With her glance she said, *They do not need your help just now.*

But oft the mistress is not near. When none look on, still I try my hand. Naught has come of it through all the autumn season, till I think perhaps a caul is what is due. So I weave this ruddy woolen sheath and wrap it tight about my charm. Its effect I guess will be full-potent. Now I long only that a beast will come to bear.

'Tis but Yule and winter—all the goats and sheep outside shiver-ing with the snows, and only the cows from among our flock lying here beside us. One is warm and ripening, but not due to calve until well into the thaw. Still I rub her bulbous belly with my foetus and slowly peel the caul-skin from the wood.

My mother scolds, but Nattfari quacks, "Leave the girl, Katla. She's only playing." Nattfari watches as she turns to weave, her long white arms jiggling fat with each strand she tucks among the descend-ing threads. Teit, close beside her, carves a spindle whorl from a bit of whalebone. In time he goes outside to strike a meal for us from among the frozen seal meat stores. Then Nattfari puts aside her tangled threads and kneels by me and the pregnant heifer.

"What have you, Bibrau?" she asks in her most beseeching tone. "A toy? What a toy! Katla, do you see your daughter? I think she would like to play with the little calf itself, the way she rubs it right out from the womb. For that, little one, you will have to wait some while." She chucks my cheek just then, which I hate anyone to do. "Now let me see what little magic you hold there."

She tries to take it from my hand. Hard as I can, I tug it back and reel from the cow's great warmth, settling with my doll before the drafty door.

"Nay," pipes my mother, "let Nattfari see." She, too, leaves her weaving, coming to take it from me, holding it in her hands, all rough with calluses from the woolen, her fingers dangling, nail tips blacked, passing my touch-taint doll among them.

Nattfari grabs it. "What a fine dress she's woven for the creature! But the weave's uneven here. Bibrau, let me show you." She takes the doll and stoops before the loom, where some threads hang low against the wall. I have no wish to, yet I follow and see her press my foetus into her lap, soft there beside her belly in the draping of her apron.

Nattfari takes up the threads and begins to twine. All the while she chatters and plaits, I watch my doll beside her belly, till my mother scolds, "Child, listen to what Nattfari says."

I glance from the foolish mesh back to my foetus with its perfect membrane.

"Daughter!" comes my mother's almost shout.

Nattfari presses the foetus gently deeper. "Katla, you have no patience. Let her be. Can't you see she'd rather play than work? And, well, I do not blame her—"

"Spoiled to laziness," my mother spits, shaking her head.

"She's still a child." Nattfari lifts up my hand and, while my mother glowers, presses my fingers close upon my foetus, then lets me go so I curl beside the heifer's lowing, where I quick begin to rub her swelling womb again.

That night, though I am sent to sleeping, I lie awake, watching about the dim-lit house as Nattfari stamps the embers of the hearth fire out. I smell the ash of her scraping them into their stone-lined cradle, then listen as she slips herself stilly onto Teit's slim sleeping bench.

Such a sound springs from there slowly, a sound as sometimes

I've known late from the stone circle with the mistress moaning, or as I've lain awake to watch my mother's dreams. Yet never came the sounds with so much fervor. By the misty moon, the thrall-man's back rises up and down. I hear the scratch of the moss-drawn bedding, and the woman there, trapped well beneath, groaning deep with Teit's yearnings. The room riddles with their motion till it makes me giddy, and I hide my head beneath my woolly sheets and push my fingers into my ears. Yet, with the morning, when they are long awake, out about the frozen homefield's chores, and even my mother seems not much to see me, I creep between their covers and smell their smells.

Thorbjorg at last returns from Yule, with not much news and no words at all of Torvard. Then the days of frost and wind and snow turn to wind and rain. When it clears, more and more each dawn, I step far upon the hillslopes. There I gambol among rocks and roots still ice-cloaked, though the breeze is blowing warmer, with the mistress Thorbjorg by me, limping slowly as I race along.

With this early spring, Thorbjorg guides me to learn the growing things, showing me how to pluck off berries while they hang still dripping with last season's icy frost, and to wrench buds from willow branches before even their leaves unfurl. These we make a store of, keeping cuttings in a pouch stitched of the tattered cloth Thorbjorg gave me on my birth day. Within it, too, come sticks and stones, clots of sod, a claw, a bone, a shell, a feather. These, she says, each have their purpose, and she chants out the kvads so I might learn.

Though I listen, I do not sing them out; I hold my voice and only sway and bob, my feet crusting up with dewy frost or sometimes twisting slightly. The mistress watches and says no word until one night about the household in the lingered twilight. We sit, all there, even the thralls. The hunger around the household is full-sated with the new spring seals just caught upon the ice-cracked fjord. All around us chore: Alof stretches skins on frames while Arngunn rubs down pounded brains for tanning; Vidur cuts fishhooks out of seal ribs; Gizur makes spoons from bits of skull; and I, because my fingers are so tiny and so agile, cut sharp needles of the finest bones.

The mistress heeds me, silent for some time as I feel her eyes like breath; until, at last, she presses me, "Come," and takes my hand.

She steps with me toward the hearth coals. There, out of the boiled bones still piled up, she pulls a long, straight limb. She holds it, looking down its hollow where the melt of marrow has spilled into the soup. She takes her blade and scratches into the shaft some marks: round spaces tiny fingers' widths apart. With a pin, she sticks them through, then puts the passage to my lips. "Blow," she coaxes. I eye her, wary. Then I try.

From the bone comes a low, stark howling—a voice not mine, yet it is my own. I jump back, terrored, yet she sets me on the bone again. The others about have dropped their choring. Even my mother has risen up, holding tightly to her spindle's strands.

"Now," the mistress whispers, placing hands about the holes, "you can sing out loud the tunes."

That night and many more, she leads me again to the stony circle. There I learn to play her doleful chants and others, listening to the wind's cold wail and the scratch of sea—Ran's fingers reaching, calling out to me—and the songs of seals and crying seagulls and the breath of Kol's white falcons' wings. Too, Thorbjorg's sounds rise up with our smoke as she teaches me how to spread out gifts: together we carve runes in flesh and bones to burn them quick upon the fire, drifting up in scented smoke to please her gods.

Soon all her kvads ring even in my sleeping. And her words, coming harsh with steam on frost-nipped air as I lie upon Thorbjorg's weary legs listening to tales of the earth's beginning: of Ymir, father of all giants—how Odin and his brothers struck him down, forming crags and cliffs and mountains of his dead body and bones, and oceans of his blood.

She tells me, too, others of the gods' deeds, but they hold no store. 'Tis the great, dead giant who keeps my grasping, and still more the little dark ones formed like maggots in Ymir's decaying carcass. These dark ones, creeping trolls, dwarves, and elves, the huldre and the haugbo folk, some who live in earthen mounds, some in woods or creeks as thin as ribbons, who hide in shadows and linger about the darkened barns. So, too, the fylgie, a spirit born to everyone, who will vex or guide as is each deserving. Even as I listen, I see them there in the very stones. True: in the deepest crags are hollowed sockets filled with eyes; their longest knobs, rounded noses, pointed chins; and, down below, knobby knees that quiver with the will to dance. I like them well, as they toy with me and nearly make me giggle. They tempt me, beckoning me nearer, till, one night, I go creeping on my knees to greet them.

Even then the mistress, with such a daring, reaches and strikes me hard and holds me roughly with both hands. "Nay, child. Leave them be! Trust them not," she says with a kind of fury, "for this world of ours was theirs before Odin stole it off. They would do much to have it back again."

KATLA

SOMETIME o'er the season, Nattfari is found pregnant. She looks about with such a reddened cheek, her skin must burn. Now she dawdles more than ever, eyes about with dreamy calm, and holds her barely rounded stomach with both her hands. To my daughter she is solicitous, coddling her with fancies stitched for her wretched doll from bits of cloth. Each she gives I snatch up hotly and throw into the fire. Seems a simple toy, yet we all know its very magic brought Nattfari's belly quick with kin. Nattfari says it oft herself and with such joyous pleasure, yet hushes up when the mistress nears, fearing Thorbjorg would have it out with draughts and potions if she should hear.

The weather passes into spring, and the light upon the hills stays later. Soon we are sent—Arngunn, Gyde, and me—upon the fell-slopes to gather new-shed wool. It would be pleasant work, but that I must listen to my daughter's music. Oh, the child plagues me with the sound. That pipe clawing up those hills—it is as the water-grims' screech, their song set to beguile a living soul. Such it seems, for I cannot shut my ears to it, even through the sheep's droned bleats. I must

listen as we pick their soft-shed leavings; too, as we sit together carding tufts and spinning until dawn. It is there and ringing when I am
sent upon the dairy hut to milk goats or sheep or our just-birthed
cow; and when I curd their milk to cheese, my arms full-thick with
milkfat's rime, still I ever hear my daughter's loathsome, brittle shrill.

It is there of a morning when a narrow skiff strikes toward our
strand. From the fell-slope's height, I sound the call as loudly as my
voice will carry. At first I think 'tis likely Thorhall coming with his
ever-hoard and gossip. Yet, as I look, I am struck to stillness: the man
who comes is capped with hair of gold beneath his thick wool crown.

The man soon shores upon our beach. Now he crosses o'er its
stones, his legs full covered with skins all patched and raggedy, his tu-
nic worn with the staining of the sea. I know him and ever would,
even from afar: it is Ossur.

The mistress Thorbjorg greets him, takes his hands, and guides him
to our longhouse hearth. I stand beside the curdle-kegs, not knowing
what to do. It is Arngunn calling us to sup which breaks my straining.
I run, rubbing milkfat from my arms, thinking not whate'er has passed
or what is next to, till I see my daughter there returning also.

She trips across the hillslope's green over the path from the stone
circle, that very crest where so long ago the cow went straying and we
both were pregnant, lowing at our fates. Oh, I hate the sight of her,
sauntering slowly through the grasses, her bone flute dancing, white
and wild on her hip. Seems her cheeks should flush from freshly
blowing, but her look is as ever, flat and wan and chill. I ply myself
and race again, bearing at last beside her, swift and silent on the path.
We bend as one through the narrow door, low beneath the heavy, turf-
bound frame, then come into the tarnished lighting of the feeble
hearth. Within, my Ossur sits, his hair shining some upon this fragile glimmer.

He does not note me—nay, it would not be fitting if he did. I take
my place among the others, beside Gyde and Arngunn, Nattfari close
and whispering to Teit, while my daughter seats herself before the
very mistress, beginning at once to nettle with her hideous doll.

Ossur turns to the mistress as we suck our meat. "Lady Thor-bjorg, I bear a gift in thanks for your good will last season."

"What good will would that . . . ?"

"For your rune's protection." He tosses quick his glance toward me. Then he moves to a corner, stooping to untwine a lengthy wrap of hide from his burlap satchel. He withdraws a strange white staff and leans to give it to the mistress. "A narwhal's tusk," he says as Thor-bjorg turns it gently in her fingers, "slaughtered on Nordsetur's seas."

"A fine gift," she murmurs. It is the length of a man's two arms, stretched and coiled softly to a point.

"It was mine to keep, for my own spear was the whale's death-spike. Some say it bears a strength to heal; and if it should, surely yours are hands much wise to use it rightly."

Leaning down, he shares the mistress' awe at the ivory's grace. Even my daughter reaches up to touch the horn. So Ossur bends— "See, child? Here's a gift for you also"—passing something from his pocket: a small wooden boat with a sail of wadmal roughly stitched. "It is just as the ship I ride with Captain Thorlaug Arnarsson." He smiles back to catch my eye—the first time he heeds me plainly—and a pleasing look is upon his gaze as the child takes the ship from him, turning it back and forth within her hand.

The night passes, light with talk of hunting grounds, great walrus tusks the size of swords and clubs twice bigger, and bergs that waft upon the waves, echoing and mocking sailors' calls. All through, Ossur watches me, his face aglow and rosy with the pride of telling. But I mark more my daughter's dally, for now she has made of Ossur's gift a small vessel for her doll.

After the fire's quelled and the soup is chill and all about lie sleeping, still he comes not near me. Nay, he says no word, though I lie awake and cannot rest, spending the hours listening to his gentle snores. Only once, when at last I drift, I dream I feel his hand about my hair.

With the morning, I rise early to fetch dried willow twigs to set the dew-light's flame. Just beyond the homefield grasses, rounding low hills growing thick with wildflowers tucked among the turf, I fill my arms with kindling before the house has even wakened. But, turning back, I see Ossur standing by the longhouse door.

As he nears, he has the smell of sleep with him, growing stronger as he lays his lips on me.

"Ossur"—I stretch back, my bundle well between us—"it has been almost full a round of seasons."

"But a single round? Seems a lifetime I have dwelt in Ran's abode, but I have lived to see it pass because of your true gift." He takes from a pouch about his neck the mistress' runestone. "I've held it by my heart, just as my heart's held close by you."

He lays his lips again, softly, sweetly, beside my cheek, and then my chin, and then my neck, and then the edging of my wadmal chore-clothes. I feel their brush, their ripe, round touch, even as my arms are pressed with stabbing twigs against my breasts. Yet his hands slip about the narrow of my waist, taking the brute sticks up within my apron and setting them cautiously aside. Then he whispers against the stillness of my breathing, "One more season's luck and I will buy my debt, and with another, enough to fend for a child and a wife. And then no man—not chieftain, thrall, nor peasant freeman—can keep me from what I would have of you right now."

Ossur bows and slips his fingers deep beneath my dress' under-sheathing. His hands are chilled with the morning's dew, yet warmer than the hottest coals of last night's fire. They burn and creep upon me, sudden close to my tortured bosom.

"No!" I whisper. "Please, I beg—"

"Hush. Only let me touch you. I ask no more than that—not unless you wish it. Not until you are rightly mine."

I gnaw my lip as his hands outstretch, gentle as they explore me. And then they pause. They have touched the mangled breast.

The strangeness.

Ossur retreats, searching now my terrored tremble. "This was done to you? *He* had done this to you? For all these years you did not tell? Katla, you did not say?"

I try to break apart, knowing he must hate me; he must fair retreat, must cast me off, must shove me fast away. But instead he grasps me back more closely, saying, "No," pressing his fingers to my lips, softly turning down my bodice's fold to press his lips upon the scar.

I gasp and shiver. I bite my cheek. I hold my cry, yet his caresses are so tender. His touch, almost as if to heal.

Even then comes Torvard's shadow—his own repugnant daughter, her face scowling up at me across the homefield's distance, clinging close to the sod-stone wall. In one hand she holds her vile flute, and in the other her wretched doll set small and cozy in Ossur's rough-wrought vessel.

I press back from Ossur so quickly, I trip upon my twigs. Some tumble down the slope. Others catch upon my skirt's hem. I stoop to pick them up. Ossur kneels, too, begging, "What, love? Calm"—edging close to me once more.

He has not seen her, and my daughter's gone upon next look. I tell him, "She was here!" Ossur senses naught but a rustle of the grasses. As if she flew! Though I know she must be hid beyond the wall, for no footsteps have I heard yet leaving.

So I can't explain. I fumble quickly to collect my gatherings, then rush to the house to make the fire, speaking not to him or to any other.

My daughter looms no more that day, even as Ossur's ship shoves off and I bear his loss in silent burning. He has told the mistress he cannot stay, for the walrus will not wait. Yet to me he whispered bitter words, though he meant them not to pain me—that his promise would turn to naught if he should remain.

My sorrow steeps all that morning. I taste him on my lips, and the growing hatred for my daughter's fiendish game. At last I ask the mistress where the girl has gone.

"About her work." Thorbjorg eyes me. "Bibrau knows her duties. Trouble her not. She will return before too long."

Yet I know my child's hatred better even than the mistress with her love. I know, too, where she would go to do such wretched chores.

When night falls and all the house is thick with snoring, I take a cloak and trek into the twilit dark, following my daughter's footpath far beneath the sky's livid vault, past the creek, to the hill where the circle lies—where I am most loath to venture. There, in the half-moon's stillness, indeed, my daughter bounds among the rocks, their surfaces aglow as if tinged with bile. I sink down behind a shallow knoll, watching the girl as if at play: bending, greeting each tall boulder, crouching to each crevice's foot to dig from the dirt a bone or feather. Then, putting up her flute, she begins her wretched shrill. Her music through the long, dead bone sounds like fear's own screaming. I ope' my eyes, force myself to notice how she dances, lifting something in her fingers, wild with it held aloft. It is Ossur's little boat, and her cold doll stuffed within! Through the air she's sailing to the sea-dark earth; and there she bends to dig down through peat and boulder and bury it. I am stunned: the way she raps the dirt down hard, then wipes her hands clean of the tiny ship, taking up again her own sordid plaything to her bitter lips, kissing hard against its rough and filthy form.

She does not tire. 'Tis almost dawn when at last she goes from the circle, her dirt-dug doll tucked neatly in her fist, her steps very nearly skipping. Never have I seen her move so light! Shaking against the heavy coldness of the earthen knoll, I listen till her sounds are nearly silent. Then I go myself down to the death-still circle, where the stones have somehow lost their vital flush. Now they are but stumps, all rigid, and about them litter: a nest of mice, small, hollow, dead; and other once-creeping things now torn apart so naught is known of what they were.

I find the place where she has buried Ossur's vessel. Not far beneath the sod is where I dig it up. Already it seems decayed, as if 'twere nibbled by death's own maggots. I brush it off with a trembled hand. What falls is dust and nothing more.

Ravaged, shaking in my fingers, this toy's gnawed edges bite my skin. I run from the circle, stealing the small ship off to the safest bounding of the homefield. In the shadow of the house, where it is warm and safely from the wind, I drop it down upon the sod, then spit upon the thing, dance around it, once, twice, three times sharp, to break the child's cursed hold.

Yet what? What little? It is all I know, yet it cannot do. Such things are weak against such vile will as hers! I fall upon my knees in quivered, hopeless want of strength. Yet, even then, I feel within my dress my mother's rosary. I take it up and, bending, shaking, I hold it tight against my mouth and whisper words, those few I ever heard my mother speak, *"Sancte Christe!"* to squelch the sight of evil.

THORBJORG

STRANGE, when Katla does such things I feel a chill—Odin, can you feel it? A shiver as she traces there upon her breast the rigid Christian cross, ever when she is most afraid. I know not why, but slough the feeling off as I go without and stand beside her, looking down to see the rough-carved toy before her knees.

Trembling, she picks it up. "What work is this?" she begs me.

I take it. Crumbling, barely buried, yet already touched by the fingers of earthly things. "Nay!" I whisper. "It is a child's mock and nothing more."

Yet, Great One, nay! By my foster-daughter's hand this work was made. To cause such reek and shed it so? Taught I her this? No. I do not recall it.

I leave the woman there and quaking, and go to find Bibrau. She is not far: somewhat sleeping, curled within the byre stall with her doll clutched in her hand, her back against a sheep, as so many times I'd watched her warmly. Now I take her up, sudden pulling by the hair, and throw her out and push her down the hill: down and down, falling over sod and willow tripping-twigs, caught on foot to the base of the homefield hill, where a storage pit Kol's dug lies lined with stinking, half-dried meats.

There I strip her bare and throw her in. I order Kol to move the stones. "Cut the light," I say, "and quell her hubris."

I hiss, "Nay, child! Think you are so wisdom-wise? Think you bold enough already and have not left some things to learn?"

I walk away clutching at my temples. I can only blame myself, for I've doted on her, taught her well and—now I fear—far too quickly.

"Three days," I command my thralls. "Three days leave her." Then I turn to Kol. "Get the doll and burn it in the hearth."

Then I go: take Teit and ship and sail for Herjolfsnaes, to Sandhavn market—anywhere to spread myself among trivial things: people, trade goods, gossip, and such other stuffs which count for naught. Go because I cannot bear to stay to hear her scratchings, hard and slow upon the sod-clot stones.

BIBRAU

SHE CANNOT DO THIS! No, she would not dare. Yet here I stand, and the cold is dripping, the cracks of glow falling slowly across the sod.

Thought I the mistress would be proud of all I've learned and turned to use here, proud that I should keep my mother thralled and obedient to her charge. Yes, I thought, to keep her from her lover. To send her man out to the brink upon a worm-bit ship—'twould be! That man she would have for me a father—nay, no father would he be to me! Yet, for this boon, the mistress with her hand on me, her glaring eyes on me, so suddenly she picked me up and dragged me toward the daylight, prickly and harsh, its edges cutting, brined with salt and sweat and stinging.

In that moment, my last cold sight: Kol bending, crooked, searching through my apron, taking out my dearest, oh—my foetus doll! Nay, he dares to touch it, dares upon the mistress' call. I feel a shout, a cry forming in my mouth. But none will touch my lips, for I do strangle it! For all the pain of his tainting fingers, I will not—not for this nor any—give my true voice out.

So I sit in this pit brooding, knowing well the smoke I smell holds my little tainted doll, sifting now through the roof sod's tangle, flying off on the cracked, rough hands of the chill foehn wind. There is naught to do but sniff it up and wait. A dull day passes, and then a night, dull, dimmer. Then comes rain, hard and slow, seeping through the fissures of my cell. Here I carve with my little finger's nail a rune upon each fast-stuck stone and more in the dirty crevices, carve them twice, then three times round, carving all the strength I know, every secret scratch which can hold my rage.

All these I think I'll turn against the mistress, who has taught me well the secrets of the runes. Now I'll bend her own sharp skill upon her. Terror on these storage walls! She herself will be soiled now, and foul. I watch the sodden earth slip down with the willing water, sweeping my dark marks off, spreading them to travel to where my only true fate's friendships lie. Deep within the earthen boundaries, to pool up puddles of my cruelest, harshest hate. Down where I know the invisibles dally. I feel them there, their mounds hard and hollow beneath my feet, while here I wait. I can wait long—forever.

Through this petty time of hours, I lie listening to the others' sounds: their footsteps outside, their thrallish slosh of mud up and down the hillside, their bells of cattle, their bray and bleat, their scrape of ship leaving shore and dunk of oars and rippling of sail. Then again, as a second day passes barely toward the evening, I hear a sound I know will bring my liberty.

Nattfari's scream. There it holds the timbre of another groaning: as a mare thick-filled and waiting for a foal to drop. Comes my mother's voice: her words muffled, cutting sharp; then she, swinging back the heavy door of the mistress' longhouse, and her slapping pads across the mud. "Kol! Alof! Quickly! Someone, come! Help me move the storage stones!"

She herself lays fingers on the boulders, prying them up and throwing them down, "Nay, girl!" reaching out, and I suppose I am meant to grasp her fingers, yet I stand there naked, arms a-fold, staring at her dangled palms. "Come! Come out!" My mother reaches down and drags me. Up I scrape through mud, even as she throws my dress about my neck. I could turn about, yet instead I follow, for I am free and she is frantic, running toward the house again.

Within the doorway, Arngunn holds a reddened rag of blood upon her hand. "Katla, bring her quickly!" Yet I slow my walk as Nattfari shrieks—more and louder beyond the household's gape.

Comes Gyde's quick-scold, "Calm yourself, Nattfari. You know well Katla's gone to bring the girl."

I step at last over the threshold. Nattfari sees me, reaching, crying out, "Bibrau! My sweet Bibrau . . ."

Knows she not how I have ever hated to hear my name aloud?

Arngunn closes the heavy door behind and guides me to where my mother kneels beside Nattfari. "Daughter—good, dear child—" she lies, stretching out her fouled hands and folding me against her bosom, brushing back my muddied hair. "How much do you know of the mistress' wisdom? My girl, we need your help. If you know the mistress' potents, find a cure to ease Nattfari's labor." She nudges me toward the heaving woman—"Go. Now, go!"—standing straight, almost bending back my arms.

Well, I think, I should not do it, for I hate Nattfari and all the rest, and the mistress, too, and my mother most of all. I should let Nattfari die, and her baby with her. Yet then I think again: 'twould be a serviceable trial for my birthing skill.

Never have I tended more than the spring's quick lambing or a pregnant heifer. Yet I know enough to find some herb. So I set a pot upon the reddened embers and brew a potion, then see the woman drink it down. Fast with thirst and drowned in sweating, she gives a pasty look as she swallows up the last. I stare upon her, waiting to see the potion's work, till my mother sudden shouts, "Daughter, fetch her more!"

My eyes some widen, yet I hide my fullest rancor, turning then, reaching for the ladle, knowing well such draughts can work to poison as well as cure.

Before I dip, Nattfari reaches toward me. "Bibrau," she begs, "Bibrau, help me! Bibrau, please!" Thrice again she speaks my name. "Here, child. Look! Here's your little treasure—your precious doll!" She holds it, dangling there for me to grasp. It is scorched and crackling, its caul cloth lost upon the fire. Yet she holds it out to me, and as

I reach for it, she shares my clutch, drawing us together near her fully swollen womb.

"Yes, I saved it for you. Pulled it from the fire. Even singed my hand to get it out. I would not let it burn, for I know you love it dearly."

My mother rails, "The mistress will not have it!"

Yet Nattfari lays it gently on her cramping belly. "It works with sheep and cattle. Why not work for me?"—laughing weak and oddly.

"*Sancto Spiritu,*" my mother hisses. "It is demons' work."

"It is a child's toy!" Yet Nattfari claims it clearly more, for her eyes turn dark as she snatches it from me and stashes it well beneath her bedclothes. "There, I'll keep it safe," Nattfari titters. "Almost as fine as the mistress' silver keys. Such was what your mother had to bear you out—without much pain or threat of death, indeed!"

"I bore that child," my mother glowers, "with more pain, Nattfari, than you will ever suffer."

"Yet now the mistress' gone, with all her clanking silver. Would you force me to bear such pain without some wisdom's comfort?" Just then another clutch of labor grips her, shuts her mouth, and fills her face up red as blood.

Gyde comes from the hearthside. "Quiet, both of you! You draw troll-wives to this birthing with your ire!" She drops to her thick old knees, setting hands about and kneading between Nattfari's thighs.

Arngunn mops Nattfari's brow while my mother damps another cloth and presses it, fat, into Nattfari's mouth to quell her screaming. The men wait outside—Kol and Alof whispering, Gizur ever at his chop, even Vidur, the shepherd boy, down from the fell-slopes, leaving sheep and goats to the wiles of the wolves and foxes. Their mumblings, all thick with fool concern, while I have stepped away and watch and hear them. I, doing nothing, because no one has asked, as Nattfari heaves and pushes and plunges and screams and curses my mother and thrice again does bite her hand, though naught has come of the baby but a thick blue veiny bulb pulsing in and out between her thighs.

After some hours, with Gyde mumbling half-twisted words—

prayers for healing hands and loosening of women's wombs—I can stand no more. I take from my apron's gape my slender bone and set it to my lips.

"No!" my mother shrieks. "I will not have that horrid screeching."

Yet Nattfari reaches for me and clutches at my wrist. "Child, play the tunes—play them out—the mistress' kvads—"

"Katla, hush you!" Gyde curses. "Let her play. Would you have her idle while all the mistress' very mysteries hang about her music?"

Then I am pleased to lay my teeth upon the bone, to watch my mother bite her lip, knowing well she fears my songs. The kvads, those oldest notes which ever god or man dared compose in the darkest crevice of remembrance—oh, how she hates these! So I, for spite, play them daintily and well, and in my mind I sing along the tune. My words are right and, through and through, I sing of my little foetus— sing so to transform my doll into a child.

A child as I've dreamed late nights, with my mother's endless scowling silenced by the heaving of her snores. Now I feel the soul of that dreaming coming born. There, in the shadowed corner where their thrallish fire's light cannot quite reach, I sense somewhat a little girl, looking a bit like me but younger still and not quite finished, with one finger stuck into her nose.

'Tis then I pull and push my melody. Another of Nattfari's screams breaks loudly. For a time, I can barely play through the sweat and shrill as they shunt dross or fan the door to bring some breath to the stale, dark stench, or send a man running to the sea for a cool cloth of salty water.

So it goes, through the dusk and quick-come dawn. Still Nattfari wails in crushing labor. Then she strangles suddenly and wails no more. I play on, for in that hush I hear at last my tune, pure and clear as if ringing off the stones. 'Tis a beauteous note, till old Gyde rustles up and lays an ear beside Nattfari's cheek. "She still breathes," she whispers, rubbing hands and then Nattfari's pasty body, pale of color, with lips some blue. "Come, woman. Come!" She shudders.

My mother chokes, "Gyde, you must do aught to save her."

"What can I do?"

'Tis then I think perhaps to drop my bone and come up near.

No one stops me as I climb close to that belly-mound, round as a meager hill warmed by the sun. I crouch and pick from between Nattfari's fingers my little foetus doll and begin to rub it slowly, slowly, rocking, rocking, forward, back, bumping gently between the mound and the thick sod wall. The chant is in me, though no sound bursts out, but within my mind again I see the little child. She reaches and pleads to me—*Pull!*—then, standing, stretches out her arms, begging to come into my own.

My mother brushes strands of hair stuck to her sweaty brow; Gyde twines hands blood-ridden in her skirts; Arngunn clings close upon her mother, watching with her eyebrows peaked, while I move back and forth, back and forth, until Nattfari shudders. Then she wakes. And then she screams. Gruesome. Gushing blood. All purple, liquid. Wet like flood. And upon the filmy froth, a body flows. Like a boat upon the fjord, like my foetus in its wretched wooden ship. And as it comes, among the gore, the remnants of a caul.

Ah! Then the heavy slap of my mother's palm. The cord is cut, and the tiny girl-child breathes. Yet no cry comes. Only from the mother—Nattfari reaching, taking the infant to her breast, rearing back with what little strength is left to bear her. Flat against the sod wall, quivering, she rocks her head upon the rough-laid stones. I draw close and see the baby's scalp is bruised and pointed.

" 'Tis just the press of birth," Gyde tries. "Sometimes I have seen it. Nattfari, feed her." She lifts the tiny thing, but I reach up and grasp the barely squirming fingers from Nattfari's bosom.

The mother does not fight to hold her as I press the child to my flat, small chest. Nearly runty as the foetus in my pocket, but this no longer a foetus, true, for its caul is cut and now lies burning on the fire. The air is thick with the scent of wasted flesh.

"She must go to her mother." Gyde takes the child from me, "Nattfari—a girl—a little girl!" folding back the cloth she's wrapped to show between the infant's spindly legs.

"A girl," Nattfari whimpers, barely touching for one short breath before she shouts, "Blue . . . The girl is blue!"

"It is just the newness of her skin."

"No! She is blue. Blue! Blue!"

They hold the child to their hearing. The little breath comes, quick and fitful. The child coughs. Such a tiny cough, it wracks her frame, rattling as if to choke as it rushes out. Then she wheezes, a mighty, terrible sound.

"Feed her." Gyde coaxes the child again into the mother's arms. "Your breast will give her strength." Nattfari coos a little, clucks, and whispers, but the child shakes and curls a fist and slightly rolls her head away.

"She will not take my breast!" Nattfari cries.

"Then help her." For some hours, the women plead and prod as the baby coughs, sleeps some, but will not drink. Nattfari, too, falls soon fitfully to dreaming, and in her dreams cries out as if in pain.

I lean and peer and listen to that child's wretched breathing, knowing well such sounds about this house will hinder my own sleep. But then I see the blackened caul—smell its tarry stench—the ashen gray, and the way the fire has quite curled it. There it lies as the Norns did knit it. Some, I know, is caught within the child's mouth, and there it does a bit of strangle, and none can grasp it out. So its ashes speak of another place where this child soon will rest. For rest it will, and not long in its mother's arms.

But I say naught. I rise and take a stick and place it in the fire's ash and watch it heat and redden as I stoke the coals, waiting till they burst at last to flame. Then I take their heat and sizzle-dry the final sap from that bit of caul. When it is full ash, I gather it in my fists, go outside the house and down to the very fjord, stand upon a stone, and throw it to the sky.

There I sit, upon a rock, with that stick half burned, swirling up the waters where the fishes and other swimming things swarm and clutch to the edges of the earth, when a rugged oar breaks through the water and a rippled sail falls softly behind a form—my mistress, now returned, and that stick of oar pulled by the newborn father.

As they near, my mistress rises and slowly trudges through the chill to shore, eyeing me with furious stillness as I dangle my rod down in the moist. Yet she moves to the house and says no word to me. I listen for the door-boards' creak, knowing well she will turn again and call to Teit, "Come!" even before the sail is wholly furled.

'Tis a long night of Nattfari's screaming and everyone fretting there within the house. I myself creep to the circle stones for a bit of peace, to sleep awhile. I am tired from my work, and 'tis my first fine rest since my cants were wasted on Ossur's feeble plaything. Only with the break of light I wake, half misted, to see Teit climbing toward the icefield's edge. There, within his arms, he bears his child. It is squirming still. I can see it as I stand and watch him stepping high upon the path, up to the ice-gripped mountains where the cold will chill the child's final gasps.

I please myself that now I will never have to listen to that child's pity-coughs again.

THORBJORG

POOR THING. Mangled, sickly. Never meant to live—yet she looked about and lay and would have lasted some small days had not Teit seen to end her torment. He took her up from her mother's arms and would have set upon the fells at once, had I not begged him linger till the dawn. That night we spent waiting for a death that would not come.

Nay. Poor thing. And Teit, bold for his quiet constancy, restraint. With first light, he did not wait, but bore her off to brook the brace of the sudden wind, to give her grace and suffer with her pain no more.

I let him go. I blessed him for his pity. Though none could bear Nattfari's shrieks, wild, grasping, even in her labor's weakness. Least of all, Katla, eyes glowering white, still chewing on her lip, trusting not at all the child who performed this deed.

True, my foster-daughter did what I myself would bare have done so well. Brought this child whole—strange fate, breathing life from a wooden chunk and a slender piece of bone. 'Twas far beyond her ken, eerie for a glimpse of what keen spirits watch over this household. Such work as this bears the mark of the invisible ones' creed.

Still this girl—her breath rang out and her suck came, weak and wasted. Life, indeed, but only for a time. Such hope destroys—Nattfari's, dressed upon a dream, stretched upon nine months and a lifetime's futile waiting. A crime, to breathe upon a fleeting flash when 'tis bare a spark. Such hope is pain. Sometimes it is best to let hope die.

I would have done if I had been here. Nary but a breath would I have spent to try to save the child. But Bibrau is young and does not know. She acted well and wisely for her practice. I cannot chide her. 'Twas not her fault. Indeed, perhaps 'twas mine.

And now Nattfari's reason's flown—up with her child. Exposed upon the fell-slopes. Waiting yet for death. "To the mountain," they term such peculiar woe. I call her madness a kind of mourning. I mourn them both—the woman and her child. Most of all, I mourn the strangeness of life's witness: that those who want are never meant to have, while those who have are ever wanting not at all.

BIBRAU

WHEN I RETURN, it is well past morning, though the coals within that house are dark and the air hangs heavy with the stench of last night's screams. Nattfari sleeps until she snores, but the others huddle low, waiting, watching, fitful, Arngunn resting with her head on Alof's knee.

I set upon the coals, stoking them with vigor. I am cold for all my rest, and longing for a fire. Yet barely have they burned before I hear, "You little beast!"—my mother's voice rising swift and sudden from the shadows.

She catches me by surprise, sweeping down upon the hearth, grabbing me by both my shoulders. She dares to shake me. Oh, her wretched touch, as she prods me to find my foetus doll. "Your fault! Yours!" as she rips it from my apron and holds it high above her head.

Then, *"Sancte Domine, Spiritus Sancti,"* in her impenetrable foreign jabber as she thrusts my foetus deep and hard into the coals.

Nay! I nearly shout, for there is smoke and then a flash of fire. Instead, I bite my tongue and leap to douse the flames, digging my foetus from the char. It is barely out when I feel more hands: Kol and Gyde grasping me about, the other men catching up my thrashing arms and kicking knees.

All the while, the mistress answers nothing. She watches, breathes no word to set them off, only stands at last and bends and takes my foetus from my hand and throws it down upon the fire.

"An end to it," she utters. "It will stay until it's burned."

They set me down. All are silent, watching the wood thing turn to flame. Then coal. Then cinder. Even Gizur, the wood-beast's maker, makes no move to snatch it out. Nor do I dare to stir to change its fate, but creep in close to watch the wood smoke rise.

From that smoke wafts up a being. None can see it drifting there but I. Within its plume, the flicker of a grinning, the muster of a finger beckoning me near. I watch him writhing: twisting like a serpent, slithering, entangled in the flare. There, beneath his savage sprite's feet, my crumbled foetus' charred remains.

Nay, the being giggles as he tempts me. I follow gladly, for Nattfari shrieks and my mistress stews. Though I hear not much beside his shrill bone music: there, within his wispy fingers' grasp, is a thin bone flute very like my own. But its refrain is so much better! Thrice again as round in tone, and his melodies dance so far above those others' ears, drowning out all morbid talk and bitter, useless pinings, so that when he plays I hear no other sounds.

Out beyond the homefield paths we travel, though a storm blows hard to shatter ice, tripping lively, skipping to his hollow tune over snowfields toward the sacred circle—the grinning stones—indeed, he knows them well.

It is there I learn his name—but, nay, I will not speak it! For if I do, he will fair'y fly, and I would miss him hard. But I can say this: that some would call him fylgie, and of that sprite there is much told.

Much cruel and faulty. So few do know the truth. But, as my fylgie tells it, fewer still have dared to open up their eyes.

My fylgie stands beside me in our circle, laughing, whispering all the words I have ever longed to shout. Longed, yet he knows I will never speak them. So his words do bite. They are vicious, mocking all the farce which shows the world of men and women false. Such and so, he speaks my mind.

That night is white, and the winds come crashing. Gliding, sliding, my fylgie leaps those slippery boulders as if they were as dry as a plod of sun-baked dung. He skips and dances from one onto another, quick-step, bounding, coaxing me to hop-step, too. So I do, because I like his music well.

Like it—nay! I hear it with adoring, thinking how the mistress' frown would plunge to see her sacred oval wracked beneath our wild, wretched writhes. It seems fine malice, and I cannot—will not stop! I bound and pant, aching at my sides, feeling my toneless laughter burst like bile.

'Tis even then I see about me the strangest vision: the stones themselves joining in our jig! Round and round, each headstone mastering the bow and crook of my fylgie's playing. But my fylgie, full up with his mischief, changes suddenly his tune. Now to a crawling rhythm, turning his melody sinuous and smooth, my fylgie sets to guide me, squirming through the cracks, through the crevices among the rocks, over stones where no foot has stumbled since the earth was made of Ymir's brow. My toes are fleet and sure as a mountain creature's as I follow.

Before too long, we come upon another, certain path, this one lighter, longer, narrower, and high. It climbs up cliffs and, clinging, rises toward a grassless ridge, crushed beneath the glacier's foot. Just there, as we reach the icy crest, the path drops sharply down.

Dark for me has always been a comfort, a mantle like a cloak to keep one warm and safe, while the bright is like a bite or a scratching nail. So I feel no fear as my fylgie leads me deep into that blackness. I welcome the chill which sweeps me, the gust of glacier's breath, the slippery stone which sucks me down beneath the ice, into that earth, and then to someplace well concealed. A hollow—so! A narrow gap. A place with no light, no wind, no sound. I know my fylgie leads me to the invisibles' abode.

There I slip and sit and linger, my eyes adjusting to the glow. Truly, there is glow—a brilliance—such a blue to fade the brightest shining turquoise on the fjord. No azure sky could contend with such a brilliance, raging in my vision as I sit and, slowly, see them all. Watching me. Waiting for me, their table set for me, wide and full with steaming, fragrant fare. The haugbo stare at me, their reddish locks tousled purple in the glow, and the sylphlike nøkks and the craggy draugs with their fingers ragged from tearing unkempt graves, and all their kin of whom I've been so often warned. They sit, small and fat, thin and lithe, some bright with the glow shining in their shadows. Some others bend and bow. Their dour gloats I know at once: these are the very spirits of the circle stones.

True, far above I could not see them clearly, but here I giddy as they cluster round—these dear old fellows, donning me in dresses made of mist and scent, binding up my hair with jewels and gold more ancient than any seen by petty men at markets. So I wear their gauzes and veils, and dance their frenzied jigs to the dissonant tunes my fylgie plays upon his hollow bone.

Then the light is gone.

I awake, lying again in wadmal, caked in dirt, my hair in tangles, clutched alone upon a cliff in the wind's sheer bluster with a quick-fall stone beneath my cheek.

I startle. I am dangled high above. Beneath, my sacred circle and my mistress creeping. Lighting fires. Slaughtering beasts. Too, Kol with his white-winged fowl. He shoos one up. Screeching swiftly, soon it nears, till its feathers flick in reach of my frozen fingers. I think to stretch and catch it—know, if I could dance among the trolls, surely now I have the will to fly—but then I think, better tuck away my new learned secrets. So I huddle closer where I lie, till the foul bird squawks to tattle-tell my hiding place aloud.

There they find me, stretching, teetered on the brink, and the wretched bird aflutter as I shoo it back with clots and burrs. After some long time, they force me down and again into the paltry stretch of Thorbjorg's homefield. Yet, even as I leave my winsome crag, I know my fylgie lingers, for I hear his whispered tune between the fissures of the glacier, singing up among the jagged rocks of the highest fells.

THORBJORG

A FYLGIE SPIRIT: not a walking soul nor a grim nor nøkk nor any haugbo living in the earth, but a fylgie, sometimes called a "fetch," and other names, both praiseful and malevolent. Such was the shade rising through the smoke as the wood doll burned.

So it seemed to me, but the flash was fleeting. Then the sight was gone. And there, only smoke and the final flame. Then the ash flowing up and down upon Nattfari's wakened wailings, so I mixed a fine concoction to help her sleep again.

A fylgie—nay! Such a fylgie's given at each birth to tender guidance or conjure harm. Fair but few should ever know their brute companion except at their last dying breath. Yet here my foster-daughter sees it rising, sensing all its beck drawing her near. And she follows. Yes, of course, she follows.

I fear the coming of this fylgie, Odin. I should have stopped it— somehow should have known. Great One, One-Eye, blessed with wisdom's vision! Now I think I hear it almost ringing on a tune—drawing our dearest, only foster-daughter to revel in its stunts, laughing loudly on what work it's done.

BIBRAU

SOME DAYS I lie about, for I find I have no will or want but for rest or sleeping. Some for eating; for now, though it seemed I had consumed so much when I was gone, my limbs are barely bones bursting through their thin skin covering. My mother, wordless, brings me meat or steaming gruel which I take from her loathsome fingers and eat with a kind of relish. Meanwhile, the others skulk about with mundane chores, and Nattfari moans and does little of much use, and my mistress sits across the low hearth fire and watches me.

My very mistress—with no word, no breath, no scolding hiss, or a kiss in love. If she knows my secret, surely she should wrap her arms about in joy! Yet she only watches, long and keen and sharp and cold. After some days' staring, I grow used to her look even as I fall asleep—her eyes like the constant washing of the fjord's tide. Like a stone on the beach beneath Thorbjorg's heavy, scraping gaze, I bear a callus on my spirit from her rough-tossed eyes.

Till one eve, long after the winter dark has come, while the others tarry close and huddle, nearly bursting from the cramp and stench with the cattle in the corners of the household and the cold too fierce to defecate outside, my mistress wakes me from my dozing with a shock—"Foster-daughter, up"—pulling me to my spindle legs and urging me to dress swiftly.

Half done am I, and moving slowly, when Thorbjorg wraps us both within her bearskin cloak and leads me out upon the bitter cold. A foehn wind whips as the mistress leads me fast along the path to where I'd danced with my fylgie's music—out across the valley to the place where my jolly fellows play. Now they lie coated hard with frost and to their very knees with the drift of winter. All trace of the footsteps of our nighttime's prance are vanished. Instead, before each boulder lie deep piles of bloodless bones.

Bones. My mistress says naught as I turn my eyes on her in question. She presses me down upon my wadmaled knees. "Look!" She points, and there are shapes cut clearly in the snow: all the runes to cast off evil. A wind sends up a spray of winter's dust which sparks my eyes. "Sit!" Thorbjorg commands. "Sit and dig. The wind comes briskly! Bibrau, clear the snow. Go now! The rune-marks must not lay hid."

She sets me down to work with barest hands on wobbly knees

until my skin scrapes thin in the biting snow, digging to keep her rune bones naked. She stands above me as I hold them up, glowing red and white with cold as if they blister. She shows no mercy. "Dig! The wind comes! Dig!" I set my hands again, gripping the ends of my wadmal cloth for mean protection, feeling tears of hate and pain seeping down my cheeks to freeze. But I will not show them to Thorbjorg. No, I punish her for treating me to such a scornful task. If she thinks she can mock me with such petty, feeble malice—me, who has made the fylgie and invisibles my kin!

Blind as all those others is my mistress, for she cannot see what has risen from the smoke—cannot hear my fylgie's laughter as I hear it: his very tune then rushing, rising above the snow. A sudden gust of warmth comes, as if his gay retort quick-heats my fingers. I see him dancing just beyond the circle, begging me with his leaps and prances to raze the bone runes and set the circle free. Yet the mistress stands above me. From what keen doubt I do not know, but I ignore his gambol and leave the marking runes alone.

The night passes with me between my fylgie's taunting tramp and my mistress' threatening tower. I clear the rune bones over, over of the snow's quick waste. When it is through and dawn slow breaks, my mistress takes me again into her arms.

Though now I do not want her. Yet she will not leave me, never again alone upon my whim. She is always at my side as I take to glean or butcher or play a simple tune, her cracked hands hovering, her breath blown hot, her eyes ever warning with their coiled caution. Meanwhile, my fylgie jounces not far about, on the hearth's edge or just outside the circle, laughing, taunting, as she treats me so like a child.

I hate her—to have made him see me so, humiliated as he tosses his head and waggles mimic of the mistress' gestures. I listen first to her rude lessons, then to his wild rants. It is the first ever I thought perhaps the mistress could be wrong.

It becomes a game that spring: Thorbjorg teaches, and then my fylgie. It is my choice to make discreetly, whose tutelage to try. Most, when I choose from my fylgie's, the mistress looks on quizzically but

lets such little indiscretions go. Till one morning, when this game's
still fresh and grows too bold.

That dawn, Thorbjorg sets my chore to cut up weeds, crumble
them, and cook them to change them into smelly brews. She shows
the method, but my fylgie thinks them best for drinking like a sweetish mead. So I drain them down to know their better power. The concoction turns my head and stomach, and the world whirls hard about.
Thorbjorg notes my stupor well, standing before me as a waving
wraith which sets my gut to tumble; so she holds my head as I vomit
across the mountain dews.

Harshly she whispers when my flush has cooled, "Foster-daughter,
these tonics aren't for mischief. They are grave concoctions meant to
heal. Think I pass you these old wisdoms lightly? When you were
younger, you bore your charge with more respect."

At her scolding, my fylgie breaks with gaiety. Against my heavy
head, his mirth bursts loud, ending in a squeak and crash.

My mistress looks about so I think she's heard his pranking.
"Nay," she hushes, " 'twas just a falling glacier's prong."

We stumble back toward home with the falling light, and, indeed,
there is a great blue shard floating down the fjord. Upon its back, I see
my little monger prancing, playing on his pipe, as the ice does rock
and creak and groan.

On my fylgie lingers through the season, always just beyond the edging of the stones. My mistress makes my chore to keep the circle
rimmed with sod-cut runes; it seems my fylgie cannot cross within
when the circle is so bound.

On rainy nights, he tricks up to the household, leaning near, his
breath upon my neck as I learn to cipher well. With my silver blade,
the very one Kol forged upon my birth, I set the runes in neat lines
across a mellow driftwood board. Yet, for each my carving masters,
my fylgie teaches another: *secret runes,* he calls them, which will turn
a pleasant tune to dissonant, twisted strains. So I set to copy, too, his
marks, but every time I try, my mistress catches my blade and turns it
from its tangent, ever back upon her straighter, duller road.

Some long nights it plays like this till my practice slab is scored about with jags and frazzle. Then Thorbjorg lays her hand and, sighing, draws my knife away and gives me hers—of ancient iron with a yellowed walrus grip and copper fastenings worn too thin and green. Strange, this brittle hatchet my fylgie cannot handle; though he gropes, at every stroke his fingers slip. Furious, he stomps his feet, stirring sparks to set the house afire. As he thrashes, he slaps the blade out of my grasp so it falls and hits the hearth's hot stone. When Mistress Thorbjorg picks it up, the blade is chipped two places on its sharpest edge.

For this I am some punished. Yet I begin to wonder, thinking perhaps indeed she can sense or see him. Nay, if she could, she would have breathed long ago some words to shoo him off. But never has she, and oft my fylgie's vowed only the keenest eyes can ever know his form. Yet I note, too, more as time hard-passes, how my fylgie stills whenever Thorbjorg nears, as if he fears what she might know.

Comes the passing of another year and I myself am turned a decade's round. It is the season's height, when Kol's white birds burst forth upon their guano-stinking cliffs. All the beasts beset within our house against the winter's cold are let into the fresher, warmer air. There is rutting near and far, with such wild beasts upon the fjord's rocks or the snow-dripped, muddy fell-slopes. Even some within the mistress' dungy byre: 'tis there we hear and then find Alof and Arngunn— caught upon a moldy bail with his twig between her legs. Arngunn's face full-flushes as she brushes hay from her wadmal, yet all know this is not the first and, like the other fly-swat beasts within those stalls, soon she will be thick with child.

It turns out true as the full moon passes. Arngunn seems well pleased upon the news. Yet Nattfari tears her hair. She screeches and crawls about the spring-melt mud, wanting not to bathe, until, as she spreads her stench, the household reeks a brutish odor even with the other beasts outside. Nay, I cannot stand it, for she follows me wherever I go, frantic mumbling about my long-burned foetus, until, at last, I stoop upon the midden's refuse. Finding a hollow leg bone, I shape two eyes and a stiff, unbroken grimace, and this I give so she can shove it deep beneath her dress and moan upon her womb-dry cries.

After the rut comes the lambing season. I grow quick-skilled, cutting cords and turning each fleece-beast free. The mistress seems well pleased, though her praise means nothing to me. Only I find I like these slick little meeklings, coated with their rime of gore. In some time I pick a favorite, a small black ball I brought forth myself. Over the warming weeks, I put it oft upon my lap and stroke its silky coat, black as the night touched by midwinter's moonrise. In time I grow to know its bleat, as clattered stones rolling on the icy strand, and how it seeks to follow when I tempt it with sweet grass, out about the steep fells, stumbling among patches of soft-melt snow and the full-grown sheep's just-shed, ragged hairs.

Not long, too, when, at nights, Thorbjorg and I begin cold sacrifice, setting pigs and goats in severed parts to offer to the gods. My mistress gives me chores: to rend the beasts and lay them on posts or in certain wafting circles, first for Odin—her chosen god—then for Thor, his son, then for Frey, the fecund god who makes things grow.

By then, my mischief game has become a taunting: I know too well how to spark the mistress' ire. For such, one night I set a beast—a white fox caught alive upon a trap—and cut it well yet use no knife, only my own bare fingers, to tear it asunder.

My mistress' eyes grow wide at the sight of blood and flesh upon the ground and beneath my fingernails. Though the bits are neatly torn and strewn, she gathers them up and rudely casts them off. Once she's cleaned her palms with sand, she rises and plucks me up and says not much, yet drags me again toward the homefield byre.

Drags me all the way, ever roughly, as she flings open the gate and finds my little lamb at his mother's teat. Thorbjorg takes him up and ties him with a bit of strapping, then gives him to me. "Come," she says, and I follow back, carrying the warm, sweet suckling in my arms.

At the sacrificial circle, Thorbjorg ties him against the largest boulder. "Such is your work," she commands, "to set this beast and prepare it for a feast—this one made for the One-Eyed god."

I feel a sudden, hateful writhing, a strangling in my throat that cuts my breath as my own heart rocks. My mistress knows this little beast is my darling, yet, no matter how I stand or glare, she will not recant. Meanwhile, my fylgie, goading with his mean-steeped tune, dances about and sings the mistress praises for her malevolence.

'Tis then I think to call him evil, and the mistress witch, just as some others do. Yet, as I start, watching my mistress' scowl and then my fylgie's jigging, somehow I know even this baleful dealing will bring me skill.

So I take the knife from my belt's sheathing. Bending low over my little darkling, with gentle fingers I stroke its silken neck. Just so, the callow beast stands calm. It waits as I turn the blade to lay it close upon the bitter black—the soft, warm throat—then press until the edging slips and I slice through.

Comes the blood. Slowly. Too slowly, I think. 'Tis just a little cut—a simple sliver pulled apart—but the lamb's eyes are black with fright and a sort of pleading. It tries to bleat, yet it cannot, for I've cut it so I would not hear its sound.

"Good, girl. Now you see the fate of falling mischief. Take the lamb's parts and spread them wide. Sit and wait till Odin's ravens devour and deliver them to Valhalla's table. Then take the skin and sew of it a cap, fine to fit my skull. Line it with the pure-white catskin your mother saved since the Althing market."

Just as she asks, I do, my own hot torment dripping, knowing each cut, each bite, each stitch, each tiny thread through the fine seal-needle's hole, is meant as if to pierce my soul. When it is through, the mistress places the bonnet on her scalp and wears it about the circle to remind me. Yet I know that pelt, poised limp atop her fine, gray frailty, is little sacrifice for the pure and perfect ruthlessness I've learned.

Rake and
Broom

THORBJORG

WHAT TO DO, Alfather—Odin—you, who gave this gift—this child? Yet now the tender thing's turned rotten, and naught I do draws her back upon our path. Naught, though I wheedle and scold; though I trick her up; though first I coddle, then ignore; though I play such cruelties as I can bear until they pain me near to sickness. She takes each appeal with myriad indifference, as if my attempts for her are wanton. As if my gifts are false. As if my love for her is fleeting as the storms.

Each day she slips further from me, bewitched with her own beguilings, led by a bare, misguiding hand. It is that hand she trusts, not mine—till no longer can I trust her own, nor what tools I've put within.

Tell me, Longbeard, why give this gift if not for good? Tell me, too, of your own dear Loki's mischief, which wrought upon the gods so many wrongs. How unlike is she from him? Tell me, when your dear son Baldr lay slain by one of Loki's pranks: a sprig of mistletoe flung upon a game! Such an innocent branch, no one would suspect it; yet the only thing in all the world that hadn't promised not to do him harm. Loki's plot, to cast it in the air on the blind god Hod's unseeing falter. Such a tiny glance on Baldr's chest! None but Loki would have thought to use such innocence to kill.

He was harshly punished, but forsaken? No, not even then. Not even he. Nor can I forsake this child. Though my hands are red with wringing anguish, and my heart—what heart is left that she's not already, in her silence, savaged? Yet I take such malice sweetly—even glad if such ill-will should ever grow to sense, if such tarnish should one day glow with wisdom. Seeing there within her fouled hand some attempt to touch a greater truth, some sight, some vision beyond my own . . .

Yet what she sees—what is it she sees, Alfather? To me all comes as creeping shadow—darkly now—and that darkness grows a cloud which swallows up all light. Just as Baldr's death draped the gods in mourning and the earth in winter's shrouds.

Is this the child's footpath, Alfather, or does some other shadow fall? I cannot sense which way this storm is blowing, only that the wind about grows suddenly quite cold.

KATLA

SOMETIME late that autumn, Arngunn bears her babies out—fine twins, a boy and girl, Bodvar and Hallbera. My daughter is let nowhere near, shoved away by Alof and sent far off by all the rest. Three days she is gone and, when at last she steps upon the mistress' threshold, her cheeks are cracked with frost and lined with crusted blood.

No one speaks or moves as the winds drift in and fly about her. Only Thorbjorg bears up from Arngunn's lying bench to shut the door against the howl. Then she draws my daughter gently in, cleans her face, and sets her down beside the fire. There, head bent upon her palms, my beast-girl watches across the embers' glower.

Watches, though she plays as if asleep. I feel her scathing grimace through her half-closed eyes. Too, Arngunn must, for she clutches tightly on her brood while Gyde wraps them in her bulk as if to protect them all somehow.

But such terrored glance does not frighten back Nattfari. From the darkest corner of the house, the mad-made woman creeps, babbling gibberish, hissing like a pesky house-cat. She huddles, speaking to herself, ever edging close beside Bibrau. There she fusses for a time, filthy fingers like tight-gnawed claws wove' through tangled tresses, till my daughter rises without even a sleepy stare and reaches for a comb to tear the knots from the woman's hair.

Through the winter, it is much the same: Nattfari as a pet upon my daughter's playing. The rest do our best to fair ignore as she strokes and coddles, then swats her off when she has a mind. Still Nattfari clings, loyal as a cur, more beast than the cows who share this homestead's frigid corners. With the spring and Thorhall's usual arriving, even he cannot hide his stun.

That first long evening about the mistress' board, Thorhall watches for a time, silent as he never is, then leans to Mistress Thorbjorg. "There are four upon my ship—new thralls, fair and hearty, just bought for Eirik Raude. I see you are shorthanded, with Arngunn's arms so full with babes and Nattfari useless but for simple chores. I'll sell you all for six of Kol's bright falcons, then set to Sandhavn quick again to buy some more."

Thorbjorg nods. So the bargain's struck. They join us, four thralls with balded scalps and eyes like sunken shadows. As the household men mend tools, we women begin at once to stitch up better cloth to patch these new thralls' tatters. Meanwhile, Thorhall bandies the babies, settling in to gossip by the hearth fire's coals.

"Eirik's sway grows ever stronger," he starts. "No doubt, his kin will claim this Greenland e'er and long. Already, his fair son Leif seems well to bear the chieftain's cloak, though Torkel Herjolfsson grows to a sturdy, just man also. Yet, last season, Torkel's younger brother, Bjarne, set sail from Iceland to meet his kindred here. On his way, fair fool, he was blown off-course and, somewhere westward, glimpsed a coast heavy-wooded, with bays a-flock with gulls. Not some far off they were, yet he steered right past—didn't even step ashore to hunt for some beasts to boil. About the halls when he arrived, he was quickly mocked. Yet in Brattahlid, upon the news, Leif ventured to buy Bjarne's very vessel. The young dolt let it go for half the silver hacked from Leif's thinnest chain; and now Leif plans to sail some soon to search again for these new coasts. Meanwhile, Torkel can do naught, tending to his homestead for his father, who is growing old and ill."

"Nay," Thorbjorg says, "such goes hard for Torkel. He is a good man, much like his father ever has been. Yet Leif is fair'y wise to the winsome ways of men."

"Indeed! He'll make a finer chief—full brave upon the seas, and bold, yet of a calmer temper than his father's. Unlike his foster-brother—nay, there is not much hope to come of Einar's eldest son."

"Indeed?" Thorbjorg asks, and lays aside her stitch.

"Nay, Torvard Einarsson is much the same—too oft upon his father-in-law's byre, setting his press upon some crying, bonded girl."

My cheeks grow hot.

"His mistress Freydis works to quell his stride. Each time he jigger-jars from Eirik Raude's own board, she sits but calmly, sucking at a boiled bit of meat, seeming fair'y unconcerned. Yet, when he returns, all tussled with exertion, she spits in his face, hisses calumny before her father and all his prideful hall, until Torvard trembles with her abuse and dares not turn a hand upon her."

"Know well, Thorhall," Thorbjorg mentions, "were she not Frey-dis Eiriksdatter, he would not stand long before countering such attacks."

"Counter? Ha! He is much changed beneath the yoke of this harsh mistress. He is so meek I think even your poor Katla would have little left to fear of him. 'Tis rumored he cannot act upon his pleasure—not even with these hapless thralls."

Such words! I stare into the fire, bite my lip, and feel the ancient scar. The rest about the house are still, eyes bent low to their mend and stitching. All except Torvard's cruel seed. There she stays, his very, vicious mirror, hid behind the mistress in the shadows' glow, looking up with strangely wanton eyes. Thorhall senses well the silence. He clears his throat and dandles with the babes. "I regret it, mistress. I meant no harm to tell the tale."

Thorbjorg takes again her thread. "Tell some other happening. Perhaps, Thorhall, some news to delight our patient Katla?"

"Aye, good Frey! For, indeed, I have something more. There is word about of her young man, Ossur. Seems he's settled in at Vesterbygd and done some well, growing prosperous on caribou hunts and walrus ivory. He's got a fine estate, if smaller than some others, and a ship of his own with a well-sewn sail. Ah, yet, don't you know, when such news reached Torvard's hearing, the lout clenched his hands and his face turned ruddy-rash. 'Twas such a sight!" Thorhall notices my cheeks are again pale. "Well . . ." He gruffly clears his throat. "Katla, spare your fret. Eirik Raude's stiff gaze and Freydis' scoldings will ever keep Torvard's plots at bay."

I bear his grin and comfort's pluck upon my chin, but there's little succor in false assurance. I know too well Torvard Einarsson's true making: this cowered masquerade is but a feign. Only time awaits his chance to pitch his vengeful rage again.

With the dawn, Thorhall leaves us at the fjord's edge with these four new thralls standing here beside. As he shouts the call for oars, he says aloud he'll bound soon for Vesterbygd and the northern hunting waters. He says it for my hearing, for he watches me wryly. Yet I stand silent and apart as he pulls up sail. Finally, as he breaks out from the shallows, he quits his game and calls, "Any message, Katla? I'll take it to him safely."

My heart is beating echo, flapping full like frantic wings, yet between here and there lies Brattahlid, where Torvard stays among Eirik Raude's own household. I bite my lip, shake my head, and wisely hold my tongue.

Still, as the chill leaves the air and we turn the toil of seed-time, I ever eye the narrow channel and cannot help but hope for him to come. These days, many ships bear fishers, hunters, voyagers, and chiefs through those flashing waters, some begging of the mistress' seeing will. At each bow's crest, my heart some jumps, yet, upon each certain landing, none bears my Ossur's message, or his shape or name, or any claim of gold or trading goods—nothing meant to carry me from this wretched shore into his warm and wanting arms.

Soon these thralls fill our emptied spaces. Svan is one: young and thick of bearing, fine for managing heavy burdens almost as heartily as mighty, twisted Kol. Then Orm, who is thin and wiry, yet skilled with club and hunting net, a fair companion for Alof with his knife and spear. Too, there are two pairs of hands both quick with goats and cattle. One's called James and the other John.

At nights, I sit about my weaving, trying hard not to shiver at my daughter's rune-scratch above the hiss of my shuttle's play and Nattfari's moans and scrabble. Till, one evening, wafts even a fainter sound, "*Kyrie Eleison. Christe Eleison.*" I start upon the whisper, facing hard against my twining and the sod-stuffed wall, yet it comes again, "*Kyrie Eleison. Christe Eleison.*" Such words are my mother's ancient calls. And the voices, these two thralls—James and John. "Lord be with you. Christ be with you. Praise be unto God. *Hallelujah!*" I cannot help myself but form their shapes upon my lips, carefully but without sounds.

Another night goes such, and then another, till a third, and, through the dim of the hearth fire's glint, the one called James settles close about my weaving. As he cleans his tools and knots some rope, he whispers, "*Kyrie Eleison,*" near my ear.

I eye him fast, then back upon my threads.

"*Kyrie Eleison. Christe Eleison.*" This time with a little singing. "You long to say the words," he breathes. "Katla, why not join us?"

"I am no Christian."

"Yet I have heard you called so, even in this household."

"In this household, yes. But I am not. Only my mother was, and she long dead—long gone."

"All deserve Lord Jesus Christ's embrace."

"What do you mean by this? What know you of it?"

"Much," he says. "Upon my homeland, I was soon to be a priest."

I turn. "My mother said 'twas not wise to play a Christian in a pagan's hall. Better, she said, hold close the light than expose its tender flame."

"Still and well, your mother was some wise. Yet Christ is near enough," he plies, "and strongest, true, where there is mostly darkness."

"Think you so?" I catch my strand just before it tangles to a knot.

"Think?" says James. "I know it so." Sighing, "You loved your mother much."

"Yes." I bow my head as if to play upon the snarl.

"Would you be with her in Heaven?"

"Heaven—she said something of it once—longing for her White Christ's arms. Yet, upon her death, she feared to ever slave at Bilskirnir."

"Surely she has felt Christ's embrace by now. She sounds a fair and honest Christian. Upon Christ's Heaven there is naught but soft and love and light. Ne'er of toil, but only one true God, great and holy on his throne. And angels."

His tale is some and more of my mother's ancient secrets. "Would you tell me of it?" I beg through a mist of sudden, harkened tears.

James smiles softly, though his foremost teeth are lost and I see his lip is cut upon a scar shaped somewhat like my own.

Comes the mistress then and hies me up to help her undress. No more that night or the next do we talk of Christian things. Yet, on the morning of the third, we are sent to work upon the fells. There I labor with the hoe and digging while James and John bend not far behind. I hear John murmur, "In my land, there are many Christians, and houses built where all the works are dedicated to Jesus Christ our Lord."

"Such a house," adds James, "was a monastery, the place from which I'd come. Truly beautiful, filled with singing. Never did we rise or eat or work or sleep without such prayers upon our breaths."

"*Sancte Christe?*" I whisper out.

"*Gloria in excelsis Deo,*" James says.

My glance turns thick with awe. "What means all this?"

"Glory be to God upon the highest."

I bite my lip. "Do women live within such houses?"

James nods. "Sacred sisters dedicated to the Lord."

I bend again upon my work.

"You must take the Christian oath," he coaxes, "one day before a priest, to be yourself full Christian, too."

"I am not worthy," I spit, digging harder at a root.

"All are worthy, Katla, who love Christ well."

"You do not know—you cannot know. . . ." I shake my head some.

"All are worthy," James says kindly, "to know Christ's mercy. No sin's too great to bear forgiveness by the Son of God."

My cheeks are hot with a kind of flush. "Mercy?" I quickly wipe away a sudden tear.

Soon enough comes Kol across the hillside. He begs the Christians off, so I am left alone upon my chore. At once I heave a wretched, wrenching sob, for they have spoke' aloud my own mother's dearest, silent prayer.

Through those warm, swift weeks, our house is draped with meat and skins all drying. Our fields flush with greening hay, and our fell-slopes bob with tufts of grazing, well-watched sheep. There is little time for talk or tender. Yet, upon odd jaunts when I can, I join these Christians on the hills. At day or eve with these two to guide me, I learn some little Latin phrasings I had only known so long in parts, but now I learn their whole and deeper meanings.

Such warming does not last. Again too quick the foehn winds blow with their chilling rains. They crack my heart, for I know such storms set fury on the seas. They will be too rough, and then the fjords frozen. Ossur will not come. Not for another season. Perhaps not e'er at all. Too, with the first frost, it grows quickly hard to step off from the hearth fire's glint to glean some greater wisdom from James or John.

Soon the nights are all but for a brief and dim-lit hour. Then, one morning, when this false dawn comes, the mistress bolts up, dripping terror from her sleep. "Nay," she cries, "the rake! The broom!" She gasps. With her rustling, I open my eyes to see her hands upon this new Orm's brow. "Bibrau! Gyde! Katla! Awake and quick. Our Orm is ill."

We rise from our sleeping benches, finding Orm thick-drenched with sweat, his teeth chattering hard as the mistress pulls back his wadmal cover.

"Hear?" She hovers, drawing my daughter near to Orm's bared chest. "The stiff sound? Child, nay, I dreamt it—the plague twins come."

Legend tells of the evil twins who do their cleaning, spreading wide the pox with their rake and broom where'er they please. And where they rake, 'tis said, only some men die, but where they sweep, they sweep the household clean.

Thorbjorg looks from Gyde to my daughter, then to each of us in turn. "I saw them come upon a vessel, the very shape and size of Thorhall's ship. And those wretched twins dared wear the faces of Arngunn's babies. In my dream, Bodvar bore the rake, Hallbera bore the broom."

Each of us grows cold with listening, and Arngunn draws her babies up. "Give good prayers," Thorbjorg says, "and offerings, all of you. Even Katla, James, and John—praises to your strange White Christ. Beg the gods for some protection, while I myself will give up prayers for healing hands."

By that very noon, the house is thick with totems, amulets, wreaths of flax and goats' and bears' teeth hung about the door, and blood dripping, burning on the fire. And crosses—James and John and I set about with what we can, twisting twigs around with bits of thread, while they teach me prayers for Christ's protection.

Still, welts have formed on Orm's pale skin. Then a spewing, green and brown, from deep within his throat. By evening, it's a bloody cough. We spend the night in turns, tending Orm and barely sleeping, listening as the mistress chants and my daughter pipes her haunting tunes.

To that cold music I hold a stinking herb-cloth fast on Orm's parched skin. I can think naught but of the ship of Thorbjorg's dreaming—Thorhall's ship, and where he was to sail after leaving our fjord, first to Eirik Raude's, then to Vesterbygd and far Nordsetur. Oh, I wonder then if it is true what legends say, that the plague twins bear their mischief-making to whichever port they hail.

George Herbert / rhythm of English poetry · or John Donne

THORBJORG

MUST I LIVE to see this house destroyed, Valfather, like each and all my houses e'er before? This time not with fire, no, but with another method, crueler. Now must I watch my people suffer and give them hope where there is none? Must I smile in the face of vilest blight and bury them when it is done?

Despite my greatest tending, within some days, this new thrall dies. Then I sense these plague twins wait in vicious humor—wait and watch us, relishing our mourning before they come once more. When they do, 'tis with a knock, a wretched wheeze and cough, and a rattle at the door. Upon this dawn, Kol bends its leather hinges back just as my shepherd Vidur crooks and crumple-falls.

There—do you see him, One-Eye?—lying, face flushed with fever, pale with sickness, his cheeks already blotched and spotted with these plague twins' horror-mars? Oh, Alfather, the boy is heavy as a man. Three thralls it takes to set him down beside the fire. Wrong to see him lying there upon a mossy cot where he's barely slept in all these seasons. Rather, know you well, he would sit through any tempest among his grazing beasts than spend one night in the warm, dry company of men. Yet now he stretches, face turned ashen, slowly wasting, as I and Bibrau tend as best we can. For all my hard-won wisdom against such malady and rot, soon—too soon—the shepherd boy does fail.

Alfather, look! As we mourn away this young one, so they come again upon the old: my fine, frail carver Gizur. He does not linger long upon such torment. Nay, soon Gizur lies quite cold, hands stiff and curled for want of a carving knife to clutch. When we set him in the earth, I cannot bear to send him so bereft to Hel's cheerless board, so I take some little pity and place his artful blade into his coiled palm.

Yet the twins do not stop with Gizur. Still they'll have the tiny babes. Oh, they steal them off even while their lips clasp around their mother's dripping nipples. Fair, but surely, they put their poison in her milk, honey-sweet so they do not cry.

Old One-Eye, listen! This is not the last. Even as Arngunn weeps her sorrow, this bane tries still to snatch her off. The mother fights and wastes and moans her mourning, drifting sometimes in her fever, bare recalling her babies gone. Then, one dawn, upon the menace's whimsy, she draws awake. Her fever's broke. It seems she will survive them, yet never have the bearing strength to mend the rended weaving of the Norns.

So the plague twins please themselves, Valfather, while you do naught—watching from your high throne, Hlidskialf. Can your all-seeing eye notice nothing of our smoke and sacrifices? Can you not see the twins traipsing still their tripping dance? Heeding not our fine protections—not our snakes or dragons carved with none of Gizur's now lost skill, not our rough-wrought throwing hammers fashioned close to your great son Thor's. Nay, none of these, nor wreaths of herbs, nor amulets all hung about nor the Christians' crosses, nor Katla's praying beads, nor any potents I can muster.

Yet note you this: some healing comes from Bibrau's touch. 'Tis strange, yet fair, as she eases breath and quiets sleep. True, and brings boils to their rupture, and joints to mend their ache. But know, Valfather, such fancy wisdom issues not from your wellspring. No, I do not trust her outcome. Her work is fair display, a neat performance as she dips and brews, piping chants upon her singing bone to sense how soon to toss crushed moss into the boil. Through her stoic mask, I sense a fouling conceit, as if she savored well each turn and groan. Yet I praise her, coaxing, "Fine!" and "Well!" and "Good, my Bibrau!"— for in such might is the only ease to come upon our woe.

Then, one eve, on the winter's crusts, when the earth's too cold to dig more graves, comes a call—a call—too well I know, for it has come before. Alfather, this time, upon a sledge and dragging horse, a strident voice above the mist and frost: "Mistress Thorbjorg, a plague does rage at Eirik Raude's!"

So, Alfather, as the horse there whinnies. I catch an earful of its scraping hoof as I sit beside my Gyde, whose once-strong hands now quake and whiten between my fingers. She, too, is caught within the clutch of this disease.

"Mistress Thorbjorg!" says the voice then, louder. "Does anybody here still live?"

I catch Kol glancing, my Kol, who knows me longest, best, and well, who has seen such heralds come and ever watched me go upon them—as so, upon the plague at Birka, where four hundred people died and I was blamed and cursed and cruelly driven off. Or on such task in Iceland, but then the sick were ill with feuding fight. They turned to me to mend what I could not—vengeance bears no tender magic! Yet for this they blamed me, too, brought their torches, flames set high, and with them smoked the frost-caked sod from the roof against the winter's dark where beneath all my household then did lie.

Now Kol bows his head and clutches at his worry-wrinkles. Yet he rises up, knowing well it is his duty. He cracks the heavy door. "Nary," he shouts, "but few, and many sickened. The plague has been about here, too!"

I feel the pressing weight as the stranger stumbles across the frost-heaves nearer. "Yet some still live! And so your mistress?"

"Aye, the mistress Thorbjorg's well enough."

"Praise to Odin's wisdom, then, for the seeress must come! Even now Eirik Raude lies between two prongs of the plague twins' rake."

Alfather, will you sound this call again? Like a hammer's strike, come to rouse me to your work—your work, Alfather. For you put this wisdom in me. I did not ask it, but you put it there with your wrenching, reaching hand—this healing and this patience and this sort of sight which tells me who's next to die but not how I might prevent it, so that I ply your might most times with sudden instinct more than skill.

Kol shuts the door and turns to face me. Gyde's fingers tighten, grasping quick around.

"I must," I say. Yet I see their looks. All their faces, not just Kol and Gyde but my broken Arngunn, Alof, bitter Teit, Nattfari mad, looking wild as she bites a bit of dirt, Katla slapping her hand to force it from her fingers. And our new men, Svan and James and John, who know nothing of our pasts or joys.

I press my hand against my hollow bosom. "Kol, you will come with me. Katla, set my bag with my healing potents. Alof, bring my cloak and leggings." I bend to Gyde. "You will be well. Upon Alfather's sight—look, even now Bibrau fixes you a soothing drink."

Yet, as I turn, my cloak close-wrapped about my shoulders, Bibrau's moon-face is but shadowed, never lifting from her brews or seeming very wary I should leave.

BIBRAU

THE MISTRESS DEPARTS with bare a glancing. With nearly not one word, she charges through the falling night to the mossy bench of Eirik Raude. She, with Kol beside her, begging not that I should join them—aid them not with my fresh and potent wisdoms, keener than were ever Thorbjorg's ploys.

Yet she leaves her party here, alone on this fjord's stretch, with not much by but the glacier's creep and my sullied fingers. Well she is wary for the charge, for I feel some heat upon my neck as she turns and closes the door. Ah, let her wonder—let her woe that my skill might kill as well as cure! Now she leaves me to my pleasure: her household in my hands, with the plague twins lending me their fine utensils and my fylgie at my elbow. Happily I will prove my mistress wise.

Thorbjorg's footsteps crush and trip across the frost; then the horse's canter fades. These thralls turn slow among themselves, then sure and suddenly I feel their eyes. Such eyes! Such fear upon my little talents! Such joy! But most, the pleasure of my birth-mare—her dread like the lamb's I'd once been forced to slaughter. Trusting so, yet somehow knowing well to doubt that falsehood; transfixed, yet having not the strength or will to flee. My mother holds my look and I hold hers as she bends and gropes for Gyde's withered fingers. And Gyde there, trying to draw her close, but already I've given her a draught to suck all strength out of her muscles, so the woman can lie but helpless, limp, her fingers slipping through my mother's own.

Like a cloying fume the sickness lingers. Some days pass before the plague twins seize the yardman, Teit. In from the sheepfold, night upon a wild storm, Teit enters, breathing thickly of the stuff of death's desire.

At once, Nattfari scratches a maddened tone: "My husband-man! Oh, my husband!" She falls upon him, clinging. She nearly drags him down into the mud, but Alof pries her off; then the new man, Svan, holds her hard so they can tuck Teit deep beneath the mistress' bearskins. There on the floor she huddles, clawing walls and clacking six of my pebbled, cast-off runes, till my mother takes them from her with a ripping grasp; and then Nattfari stands and rabid-stares while her husband aches and foams.

Fast, Teit's sickness worsens, faster even than old Gyde's. My fylgie pleads with me—*Kill him and her and all of them—make quick work of it!*—and chides me and stamps that I should hesitate to do it. I am tempted; for the house is cramped and thick with stench and bowel; but I have no wish to linger here alone without some thrall to clean and milk and scrape seal oil to warm my stew.

So, instead, I watch them dying, lying there within that house. Worse than death itself, for death can be swept and cleaned and tucked into the darkness of forgetting. Yet dying stays and stinks and lingers, demanding food.

Their brews I make against my fylgie's leanings, mixing bitters of some brawn instead of poisons to tempt their fate. 'Tis a little thing, a sprig of juniper, a snap of scurvy grass, a shred of fungus scraped from the circle's rocks. And then to heat the brews to boil and, while still burning, smoothly feed them down. About that work, I mostly put some other hand: my tremble-mother's, who suits well to do my bidding, following my silent points at the end of a rune-carved twig I've made much like the mistress' own. Just so, I press my birth-woman there to serve me: forcing a filthy rag upon her fingers to wipe some spittle from Gyde's plague-fat lip, or a fetid bowl of Teit's sloshing waste to toss away. My mother's hands turn coarse and red, her scar-wracked face looking worn and thin and graying, as my fylgie prances and kicks and dances and titters, pleased to see my mother made my slave. So we plot soon she'll fall under the plague twins' stroke; yet she eyes me always with a wary watch and manages somehow to keep well and away.

Yet how does she, when I rarely give her anything to brace or cure, nor let her sleep enough but so she'll fail to foul up my chores? Oh, what does she but pray her Christian pleadings that twist up smoke and skew the music of my healing pipes? She even turns to those new slaves who call this Jesus Christ their own. Each night they teach her their half-wit gibberish—all their prayers, where before she'd known but foolish one or two. Yet now they let their Latin tumble—"*Kyrie Eleison . . . Christe Eleison . . .* Lord be with you. Christ!" tangled on her tongue, and those two, so quick correcting, growing bolder with their pagan mistress gone. Soon all three to-gether cry their Christian chants, while my mother fumbles in her apron's pouch for a fistful of her worthless, rotting beads.

"Rosary, they are," she whispers once, as if to teach me, "given me upon her death from your own grandmother's hand."

My grandmother's! Ha! If they were such, then but a bond-slut's rubbish. Yet my mother presses them with their clack and clatter, adding rumble to her rasping sounds, wearing down those wooden gobs till they are but lopsided grains, and prays as if 'twere hers to conjure this fool White Christ to magic-heal all these plague-trapped slaves.

Then, upon a night, my mother grows still bolder. Within her wretched pleas one word I recognize above the rest—"Ossur," sudden from her lips, "Ossur!"—rising up on falsest hope he should be saved. He? Saved! Ha! Now I know too well why she's been praying. If I could send the plague twins on to Vesterbygd myself, so I would; but, in truth, I have not yet learned such skill.

Still she does defy me, even bends as I busy making Gyde's sick-cure, whispering in the swollen woman's ears, "Gyde, remember all

that Thorhall said of Ossur? Soon he'll come and take me with him!
Yet, Gyde, what if this plague should take him first?"

And the mistress' woman moaning, begging, "Katla, hush you.
Let me sleep—"

"Yet, Gyde—"

"Take him? Calm. Such fearing sends the evil eye."

"Think you so?" my mother begs, chewing to the bloody quick
her finger. "Yet, Gyde"—she will not silence long—"Gyde—all my
hope—to see it waste—"

"Hush, girl—even silent worries call the notice of the Norns. Now
let me rest." Gyde turns away. Such is the quality of my mother's
mercy, for "mercy" now is the word she relishes most, learned upon
the Christians' teachings. Thinking only of herself, she vexes Gyde re-
lentlessly, till, at last, I send her off and press the poultice to that sick,
pale brow myself.

The woman breathes relief beneath my pressure, while my fylgie
plies me and dances an evil dance, malcontent as I until I hush my
mother up. But how? How? I dare not kill her. At least not yet—not in
any obvious way. Only I might hurt her most by bringing deaths
about that would cause her deepest, truly tender pain. At first I think
soft Gyde, but no, for she is of the mistress' bosom. But then I think of
those of somewhat less account—these Christians, John and James.

Indeed, that very night my mother sits among them and mumbles
soft their drooling, "*Confiteor Deo omnipotenti. . . .*" From them, too,
garbles, "Upon this plague, only Jesus Christ deliver us!" as if some
other, surer god cannot as well oblige. Nay, theirs is a sickness worse
than any these plague twins have delivered—as they eye me coolly,
shying back when I proffer up the very best of my mistress' brews.
Even as I set on them a truly healing mixture, the one called John
reaches out to stop my hand, and James whispering, "*In nomine Patris,
et Filii, et Spiritus Sancti,*" and my mother mocking at their movements, just the same but smaller, almost hidden from me, somewhere
close behind.

Nay, it is the last they'll have of all my mercy! That very night,
upon mid-eve, I trace a rune-curse as my fylgie shows: dug deep into

the earth, the sharp-edged runes before their sleeping benches. Then I cover the scratches over, thick with feces, then thicker still with dirt to hide the smell. With the morning, there they'll trip upon their path with nothing left to break their fall.

Within one week, both Christian dolts are languid, frail, diminishing. My fylgie and I would dance upon such hoax, but, to fool my mother, I scrape and chore and mix up curatives to press between their lips. So—yet with a secret smirk as they struggle, wisely fearful of these drinks, for these are fully spoiled, as they well suspect, and the poultices fine-packed with naught but worthless dung and mud.

Quick the plague within them festers. Well before the last, the Christians know their lives are lost. Still I wait for some regretting, for some soft mention of their deathbed's surest cause. Yet they say naught, only, "There is no fear in dying, for we will lie at last within our own Christ's loving arms."

Pitiful arms, I think, frail and weak as wind-wrenched, dangled twigs. Yet my mother pleads, "Nay, you must not die!"—shaking her head about in splattered anguish. "How can I live without you here within this house?"

"You must pray," each Christian counsels, "each day and many times, your just-learned prayers. Then you must fall before a proper priest—for surely one will soon reach even Greenland—fall upon your knees, bow your head, and pray aloud in earnest, 'Forgive me, Father, for I have sinned.' "

Sinned, indeed, it seems to me as my fylgie dangles from an eave, playing them both as puppets with his music-wand. I watch and listen as each man breathes a sudden gasp, then coughs each a cough so hard each chest does rise and writhe and fall in rhythm with the last. Then one of them—John or James—it does not matter which—takes my mother's arms a-tremble, "Please, upon dear Christ," clutching at her spit-stained sleeves, "place a cross to guide our wasted souls!"

That very eve, my mother twists willow bits into worthless roods, planned to place upon their putrid corpses. True, when the frigid night is through, naught is left but some smelly flesh we lay to rot beneath two roughly gathered cairns. There my mother drops the crosses down beside some many tears. But that night, I creep quick back and tear the willow twigs myself, until they break and scatter on the winds.

When I return, my fylgie again is filled with frenzy, flying up about the rafters, stirring ashes to a popping cloud of dust, stomping feet that I should cast such curses the same for all the others. *Nay*, I ply him, *silent, still!*—to wait and hold his storm. Such, I moor him, tempting only that I torture so we might pleasure as they linger, suffering long. Then my fylgie sits upon the hearthside, fed but brooding, hushed, while my mother's face flushes white and body rocks as if struck by winter's windy mood. At least she's quieted her Christian chanting. I please myself upon good fortune and set to test the rest my budding healing skill.

For a time, in fact, both Gyde and Teit seem better. But sudden Gyde again falls weak, then, slowly, so Teit, too. Though I ply my might, I can do nothing till I notice that my fylgie, on an eve, silent while he thinks I sleep, dances about some twirling mischief even I do not yet know.

I rise in fury, for my fylgie's lied upon our pact. I bend to the sod, scratching rune-marks as my mistress taught me around the sickbeds, sharp and clear and hard, the very kind I know my fylgie loathes. Then he can do naught but rage and thunder; and that he does, calling up a wild storm. It kicks and thrashes and rattles just beyond the mistress' hall. Then, with a burst, the door flips back and slams against the thick stone wall. Winds send bowls a-tumble such as I have never seen; a broom quick-snaps and falls into the hearth fire's sparks. Quickly spent, they spit and sizzle, then smother cold. Nattfari wakes and tatter-shrills. Fever-headed Teit stumbles in the dark upon some instinct to help calm her. Yet Alof holds the sick man down. So, my mother bends to light a bit of fire, and when she does she sees my runic scars upon the ground.

The house is dark but for the bright aurora glowing through the doorway's gape. By that eerie air, my mother sets upon her chest the Christians' cross, then speaks their words, *"Per signum crucis de inimicis nostris libera nos!"* Fast and furious, she snatches a bucket of meltwater and douses the runes I've so keenly drawn. Nay, the wretched fool! I nearly break my breath to screaming. Nearly, but there is not time, for, at once, my fylgie snickers as he jigs about. Then comes Gyde's choking, coughing harder. Lo, I bend into my mother's mud and begin to scratch the runes again, but the slosh runs thick and will not hold them.

Gyde sputters till her body's wracked. Arngunn falls beside her, propping her to sit, then lie, then stand, but then Gyde seizes on a fit of shaking. She quickly pales—so quick as if her blood had drained. Nay, Arngunn holds her mother's pallid cheek, tucking close her blankets, stroking back her thick, rust wad of sweaty curls.

Then again my mother dares defy me, muttering softly against the woman's chills, "Kyrie Eleison. Christe"—with all the spike and pepper of that Christian name—"Lord be with you. Jesus Christ"—while my fylgie prances and pipes his vile tune.

By his grin, he thinks he has me beaten. But I will not let him—not even on this mischief-ruse. My fury breaks upon my fylgie. I run to fetch my own bone flute—but cannot find it. He's hidden it well away—within the midden, with the bones. At last I pluck it out and wipe it clean. Fast and frenzied, I begin to countermand his playing.

"Listen," Gyde cries out at my tune's climax, "comes the shepherd's music! Hear it?"—still shivering, shaking, choking, her head now heavy and white like a sheen of moonlight spread across Arngunn's tear-stained cheeks.

Arngunn can only bite her tears and whisper, "Mother, hush."

But my own mother brays, "Gyde, you know 'tis but the child's foul playing."

Foul.

Foul.

Foul. Playing . . . This.

On my mother's breath, I drop my tune. I let the bone flute fall, dead upon the muddy earthen floor.

My fylgie, too, hushes his wretched tittering.

And the thrall-folk, all of them, stare upon me, frightened with my sudden still. Only Gyde, who cannot help her cough, fills the room with bitter sounds.

My fylgie slightly smiles. I see his grin. With a breath, Gyde reaches, grasping at her daughter's cheek.

"Arngunn, such a lovely brightness!" So her hand wafts up its last, then meekly falls.

THORBJORG

STRIDING FORWARD I, toward Brattahlid's death-darkened hall, upon the hill beneath the looming mountain Burfell. 'Tis the time of season when the sun rides low upon the land, and all about is tinged with gloomy glow as at the brink of ending.

Much alike is aging Thjoldhilde's face, flushed with dread as she opens out the door. Fast she falls upon her knees. "Mistress Thorbjorg, thanks and praise. You come at last!" I look on her, Eirik Raude's long-suffered woman. "Do aught," she begs, "and all you may."

"Aught," I say, "or none. Only Odin's wise-wife, Frigga, can know the future."

Beyond her are more faces round the hall: thralls who stand, wan and thinnish, their number lessened by some half a host. Too, freemen staring from gaunt, dull eyes. I see Thorhall not at all. Farther still, beside the master's bedding board, are Eirik's three strong sons, Thorstein, Thorvald, and Leif, not touched yet by the sickness, but looking weary. Leif stands tallest and most like his father, whispering harshly, "Mother, let the mistress pass and give her room."

"Aye," I mention, "and a pot to boil. And, if you can, sing some the ancient tunes."

"Tunes . . ." Thjoldhilde trembles.

"Such kvads as are ever sung to draw the Norns' rough knitting tight. Of late, I have heard them oft, but only by my foster-daughter's playing. Hollow are her melodies, for her pipe itself is dead. 'Twould be strange relief to hear a human voice raising them again."

Thjoldhilde sings, but her music shakes with wear and worry. Hoarse and forced, she strains ever more as I lay a hand upon the blight: there Eirik Raude, his face marred with pox, and wheezing hardily. Upon his chest, the hair is thick with gray and sweat. Coming spit and sputter, he barely moans as I press my palm.

"Kol," I whisper, "bring my sack." I take up herbs from the sealskin. The draught I mix is strong, but the music's stronger. It rings in this desperate air, spreading through my fingers' joints, seeping strength into my hands. There, now—the god's touch—*Odin, now I feel you.*

Reaching out, I clutch the knife to shape the runes. As if the very tunes themselves do prompt my jagged blade, I carve the string of wisdom-cuts, there above the sickbed, such wiles to ward off twisted evil.

Soon Thjoldhilde's voice is rasped, and all I've done is nearly finished. Naught is left but to pray and offer meats. I go with Leif to the byre stalls to pick goats and cattle with the thickest flanks. He bends to take a yearling calf I have assigned. After it is slaughtered and all its sacrifice laid out in Eirik's hof, only then I ask, "What has come of Thorhall Hunter?"

"Thorhall?" Leif gruffs, looking over the beast's bloody parts. "He was not yet dead when last we saw him. He has gone to Nordsetur to hunt for whales and walrus. He sent a six-oared boat thick with hides and meat just before the fjords froze. 'Twas some weeks ago, before the plague twins set their rake upon us."

So 'tis best—Thorhall, stay back. Keep away. Or go off even farther—to Ubygder, the uninhabited places. Hide within the crevices and cracks where no one's known to dwell; for the plague twins follow where'er ye wander.

That night, they light the pyre's flame upon the hof, and for nine days, I command them not to stop its blazing. On my require', they slaughter meats, cutting hearts of every beast which falls. These I eat in a soup of milk from a pregnant udder. Odin, my tongue is yours; thus you savor, too, their sacred gifts. They know it well and say it so aloud and ever watch me.

Days pass in singing, slaughter, fire, fretting, waiting while I tend the chief. All of Eirik's sons stand with their muscled backs behind me as if, through their sturdy brawn, no prong of the plague twins' rake should pass between. Still the bitter twins claw about, rummaging their tracks for what litter they have scattered. Such, one and then another falls. I turn to heed them—mostly thralls—but Thjoldhilde ever pries me back to Eirik's groanings. She tears at the hemming of my dress, though there is nothing more that I can do. Still, to quiet her, I must leave Kol to do his best. He conjures what he can with his own Finn's magic while I sit and hold the ailing chieftain's hand.

From that sleepless gloom, one night comes another breath-caught rumble. More a cough, as I have heard these days, so many I hardly heed. Yet this sound seems somehow odd, familiar. When it comes again, I know. I am bolt awake. I turn my ear to listen. It is Kol.

I stumble first across the bare earth floor, finding my way by the very hall-posts, one by one splinter-carved of driftwood, till I come to the corner of the hall. There the favored slaves and sick ones lie, their legs entwined and splayed, upon a sod heap. "Kol." I lay my hand and lean against his chest to listen. I smell his breath.

"Mistress, it is naught," he says. "Nothing but too little rest and a winter's chill."

But I smell upon him, in the sour of his sweat, the scent of creeping death I've come to know. "Perhaps you're right," I whisper, "yet I'll put a draught to boil, for I'll need your help to heal upon the morrow."

I set my hand to the great iron pot, making my way to wake the embered fire. *Nay!* I think—I pray. *Not my Kol!*

So, Great One-Eyed Wisdom, will you take him from me? My bondsman—nay!—Kol has ever been my fair companion. Better than a bonded slave or a faithful dog. He's stood by me as has no other, done my deeds and supplied me well. Too, in truth, protected me as none I've ever known. Saved my life before, saved it more than once. Old Cruelty—will you have him from me now?

Wretched thought! I will fight you for him, god of my gods, breath upon my breath. Everything I have ever known you have taken from me, bit by bit. But Kol—I swear upon it, no!

I mix the draught, feeling curses on my lips, " *'Down to Hel, bane daughter of the trickster Loki, whose meat is hunger, whose bed is sickbed'*—I will not give him up to straw death, to be entertained on hollow famine. He should feast at Thor's thick, oaken, Bilskirnir board! Nay and go! A worthier death than this my faultless friend deserves."

So the word comes, "friend," with a puff of steam rising on the chill. I watch it drift and realize this word is fearful, honest. "Friend." But for Thorhall, never have I had another. "Friend." I fall upon my choring, whispering, as I feel the fire burn the cold. "Friend," as I stumble through the death-dark hall to press the draught down slowly to Kol's dry lips. "Soon you will recover," I say. "When this plague is through, you'll have your way. I'll give you freedom, for well, my Kol, you have deserved it."

Kol looks on me with such a pale and eyes so shallowed. "Freedom? Lady, think you, with my Finn's knots and all my magic, I could not have sailed off long ago? If I should ever leave your side, 'twould be at death's own battle. . . ."

He lifts my hand in his, my old, gnarled claw, and lays his lips upon the very knuckles. Gently, for his lips are cracked and rough. I feel them wet on me, the scent of my own bitter draught which should make him sleep.

"Hush now, Kol, and rest," I whisper gently.

He rolls away while I creep, with the others all about at snoring, moaning, grunting, to take from my sealskin sack a bit of rowan twig. This, which I have carried since the ancient eastern forests; this, the very last, most precious, which I have kept but for the keenest hour; this, which I have hugged against my breast so oft, the bark in places has sloughed away. This I take and sit beside him, there amidst the stinking thralls, to carve anew a precious runestick with my blade.

"Here." I shake my hand and hiss, "Old Graybeard, look! I carve your utmost sacred visions. Here, your secret runes! Here, your hallowed power! Here, your wisdom's recipe! Such I'll lay them out before this poor thrall's feet. Better here than any other—better than any freeman born, than any karl or jarl or chief! Here, for your own sake, tucked away so no cold eyes may stare in wanton wonder. And fair, beseeching, to be meek before my humble master, here I bend and tend upon this thrall so I might learn at last to rightly heal."

It is done and the stick well hidden among the torn-moss mattress clots. There I sit and stay awake and ponder, frightened as I've not been—not in very long—but twice before that I remember: first upon my sisters' slaying, and then again upon the night when my husband, sons, and all my household burned.

There—that night—as if singed upon my memory, I feel the heat of it, the pain as Kol dragged me from that fire, yea, for all my pleading, "No!" My body then was but a charred and stinging mass. But he healed my flesh with some strange concoctions I could barely speak but to speak against. Too, hid me down beneath the tenting of an ancient bull's skin beneath the frowning shadows of my children's fresh-dug burial mounds. Kol showed no fear of them, as might a thrall like any other. He stayed with me, brought me food, stole bread and mead and meat at risk of his own survival. For some long weeks, above we heard them search among the char and stone and wasted house-frame for my own ashy bones. Yet they found them not. And when they left, though I could barely stumble, Kol plied me up and led me to the fjord's edge. There he set me in the soggy hull of a rocking skiff and rowed us both, silent, on the moonless waters.

There—and then—and yet—I wake, fallen rashly over Kol's fevered bosom. Above, Thjoldhilde stands. Her fingers shake, white, gripped about my gnarled wrists.

"Mistress Thorbjorg, treat you now your own foul thrall and fair neglect my mighty captain? I beg you!" She dares to pull me up upon my shoulder, as if I were some barest slave.

I steel an angled look on her, only half alert yet seeing clearly Leif and Thorstein rising.

"Mother," Leif calls, fearing not to wake the household, "dare not speak upon our favored guest that way. Mistress Thorbjorg, for my father's sake—I am fully sorrowed—"

Yet I am fitful, quivering from my dream. My voice is harsh as I hold it, low: "Should this man of mine lose this sickly battle, then all about this Greenland gravel will be naught but draugs."

I say it so, and sudden know it true. 'Tis fairest prophecy as ever I have breathed.

Well, Thjoldhilde believes it. Thorstein, Leif, and Thorvald, too, plying all their house upon my call, sending slaves to cast their hands when there is nothing they can do. Yet I set them chores with mighty terror. All my orders they hear and tremble and unfailingly obey. So I turn their heed to Eirik's ministerings while I bend to tend my Kol.

Days pass. Nights. Still he sleeps, lying on the straw. Bleak, black marks bear in and out upon his throat. They stiffen, harden. Soon they'll thicken, choke him, creamy white dripping from his nose. Then all will sudden cease and dry. Then—last—my Kol will grow slowly cold.

Nay, for once I'm frightened, frenzy beating at my breast— Alfather, have you deigned to set me low? To test my skill at my own man's risk? Challenge me to see what I can muster? Well you know I can manage much. Yet this?

Alfather, no. You will not have it.

I lean and whisper, "Kol, press upon them. Those twins are fat and sated now. Fight them! Yes, their greedy gleaning. Fight! For I will not lose you. . . ." This last I whisper, fearing yet to speak. It does no good. Daily Kol grows weaker. He barely knows me now.

Then, one night, he grips upon me with all his lingered strength: "Promise . . ." he pauses. "Lady—Mistress Thorbjorg—make my grave upon the meadow beside the sea, for I love to hear it there—the washing waves. With a skull of walrus—that beast is fierce—his and mine should face the east—together—toward the frailest sun. Too, my bear-tooth tokens—set them about my neck as they've always hung— though I know it is not custom to bury thralls among their precious things."

I hold him. As his eyes slip closed, I force him back: "I will not have it so!" Rising up and turning, there and then I begin to chant the sacred runes. One upon another, entwined in twisted trails, such sounds as should ne'er be uttered, yet I sing them boldly. Thjoldhilde raises up her head from her worry over Eirik Raude; then Leif, upon my brutal tones, then Thorstein, Thorvald, soon all the freemen and the house-thralls. Out of Brattahlid's tightest passages, they stand beside me now, listening from the shadows of the hall.

From my tongue slip shapes which none about can realize. Yet I speak them—name them, one upon another, chant upon my chant—bearing Kol's hands up, icy chill within my own and heavy, till my voice grows hoarse and my tears stream down. "Algiz! Nauthiz! Teiwaz! Odin! Say you! Hear you! Old One-Eyed god, I bare your secrets out! All of them which I do know—I have the strength and so the daring. What you give, I turn and speak aloud, and from my heart, shouting so you cannot help but hear!"

This last, and Kol is groaning. I ease him back. "Lie quiet now and still." First I think—for the angry god's sake, nay!—he has doomed my man to dying. Yet, as I watch, I see Kol sleeps. "Hush," I whisper, setting fingers by his lips. Gentle warmth I feel, and easy breathing.

"Mistress, will he live?" Leif steps behind me, his hand upon my back.

Barely can I find the strength to nod. Yet I do, some slightly; then take Leif's offered hand so he and his brothers help me find my way to rest.

All that day and then the next, the mistress Thjoldhilde wracks with grateful sobbing. And in the end, Eirik Raude, too, revives. By the Yule log's light, he is well enough to praise Thor's might and cut a fresh-killed boar to mark the feast; while my Kol serves me, limp and frail as he has never been, too weak to stand, so he sits beside me, pouring my ale, cutting my meat.

Upon that bitter feast, Eirik praises my keen prediction. "Thorbjorg, to see a slave upon the plague twins' turning? Odd! Yet so you saved my life and all these others and surely our whole Greenland."

I listen, most in silence, for I know too well my pleading's truth: 'twas simple desperation—vile daring—little more. Still, with talk and gossip spreading, by spring they've made of me a seeress even more than I was before. As my reputation grows, I bear the weighty burden. I have no strength or will to fight it back, knowing well my hubris and its fair recrimination. For challenging the highest god upon my selfish need, I know he will wait—Old Longbeard is full-patient—wait, but one day surely strike me down.

KATLA

GYDE IS GONE, now cold and stinking sickly, lying upon a pile of stones above these others' stretched-out bones. On this rock-flecked heap, we stand striking at the earth with shovels. Made of caribou bones, they should be tough. Yet the ground is tougher. It will not yield. In the end, we set a rock cairn above her corpse, bare enough to keep back the foxes and the wolves.

I wipe my cheeks where dripping sweat mixes with my sorrow. It is the first warmish day in all these months, and the stark light shines, cloudless, blinding if I lift my sore eyes up. Yet I have no wish to, nor to catch another's sight. All blame me for our woman's dying.

As well they should. How could I be so foolish? Surely, if I had thought—all these years, and what the mistress has taught my child. Yet, for fear and crying, I could not stand her noise, like a terror's cackle, and the wind all blowing round, and the dark and night! I was certain 'twas a haugbo's taunt. Or a draug—come the walking dead to gather more. Surely, I thought, she had called such demons with her music. Never had I thought she should ever try to heal.

Now it seems my thoughts did lie, for she stood furiously playing on her screeching pipe and only stopped upon my call. "Foul." Foolish! Dared I cast it off? It was the first ever what I'd said had any weight upon her. Yet only then did Gyde fall deathly white and gasp and crumple—only then, as Arngunn fell about her chest to listen to her heartbeat still.

Then my eyes met my daughter's. There, a sort of blame which has never mourned or known a sense of guilt. Such, she turned just then, and I did not stop her as she made again her runic marks— figures in the mud—this time with sticks the mistress used for prophecy. And the wind did stop its blows upon them. For some days Teit full-slept, then gradually grew well.

He stands now strong enough, quite clearly healed; and no others since have fallen to this cursed blight—none so long as my daughter's wretched marks remain. I sweep around them in that house, feeling all their eyes as if the threat of death lies before my careless broom. I endure it. So I must. Certain guilt should bear such certain pain.

Too, now I listen to my daughter's music and try to hear it with a different ear, with some small thought that perhaps her sounds could please. But upon this woeful graveyard, her strain is grating, bleak. Oh, my daughter's craft! She knows now full well its power. Her sounds—she bears them on me with a glower. How she bows her head in mocking of the mistress' poise, then raises up, gangly now with all her youth, her hands upon her playing bone already growing larger, her face with its ice-orbs blue in their skin like winter moon.

They are Torvard's eyes, wicked as they mark me. Cold. Ever cold as ice. And her music biting, falling sharp, crackling, as if each note should twist and break, as if each tone should shatter. I turn away, yet I cannot block my hearing. So I try to block my thoughts, to think upon some fine distraction, some beaming reverie both lovelier and louder: the thought that might, among these blue-flecked heaps of icebergs, come one day a rough-hewn skiff which will take me from this sound.

A rough-hewn skiff with just one man aboard: how I cling upon that lovely longing! And the picture of a land we've drawn—what land as might already be his—which we will work together, him and me. Oh, the land will be coarse, but 'twill surely be a pleasure with him bearing his back up toward the sun, and me with my kerchief damp with sweat about my brow, and both our feet in muck as we haul manure to plant our furrows, and my fingers sticky with the sour milk shooting from our goats' and cattle's teats. But the milk most sweet because it will be ours, and our homestead small and drafty. I know we'll dwell alone and lonely, with no goods to trade for thralls. Yet better I should thrall to him and he enslave to me. To be enthralled by one's own choosing would be no slavery at all!

Such, yet at once I turn my thoughts, for such joy quick draws the evil eye. Death is all around. Already Ossur might be fallen to the

plague twins' glee. So I scrape again upon the hillside's muck and banish out such hopeful musings. Instead, I gaze off toward the fjord's
broken crust and feel upon my lips again the shape and whisp' of the
Christians' teachings. In these I have found, much like my mother
often said, such comfort not even death can take away.

Yet, as I look—there is movement in the fjord's flow. Upon the
froth, a skiff and sail and oar. It is but a dream! Yet it makes its way,
hauling forth with fits and jerkings. I am standing, stunned, while all
about are shouting, "Who's upon it?" "Come and run!" " 'Tis the
mistress Thorbjorg back again!"

"The mistress," I whisper, calming my heart's wanton patter. I am
ashamed I should not have worried in all this time if the mistress
should come home.

I follow with the others to the water's edge and the skiff's rough
rail. We help them set their feet upon our home-yard's stones. Fair,
through shouts and proddings, through queries most of Eirik's health,
there's a sudden still. All at once we see poor Kol standing bare
aright, leaning on the mistress' elbow.

"Kol," Teit starts, "it is good to have you." Yet Kol's a pity of himself, a wretched shame with what the plague twins left. Too, we sense
the mistress' hush as she counts what of her house remains: we are
now only eight, when before the plague we had been sixteen.

She bites her lip and asks, "Of those lost—they all are buried?"
Our nod is the last then spoken of any woe. We turn our faces boldly,
never mentioning our grief again.

Through the slush and mire of the springtime thaw, up and down the
homefield grasses, our Kol struggles. Oft I help him walk to gain his
strength. Upon old Gizur's cane we go. Kol drags one foot and then
the other. Reaching hard, he falls to grasp the stones he himself once
gathered on his back to build the homefield wall. There he rests,
breathless, leaning heavy on his hands.

He props himself and whispers toward the distant cliffs, "There
I bore down falcons," reaching, bending fists as if to tame an outstretched wing. "Well, I can remember. . . . I did it fair with wit and

brawn. . . ." He sighs as if such feats were long days past, not just one year ago.

In time, Kol regains some his strength, but will never be what he once was. I see the mistress worries, first for Kol, because she's kind, but then, because she's wise, for the welfare of this household. For here, 'tis true, with some few grasses growing and bare but barley and less again of oats, there'll soon be little for the sheep to graze on, and less for us without much hunting or killing off our meager stock. With nothing left of the brilliant falcons, nor anything else of worth to bring to trade, I know she fears soon we must be sold—each one to another chieftain's household.

Weeks pass, and we make no move or plan to set upon the Al-thing. I'm glad, for 'tis a traders' and a slave-ships' fair. Yet, finally, the mistress calls to raise our battered sail. I'm sent to sit on the skiff's boards, though I pray the wind won't rise. But Kol's Finn's whisper-ings soon blow it up in certain gusts. It takes only Svan's swift master-ing to train our household toward Gardar.

As we near, we see but half a crowd of ships upon the shore. They are a grim reflection; and the scents about seem a wafting frailty of some distant tinge of revelry; and the calls, the cries, even the bleat-ing, braying, blurting of the beasts, but pale echoes of a finer sort of din. The faces carry sallowed tones and deepened shadows. All the talk's of counting off the dead.

So, when Einar's old house-thrall Hallgerd comes running across the homefield, all her bulk is a shaking, sagging shadow of her former self. This Hallgerd, who for all my youth but taunted and ill-treated me, now stretches out her arms and lays her cheek upon my shoulder with some hapless tears.

"Katla, oh," she cries, " 'tis good to see you! After such—oh, what terror was this plague! To see those tortured babies, those old men set to serve at Hel's hard throne. But I fed them well and treated them with all my knowledge—crumbled lichen on their lips and pressed with fatty, running poultices. But none of it would heal. None! Noth-ing I could do would cure them! Then the mistress Grima feigned al-most to die! But I implored her—who but she should run the master's house? Freydis Eiriksdatter? Nay! With a heavy hand and a harder fist! She is worse by far than Torvard—Torvard even!—oh, and you know well the miserable weight of him."

Quickly I see Hallgerd's sobs are turned to taunting, knowing she has twisted up her tale to scrape the healing scab from my ancient wound. Only then I notice Inga standing, stock and sturdy, with a child of some six years at her apron's edge and another hardy infant in her arms.

"Inga!" I run to kiss my dear friend's ruddy cheeks. "Inga, you look well and cheer! You have survived the sickness. And your children, too. They are fair and—"

"Not mine, Katla. They are the master's daughter's."

"Torunn's?" I sense in her some sorrow. "Einar's daughter's gone?"

"She survived, and her two boys, and some two others also. Yet the husband that put them on her, though strong and bold upon the seas and fields, was tripped upon the plague twins' path."

I shake my head. "Tell Torunn I bear her grieving. Yet what of yours, Inga?"

"Hush!" She turns her eyes.

"Your children! Pray—" But I hold my speaking. "What of Snaebjorn?"

"He is well enough." She pats my hand, bites her lips, and keeps her head away.

Then she laughs. "I think," with a ring of red about her glistening, emerald peering, "only those who are good are taken off, and those who live. . . ." She sets her gaze upon the Gardar plain.

There, far off, Torvard leans upon a woman's shoulder. From her size and strength and bearing, I know 'tis Freydis Eiriksdatter.

"Torvard was heavy with the sickness, Katla," Inga answers my unspent gasp. "But now, you see, he has survived. 'Twas Freydis' doing. Freydis—for Torvard seemed more pleased to die than live. Strange it was. He fought it not, but seemed to drink the sickness as a fragrant nectar. Yet there was Freydis, quick-kneeling at his side, feeding brews she made upon her own wide wisdom's reaching—such strange concoctions of cattle dung and the beetles mingling in the byre's cracks. And with such swearings, Katla—chants and word spells as never I have heard! She fought the plague twins, too, with threats upon her husband: 'You'll not have your straw death, Torvard! No, though you do deserve it for your thickness and your cowardice. But I'll have no husband dead upon the straw. Only a husband proud within Valhalla's halls—and this I would rather have some soon!' "

"Such she spoke to him?"

"Aye, and Torvard did not answer and seemed almost to cower in his bed, if cowering he could, upon his weakness. Yet, quick enough, Torvard was healed and rising. 'Twas, I think, the fright of her which bore him up, for, most like, Freydis would have found some way to torment him even upon his doom."

"Such as he deserves."

"Aye," says Inga, then no more. We walk in silence, spying at the sparse-set booths and the sundry, wretched items. Suddenly there comes a ripe commotion. Seems another ship has tacked about to moor, though it is a poor one: its sails flapping, barely tattered rags, and its planks squeaking loudly as they press upon the shore. Still, its hull is thick-burdened with skins and bones and such, so perhaps there'll be some wealthy, storm-swept merchant to tell us hopeful tales.

Nay, a wafting silence falls across the crowd. All see clearly: this is Thorhall's vessel. And well 'tis whispered, for rumor's quick to flare, that this wretched plague had come off of Thorhall's boards.

The men about the ship bear heartily their bustle, shouting for help from among the throng, yet none dares send a single hand. As the men upon the ship look askance, even then I see among them a blondish pate and familiar visage.

"Inga." I clasp her hands. "Do you see him?" Ossur's face, some thinned, but fine before my gaze.

"Aye," she answers. "Yes, I see."

Just then, across the field come men from Einar's household. Rushing, bearing half-split byre boards, their edges long and keen, they make their way toward Thorhall's ship with cutting curses. "Send him off!" "Set him back to drown!" "Off with Thorhall and the plague twins with him!" "Hold him still so we can beat him heartily before he wastes!"

"Stop you there, before a riot comes!" All turn to notice Einar. Standing tall and still and finely grayed, my old master parts the portal of his hall. My own mistress Thorbjorg stands beside him with my daughter at her hand, and, too, old Kol, leaning heavy on Gizur's driftwood cane. "Mistress Thorbjorg says the plague is finished. Come, leave this man alone!" Einar shouts, yet the crowd still bustles until Thorbjorg herself raises up her hands for silence.

Her sleeves slip down, showing thin, white, bony arms. There she waits, though silence comes but slowly. When it does, she takes her narwhal staff from my daughter's keep and makes her way among the hummocks, carefully over the rattled stones, measuring each footfall toward where Thorhall stands.

"Seeress Thorbjorg," someone shouts, "will you greet Thorhall Hunter now, when you yourself said the plague twins traveled with him?"

"Aye," begs another, "set him back on Thor's angry bolts! Sure a storm is brewing on the vault of high Valhalla. Send the traitor and his cursed vessel to it!"

Still the mistress walks, through the grumbles of the crowd. They let her pass, for they seem to fear her as much as Thorhall or the very twins themselves.

At last Thorbjorg sets her feet onto the gravel and then into the cresting surf. She reaches up toward Thorhall's splintered railing.

"Welcome, friend," she says, "Old Odin's eye's upon you."

"So it seems here, woman, and some other eyes as well! What way is this to greet such a wondrous butcher?" Thorhall bellows out, "Don't these misers know I bring down riches from the barren north? Walrus ivory, oil, cord, and the warmest skins in all the settlements from here to Iceland. Say, yet, why these threats and cursings?"

"Thorhall, there has been a plague."

"A plague?"

"Hush. Come and I will tell."

"Nay! I'll not come upon it, but, rather, sail to Norway fast to save myself."

"The plague is over, Thorhall. It came with you and seems now gone."

"Nay! There was no sickness upon myself or any of my sailors."

" 'Tis like, for it is said the plague twins never leave their mark where they have bed and board." The mistress tells it loudly, so all the crowd will hear. "Come. Let him pass, and all his weary crew! They are no danger, now the plague twins have tired of their raking chores."

Just so, the mistress takes old Thorhall's ruddy palm. Together they walk across the stones, then onto the muddy sod, the mistress clinging to Thorhall's arm, and all the crowd still wary, watching, some few with red-clenched fists splintering about their byre-boards. But at last Thorhall passes, and then, slowly, all his men step ashore.

All of them, some still stumbling from the ocean's bounding, their giddy vigor now subdued, their gazes fixed with wary fearing. They peruse our plague-sapped assembly as if hollow draugs stood upon this beach. Of all these, at last comes my Ossur. His visage and his cheeks are touched with pallor. His eyes do not turn. Nay, they look ahead, as if 'twere more of cause to see his fellow's balding than to search the crowd for me.

I follow quick, but cannot reach him. His steps are dull as he walks right past, bowing his head upon the sight of my stern mistress and my daughter. With the crowd, he dips into the massive Gardar hall, where sailors, freemen, and all the chiefs are set before a feast. So, with Inga close beside, I go myself to work upon the meal.

Nay, I move my place across the siding of the hall, but he does not turn or bear some whispered word or cast even an eye toward me. There among his fellows—at first downcast, but, with passing ale-horns, growing ever rowdy—he lowers down his head, barely looks about, seated not far from his very captain, and there my mistress upon old Thorhall's arm and my daughter at her knee.

Thorhall brags, "In these wild places, only the boldest man can make his way. Sometimes better by wit than too much brawn. So I've learned from my fellow Ossur Asbjarnarsson. Aye"—his hand falls hard on Ossur's rounded shoulder—"seemed this man at first was but a meekling till I came upon his wisdom's worth. We were to sail before the winter's deep, yet the cold came upon us quickly. We had not much food and were fit to starve till Ossur spoke: 'There are caribou upon those slopes.' So off my men went all together, hunting, but there were no trees to hide in, the snow was thick and squeaked, and these bucks were fleet and unwilling then to die. We had not much luck until Ossur spoke again: 'Set a simple trap, somewhat like my uncle's old contrivance on the Norway slopes.' Well, but it was clever: to drive them down a narrow ridge to the edging of an outstretched cliff where the bucks could choose to jump or die upon our spears and arrows. Ah, they fell, sweet and tender, already almost split to cook upon our heated coals!"

The company bellows then with laughter. Ossur's friends pledge their praise and raise up horns. And Ossur, eyes some red with drink, answers with a horse's leg-bone shaking, thick and hanging fat with meat.

So I see how now he's different. His glance has moved from hunger to a gloat. His sight has lost its long beseeching. And the free-women watching also note this change, for their eyes are touched with sudden craving—nay of course, as he bends over his feast, for Ossur seems a richer man. Rich, for he is strong and healthy. Rich, for he is a hunter and said some wise.

Across the feasting board sits Torvard with his wretched frame, and his glassy glancing fixed on Ossur with a hateful, jealous gaze. The conversation's turned to the remnants of the settlers: how many households waste, and what barest hands are yet enough to cut the winter hay. Says Leif Eiriksson, "We'll send a ship toward Norway's court to put our cause before Tryggvason."

"Tryggvason?" Ossur speaks. "Now is he the king?"

"King, or last we heard, crowned as was his father's grandfather before him."

"Ah, well—"

"What, sir?" asks Leif.

Ossur says, "Only I know him."

A brighter flush crosses the freewomen's cheeks.

"Know him?"

"So. I stood among his troops upon King Ethelred at Maldon."

"Well, then, Asbjarnarsson, you'll come upon my ship and give us aid."

Ossur's face turns rusty. "Nay, I'd think Thrain Ketilsson would do much better. He was with Tryggvason, too, upon those fields—"

"Know you not Thrain Ketilsson was plague-struck and has perished?"

A chill rushes over Ossur's features. "I knew it not."

"Then you will join us? Come, for your foster-brother's sake—"

"I'm not well met to face a king."

"Yet you were a friend to him."

"No," he balks. "No friend. Only set upon the same dread blood and roil."

"Yet he would recognize you?"

Ossur nods.

"Then come to help our cause. Only greet him, then I'll sit myself to do the bidding, bringing knarrs and settlers to our banks. It is a good campaign. After so much plague, think you he'll treat our mission justly?"

Ossur flushes. "I do not know."

Yet I think: Ossur, if you should ever meet this king again, 'twould be in fair disgrace, not wise negotiation. But he speaks naught now of how he cowered on that battlefield, how he killed no foe but a Viking kinsman, then upon Tryggvason's mercy whiled his days at women's chores. Ossur mentions nothing of this. Through the soot and smoke and grease and splashing mead, his face turns bright as he discusses the mind of this new king. *Ossur, such pride's too quickly cut by swords!*

Still, I will not harm him. Already he does too much harm upon himself. Instead, I bite down hard my wisdom, pass the mead bucket's ladle into Inga's busy fingers, then turn upon my heel and go.

Out toward the fjord's crash, where the waves are sharp and beating, I barely see where I am stepping, tripping beyond the smoothing slope toward the water and its icy flood. I think to be strangled by its chilling touch—better that than live with both lost hope and fouled love.

Foul—I take a step, listening to the cold stones jiggle—

Foul. From high upon the Gardar green comes a sudden, terrored shout.

"Katla!" I hear my name. "Katla!" Upon my heartbeat's hammer. "Katla!" The sound grows hoarse and louder, rumbling thunder: footsteps falling hard across the earth. I tear away, fearing, knowing surely I have lived this day before.

Fast upon me—the surf like blood pounding in my ears. "Katla!" Now the sound grows close. The rocks behind me jitter, crackling under footfalls' force. He grabs me, pulls me. "Katla, please!"

Ossur drops before me on his knees.

Ossur, bearing lips and hands, all wet and hot and clutching. I tremble back. He lurches forward, takes me by my waist, his face flush with tears pressed against me, his lips to my belly. Through the wadmal cloth, I hear, "I'd thought you'd fallen to the plague."

"Thought?" I can but whisper.

"I saw your daughter, saw Thorbjorg there, but saw not you! I thought indeed—"

"You barely looked with the slightest seeing."

"When I thought I'd lost you now forever, I could not raise again my eyes."

For a long, hard time I can do naught but hold him through his weeping, high upon these death-bound stones above the fjord's lap and splash and foam. Ossur speaks not much but clings to me, his warm arms strong against my thighs, his head tucked close about my hips, safe beneath my palms.

Yet, as his breathing steadies, again comes to mind the truth upon this dawn. I speak at last aloud: "There is little joy in this uniting."

He looks on me and draws some back. "Katla—say you do not love me?"

"I cannot love that you will ever go away."

"Away—"

"So Leif Eiriksson would have it."

"To Tryggvason's court," he sighs.

"Ossur, 'tis a fool's journey," I stammer short, knowing such words will cut him to the heart. "You must not go. You cannot, or be disgraced before this king."

Ossur turns to me again. "Katla, know you well I cannot refuse, or be disgraced far more before these Greenland fellows. See I am respected now—even liked? Perhaps I can court such favor with Tryggvason." He hushes me. "Upon this chance, if the king takes kindly, I'll return with gold. Then I'll take you rightly with the reddened sails of my own vessel—a proper master's ship—"

"Ever full of ships and fortune. What of walrus ivory and caribou skins? Is freedom never bought with lesser things?"

"I've made not near enough to buy you, even as a slave. Ne'er yet to claim a bond-free wife. But one more year—"

"One more!" I grieve. "Such times grow long with waiting." I shake my head and stroke his jerkin—lightly at first, then with means to scratch.

He takes my fingers up and kisses them softly. "Here." He eases from the folds of his woolen shirt a fine-carved comb. "Of caribou bone. I made it for you through the darkest of this winter. In Nordsetur, to keep warm, I had only to think of placing it within your hair."

He reaches. His fingers touch beneath my kerchief. The comb's teeth are firm and smooth and chill. "Remember me by this," he says. "Wear it even till the day of my return."

Ossur holds my face. Pressing close, I feel the grizzle of his cheek, smell his scent, sweet and musty as the dew upon the moss. Tears come at last, just as my wisdom's warnings, absorbed into that mat and fur.

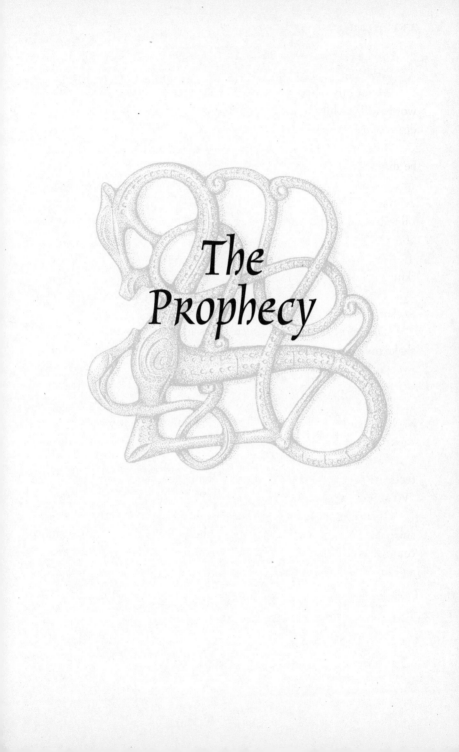

The Prophecy

BIBRAU

So he went to her, the fouled weakling. Went when I'd thought my evil eye had blinded him to her at last. With all his jester's prancing, his frail guffaws twined among those freemen's laughter. Their sounds came fierce while his but squeaking—the sounds of a mouse masquerading as a man.

Still I snickered at such feigning wealth and wisdom, that they should all believe him of sudden greater value now. With all those freemen's ugly daughters glimmering—it was enough to watch my mother's gloom, to see it fester, rot, and harden from disbelief to fair despair. And then she was gone. I listened for her footsteps, hoping, even through the mighty clamor of the crowd, I might hear my mother's wails.

Yet one breath and my savory sweet turned bitter. Ossur came awake and saw her fly from the Gardar hall. Nay, I lost my clutch, for he was fast, leaping from the feast, shoving other guests aside, leaving Leif half answered in his query. The crowd then hushed, for all had listened to the two men ramble. Never had they seen a freeman run so quick to catch a filthy thrall.

But now my gaze falls sharp across the feast hall, where a different rattled growling hovers above the meat-greased board. There, sunken eyes cast hard in an ashen skull. Bare at first I recognize, then keenly I remember—here again is the one they call Torvard.

Torvard, who once made such mighty mock upon that distant Althing horsefield and nearly had this Ossur in his clutch, but then was crushed and let him go. I have heard him called a lout and fool by

Thorhall and some other freemen. Still, his very name sets my mother's fingers quivering; his very shape turns her eyes to tears and flushes her face with anguished woe. To me never was he more than a lumbering oaf blustering with his stocky bulk more than with any wit. Yet I remember he was daring once—this Torvard spoke my name out loud.

Boldness! But now it seems such gall has pickled to a rot, and that rot has seeped out his fevered core to spread upon his very surface. There he sits beside his mistress, Freydis Eiriksdatter, tall and feasting, proud, while Torvard hunches and nibbles, stinking still with the plague twins' stench, eyes tucked close, lowered down, as he grinds his meat, cutting slowly into tiny pieces. No longer bold or broad or even very weighty, he looks somewhat like a desiccated toad.

Across the table's distance, Torvard rises slowly, his face squeezed tight. "Will this man go off," he croaks, "with Eiriksson to Norway while I stand before you, a chieftain's firstborn son?"

Leif speaks: "My law-made brother, think you not 'tis of some value? Ossur Asbjarnarsson knows the king."

"So he claims. Yet ne'er before was he any' but a wastrel."

"Wastrel?" Thorhall bellows. "Ha! You should see him at the hunt—"

"Let him hunt if it suits him best. Let a chieftain's son speak for Greenland before this king." Torvard clutches the table, his knuckles gripping white.

Leif humors, "Torvard, come. Your hand is wasted by this plague. You've not the strength regained to sail before the fjords freeze."

Torvard unclasps the board then. He raises his palm, reaching out for his wife's half-brother. And Leif, holding back a smirk, sparring somewhat, grabs it up, 'most in jest, till Torvard grasps him hard.

Soon, across the feasting board, their hands entwine in a forearm's wrestle, elbows jabbed into the splintered grooves. Torvard stresses and strains; his face turns ruddy, sallow cheeks puffing, thick and fleshy-full. He clenches and squeezes and twists, while Leif's arm stands firm and the freemen shout their mocks and jeers.

Leif soon wearies of such droll display. In a breath, he thrusts down Torvard's fist with but a subtle turning. Torvard seeks to fight again, but Leif shoves him back till Torvard bumbly-topples. All about, the long-hall rumbles with the watchers' roars.

From a spray of dust, Torvard sputters, "Perhaps I'm lacking now of strength. But that man Ossur is not fit to meet a king. His worth is lowly, his tastes are lower still. See how he chases after slaves!"

On this fair point, at least, I quick agree. Yet Torvard's mistress Freydis follows. "Fool husband, think you now you have any cause for pride? At least this Asbjarnarsson goes upon that thrall invited, while you must take your maids by force if you are to have a maid at all!"

Half the hall fills bold with laughter while the other half—mostly thralls, as my mother knows—nearly quiver in their still.

Torvard presses to his elbows. "Woman, I would have you so yourself, if you should dare to rouse me."

"Rouse?" Freydis spits into his teeth. "Husband, you have not the strength to vanquish me. Spare your hollow threats. When people taunt we have no children, do not deign to claim it is my fault. Make no mistake, all about here know you can do naught of worth in bed."

The watchers bellow even louder. But I care not, for all at once I sense Torvard—his eyes upon me, and something deep and darker— his torment so much richer than before.

Oh! Just then Torvard takes his mead-horn, slings it back for a thick, coarse draught, then lets the empty drink-bone roll. Reeling about, he totters, staggers fast and closely, lingering behind me where I sit, just a step, before he lumbers toward the great hall's door.

So I follow like fine temptation, smelling sweet mead on his breath. I slip through the crowd, small and silent, stooping as a hovered sprite in among the shadows, to watch him stumble across the Gardar plain among the hummocks and the stones. There Torvard trips across the frost-heaves, trembles, tumbles over lobbed and mottled grasses, crumples fast in all his frailty's cower. I dare creep nearer where he thinks he's hidden, his thick-set body molded to the mossy heaps, his face glowing upon the moonshine, streamed about with tears.

Tears! As no man's eyes should ever bleed! So wrought and rich as vomit from his soul. Yet up they come as I watch and feel my stomach turning. Sour. Sickly. Nay, a sudden strike—a sickening of my own.

Oh, rare misgiving! Rare, and yet it comes: a thought no thought of mine has ever formed. Yet is it this—some feeling for this fleshless boil? To harbor such compassion, nay! Yet this pity writhes in me in all its putrid strain. Somehow I cannot quell the anguished wrench as I stare at Torvard tripped upon the knolls. He lies helpless on that rutty soil, with the milky stars mirroring the rising dew and his spurt of tears. He heaves, and so I hear his wailing, even as I think to reel away. Instead, almost against my will, I creep nearer. Sinking low among the hummocks, I curl up small, if he should seem to hear or dare to send a look my way.

Lo! He notices not, but boldly hisses, "Curse upon that savage rune-witch wife!"

'Tis then I choose to stand at last, towering above his huddled skull. He looks up, strangely seeming seeing nothing, lifting to his knees.

Then, very near, his crimsoned eyes stare flush with mine. Such a sudden, steely vision! My heart quickens with a shriveled shake. He cowers first, then shoots up arms and takes me boldly by the chin. Never have I borne another's grasping! Ever from my mother most, but rarely from the mistress either; yet this man, this weary weakling boldly pleading, takes me close and holds me hard—his cold flesh steaming up, his eyes in all their glassy seeping cutting as if to see me bare.

"So"—he speaks—"so alike, as if a mirror. Anyone can see!" He looks then upon the moon, curling eyes within their sockets back almost beyond all vision's start. And for a moment, truly I feel terror—

Terror? What? Afraid of a weakling man! Torvard? Foolish! Never! Nay!

Yet I cannot pry apart as he clasps his fist about my neck, then drags it slowly down my dress, hanging wholly on the wadmal tatters. He clings to me and cowers down, close to my belly, slipping slowly

poetic
scansion

almost to my knees. Then he suddenly throws back his head and howls.

Wild-laughing, he thrusts me off. I fall away as his voice comes hurtling, piercing sharp my ears. My heart is pounding, lashed beneath the fragile skin between my half-formed breasts. I tumble, crawling, terrored but to tear away.

Then some footsteps falling—I turn to see my mother. Full of wrack and pain, she's run from somewhere in the field's long shadows—fast as ever I have seen her up that slope—and there her vile Ossur close behind.

"Never!" She sweeps me back from Torvard's touch. "Never! Never be so near!" With rasping breath, she spits and grabs me hard about my arms as Torvard stretches, wild, stagger-grasping, drunk, toward us.

"Katla!" falls my mother's name from Torvard's lips.

Strange to hear it, as my mother's face turns from red to ashen. Quick, she grasps and holds my wrist.

"Katla!" Torvard's voice spreads, needy, desperate, across the empty fjord.

"Come!" my mother shouts and tries to drag me.

Drag me—nay! Would she? No! I thrust her off.

"Katla!" comes again his wretched sound. And then the word which none but he dares utter: "Bibrau!"

My name across the Gardar plain.

"Bibrau!" again.

The sound scrapes coarsely up my spine. I shrink against it, cold and shying, a cringing terror I cannot thwart or claim.

My mother's arms draw me quickly to her, then her coaxing, whispered soft as she thrusts me back, "Run from him! Run!"

So I run.

Stumbling, panting with some anxious breath, my ankles twisting from the treachery of the misshapen earth, I fly until I hear Torvard's resounding "Flee!" across the slippery dew. "Flee, as ever cowards!"

So I stop. There dull Ossur's running, and my mother lashed upon his arm, and foul Torvard, a huddled heap like a pile of frozen sheep's dung. Nay, my frenzy burns to loathing. I, afraid? Of this pitiable fool?

Again he howls at the slivered moon. Then, from off the mountain far above, trips a subtle gambol. Where the icy glacier dribbles down, upon its sharpest, most impossible ledge, my fylgie hangs by his slimmest finger, and from his pipe he shrilly shrieks his harshest dancing tune.

THORBJORG

"THORHALL"—comes a flush upon me—a strange sensation—is it cold or hot? Then a whipping strike battering at my vision, then suddenly at my heart.

I seize the mead-horn tighter. It jitters, jarring. Thorhall notices. His old eyes linger hard. "Mistress, tell me. . . ."

I would cry out, but can barely whisper.

"Are you ill?" he asks.

"No." I nod my head.

"So . . ." Thorhall knows me well.

All about the Gardar table, talk and cheer, yet I can bear but quiet as my body quakes: *Odin, One-Eye, it is you who calls. You, who use me so at your will and with no discretion, with no thought of my own misgiving, here in this public place, before all this mired congregation. So again, yet I can do naught but feel your chilly rush, your terrifying tremble!*

Still I hold my head upright, but at last the mead-horn grows heavier and falls. The blood-red mixture drips and drains into the earthen floor.

"She is taken by her god!" they shout. "The seeress will give prophecy!" These others crowd about, closing off my air with their short, hard gasps. They steal my breath even from my lips. Know they not, this thing which comes is not for show?

Thorhall hies me up within his arms, into the thickest shadows of this chieftain's hall. Smoke mingles there with the darkest mossy clots. I can bear only the barest light, the softest, whispered sounds. "Go," I rasp, "get the girl!" Thorhall runs to find Bibrau.

I am left with Kol—my Kol, who's seen me thus enthralled more than any other. Then Leif Eiriksson comes and soft beseeches, "Mistress, will you speak some portent on this voyage to Tryggvason?" He catches up my hands, as did his father so many years before.

. . . Fourteen frigid rounding seasons since Eirik Raude looked white and hiding on his isle, Klakkeyjar, in the heart of Iceland's Breidafjord, outlawed and banished, yet full of hope and begging, too: "Tell what the gods can see!" He had sent for me, cast a skiff in my direction. I was barely rescued then from the fire and my household's murder. I could not yet walk without Kol's stiff, guiding hand.

Just so he holds me now—my ancient, faithful servant. But Kol is thinner, older, weaker than he was before. And I am weaker, too.

. . . Eirik Raude, back then, bright, sure, and full-strength hearty. When I'd spoken for the One-Eyed god: "Go to this place, this Greenland," he took my guess and, as fair payment, took me with him upon his masters' ships, across the sea with its icy teeth, where none of my enemies should fear me. What I did not tell him then: if the sky from which he fled was dark, so the clouds ahead were shaped at least as shadows.

Now I lie, sensing only barely this long hall's distance: Eirik Raude, somewhere far across the fire, and his son Leif, bearing well his face—wide-stretched, wary, eyes upon me, tremulous as I grope for a glimpse of darker fate. Through this vision, soft and wanton as a drifting fog . . .

There, before me—a great white hammer. Nay, it yet transforms into a cross, lean and thin as the Christians make it. Hanging from it, a long, dark man in a long, dark robe. Around him, candles burn, tapers dripping waxy, and scents so foreign, thick with smoke, not of heat or cooking fire but a kind of putrid purification. The man descends, holding out a heap, heavy in his fingers. Nay, he bears a stack of crackling leaves, thick and bound up within a leather sheath.

Such stuff! What I see is not of any proper vision, not of Odin, nor of Thor, nor Frigga, nor Freya nor any figures I should reckon. Nothing but that long, thin form with his long, thin, clawlike fingers and his crumpled leaves, and on these crawl a tiny, curving scrawl. Yet there I notice, at the very corner of my vision, *my woman Katla kneeling at his feet. Now she sweeps the Gardar floor....*

I fall from Odin's keeping! All about me, shivering as the god seeps out and my arms are tingling and there beside me is Bibrau—the woman's child. My foster-daughter, covered damp with sweat. In her eye is a look of terror as I've never seen. I touch her cheek: it is red and hot. Always but a frosty mask before. She cannot know what I have witnessed, yet some fear has struck her. I feel her hand. It is stiff within my own.

Then comes Leif, anxious as ever was his sire. "Mistress, tell us, what upon our journey? Can you say?"

From my lips I try to form some words—"Let me rest." Yet Leif's face, so bright with hope and needing. I close my eyes and sense it clearly: it is Leif who guides this black robe here.

"Go upon it," I tell with bare but breath, for no words were born which could ever change the course of fate. "Go in striving and, with your return, discover then the whole world changed."

Leif takes my words for mighty promise. He beholds his fellows set and wanting there about the hall. They turn and cheer and raise their horns, first for the gods and then for me. Then Leif feeds me from his own thin cup, a thick and hearty draught of mead.

KATLA

UPON THE MISTRESS' CALL, Thorhall scoops my daughter up and with her nearly flies into the Gardar longhouse. We come in breathless, close behind. There the mistress lies, pale and slightly greening, while all about are freemen boldly cheering of triumphant voyages abroad and somehow the whole world changed.

Even then they draw my Ossur from me, turning his hand upon their drink—a shout in praise of this Tryggvason, king.

"Have you heard, husband?" taunts his wry-wife, Freydis, as Torvard staggers through the door. "While you were out upon your seething, the seeress prophesied their Norway trip will fair succeed!"

Torvard stumbles weighty, wearied on this news. He says naught, but scowls dully at the hearth fire's flicker.

My daughter stoops before the mistress. Thorbjorg's fingers twine about her reddened own. Within her eyes is a troubled fever.

"Katla," Thorbjorg whispers, "go from me. Out. Gather wood to set a fire with a purging flame. Foster-daughter, you go with her. Be sure she bears the blaze up to the midnight's brightness—and get for it these god-offerings: a newborn pig, a half-formed goat, a full-grown pregnant ewe. Go to it! Off!" She thrusts me up with a sudden, powered shove. I stumble back, but my daughter's clasped about the wrist by the mistress' claw. "Child," she whispers, clutching at my daughter's pallid cheek, "foster-daughter, what demon have we seen?"

That night, before the strange-commanded fire, I help my daughter throw down sod and stuffs to raise a smoke cloud up. So, and I'm her butcher—with the mistress' jagged knife, made to cut the living foetus from the ewe. Then, with my blood-fears blinding and my mother's Christian whispers, "Sancte . . . Domine . . . ," I must split the half-grown goat to pieces even as it bleats out loud. Oh, to endure such gruesome service! My daughter with her pipes pitched high nearly glees as I sicken from the stench and bleeding. She bears no pity, but sets me down to slave upon the flames. Then she herself kneels to slaughter the suckling pig. To watch such joy upon her grimace—as if the feral, grisly task should tear away her terror of this eve.

Terror, indeed, though she would never claim it, nor comprehend how I protected her from Torvard's fouling hand. Yet now such anger's in her fingers' grasping, such thrust upon this pig's entrails as she pulls them up, then throws them down. And the pleasure in her—sniffing deep, as if to suck the life from the flesh-burnt air! Oh, this daughter—born out of my body, yet naught of me nor any of my mother—this child is a blood-let beast, just as her sire!

The dawn comes slowly from the murky summer's dusk, but at last, with its vapor, the wild flames are finished; the bones charred down to soot and crumbled, blackened coals. So, the bleating, mewling—dumb—lost upon the morning's howls. And I, thick with blood, wander-wearied, nauseated with no rest or food. Upon my daze, I choke small comfort from my lips, "*Kyrie . . . Eleison. Kyrie . . . Kyrie.*" Too tired to think or know which words I'm choosing, yet the sound of them, gentle phrases drifting soft, entwining with the tails of smoke and white-flecked ash to slip upon the winds. Just so, my daughter hears me. She hears, though most my words she has ever fair ignored. Yet she hears me well, for upon her face I see what's almost claimed a sneering, as near-to as ever I have seen emotion there before. This sneering taints her scowl; her gall is peevish. She listens hard, almost till her grimace leans into a scoff. A scoff—my daughter? Nay, she would not stoop to make such sound.

My daughter—caked in blood, her rags full-soiled with entrails, feces, flesh from off these slaughtered innocents. Her stink is foul and her face is worse—cold-worse for its sudden, pale, sated calm.

"Nay!" I say, and find I'm nearly shouting. "Why protect you, wretched beast? Why, when Christ himself would forsake you with his mercy? Daughter, know how near you came to certain, painful ruin? Be grateful I should care enough to keep you from such harm!"

I hear my own words pealing off the ice-cloaked cliffs, satisfying, cleansing to my blood-soaked skin, bounding toward the distant Al-thing grounds as if they could absolve my soul. But there, bounding back—coming slowly up the ridge—my mistress Thorbjorg clinging to old Thorhall's jerkin.

I push my daughter toward them and am vicious, pleased to see her run. "Go," I shrill, "down to greet the outcome of this rueful toil!"—glad as she falls into the mistress' welcome, her arms about her, her straw-gold head within the mistress' palms, then standing proud between them both wearing her blood-soaked garb as if she bore a prize.

"*Benedictus Dominus! Kyrie Eleison!*" My furor leaps to screeching.

Thorhall bellow-warns, "Upon Thor's hammer, Katla Christian, hush all rot of Jesus Christ! Off your tongue, ne'er to speak it—not if you should choose to live!"

He comes upon me, and from such a man, bounded up in skins and heaving, bearded, he seems as Thor himself, raising his hammer-hand to strike.

"Nay!" I scream, and cower.

"Thorhall, stop! Let her be." The mistress moves between.

Holding my daughter's hand for steadiness, Thorbjorg kneels before the ruined fire, reaching out to feel the last coals' heat. "On Odin's watch," she whispers to the ashes, "now let all such wary visions burn." Then some sounds of secret runing. My daughter takes her pipe to play the mistress eerie airs. We listen till the music's caught and dances beyond the fells and glaciers. When the air and ice crackle crudely with their rhythms, at last the mistress stills her tunes.

"Go." Thorbjorg barely sees me through the shadows of her rune-cloaked sight. "Katla, go and drink and wash upon the Gardar spring." I try to rise, but my limbs are feeble. The mistress comes and takes me by the hand. "Katla, have good faith," with a tone of goodly kindness. "You've done well upon this chore."

THORBJORG

IT IS DONE. So it would be done: a mighty sacrifice is made to steal this vision. To seize it from the air, wrap it round, heavy in burning flesh and stench and blood. Then to cast it off, drive it on the foehn winds. Come, winds! Come, the howling madness! To set this strife upon the jagged cliffs, to drown it in the frigid seas, to batter it with rocks of hail, to tear it but to wasted tatters—to naught but cinders— ash upon the lapping flames!

But the flames, as the winds, do—and have—and forever will— recede.

What strength have I to change our fate? Alfather, what wisdom to tie the fraying threads in the Norns' taut weave? Yet I have ordered everything you taught me. Even sent my woman to unmake her destined duty: burning it in fire, drowning it in blood. As if all this could expel the dream. ⤷ 3 Fates rule over Odin, Thor

Still, my Katla—listen!—e'er she spits such fateful words out from her lips. Those Latin prayers. She speaks them over, over, her hands still trembling, still caked with death, still thick with magic, slippery still with blood. To these words she turns—not to you, Alfather—not even after all we've given. And naught I've done—ever to her kind and good—will set them from her lips again.

Yet she's a gentle creature. She works full hard and wants for naught but love. Love and succor. Though love knows naught upon such visions. Succor cares not upon such dread, but only comfort and longing arms in which to dwell. She cannot see what she herself will usher. She cannot know.

Nor any of them. There those freemen, standing now about the Althing ground, wretched after a night when none could sleep for the flash and fire. They smell the soot and ashes, stumble up upon the blood-sopped earth, footsteps crushing the smoky morning's dew, begging but to have my vision. Yet what can I give them? Nay, I cannot speak it out. It is not mine to share what is barely mine to know.

I wave them off, calling for a breath of distance. They ply me, prodding first with words, then more with worthless beads. I want them not. I thrust them off. Still they press, cold upon my hard, wracked fingers. Such tripe I fling upon the rutty ground; but they pick them up. "Mistress, if you see such fate, then tell!"

I turn away. I turn to you, Alfather, to give me words. What should I say? Ever have we stood but close to charge such destiny. Yet, when I reach, your hand is lost. When I listen for your breath, there's a gape, a gasp, an unfilled sighing. I tremble at the void—ne'er before— to draw such silence from a god.

Still they come, though I have naught to give them. Naught but words as can be twisted on a thread—worthless without your vision's guiding. Then Kol whispering beside me, honest warning on our winter's loss: "With my strength to fetch the falcons gone, and all our household wretched, truly we have left but little means to live."

Is this, then, as you would have me—forced to cheapen your esteemed craft with base economy? Begging baubles and petty trinkets so my household bare can eat, when the gold I seek is far beyond all price? Yet they beg me, proffering to me, coming closer, trammeling the air. You will not speak? Not say one word? Their eyes beseeching—

And my own people thin and wan and too soon starved.

Nay. I reach. I take a single strand. Cold and callous are the beads within my fingers. I make some sounds: empty words flowing as sweet milk from my bosoms—barely crusting on my shriveled nipples through these breasts, now hollow, flat and hard as stone. Yet this fragile stream—it is what I have to offer—all that you have left me— breath and brittle bone. Still I know I can—I must try to feed.

BIBRAU

FIRST, the mistress' vision. Then the pyre's flames. And now, upon this very hillock's lingered, languid smoke, come peasants, freemen, and their heaving mistresses, with their hands chock-full with bits of shining stone. Some with gems, some amber, some with garnet, some with bags of small glass beads or a clanging sack of coins, others tripping to our sod-built booth with gold-wrought brooches, coils of walrus cord or seal-intestine line, or meal or meat or whatever they can muster, begging but to give the mistress booty so she will read their doom.

Oh, and how these freemen wheedle, demanding fates, promises of harvest, births and deaths and sicknesses—all ill! My mistress, loathing first—yea, fair denying the value of such requests—in time is pressed, and finally she yields.

So she sets down twiggy runes or reads some fortune in a pile of picked-clean bones, rattling them first, then thrusting them from between her fret-bit fingers to let them fall down hard upon the muddied sod. And here I lie beside her feet, watching those rune-twigs scatter as she, quieting the crowd, bends and spreads her hands out wide above. Then, mumbling first, she spits such petty magics as should placate and appease their woes.

But all her words are false, I know. And well she knows it better. On the start of these purchased casts, the god quick left her tongue. Still it wags, filled with mock but naught of meaning; and for all her lies, these fool-men pay us well. Even Leif, bending low before the mistress, placing a sack of cloth, soft and black, into her hand. Within, a lump of tarnished, unworked brass, and upon his lips a pleading to twist the winds and bend them to his jaunt—bargaining his longship's fate before the all-forsaking seas. I think to cast my own upon his query, to see his ship hard-fail and send my mother's love adrift. Yet I have no chance, for the mistress takes that tarnish, saying, " 'Twill make a splendid tip for the narwhal staff Ossur Asbjarnarsson once gave," and, with a quickish eye on me, hands it to Kol.

Kol takes that lump in all his plague-sick weakness and, with Svan's strong arms upon the bellows of the Althing smithy, makes from it a gleaming coil. Mating it upon the mistress' bone, he inlays it with precious stones she has garnered from her mischief. Those he does not employ, he sets for me to stitch upon a cloth, dark blue, of the softest pile and thickest heft, to make a mighty mantle for the mistress' ploys.

Strange, it pleases me to thread them there, glowing, glittering within the dusklight's failing—ringing a raucous, gaudy luster about the hem, and some glassy beads of brown, red, yellow specked about the necking and the band. With each I stitch, come large or small, I hush a secret chanting meant to mark the stone with a vicious power.

In time, the cloth grows weighty with my meaning, till, at last, I fit it with walrus binds, then wait for Thorbjorg to come and please to try it on.

But she does not. Nay! Not once through all the lasting days of the Althing season. Not even as our gifts are piled high within the railing of our skiff. Not even as we lash our plunder and sail from Einarsfjord upon the fortnight's dawn. Nor does she look as I hold it close upon that dewy gloom, but only gazes toward my feckless mother clinging to the skiff's low rail, at her tears falling thick and fretting loudly over Leif's fattened ships and her lover's feeble farewells.

Just so, we turn our tidy profit and our dipping rail toward home, returning to Tofafjord's waters with five fine invitations fixed to play the sham upon some other farms. I am pleased to do it, but the mistress lingers, broody, and is much loath to go. For some few days she sits about in such or silence, her hand gripping white about her narwhal staff. Then, at last, she rises on a midnight and trudges out into the dark toward the circle stones.

I dare creep after, there to see her stand, her hands raised up, singing praises to the ancient gods, then twisted talk of the roots of old Yggdrasil and the ways of springs to dribble and to dry and the fountain for which Old One-Eye gave his sight to drink—songs even I have yet to learn. She sings and sings until, sudden trembling, the mistress buckles. Bare upon her knees, she cries an anguished note, as if the god himself has struck her with his broadsword. She crumples, rolling on the ashen sod, then turns and looks and finds me, even as I slip among the phantoms.

"Child," Thorbjorg shouts, "go off, if you have some love for me at all!"

Love—for her? Nay! What is love but simply useful? Yet I turn upon her scold, falling down the path and across the homefield grasses. Well I know some uses for her still.

Through the wretched wooden door, swinging heavy on its leather hinges, I go to sit six long nights while the mistress stays apart. Through the waning light and a heavy fall of hail, I wait as she fasts for six nights longer. Then, at last, she comes, dew-dripped, her face awash with white and weary, at first saying naught, staring at the hearth as if the sense of warmth were odd.

My mother leads her by the arm and sets her down before the fire. Kol bends before her feet. He takes her hands, both within his own, "Mistress, what say the watching gods?"

Thorbjorg barely moves her head. "They speak not, nor give me any symbols, save only one, whose note tells me surely we can do naught but go where we are called."

So we are to go! I nearly dance, then seek to show her my handiwork at last. Fetching the cloak from my sleeping corner, I fling it out with a rippling sound. As it falls, all the shadows and shimmers flush with fire.

"Fair impressive!" says my mother then, and with her praise almost all pride upon my work is lost. But the mistress stares, letting fall her hand to stillness on the cloak.

" 'Tis fairly done. Well and rightly for this trespass we'll prepare."

For some days more we do but wait, I barely sitting, fidgeting much, kicking at the hearthstone ash and the pounded flooring. Till, at last, the mistress turns from her sighs and orders: "Foster-daughter, bring my pouch."

I race to the task, taking from her waist her silver keys to open her e'er-locked trunk. From within, each twiggy bit and precious potent I bear upon with glee, tying them well and tightly, breathing on each an unspoke' charm. Then I go and hold them out to her. She takes them from my hands and, slowly, bumbling as if upon a dream, ties them to her touchwood belt—the one which old, dead Gizur once had fashioned.

'Tis a hefty sack falling low about her hip, but the touchwood curves full-neat and holds it well about her waist. She stands and calls, "Fetch the cape. And Kol—good—bring my cane."

So we all go running and stay up late that night, pleased to dress the mistress vainly. When we are through, Thorbjorg stands with my mantle draped about her feet. Such glitter-stones glow like stars before the meek hearth-fire moon. Well, it is a fine display—a fair, imposing costume! But my mistress, though she's barely set her hand upon the narwhal's brass, quick commands Kol to fold the garb away.

THORBJORG

TRUE IT SEEMS, yet ever, always, I am caught upon a path unwanted, forced to yield when all my wisdom screams to turn away. Hard-wrought. Yet I go upon it. Odin, look. You see? I go, though my soul knows ne'er but rot, my tongue the taste of fruitless spoil. For all these years, set to serve upon your step, to lead me to this degradation.

What is pride? To what purpose? To serve you truly, Alfather, was ever all I sought. Though you neglect me. You reject me. You send me off on pitiable tasks and leave me, neither speak nor listen to my sorrows, e'er alone with your empty cloak, never your guiding hand.

I am your servant, Odin. Hear me, out about your work with naught but some threads of knowledge torn rashly from your shift? Yet for these—Old One-Eye, Great One—they come begging.

I will do my best. I will tell them what I know, though most I will speak little that's coherent. Naught that's clear, for, if I should, might I not say, "Little more do I yet know than all of you"? Yet I will forge the fake you have forced upon me, with mimicry and magic sparks. You have laid me bare, set my legs apart—propped wide in mocking of your proper service. Why? To test my strength for what's to come? In faith, then, tell me aught that I might listen! But since the Althing feast, you only come in dreams and cold misgivings, in sudden, fright-ful shocks: a broad white wave borne to wash our shore with fierce mutating, but nothing more.

You are silent, though I know you listen. I sense your unremitting hiss in the utter still. I step forth because I must, my arms out-stretched though my hands are nearly empty. I go—I will serve—with naught of tools or any but my hollow moans.

BIBRAU

DESPITE her odd reluctance, with the dawning's rust we set our skiff into the shallow harbor, with Svan and Teit about the oars and Kol upon the rudder. Kol is fair'y feeble, with nary but a Finn's knot tied to speed our pass. Yet it is enough to ply us out from Tofafjord's dullness.

All that autumn, we sail the ice-flecked fjords, first to fat old Ketil's farm, then to Thorbjorn Glora's misty islands, on to Arnlaugs-fjord, and once even to Eirik Raude's fine stead, in time to nearly every chieftain's hall. At each fair farm, they treat us with fancy feasts, with shiny copper trinkets, pins and arm-rings thick bejeweled, some forged in bronze or silver, others gold or cut of fancy walrus tooth; and all of these the mistress first refuses, until the freemen soon insist.

Too, upon each farm, they fall quick to fawning—feigning cheer to see us alight, mocking just to have our pleasant company. Though, as each feast grows long and our bellies full and our thoughts press near to bursting, ever then does the master of each high house rise.

"Lady—Seeress," each one says upon his turn, bowing low, nearly kissing on the mistress Thorbjorg's jewel-hem, "would you kindly set your rune-twigs out upon this household's fate?"

Ever then the mistress rises, turning swiftly, scowling some, and nearly scolding, "Know you well what little good 'twill do to beg upon the Norns? Their weave is ever hard upon its warp, twisted up and bound to shift and fray."

Still they beg, "Lady, do us favor—for this lavish feast and that hefty band of gold wrapped about your arm."

Till she tosses her roast rib-bone hard upon her platter. "I warn—the future can't be bought or begged or stole'!"

Yet finally she turns about, sending me with a chin's thrust off to fetch her sack of potents. I eye her close as she takes them up, shaking, speaking slowly: "Think—would you have such vision? Would you see what I have seen—know what I yet know? Oh, you would? Yet, if you should, you would not truly want it. Nay, you'll have your sight, for what it's worth in sorrow, and blame me not if these twigs tell you less than naught at all."

Then she clutches her twiggy-marks, craggy in her fingers. Her cast rattles, then crashes quick, scattered odd across the ground. Naught I've ever seen upon such twisted spreads, as they roll beneath the table-board or sometimes trip over the thrall-tramped path to the fat-meat kitchen. Still the mistress bends her back and spreads her fingers, thin and shaking, over the runes' rough grooves. Then she breathes some cryptic chant even I cannot decipher. 'Tis enough, for her words ever bring the freemen's gasps, though she says bare a bit, and less of any meaning. For all these chieftains' finest yearnings, Thorbjorg speaks not a single honest spark, but only curls her lips to please.

So it goes, first at one hall, then another. After each, Thorbjorg never lingers, but ever turns us swiftly off, begging to have another farm to call—one "over the high fell-slopes," another "by a distant fjord." Though most there is naught to such requests, only the mistress' grief that again her sight has foundered.

Still, with these cryptic cants, such fancy invitations flourish. Prophecy is what you make it, and Thorbjorg makes it well. Full grows our fame, our sacks some stout, our bellies firm and sated. Though the mistress takes no pleasure in the trick. Six long weeks she strikes her senseless notes, seeming ever clouded bleak. Though, for all her loss of pith and tongue, she never begs me lend my own magic's winsome timbre.

Nay, and well she should, for, as she casts her stumble-notes, ever I sit upon some darkened corner, scattering my own. Such bones and twigs I toss across the ashy dust, setting them to strike as does amuse me. It is a wily dance, waving hands while hearth-hags stoop to guess my meanings. Even the invisibles spread quick-quivers on my lips; but for such thrall-dull fates, I am loath to speak them.

So it goes till, late into a winter's eve comes a knuckle's crack against our door. We've been home not three crisp nights. Bare have I set upon my own sleep's patience, but the call presses hard with breath to frost our door hinges' creak: "Mistress, pray, come at once upon the birthing of a child!"

From the tone, I know 'tis only Arne Thorbjornsson, a freeman living on a distant spit of Herjolf's homestead. There he bends his back at peasant's labor, year by year, to pay his debts in sheep and woolen cloth. So he ever hopes—and speaks it ever boldly—to bear up wealth enough one day to claim his own small farm. Well I know, for I've seen such mean folk often—far too oft upon my mother's boot-less Ossur. They are much alike—thick to have their pitiable pride, quick to play upon each chance which slightly favors. Yet he, at least, is wise enough to wed a freeborn maid, while Ossur pines still upon my worthless mother.

Kol opens the door. 'Tis no surprise this Arne nearly crawls upon his knees. "Mistress, come," he begs, "for my wife will lose this child. Already once she has lost—our last—gone upon the plague twins' sweep!" He whimpers much, till I would have thought Thorbjorg would turn him out with a hiss and slap; there are thralls enough about to do the midwife's duty. Yet, though he is of no account and cannot pay us rightly, Thorbjorg spends no breath and scarcely time to wrap our cloaks. We bear out fast upon his sledge and horse to give him aid.

This time the house is not near so warm, nor the food so lush; and the smoke so thick 'tis hard to see beyond the cooking fire. But there within, as Arne leads us through the stench, lies alone upon a moss-hard bench the woman Ingibjorg Erlaugsdatter.

Woman? Nay! But a pit of a brightling, bare fifteen years old, though some two years more than I. Plying at her labor, she clutches her housewife's keys. Pitiable keys they are—bare but silver slag, broke and turning black with tarnish. Yet she grips them till I see her hands grows red, then white with toil.

When she catches our sight between her writhes, she nearly lifts up from her lying. "Husband, said I bring the midwife, yet you bring the very prophetess herself!"

"The seeress was at home, Ingibjorg. 'Tis fortune and a portent for our baby."

Ingibjorg cowers. "And the changeling, too . . ."

On this note, I feel my vexing rise.

But the mistress sets me hard about, passing me her staff and cloak upon a scowl. She presses me back and bids me send this Arne off to wait on the dim-lit ice while she bends and tends between the woman's thighs.

There I return to watch as Thorbjorg prods about—in places, well, I am curious to know. Yet she keeps me back. Nay, Thorbjorg will not let me close, forcing me instead to the pettiest of chores. To holding light yet not too close to burn, to fetching her healer's pouch, then to mopping this Ingibjorg's sweating brow. Oh, it is ill and mocking of my skill! Yet I hush, knowing the mistress watches me keenly. And this Erlaugsdatter watches also, though she with more cold thought of her own need than any of my ill-will.

Such it goes for some long hours—I cutting jagged chunks of ice from the roof's long spears, holding them to drip into her mouth's parched cavern. Nay, with my face a stony mask of fury, listening to my fylgie's cackle ringing off the house's low-slung beams. I gnaw upon my rage and long to bear these frosty points into a barb; but I hold my still full-tight, until at last I see . . . Nay, in this will come my craving's remedy! To touch such mortal, birthing fright with a fawning, fleeting calm. Indeed, to give this Erlaugsdatter false-ish comfort. 'Tis simple—but a twisted little hand, the slightest feigning smile, and—fair!—I will belly down my mistress' doubt and even this belly-woman's pride, till at last I have what is full and rightly mine!

Though the plan does taste of pit and cloying, I swallow it down hard. When next Ingibjorg grunts and begins to sweat, I merely gentle up my mopping stroke. She looks at me some oddly, sensing well, if she is wise, I long to press the filthy cloth down rough. But she is dull and even smiles at my trick, suffering my ministrations as some kindness. Then, when she is set upon with newfound pain, I let her hold my fingers tightly. I bear her clutch with stunning patience, noting well the mistress watches, saying naught, but in her eyes quick-blazoned, fond surprise.

On it goes, we three together, waiting for each grip and scream and moan. I bear upon my face the grimace of compassion, while, between her struggles, this Ingibjorg chatters, drifting, weary, wound in nervous dread. "Well, you know," she peeps, "my husband, Arne, was once Torkel Herjolfsson's dearest playmate. This child who'll soon issue forth will be fostered at Herjolf's stead. This son will shape the future of our fortunes. . . ." She muses far overmuch, then gasps between her strains. "Mistress Thorbjorg, tell me—pray—should I bear a son?"

Thorbjorg, upon her request, bites her forelip gravely.

"Mistress—I mean no greed. I will pay you well for aught your trouble—"

"Woman, hush!" says the mistress. "I'll take no wage," then pries the pity-keys from out Ingibjorg's damp fingers and presses them into my cold palm.

I look on her.

"Bibrau, hold them—here—above the woman's bellied core."

So I do. Ingibjorg shudders, though she tries to grin.

"Fear not the girl," Thorbjorg counsels as I dangle the slaggy bits barely above her.

"Nay, I'll not . . ." She looks on me full-frightened.

"Foster-daughter, hold them still. There—wait and watch their turning." The keys slow-drift, ranging from their place though I move them not, barely breathing any. At last the mistress bends and takes a bone from out the hearth fire's ash. On it I know to scratch a subtle rune-string. I carve it well, tracing deep and down into the marrow, then lay it by the woman just as the mistress shows.

"What shall he be?" asks Ingibjorg, anxious. "A man-child?"

So I nod.

"A son! Dear Frigga, mother of the gods!" This Ingibjorg sings and clutches on her belly-bloom. Only the mistress bends and takes again the bone I've carved. There she sculpts more upon its edge: *This trinket ply against the fate of child-bearing.*

So I know the twisting keys have told her something more than she had sought. Yet Thorbjorg says not what, only sets me burning oil lamps to ward the mound-ones off. Then she calls me near, and we two together rock with Ingibjorg as if she were a child, I gnawing on my singing pipe as Thorbjorg murmurs ancient tunes of the frost-giants' doom, how Ymir's skull became the overarching sky, and how, from his body, the Norse gods formed the world. //

On and on, so it seems for endless hours, for days almost, with this Ingibjorg wracked with pains like the gripping slither of the Midgard snake. At each I am quick upon it, remembering well my feigning place. I take a cloth, raise up Ingibjorg's fingers and bear her weakening wrench, while the woman stinks the hall with sweat and wailing.

So it goes, she looking ever paler, till, at last, upon the early dawn of the twentieth hour, comes a sudden, sweetest pause. Indeed, her brow drains white and quickly cold. Her wretched shrieks grow quiet.

The mistress begs me oddly, "Child, stretch your hands inside her womb."

I heed her, in sort quite stunned and only half in hearing. Yet the mistress hisses, "Foster-daughter, do it now." I realize only then that Ingibjorg has swooned.

Still her body writhes, pressing all the while against the baby. With my slim white hands I part her red vagina. There my arms, bare, thin, and taut, are quick-clutched from deep within, her womb against them ever pressing hard. Thorbjorg begins at once to beg me answers: "Daughter, do you feel the child squirm?"

I nod.

"His forehead—can you tell—does it come first?"

I screw my brow.

"So, his heels? Will they come sooner?"

I purse my lips.

"The cord—do you feel it wrapped about his throat?"

With this final nod, Thorbjorg leans to me. Calm, discreet, she tells me what to do. The mistress begs my hands to grope and find the narrow wrapping. Feeling for this child's nose, to stretch it back and turn the baby round. All the while, the mistress mumbles magic words, calls for breath and a wider path, a pleading up to Frigga, mother god of Baldr and of Thor, and another prayer to Frigga's handmaid, Eira, who taught wise women such birth-attending skills. To all and any who will buoy her as I work. Too, I hear the mistress' anxious tone. I look on her and then on Ingibjorg with a sort of tremble I had not thought to feel. 'Tis the first I've ever thought, though I have known it true, in birth a woman can well expire.

I close my eyes against the blood and stench and smoke.

"Have you done it?" begs the mistress. "Untied the cord?"

Of a sudden, the strength of Ingibjorg squeezes down upon my hands. So come screams—first the mistress, then the mother, for she wakes from her murky torpor only to see my head between her knees. Her moan bears out, and she shoves me full, and then the babe comes quickly, thrusting spew and wrack and sack and waters gushing forth as the dross and wreck of an aged belly-sack of tendered cow.

Even then, the husband, Arne, bears back the long-barred door and finds us all lying thick with fluids and blood, the baby stretched out full across my thighs.

"Changeling . . ." he gasps as I sit bleary-eyed but with the infant fast within my grasp. "Changeling . . ." He steps to set me off. Just then the mistress bends and takes the babe.

She cuts the cord and sweeps him from me, to put into the father's arms. I fume and rage—that she should dare so vicious take the child I have torn into the world! I rise and reach for him, but Thorbjorg thrusts me back. Then from the lying bed I hear this Ingibjorg mutter.

"Husband, quick and name our son."

Says the man, full-quaking, "Before mighty Redbeard, I call this child Thorbjorn Arnesson, and bear him forth to bring our household's name full honor!"

Such words to keep the child safe—from changelings! Even Ingibjorg, whom I thought I'd cozened kindly, is wont to keep him safe from me.

For some lean time I still, until the afterbirth is cooked and fed out to the gods, till the mistress spells for the father how I helped upon this birth. For this, Arne offers paltry sips of watered mead, but he gives no look or thanks toward me. Instead, he calls about his neighbors. Begging yardmen gather round an open bucket, where they drink foul sips and pass the child to their milkless breasts. Meanwhile, I and Thorbjorg stay within the house and watch and tend, even as this Ingibjorg Erlaugsdatter dies.

She slips away, full true, much of her own accord. I myself do not one thing to set her on that bearing. The mistress must have known, for she sits distressed and holds the woman by her fingers. Through the passing hours, Thorbjorg takes no drink nor sleeps; though I think it strange and somewhat striking, she notes not my fylgie tapping rhythm on the household's beams.

At last, saying nothing more, Thorbjorg opens wide the door so the men outside may see the corpse lie rigid. We sweep full fast away after Ingibjorg's body is buried, covered up with pebbles and my mistress' death-protecting runes, dropped into the pit to settle hard in Ingibjorg's stagnant palms.

They say the woman's death was no one's fault. Even, as the rumor spreads, some mention I myself brought that child living. Like as not, most are suspicious on that truth, for they look on me no little leery and give me still so little thanks. Yet upon that morning my reputation slightly alters from demon sprite into a somewhat healer.

Blood

THORBJORG

EVERY DAY, I watch her. Well I see her power grow. Where before there was but scratch and ire, now her vision is so soft and honeyed, in these peasants' eyes she has grown to near a seeress, too. When we ply upon a house, two bowls are filled with meats and hearts and livers, two pillows set before our feet, two places laid with feathered moss to bed. For this she pleases. A warmish glow comes behind her austere frown. But she sheds it quick and moves about, never breaking with her stoic silence. And though she spends no words, they turn to her—some days, often, more than me—and bend about her all their woes.

She is everything we'd hoped, Alfather. All that we had wished—throwing down her certain casts, marking runes with a fair and wise-ish wisdom. These many months, never speaking out, ever guiding them with meaning gestures. And when there's need—for such fates as these come oft—plying a soothing touch on each doleful, trembled hand.

Still, I cannot help but sense a coldness beneath her touch, an icy glaze upon her sudden melted vision. Could it be an error in my sight? 'Tis clouded now more than it was ever. Yet I cannot trust, as before these freemen she is even pleasing, biting back her cheeks as they fawn about and press their smallish gifts into her fingers. Nay, so changed! From full disdain to fair compassion's manner, as she takes them up and even lets them hold her hands.

I should buoy upon it, watching close her gentle gestures and their hard, strained faces as their terrors ease to calm. And they, gaped wide, their lips half bit and whisp'ing awe—"Silence is her craft!"

Well, I think she likes this bit of homage far better than all the petty baubles we receive.

Old One-Eye, still I dare not question. Better they should learn to trust—to find some solace in her certain feign. For, if her hands are false, at least they bring some comfort. While mine are cracked and worse than crippled, futile, brittle to the bone, as some ancient sea-ice long since severed from the mighty glacier—drifting lengthy, caught upon a fjord's shoal—lost upon my soul's own course, cut away from your hard need.

KATLA

'TIS AS IF the seasons pass but with no feeling, growing cold, then warm, then cold once more. We lie in wait of driving snows. Finally they come, whipping at the longhouse walls, covering the door's tight cracks, flying till the smoke-hole drops a pillar of sooted slush all about the hearthstones.

My heart is cold as that black slush. 'Tis near two years since I have heard from my Ossur.

In all this time, rarely have I left our Tofafjord. I have not wanted—even shied upon the tempt'. Though my daughter does so often. She comes and then she goes; and at each returning, comes back ever different. Changed upon her passions—with her walk grown proud beyond mere brazen. And her bearing: even when she stands against the wind, it seems somehow to part about and does not blow her much around.

Such changes frighten. Yet toward me, too, this child is transformed. Before me for a time she's meek, almost solicitous, with a tender touch and a heeding nature. Ne'er before was such gentleness her wont. Such as it is, I should rejoice, drawn as I am by some shadowed tie of a mother's feeling. 'Tis true—she is some part mine, still my pain and blood. Yet, in a blink, her newfound nature withers, her fair

compassion turns upon a mood, and she is as before: scorning, wrath-
ful, in some swift, distant recoil.

When the mistress sees such wanton temper, she succors her,
"Foster-daughter, bear some little patience. Gentleness is ever wisdom's tread." Then my daughter shies her gaze, nodding some, as if
she welcomes Thorbjorg's urging. Then she turns to me, her face now
soft and calm as ancient friendship, the cold moonglow set there
seeming almost benign.

Nay, I understand but little, and less of what the mistress tells,
something of Bibrau's healing nature and the way she's learned so
quickly spells. Yet I do as I am told, for the mistress sends me oft about
their work—to gather ice-caked moss from off the bouldered slopes,
to sop up dew from glistened willow boughs—till I am grateful for the
late-come spring, when the frigid glaciers at last begin to gush, for
then I'm let to go upon the fair fell-slopes to chore at simple, useful
things.

So, of a morning, I stand before the hall collecting smocks in need
of spring's full-washing. Each among the household comes: Teit, Svan,
and Kol, ashamed to lay their filthy tunics by; Alof and Arngunn, setting theirs upon the stinking pile; then the mistress with her well-
worn shroud. Only Nattfari sets to fuss. We must fight to wrench the
wadmal from her, knowing well 'tis full of lice and must be boiled first,
then scrubbed. But then I wait—my daughter does not come—till the
mistress tells me, "Wait no more, Katla. Go about your duty."

Far she must be, as she is oft, likely howling at the waning moon
or dancing at her stony circle. I do not care, only please to walk the
path alone. 'Tis not long till I am over the slightest hillslope, then slipping down into the narrow valley. There the snows still cake the earth
in cracks where the sunlight cannot reach, though some rays dangle well above, spreading hints of warmth upon this last of winter's
breath. Across, the first coarse stretch of faded moss is flecked with
new growth's green.

I bend to my work over waters' rush, crisp and numbing to my
fingers. The ripeness of this dale grows well and wild, however lone

and wistful. It seems to me as some precious chamber for my heart. I sigh and cannot help my thoughts, drawing hard with longings for my Ossur. These I cannot suffer. I turn again upon my task. But not some six strokes on, I catch, from the corner of my vision, my daughter bent upon the selfsame chore.

Strange! By this very creek, not far above, she is crouched upon some shapeless washing. Never yet nor e'er before has she lifted up a hand to do such dull and proper work. Yet she is seeming eager, her strong, thin back bent upon the task, her hair unbound like a quivered drape about her, pitching in gentle rhythm, glinting golden in the chilly sun.

I cannot keep my eyes from drifting, ever and again, until her chore is through. At last my daughter rises. Now my fingers bumble to my lips. White and wide and bare—she is naked as I'd never thought to see.

Oh! That shape—that shape of hers I know. 'Tis fair. . . . 'Tis ill. . . . 'Tis ever as was mine! Such fine, slim limbs reaching out beyond their call, hips but a little rounded, a narrow waist, and arching breasts—so small, impotent, coy. Oh, her breasts—her breasts—they are my own, even as they might be still—and then I think, *Without their wretched scar.*

I cannot look. I cannot turn my eyes away. I cringe as she rises with her arms outstretched, pausing now as if to flaunt such virtues, holding her soaking dress aloft like a billowed sail flying on a well-wrought mast. Then sudden turning—oh, her stinging look! She turns it plain and hard on me.

Her glance is cold, her scold so harsh, her eyes are fiercest gazing. Her arms raise up and, with a breath of wind, she ope's her hands and lets the garment fly.

It tumbles in the grasses. Her look, like fists thrust from out those eyes.

Those eyes—I know so well—are Torvard's eyes.

My limbs do tremble as I step across the sod, coming slow and close. She makes no attempt to stop me, but watches even as I stoop down low to grasp the sopping gown. There I glance upon the wadmal's dankness. In terror, I see what I must know—the reddish stain clinging to the fibers.

Now I look upon my daughter standing, hard with such conceit— as if she knows this body's purpose and mocks me with intent to use it well. And then I know: never yet have I escaped my fate. It stands before me, all that he had wrought—grown into a woman. I try to reach but one last time—now with a palm outstretched as if to snatch her scorn away. To tear it back with my sharp, hard fingers, cracked and aching. But my daughter almost sneers upon my stroke, lost as it is and spent upon the empty air. She turns her gaze beyond, toward the fjord and its looming glaciers, toward its frigid ever-wind. And then she goes.

Yet, even as she ventures—I swear, as my daughter walks but bold and coldly, naked to the nipping breeze—I hear almost a muffled tone, a somewhat sort of laughter, as she drifts away, soon swaddled up in moss and mist. . . .

Yet there is no din.

There is no laughter.

Nay. Of course. There is no sound.

BIBRAU

WITH THIS warmish moon's full, I am counted fourteen winters, feeling well my power's weight growing heavy in my hands. Too, my body stretching long and lean and narrow at the waist, my flesh rising full upon my chest, taking on a bulbous shape. Well I know that shape holds power; I sense it in the sudden looks of men.

My monthly bleeding—'tis such a simple thing, and long past wondering. So oft before I have seen the mistress tending others on such woe. Yet I had not thought that, when mine came, all at once 'twould show me altered, so far mutated that even I myself would sense me full-transformed.

With its first-come dribble, I step upon a spark and quick-trip through the frigid night to the sacred circle. Here, while my mistress and her household numbly sleep, I stand before those subtle, silent watchers. For them I bend—for they who have ever known my course—and take a finger's flick from where it is dripping down my thigh. Small and slow, with it I paint a rune of rust upon the foehn wind's breath. There it glimmers slightly, moist beneath the full moon's cast, till I hear my fylgie—his music full and fair and flying.

Ah! I bend again to behold the treasure of all my full-fold woman-hood, dancing that night late into the hours while my fylgie plays me jigs. In his airs, he lyric-counsels how this bloody clot is made for cast-ing spells to set on tongues, to twist up foul lies to bear as truths. Oh, he's merry in his mischief as he sings—

> Unlike the blood of beasts or petty men
> such blood to cleave and leave no trace,
> to sicken worse than wounds.
> Sometimes a poison to be dipped!
> Sometimes to draw a bounding—
> and, true, sometimes to play upon a want—
> soft and fair—to charm, seduce, and curse!

So he brays, then bends to set such mighty chants in motion, rising upon the stones and frenzy-leaping, his narrow pipe cast rich and loose and high. I join him in his bandy, welcoming such torments with my own tarnished praise and sullied, vicious drools, with turns and twists and uncouth twinings, with writhings-up and slithers in the chill.

Until, at last, we weary. Then I and my fylgie throw ourselves upon the earth and lie, watching our hoary billow-breaths, as my fyl-gie urges me in secret gaspings. *Catch these clots,* he heaves, *and save them upon each full moon's rise—store them well in a small, tight pouch—stitch it up of chicken's skin and tie it round in gut—and there they'll gain in strength and certain, secret magic.*

Ah! Hail! Then the fires brighten and light the circle's ever-watchers. We know, as we heedless-breathe, the mound-ones grin and glow beneath the nimbus moon. We please upon it—giggling, rolling across the grasses—aye!—our limbs and bodies fast entwined—till the sun glows up and turns the world from black to gray to dawning.

Then I roll away and, when I look again, my fylgie's gone.

'Tis not long before Thorbjorg comes. She finds me by the stones, there shivering on the dew-dripped grass, bare and streaming honey sweat, glee'd and wanton breathing. Heavy tutting but saying not one word, Thorbjorg wraps her cloak about, then bears me hard upon my feet, her arms about my naked shoulders. She leads me sound and quickly down the mud-dropped path. I would fight, but my limbs some limp with a weariness I had not well considered. Even then, for all my falter, the mistress' limping gait and mine are somehow out of step, mine tripping lightly over the hillocks' crests while Thorbjorg's step is ever heavy, pressing down.

Still I think 'tis wise not to bold my stare or set my eye against her. Instead, I choose to counterfeit my glance till the mistress thinks it frank and rueful feeling. She turns quick upon a cure, warming her worried stroke to smooth my tangled hair, drawing me again inside the homefield bound, tucking me but neat beneath the dusty roof beams: so thick with gloom and stiff inside, hot with all the household's stares—all those bond-cows who ne'er have thought but to waste their precious blood for bearing young. All of them with their bellies bent, wanting thickly to be filled—a fetus quick beneath their hearts and angry-kicking. 'Tis all they know for such precious, ripened stream. And worst, the foul heifer whose body dared bear me!

Well I know—already I have caught upon such finer force, such subtler sort of magic locked within those dripping clots. And I will use it. Yet for now I must endure their petty women's talk—such as "Well, you will be weak at first—you'll wad a cloth to stop your blood . . . ," each clutching on my hand and giving me some worry-preening. "Nay, I'll show you how—then you'll learn to clean yourself. . . ." Fool speech and feeble counsel. I far prefer Nattfari's rabid sniffs and scratching paws.

Through those next few days, while my blood still flows, Thorbjorg does not let me from her. By the amber light of each my blood-night's dusk, she lies beside the fire and whispers in my ear. Well I listen, for she speaks this blood-sore's subtle dealings—how to cause a love or cure it of some pain, how to turn impotence to mighty pleasure. What she teaches is fair enough—all and naught of what my fylgie has yet mentioned. Though through those nights I see him taunting, sometimes by the smoke-hole's spark or swinging from the low mosseaves. Soon I grow full-vexed and turn at last to try to hush his hissed contempts. But then my mistress sees my look. She stills her speech. For a breath, I think Thorbjorg will strike me. Instead, she draws back, slowly rising, slipping me from her grasp's embrace.

Away, away, so I pray at last she'll leave me. Instead, she bends to draw a rune—deep and cut with her crystal point into the earth— then another in the sodded stone wall, another beside my sleeping bench, and another by the homestead's door. There a final last before the hearth fire's heat, till I see but clearly a fixed and cringing figure: my fylgie, red and huffed, froze' and rare upon the spot, singeing slightly in the smoke. Off his fancy cloak, some fire's tongues are rising up. There they dance about his silvery limbs and tease upon his spindled, knobby knees. And though his eyes speak pleading, bent on me with a certain rancored bruise, when he ope's his mouth, no longer can I hear his screams.

THORBJORG

I CANNOT SEE what tempts her. Can only sense the chillish breath, the warning waft, the strangeish eye—my foster-daughter's drifting, when all my talk should draw her off, should lure her close, should fare and feed her. I careful-craft my speech to tempt her near.

Tempt her—nay—tempt her now with dangerous lore: with unwise runes and vulgar casts I ne'er would lay before her wisely. Yet I do it—aught!—I do it, fair, and turn my talk upon most baleful tones. Though I know already it is far too late: the vicious sprite has merry-mixed his draughts and set about to tell her all.

So already he has taught her how to dance upon that rouge-ish glow, how to paint the runes in her own rich blood. Her finger's marks upon the stones—I saw them small and crackling, still slightly bright, barely dried upon the dawn. Her runes, all twisted up and turned about, set inside out as some magic script I had ne'er yet for her fashioned. Though I know it well enough—have hid it off and waited lowly—waited till I could give it out when I'd thought her rightly honed.

Rightly . . . What have I to judge? My sight is bare a shadow of its own shade; my voice now echo more than tone. Yet she hears the sly one's notes full-clear, though they are tangled up and tainted. Is it aught? She hears far more than I—for I am deaf without your certain voice, blind without your guiding hand.

I can but lean on her to find my feebled step. I must trip in rhythm with her own. Alfather, is this as you'd have me when such dark and foul portents draw so near? I feel them in the nights, not in dreams but cold misgivings: such shapes upon the dark which eyes may see only when slightly closed. I ope' and turn about, but the hall is dark. The silent eaves. The fire's rightly smoldering. But by its light and the narrow spark of stars, I sense within the shadows: we are not long upon this land alone.

Alfather, can you see such fate? Who comes? Not these demon sprites, these bare, ancient invisibles. They are aught enough, but it is something more. Something strange and savage in its view. Yet I feel its mask. It takes a kindly shape. What shape? I cannot tell. Nor, I think, can you.

BIBRAU

SOME SPRING and summer pass, and then the autumn; and with each rounding of the moon, I bleed. I keep my clots just as my fylgie taught, well stashed within a tatty bit of chicken-plucked-of-feather. Soon enough there comes a hefty weight to that dark and sticking dust. Indeed, such potent grows mighty with withholding.

Yet, beneath my mistress' sight, the time is fret and taut. Nary but a breath I breathe but she watches on me keenly. Still I hie about with my most meek and mellower expression, all the while feeling the sack dangling between my swelling bosoms.

So I bide, day upon each dark, as we work our prophesying ventures. Thorbjorg is frail and weak, waking nights to stare upon the dust-rot eaves; in days, shaking hands above the rune-struck casts as a beach-bound sprig of heather. I know she troubles: 'tis ever as I want, she leaning on me, heavier with each passing footfall. It will not be long before she trips upon the path. On her fall, I will welcome-vaunt my new-brought powers.

So it comes, long into the foehn winds' howl, a call to bear toward Herjolf Bardsson's farm. It has been some while since we last plied upon that house, though we have been full-oft with invitations. Nay, I think Thorbjorg shies upon each chance, fearing her ancient friend should see beyond her jewel-struck cloak to her hand's hard tremble; for once she told that Herjolf's known her well and long, even since her husband and her earliest prophesying days. Yet, this time, though Kol urges her to wait at least until the ice has firmed enough to bear a sledge and horse, Thorbjorg only shakes her head, pushing him off, then softly moans, "The message says Master Herjolf lies near dying."

Ne'er before have we rowed so swift through such ice and crag. The moon is not yet full when we drift 'neath Herjolfsnaes' high-cape rise. Beyond, the bay hangs with dewy desolation. Where the cove most ever bustles, that night bare a ship is beached, and those only set with some minor thralls to strive to keep them from the waves. As we paddle close, such thralls abandon all their posts, bending as a cast of claws from some shipwrecked draugs through the shroudy mist, lending out their hands to draw us nearer. The gravel scrapes against our skiff's old hull and rattles at the midnight's still. When the mistress cautious-steps ashore, her cloak's hem clatters, falling heavy on the snow-slipped bank. At the sound, these stumble-thralls draw back as if the tone itself were full of augur.

We trudge our way, pausing first before the master's hof— Herjolf's praying shrine to his favored godhead, Thor. Thorbjorg presses me off and bends but stiff within, there to lay some clutter down upon the altar: so, a slim goat's bone nearly cracked with dull and shaking runes; too, some thin breath-wisps barely trailing on the chill, shaped into a sacred invocation.

Not far from shore and anchors, Herjolf's homestead echoes back the wave-stones' crash. At its gate Torkel Herfjolfsson waits, bare a shadow against the sod-stone wall. Tall and woolly-bearded, he stands but well upon his master's fate: all know he'll gain the most of Herjolfsnaes' great wealth with his father's passing. Yet Torkel seems not much to hunger for such boon. He sets upon us, seeming doleful, dark of eye, nearly breathless, as he speaks: "Mistress Thorbjorg, it is good and not too late—you have come, praise be unto Thor."

He eyes me once, then bows his frown and leads us from the frigid draught into the dark and smoking hall. Within are watchers—freemen, peasants, mostly thralls. Many cower, some looking odd or ill, others daring but to bear in bins and platters such stuffs as lay-folk think will bring some healing cure. These they offer up as Thorbjorg passes; and though she chooses to fair ignore them, I think to lend some tender spice to this vigil's brew, passing my hand in feigned intent over their useless balms.

Torkel moves us through the hall till, soon, we stand beside the hearth fire's glow. There Herjolf lies asleep among such skins and heavy woolens piled high, seeming slim and frail, small and wretched, as he has never been. Around him hover kindred, even one of whom I have often heard: Torkel's coward brother, Bjarne, who plied so meek upon those newfound seas. There he stands, full again afraid, with ne'er as much to gain upon this loss, tugging close his bloated, red-cheeked wife who looks to bear out soon a half-ripe, wit-dull child.

Too, among them all at once I see an odd familiar—a boy clutching close upon a beast-carved beam. I know not why I know his face. Barely blinking, he watches me piercing-closely. Strange, such pluck, for he is but a stripling, near to my own age and growing fast into his length and stride. Almost I would like his look—bright of hair with a bit of green about his eye and a boldness to his lip, his staring but a dare, an almost provocation. So much, I think to toy upon his gaze, so

I stab him with a spiny view till he—milksop—turns his gall and slips into the shadows.

Then there's Herjolf's goodwife, Torgerd, crouching. Barely does she raise her eyes but thrusts a stick down quick into the hearth-fire coals. The motion sends up fragrant smoke, which cuts the pungent stench I smell upon the air. Of turf it stinks, of driftwood rank and oil's muster, of sweat-dried leather, the musk of thralls and men. But most, it smells of pending death—a pleasant odor.

It floats up heavy as Torgerd turns her stick about the ash. Yet my mistress bends to clutch and calm her fingers. "Woman, tarry not, for, though such work can do no harm, none of very good will it do either."

Torgerd turns her gaze. In her eyes is such a tearful redness, enough to match the fire's blush. Yet she lets no drop unseemly dribble as she waves away her smoke. "Again and welcome, Mistress Thorbjorg—Little Sibyl. You have come. And your bond-girl, also."

"Apprentice," Thorbjorg mends.

"Apprentice, yes. I have heard some well upon her gifts." But still she eyes me hard and wary.

Torgerd leads my mistress to lean her hand on Herjolf's grizzled cheek, listening hard to his dark'ning breath, hearing clearly as he wheezes. Torgerd whispers, "Each night is as this, as if a she-sprite sits upon his bosom—a nightmare, nay!—but close upon his chest. And though he hacks and shakes, never will she rise. Upon each gasp, she seems to steal his very breath. . . ."

Then, as if to prove her woe, her husband cruelly quivers. Yet, with the quake, the chieftain sudden wakes. "Mistress Thorbjorg," he merry-croaks, "it is good to see you. . . . Since the last, we have many words unspoke'. I think I would have them of you now, if such words bear fateful meaning." Yet then he shakes with choking on some bile. "Torgerd! What way is this to greet a friend so old and honored? Ready for a feast, if such is still the custom, as might and ought within a chieftain's well and prosperous hall."

Slowly rising, Torgerd steps away, saying naught but only shaking slightly, her eyes welled up with bitty tears she dares not blink to shed. Too, my mistress Thorbjorg unbends her limbs, turning back from the scent and shade of death, eyeing hard instead this household's woman with a gaze as if she knows her troubles well. Torgerd notices not, only turns upon her worry-weighted sons, begging Torkel first and then Bjarne to bear their father up and steady at the table-board.

They lift his withered frame and prop him on his high-seat's pad; and as full a feast is laid as if Thorbjorg and I were fair returning warriors. Yet Herjolf does not hunger much. He mostly sleeps, and when he's not, he coughs, till the mistress Torgerd rises with trembled hands. "I beg you, seeress, set a cast of runes upon this soil."

Full dread weighs on Thorbjorg's step, but she wavers not, calmly prying up to stand before this household. Her arms raise high into the rafters' vault. She presses her lips and from them come the kvads. She sings with an awesome fervor till the rune-twigs tremble in her fists. Then she rolls them hard away across her palms. Still they stagger, tumble, strew, cast about, as they have for days and nights so long. Upon her face, a troubled tinge as ne'er before it has so struck. Yet there it stays, and, some but slowly, the sound about the house grows hushed.

"Foster-daughter," Thorbjorg whispers low, "come by me and throw this cast again—more gently." Gently . . . "If you please."

I look on her, bare a mask to hide my giddy. But swift I bend my brow, then move across the rigid hall. Slowly, heavily, feeling all these watchers hiding low beneath the hanging struts, tucked away into the long-hall's gloom, gnawing first upon their lips and then upon their fingers, just as the dragon-beasts anxious-carved above their heads, gnawing jaws upon their twining tails.

I kneel to gather the scattered runes into my hands. When I take them up, I feel them frigid. Cold upon the mistress' touch. Yet in my own comes a swift and sudden vigor. A livening. A quickening. Some subtle shake as they begin to thaw. Then, slow, a heat, till soon I can barely stand their burning. Then, all at once, I let them drop. Slowly, slowly the rune-twigs tumble.

Thorbjorg eyes as if they drift down from some mighty height. As well they must—from Odin's very grasping. Yet I can see them well enough. In truth, I need no runes to tell this cast's prediction. Bare it is, and written all around. Yet, all about, eyes gape, wonder-gasping at the fall.

I let her try: Thorbjorg bending, stretching out her palms above their pattern. She sudden shakes, and soon from out her lips come cryptic lisps mumbled forth as somewhat meanings. Meanings? Nay! As ever, her voice seems wandered off and sounding odd. Her lips some tremble, then one tucks hard between her craggy teeth. So I know, though Thorbjorg dares not tell it out—she cannot call this cast aloud.

I draw up close, for I can bear no more to watch the mistress fumble. I drop upon my knees and set to stretch my hand above, guiding hers as, long ago, she guided mine. Oh, her chill some warms as our hands there hover, drifting over the rune-twig's lore; she seeming to sense again as I soft-guide her sight within my own. Then her lips whisper, then mumble, bearing slowly back some strength. And though this time her words are coarse, they are closer to the rune-truth's meaning.

"Upon a sharp'ning sword, hard cast! Uruz—the sacrificial beast. The runes of blood flowing. A journey—rhythm of the soul. Cold. Far off. The empty space is filled with bearing. Odin's runes—life and death come quick, retreat, and then are gone."

Strange, when after all is done comes silence, then slowly, rumbles from around the house. The call is crude but clear enough—the master soon will perish. 'Tis only time to bide, and naught that any all can do.

That eve, when the feast is solemn finished, Mistress Thorbjorg bolsters Herjolf back upon his sleeping bench, then gestures me to bring her sack of cures. I bend beside her as she raises it up and draws such clutch of herbs as once my pity-mother plucked from off the Tofafjord dews. Thorbjorg takes them gravely and hangs them round the chieftain's cot, then takes her runestick—the ancient rowan etched with cuts and its crystal flashing. She raises it slowly first, then firmly lays it down—there, upon the man's hot form. Through the night the stone glows soft as Thorbjorg sings out chants and tales, calling lowly forth the fight of gods. Then, slowly rising, the sounding clash of Thor's hammer striking hard against the ancient frost-giant foe—

such heated battle cries which have ne'er yet wrung upon the plain at Ragnarok, yet soon enough will spill the gods' rich blood and open up the mighty gates of fair Valhalla.

Thorbjorg sings to spur Herjolf with such bitter battle, and her brittle breath rises against the hearth fire's smoke and drifts as the slightest fume ascends through the roof's gape-hole into brutal darkness. Yet I know no rally's cry to turn this fortune's fashion. Not one jot of hope or any of the mistress' dull entreaty will change the course of the Norns' fair weave, nor cast more than a comfort's useless sigh.

I know, yet watch and listen as Herjolf's kindred wait around the house—Mistress Torgerd ever bearing close, her hand about her husband's fevered forebrow; Torkel situated fast above, casting death's dark, hungry shadow; and Bjarne gnawing, useless, on his ragged palms. So it seems; yet, in time, even they each fall asleep, till only I and Thorbjorg tend this death's dark journey.

"It will not be long, old friend. Not long. I sense the Norns weave tightly."

"Thorbjorg," comes Herjolf's rumbled voice, and his hand, outstretched to hold my mistress' own. "I would have liked," he croaks, "to see Valhalla—to scent the mighty roasting boar—the Yule log burning nightly. To share such wit as would win a warrior's pride—waiting, rare, to fight at Ragnarok, the proudest-ever battle . . ."

"I know it well," the mistress caws.

"Yet this bed of straw is not a warrior's cot. 'Tis a coward's couch—a weakling's feeble bier." Then he gasps and coughs and sharply clutches on Thorbjorg's arm. "In my youth—my battle mail thrice cut, my sword once cleaved, yet still I fought. . . ."

"Oft I heard my husband tell it round our own hearth fire."

"But a little longer," Herjolf begs, "enough to sense the springtime's thaw—then to go to sea—to fight the Midgard serpent. Or even till the Yule—to feast upon that season's boar . . ." He spits a watery gob, which sticks upon his throat like a choking shroud. "Do not let me die. Not upon the wasting straw!"

My mistress listens, her poise some quaking. "It is not for me, old friend, to turn the weaving of the Norns."

Herjolf heavy-bends his head. His breathing rattles with its stale death-note. "Seeress, tell me truly—only those who die upon the sword—"

He retches as the mistress answers: "—do dwell in fair Valhalla."

Their eyes fall deep across the darkness, as if death itself lies there upon a bier. Yet slowly then does Herjolf's vision lift, and Thorbjorg's follows toward where are hung his age-worn battle belt and sword and dagger upon a dusty peg.

Weary-weak, Herjolf's hands reach out. Thorbjorg pauses but an instant before she rises up, then hands them down. Heavy more of import than of heft, the leather there is brittle to be broke, the metal almost crumbling in their fingers. Still they clutch each precious bit, staying for a time entwined, two hands upon one tarnished, bronze-bound hilt.

No words are then but the fire's flick—that very last while still the embers smolder. Thorbjorg begs me help her raise the chieftain up. For all his fragile frailty, Herjolf is some heavy as we together stand him steady on his limbs. Then in his Viking armor we dress him swiftly. With a gasp and glee, Herjolf straightens fair and fine, seeming even better, almost comely in the health of youth's lost shadow. But only for an instant. With eyes set hard upon the mistress' glance, he gives a nod. We let him loose. He poises on a breath, then slowly teeter-topples. He falls then, happy last, upon his sword.

The night beyond passes slowly, while outside grows grim and sharp with frost. Still we have much to do to wrest from this grisly act all unseemly evidence. Says the mistress, "Come the dawn, the household will awake to find their master laid with certain dignity."

Dignity, cold and dead beside his sword. With the morning, the blood lies old and crusted on the blade.

"Nay, my husband!" Torgerd bursts, full-bitter at the sight.

"Yet he had no shameful straw death," says my mistress as the widowed woman falls on her husband's wound. "He longed only to die upon a stroke." Then, leaning weighty on her narwhal staff, Thorbjorg hammers thrice, tracing a circle with its tip. Spitting in its pounded dust, she etches within the scribe a rune.

"Death's mark." Torkel Herjolfsson bends above the grubby scratch. "My father will yet have his want. Praise be unto Thor." He cries, "Look fair upon the Norns! Herjolf Bardsson will rise mighty to Valhalla!"

THORBJORG

EVERYTHING DIES. It is the past. It is the future. Slipping slowly toward a rot, turned and tossed, swept upon the winds. So I mourn for Herjolf some, but I cannot sorrow. There is no death in death itself. Only for those left behind upon their grief, who must cross the paths the passed one walked—but for a time.

So. Yet, more and more these days, around me there's the smell of death. None note it much. None about but I. The empty echo—the restive still, such as on a ruined habitation: smoke-charred beams, boulders caked in ice, withered grasses set between such cracks, and a pathway overgrown, near full-erased where once it had been well traveled. Nay, in this death I walk. I wake and stand, though sterile is the morning's dew. And move about, an empty husk myself, dried and blown and caught upon this ruin's crags.

What is to come. What lingers close. What these others all about me still cannot fathom. Yet ever it will come—as they to me, begging for some lean, uncertain tidings. I tell them what I may—what little well I can. But the murk is thick. My master's voice has grown quite still.

Even as I reach above the runes, the thrill of life is seeping from me. I feel it as a sucking rush draining quickly out my fingers. I cannot stop this tide. Yet their eyes—upon me ope'd as if my touch could bring the healing flame—glowing brightly, reflected on me from their cheeks, sensing not this is the fire's final embers.

Sometimes there's a glimmer in the dark—and the god's thumb reaching—brilliant once, though now barely perceived. And a scent— such a scent—strange and thick with the sweetness of a rotting. Such as I knew it once—upon a distant market—where? Well now I remember, and somewhat how that scent was termed—by foreign names, fitting crudely on the tongue. One was frankincense . . . another myrrh.

BIBRAU

SO THE EARTH is cut, hard-bitten though the soil is, and Herjolf set within with all his arms, his shield, gilded metals, feasting foods, his slaughtered horse, and five thralls slain to serve his death-bound journey. 'Tis a proper Viking's burial, with even a wind-tossed skiff which lost its mast upon a storm, now scrubbed and patched and carved to lend Herjolf his bier.

The procession lingers on that windswept slope. My feet grow cold for standing still and listening dully. Yet, as I silent-mock such speechy praise and fond-remarked bemusings, there again I see the boy.

He is among the mourners in the middle of the soppy crowd. Each time I look, he slips away, yet somehow stays his bearing—always at the shadow of my sight, digging in as a bit of cutting dust. And on his face, that certain bold demeanor: such a look of blatant loathing as I've often held myself.

There again, I find him at the funeral feast among its mighty toasts to Thor's and Odin's wisdom. Among such boiled meats of pigs and goats and horses, the boy sits some far off yet near enough that I can see him fully. From my place, bare and clinging on the edge of the bond-thralls' bench, I gape until I sudden realize why I know his glower. At the hollow of his neck, a sharp-etched blot—a blood-mark mars the thin, pale skin. So I know him well enough for the boy I would once, long ago, have murdered.

Even then he stares at me, such wild malice in his sight, almost as a whetted finger reaching out to scratch. I turn my head and tear into my horseflesh—hungry from such eyes, like breath, boring, reaching, hissing. Never has another dared! Yet he sits quite still, full-quiet at his distance. Though his eyes keen sorely. Oh, I cannot bear such sight! I charge up then and race into the chill, black evening.

There to stare upon the stars and let their frigid distance cool me, glowing with their hard, white frost while, like the curtains of Frigga's gown, the aurora floats across the moon. Slowly I come to calm with the icy touch of wind across my fevered forehead. Yet, sudden, soft, a new-bound footstep sounds behind.

"So," he says, "you recall me now."

Such a churlish voice. I turn to glare. The boy stands before me with a mead-horn in his fist. His breath smells thick with guzzled drink. He should be afraid, yet he laughs a little. "*Changeling* . . . you have always hated well that sound. Yet what better word would you have me use—*Bibrau*?"

I bear my hand up hard to slap. He grabs my wrist, surprising strong about his grasp. "You think I know only your name? I know much more of you," he scoffs, slugging down a bit of drink—so unmasterful at that skill, I nearly laugh upon the gesture. But instead I curl my lip, then take my chance and rip his grip away. His mead sloshes up and splatter-stings his brazen eyes. Then I whirl and strike him firmly.

"Bibrau"—he catches my arm—"Bibrau, Bibrau"—and holds it. A drop of blood comes from his mouth. "I've known your blows before. You did not kill me then. Why should you do it now?" He takes my hands—both of them in his, smelling sick with drink—and brushes the blood from his lip with my bare knuckles.

"I am Gudmund," his stinking breath steaming on my fingers, "Torkel Herjolfsson's firstborn son. It is my grandfather's death-feast you have dined upon. I saw you standing well beside your mistress through Herjolf's ebbing eve. Upon the midnight, most like you stood beside her at his death. Merry, girl, perhaps you helped her thrust the very blade? It is whispered round, and would not be hard to fathom. Now all wonder where his fated soul will walk. Three heavy stones placed upon his feet, yet it will not be weight enough to keep him still. Just so, it was not his right or proper want to die, but a fear of Hel.

Better he had fought to live and fought to die! Though my father says, Be glad the witch kept Herjolf from straw death's taint. I say, Better wise to eye the imp beside the seeress—for I watched you toss the runes which cast his fate, and I swear I saw you twist them up and break them."

So he dares to speak. I would shrill upon his talk, but will not give him satisfaction with my sounds. Instead, I watch him suck the dregs of the mead-horn's droplets. "To Herjolf Bardsson," he drunken-lauds, "my blood-born kin and brave grandsire!" As he swallows all the drippings down, I lick from off my hand his blood.

He watches me contemptuously. "Try to taunt me. I am not afraid. I've seen the worst that you can do." He smiles then, as he had not dared so many years before. Yet I see just then the moonshine glint upon the twisted grizzle not yet risen full upon his chin. So I think, This boy is bare become a man—and then I know he's seen nothing yet of me.

For some days more, this Gudmund casts about his gaze, like a sword he is not yet strong enough to handle. Most he tries to mock me, to banter some and saunter, jaunt about. When it pleases, I find it sly to simply slip before his eye. And when I do, Gudmund feigns to hurl up bitter rocks, which I know, despite his ire, will ever miss their aim.

We stay at Torkel Herjolfsson's homestead three more weeks, till Yule. Each night, as Thor's feast-log burns, the household crowds full up with guests, mostly freemen and winter-stranded merchants bound to curry favor with Herjolfsnaes' latest chief. Torkel treats with them all, fêtes most, and turns away but none, till I grow sick and tired of the fawning lot, so slip from the pander's noise to sleep within the cattle-comfort of the byre.

Into the dark beyond the longhouse's glow, I step where there is no moon. The snow is dense as the wind has blown it. The path beneath my feet is lost but for a knee-deep stretch through which I slog but slow. Yet not too long and the door hinge creaks behind me. By the rhythm of the breath, I know it is Gudmund.

Well, if he likes, let him follow on his fate. Just so, I slack my pace and wait as I hear him come. Bare but he does 'tempt this time to clutch the edging of my woolen cloak. I do not fight. Nay, I bear his tug as he dares to turn me round.

Step-thick in the snow, Gudmund takes my forearms. "Bibrau," comes his awkward grunt, "are you far above our petty little feast, or simply dull upon our bond-thralls' winter banter?" I stare. "Perhaps you'd better soothe to hear the latest freemen's gossip? They say Leif's ships have returned." I dull my eyes, as if such tatty bit of buzz should tempt me. "Just before the winter snows, after two full seasons feasting well upon Tryggvason's court, returned with riches fair and fine reports, for they say Leif's found lands thick with grapes and wild wheat. So he's claimed them well and called the place Vinland. . . ."

Then a shadow casts across this Gudmund's brow. "Nay, such lands as these should be my uncle Bjarne's, for he found them first and should have claimed them. But now we stand bound e'er again to Leif, as all this Greenland's bound upon his father." Gudmund grumbles low, almost to himself.

"Nay!" he balks. "Never will you know such grief, nor such brave and bold adventure. Forever you will be a thrall, though you act as if you're something better. Apprentice to the seeress? She will not live long. When she's gone, your fate will be full wrought to scrub and scrap and bend upon your master's knee, while I will be far off upon my longship, to make my claim and be a chieftain just as Leif or Eirik Raude or my own grandsire."

So he says, his eyes bright with vicious boast, as I turn my face indifferent. Then he spins around. Swift and close, I feel his hands upon my limbs, hard, strong and strange insistent. " 'Twill be me someday— with a fjord named upon myself and a shipload full of thralls like you to mop my decks and warm my bedstraw."

I watch the air of his breath-steam rising. Just then a strangeish tingle comes upon his gropes—awkward though they are, as his hands some shake while he lays them close about my collar. I know but well a spell to break his grasping with a single stroke, yet I do not ply it. Nay—so close I feel his heat upon my neck's bare skin, and his boy's heart beating fast against his pigeon chest. Even through the cloaks and linens—frail and narrow—it is there as he wets his lips and bends a little close. Odd at first, the way he twines his hands about my shoulders. And the sudden beating of my own heart. Sudden, too, my fylgie's sounds.

Oh, his little tinkling! His rancid little chirp. I know full well this kind of music. My fylgie's come at last to guide me in this sport.

This Gudmund barely counts for a pity-child! Still I think, indeed, it will be a merry bit of fun, with my blood-dust dried and ripe and ready to ply my practice. Oh, I listen well to Gudmund's drifting words coming hot and close about my winter hearing, while the wind full-howls across his dead grandsire's homefield rocks, and my fylgie's jingles twine upon their pitches. When I hear full-clear my fylgie's mirth—so and such, his rabid, brutal teasing—I know just what to do. With Gudmund near about my cheek, I reach my teeth and bite him hard about his lip.

'Tis a juicy hunk from which he bleeds, fat and pink, as he thrusts me off—hurls me hard into the snow so it crushes and crunches beneath my wadmaled back and my woolen sheathing. There I lie, listening to its subtle squeak and to my fylgie's shrilling glee as this man-child's eyes change from strange, clouded desire to raging horror.

I squirm upon my feet, tucking well my cloak around me. For a breath, I think to run and let him chase. But my fylgie coaxes me to linger soft, slowly, through the snow. So I ease my pace. And Gudmund stares. Never have I seen such eyes—so strained. But he does not come. Nay, instead he shouts hard across my path, "Go, then, Bibrau—proud as ever was your mother. Once, before she bore you, well they say, she was full proud as you, and fairer! Yet now she's damaged, wasted flesh. So will you be yourself one day!"

I do not turn, for my mother's pride is no concern of mine. But Gudmund hisses louder, even in a whisper, "And I know full well what man made her that way!"

The Christ
Has Come

KATLA

SOME WEEKS PAST the hour of Herjolf's dying, Thorbjorg returns with my daughter well beside—fair comely, with a strut upon her step and no seeming sorrow for what she must have witnessed. The mistress notes it not, for she is strangely changed herself, lost of all her tranquil calm. By the dawn, Thorbjorg masks her dread with a quiet, caring gesture, while night upon each night, she anxious stokes the fire's flame and spreads upon the earth her wisdom-runes.

When Arngunn begs her, "Come to sleep," the mistress lies awake and fretting; or if she finds some slumber, it is fitful, often waked by dreams. Then she cries out to the shadows, "Nay! Get back! Get ye away!" One night I go to her. There she sits with all her midnight shaking, her back a-quiver, arms wrapped hard around her heaving chest, face some glittered in the embers' glow of tears. I bend to her gently, try to take her to my broken breast to comfort, as so long ago she had much done for me. Yet, barely in my arms, she shudder-trembles, pressing me fast back.

"Katla, nay. Get to bed with you." Then, begging Arngunn, "Go and fetch my foster-daughter to me."

Arngunn raises up my girl from where she huddles in the homestead's gloom. Bibrau weary-wakes to stumble-sit beside her. She bides the mistress well, tucking knives of silver to protect amidst the bedding moss, turning Thorbjorg's shoes about so the nightmare will trip when next it tries to mount her sleep bench. Then my daughter sits and watches. But keenly, just as Thorbjorg snores, the girl turns her back and gathers up the mistress' runes.

I take no comfort in my daughter's feigned heeding. Yet none
about do note it odd; so I think perhaps 'tis I. She pricks in me such
harsh, confused feeling. In my daughter's gaze, I see a callous, baleful
glow. Such as it is, I close my eyes upon dark vision, and by daylight
stretch my mind toward thoughtless, needful things: to setting hot the
fire, then a pot of water and some salted meat to boil, humming softly
to myself till I find some soothing in an ancient rhythm, a solemn
music my mother used to cherish. "*Ave Maria . . .*" goes the tune.

Soon the winds about the household blow with the scent of
spring, and old Thorhall belly-roars across the greening cliffs. "Come
again at last! And this time with no plague twins clung—I swear it so
by Thunder-Hurler Thor!"

His sounds ring off the icebergs' edges. Down the sun-drenched,
muddy bank, we slide and stumble o'er the snow-caked rocks to watch
his skiff slip closer to the strand. Slowly Thorbjorg follows along the
homefield slope, my daughter posing as a crutch far better than the
narwhal Ossur once gave. The men rush down to pull the hunter up.
Thorhall takes such hands to aid his wobbled sea-gait, yet beneath his
cheer I see his look is worried. He catches quick on Thorbjorg's glance
as he steady-steps some close upon the sea-bank's rise.

He reaches out to take the mistress' hands. For a time they hold
but firm and roughly. Then he spies me out, "Katla Christian,"
whistling, "there upon that rock! I bear you news."

"What news," I stammer, "good or ill?"

"Good for you," he gruffs, "if for no other."

"I hold no hope to hear of Ossur."

"Fool girl." He squints, the sun snatching round his wrinkle-
scratched eye corners. "Such news as yours I've run this icy sea to
tell!"

"Then say it out." I come up closer. "Is my Ossur home?"

"Aye, that—and well and borne upon the court quite brightly.
None about would have thought it such, yet there he was, and somewhat reckoned fairly. He bids on you a message." Thorhall pauses,
catching queer the mistress' glance. "Says your Ossur this: 'Your
Jesus Christ has come.' "

"Jesus Christ?" I ask, confused.

"Aye. Or, so, his counterpart."

"What Christ is this," I beg, "risen from the dead?"

"Much the same!" Thorhall grumbles. "A smelly priest in heavy robes—a pasty, black-clothed weakling!"

"A priest . . ." So the Christians James and John had ventured—fair!—someday a priest would surely come even to this Greenland . . .

The mistress moves then closer. "How comes this priest?"

"Stowed on Leif Eiriksson's home-come ship by that foul King Tryggvason."

"Tryggvason?"

"Aye, the mighty warrior himself, turned into a mighty sop! So the king claims now the Christian faith, and presses all about to turn aback from our own Norse gods."

"Thorhall, calm," Thorbjorg hushes, though upon her eye I see some woe as we trudge the homefield slope and settle Thorhall to warm beside the low hearth's fire.

Still the great man chafes: "I like it not, Thorbjorg. Says Leif we must heed this priest, for it will do much good for trade. Such as it is, Leif's thought is fair, for now these Christians will not barter with the *infidels,* as they call us. Yet says his father—and I trust his cutting wit—'twill be the last of all our greatness. . . . Nay, even now this priest goes about always with his riffled book, always pointing, shouting 'Sin!' upon the slightest harm."

"A book?" I whisp'. My heartbeat quivers. *Sancte Christe*—as so oft the Christian slaves and even my own mother spoke!—of a book so filled with words for sin and greater prayers for hoping—

". . . Nay, Thorbjorg, I have looked upon that book. 'Tis nothing like your scratches. But a strangled scrawl showing naught but words of punishment for evil."

"What call they evil?" Thorbjorg begs.

"Naught but to fight for right and to go a-viking for goodly gain and to avenge upon a foe! Says this Christ to 'love thy neighbor' and 'do to others as you'd do upon yourself'—sure, sure!—or some such rot. Such talk will fatten us as sheep for slaying. Already I have heard of bloody wars fought for Christ upon the eastern shores of the Baltic Sea. So you see they love their neighbors well."

"Nay," says the mistress, almost to herself.

I try to speak. "Said my mother, Christ was born the Prince of Peace—"

"Peace?" Thorhall charges on. "Peace! Worse, this priest preaches loud for mercy and forgiveness. Forgiveness? So, who's done you wrong should pay the price with but a cheek bared, turned in waiting for a kiss!"

When you're hurt, my mother mumbled as she kissed away some pain of taunt, *you must turn the other cheek, so the Bible often says.*

"And worst, for a sin of murder, this Christian god does damn to Hell—Hell it's called, just as our own Hel's frigid premise, but this Hell of theirs is hot, not cold!"

"Hot?" asks the mistress.

"Aye, hot. What punishment is warmth? What luxury! Let me lie in such a place, as at Thorbjorn Glora's steaming spring-pools—aye! Dunk me in to soak and soothe and wrinkle for all eternity! What Hell is this? No unforgiving torment as to freeze till Ragnarok, which serves such cowards right and does them well."

A fiery Hell, like the mouth of the mountain Katla. Katla, the fire beneath the ice, the burning pain within my breast, my child, from which was took your name.

" 'Tis true!" I cry. "Such a hot and burning, dark and red with fright. My mother said she knew such place, and never would she beg to see it! But the other place is Heaven, with angels dressed in white and singing, crowned about with gold and glow—so my mother told—"

"Katla!" the mistress harsh dismisses me.

Yet Thorhall answers, "Thorbjorg, such—'tis nearly as the priest there calls it."

Thorbjorg eyes me still. "What say the others?"

"Others? Beside this priest, Leif sailed into Eiriksfjord with a shipwrecked chieftain. Out upon the dim-lit brine, seems Leif heard voices on the bergs. So he sent the priest to look beyond the bow. And

there—wide Odin's watch!—stood Thorbjorn Vifilsson, Eirik's ancient ally, with his daughter, Gudrid, who proclaims herself to the
Christian faith, and others of their party, all bound for Greenland but
stranded on an iceberg's wake. Yet, even while they were fixed beneath
its silt-crest brow, this Gudrid sang out, 'Such good fortune comes
proclaimed—a sign for the risen Christ!' "

"Nay," Thorbjorg whispers, "even when their fates had been so
nearly severed?"

"Aye, and no thunder came, nor any storm, nor any single
mishap, till Leif set them safely on our shore. Yet Eirik Raude, though
full-pleased to see this chieftain-friend and daughter, turned eyes upon
the priest but once—pasty-white and cloying as the byre's dust—and
nearly hied him fast and to the brink till this Gudrid's gentle face
and pleading. Nay, she keenly drew him off, for the lady is full comely
and persuading. Yet, Thorbjorg, it is foul, for now all Austerbygd sings
loudly, 'Leif the Lucky!' for their fate. All the while the priest with his
sog-warped book claims such fairest chance in the name of 'Jesus
Christ, the Son of God!' "

Thorbjorg shivers. Again she lays her eye on me, looking keenly
moments long and strange and twisted in the fire's flick. Beneath such
gaze I soon should burst to flame. Yet, in time, the glimmer in her
eye-light softens. She reaches out and strokes the quiver from my
cheek, noting well my tears held back, my lips pulled thin and cracked
with harshest bearing.

"Katla, would you see this man—this priest—this Christian?"

"I would," in the faintest little whisper. "My mother would have
wished it."

Thorbjorg spies far off, then to Thorhall, then strangely dark on
Kol, then dismal on my daughter's ever-gloom. "Yes." She shakes her
head, and now is kindly as she cups my chin. "So you would. Then I
would go to see him, too."

Three days hence, we hoist our sails to Eiriksfjord. With the ice still
thick, 'tis three days more till we touch upon that shore. Yet, on that
last, I stumble out and feel my steps fall, ill and shaky. I gird my

strength, for there seems an earthly glow about the air. There upon the slope: a milling crowd. From among the clumps of thralls and freemen, I hear intoning, "*Pater noster, qui es in caelis, sanctificetur nomen tuum.* Our Father who art in Heaven: hallowed be thy name. So Lord Jesus Christ taught us these words to pray."

"Jesus Christ," I whisp' into my fingers. I take some steps, but Thorhall holds me back.

"*. . . Adveniat regnum tuum. Fiat voluntas tua . . .*"

I look on him, then upon the mistress. Thorbjorg's face is pale as she gazes far beyond, up Brattahlid's stark, spring-bare hill.

"Woman, would you go there?" Thorhall asks me.

"I would—to hear this Christian's words."

"Yet, when you do," he cautions, "remember well who once had healed you—wrapped your wounds and shielded you from terror."

I nod, then pull from Thorhall gently. I turn and, almost at once, begin to stride. And, striding, find I cannot help myself but run— quickly, tripping, falling on my skirts. I gather them up. My legs are heavy from the sail, yet my judgment draws me, breathless. I am panting now, sweat oozing up between my breasts as I reach the flat where the crowd is gathered. And there, crashing through as if I part the waters, sudden I am fallen to my knees. "Forgive me, Father . . ." I sink before the long black robe. ". . . for I have sinned—"

"What is this?" The crowd is hushed as this God's man bends before me, the single symbol of his faith dangling before my eyes. "Woman, where did you learn such phrase?"

"Father," I stammer, "I have sinned. I am no true Christian. I am foul, tainted, yet so long beheld my mother's prayers. Long ago I had listened to their angels' music, yet come upon this Greenland, lost. Then, from some Christians—slaves—both dead upon the plague twins' sweep . . . And now you've come, when never had I thought I would ever hear them sung aloud again!"

The words spill from my lips as if they had waited all these years to flood. So this man, this stranger—priest—looks on me with such a sudden praising. Within his eyes, a warming glow, and lips, small and gentle as a babe's. In my gaining courage, I fumble in my skirts to find my mother's rosary with its worn and wasted cross. I hold it up and lean my head upon my bead-clutched fingers. There the priest-man lays his hands upon me. He whispers, "Tell me, woman, what is your name?"

"She is Katla," someone answers from the crowd.

I look up, frightened to see who should speak my name so boldly. There, just above my face—somewhat older now—yet gentle is his smile—

"Katla." Ossur bends upon the soggy earth, taking both my cheeks into his fingers—

The God's man begs, "Ossur, you know this woman?"

"Aye." He stands aback. "She was bonded once to Einar's house. But there she was much ill-treated, and now she serves the seeress Thorbjorg. Father, you must give her up to Jesus Christ, for in her heart she has always been a Christian, even long before I or any of us knew the call."

THORBJORG

'TIS A SIGHT from out my vision. She bending on that ground, and that long, black robe with those pale hands dangling. Thin and frail as a withered corpse, and yet they move.

A single man upon a hill—is this what your sight has shown? Alfather—this, which could stop your breath? Which could turn such arch upon your ancient wisdom's brow?

Nay, in his tattered robe, bare a sheath to cover well his form. Yet those hands—reaching out and gathering around him—all that crowd, to hear such words. Strange sounds, so raw in shape as to bear no weight or meaning. "Set not yourself above your brother. . . . For-give his every trespass. . . ." Can these words so catch? His voice is hollow-strained, strident in its screech, yet it flies across the fjord as a fulmar's caw to strike the distant cliffs. I hear the break of ice even as it clatters down.

Perhaps upon such simple purchase has ever come an end. Already I feel the subtle draining. The circle's drawn, not around my feet nor before your sacrifices, but around that cross—ill cross—so very fragile, yet set against that robe so stark as if to part the wafting of the very seas.

It is the nature of the tide. So strong, and yet each lap upon the beach seems gentle. Is it e'er before a storm, the waters look so meek? I know, when it comes, it will pit and smite and cleave.

Will this, then, be the fateful Ragnarok, the great battle coming soon of wit and brawn? So long have we been promised—when the will of gods will meet the face of evil, with the Fenris-Wolf caught hard upon the Norse god's throat, and Loki leading fire, and even Thor unmatched against the vicious grip of the Midgard snake.

Yet now that face—that evil—bears a shape: now long, white whiskers. And long, black robes. And leaves—white leaves falling down from long, thin fingers.

What kind of swords and teeth are these?

BIBRAU

AND NOW she is a Christian. Ha! A Christian. So it seems to her right to leave her chores, her kindly mistress, and even me, her very blood, shivering on this wretched shore. So to go—to trust this faith with which she has ever been enamored, but of which she knows not more than fourteen words.

Such a thing I would think she could not fathom. Yet she does it, openly, there before the crowd. And perhaps it seems not strange that she should wish to follow such a pale, pathetic god. A god not god but mortal, a dead man of no might, lying limp, pined, and pinned upon that cross—an ill-made spindle set upon its spine.

Just the same, she runs to it. Runs! Up away, while we, all panting, linger. And after some short time, she bare returns, slogging, drenched, along the bank at the center of those Christians gathered.

And all the mistress thinks to do is lean upon her gilded cane. "I claim only the sweat from off her back. I cannot now nor ever own her heart's true leaning." So she breathless answers as my mother, looking pale and stricken, shivers from the icy water's dunk, her footsteps slow, her skirts pressing flat the new spring grasses. But on her face—such a look of gladness! With Ossur's arms ringing about her, and the priest-man's hand gripping at her wrists—drawing her onward as toward some bridal bower or a sacrificial flame. And a one whose voice raises up, *"Ave Maria, gratia plena,"* my mother's paltry words sung ever sly and low in the byre's corner—only now they clang out loud.

So, and she should go. Go! That night she stays mostly among them: there beside the shipwrecked Gudrid, who teaches my mother songs. So thin and frail as a raven's screeching, their Christian music scrapes across the air, breaking the dizzy riot of the feast and drinking, the reckless dance and games and wrestling fights.

Ah, but I am glad enough to see her off. I turn my tastes to Eirik's board, sitting beside the mistress, watching these fool Christians refuse to eat. Nay, in that red-glowed night, when such fine roast meat is set before them, their priest, the foul-man, shaking, takes his book and points: "Such horse's flesh is pagan taint. No Christian ever should eat of it again!"

"Why?" asks even Leif among these newborn Christians. " 'Tis ne'er but the finest meat upon my father's table—"

Says the priest, " 'Tis set with pagan rites. Leif, heard you not how your father slipped profane words of sacrifice upon its blood?"

Barks Eirik Raude, " 'Tis sanctified to Odin, as is proper. Astride such a horse will Old One-Eye race across Valhalla's fields to strike upon that final battle."

"Battle?" argues the priest. "The Son of God ever preached against it."

Eirik challenges, "Would your Christ then please to sit astride an ass and wait for death before a sword?"

"Well enough, for he would turn the other cheek. So the greater fight is ever won."

"Turn the other cheek? I would believe, for there he rests upon that cross—already dead, and someone surely put him there."

Snickers spew about the feast-hall then as some other Christians near to listen. Upon that very spot even my mother dares to shy her cheek, clutching up with Ossur at her side and that Gudrid by her ear.

"Aye." The priest nods, his face some crooked. "Indeed, someone— a brutal beast. Such, that beast was Man! So I tell you, Christ came to preach to Man's more gentle nature."

"Gentle, so you say?" Eirik scoffs. "Then here's a beast, more gentle for it's cooked." Again raucous guffaws, while the priest turns red and my mother blanches and cowers.

"I say no Christian e'er should eat of it!" cries the priest. "Even you, good Leif, to show them Jesus' way, eat it not! You pledged your faith at Tryggvason's table. Or would your word and deed upon that night be feigned?"

"Feigned? Nay, know you well, good priest. Yet here's my father—"

"Your father? Would you honor Christ and Norway's king, or play your blood-sore's pagan heresy? Know well whose promises both bind and aid you—the king's here now upon this earth, and God's in his true Heaven well above."

"Indeed," Thjoldhilde ventures close beside her husband's ear. "Eirik, we sent Leif off to bring us trade. This man is brought and is wont to aid us."

Leif whispers, "Father, pray, be still. Quell your talk, for naught will come to us if we're not Christian. The priest here is our guest—"

"Guest?" Eirik murmurs. "Yours, indeed, not mine. Priest, you come upon my shores unwanted. For my son alone, I treat you with some patience. Yet I am no Christian and will have none, not upon my table-board nor hall nor e'er about my byre. Your god with his chary weak insults my gods. Your frame betrays my fashion. And your lips' dull speech knows naught of prudence's kind. But I'll give you sound advice—some fine from One-Eyed Odin's word. He says—and heed, for I know how well you like to quote—'The unwise man among strangers, be he spare of speech; none knows he is naught of worth, but that he open up his mouth too much.' "

At that, a roll of laughter curls about the crowd. Even I shy back my lips into an almost snicker. Eirik Raude catches quick my humor. Quaking some, he snatches away the greasy plate. "Even this dull thrall knows the worth of what you waste. Go hungry, fool, and all who follow after. This fine meat is fit enough for proper, war-ripe chiefs; and there is nothing else to eat this eve upon this board." There he sets it down before me—this fine, fat meat, steaming up with scent—far from the sour priest's touch and before no other. I look on it—the beast lying thick and juicy, smelling savory and somehow sweet. So I take the tainted portion and ply my mother's bit as well, and eat till my stomach aches from so rich a feasting.

Such as it is, some few days after, late upon an eve, comes Thorhall to us, straight from Eirik's side, and hot and red with ire. He sits beside the mistress in our rough-hewn booth, heavy on our earth-carved bench. Silent for a time, then he hisses lowly, "I'll do well to cling to the old Norse gods till the Norns tie off their final binds."

"So you should, old friend," my mistress calms in seeming comfort.

"Aye!" Thorhall caws. "And ever heed fair Thunder-Hurler's might. And follow in Old One-Eye's ways!"

"As will I, Thorhall. We are too old for finer mischief."

"Mischief! These gods are fine and have served us well enough. But some about—have you yet heard? Eirik's own mistress, Thjold-hilde's taken to this new faith as none had thought. Nay, turned upon but fast and firmly! And Eirik now is fuming, for she has sought to build a hof—a 'church,' they call it—at Brattahlid itself—a fairish frame of sod and chink and grasses!"

"Nay," protests the mistress.

"True, if she has her wanton way. Though Eirik rails and riots against it, and shunts her paltry shrine far off beyond the homefield's bounds. But already she's set her slaves to gather driftwood from the fjord's edges. Even now they cut tight sod from the hillside's breast. So Thjoldhilde plans to build a sturdy roof, and walls so thick 'even the foehn winds will learn to whisper.' So she says; and in all this, swears she'll not bed with Eirik Raude, never more, till he becomes a Christian, too."

"So says she?" Thorbjorg answers soft, bending down her hand to rough the fires' coals. "What says Eirik?"

"Naught, for Thjoldhilde's loud, shouting from where she mingles among the Christian rabble: 'Husband, perhaps if you'd loved your neighbors and turned the other cheek, we would ne'er be on this distant rock, outlawed from Norway and Iceland both for your hot temper!' "

"Such"—Thorbjorg laughs strangely—"is Thjoldhilde's honest wisdom."

"Wisdom?" Thorhall shakes his head, grimly draining ale from a carved goat's horn. "If true, then a toast to Eirik's beguiling prowess. If not, then to his forcing skill. Yet already I see this crowd of Christians numbers."

Some three more days, and on each, chieftains come to Eiriksfjord. As Eirik's runners spread the news, soon sails fly up to catch the wind. From Siglufjord, Alptafjord, Ketilsfjord, and even Einar's farm, Gardar, one by one, they fill Eirik's port to a gathering near as vast as true midsummer. Though now 'tis icy-crisp upon the dawns, and at nights the murk-cast sky is set alight with burning fires. Above one of these, my mother's god's-man stands just beyond Brattahlid's homefield bound, spitting out his tales of Jesus' woe and torment. About him draw dim-wit thralls and even trifling freemen, hovering near to hear the strange, eternal bane some fiend called Satan threatens will be ours if we refuse to yield.

Yield? To whom? To him! All selflessness and mercy, prancing in his chalk-bare feet and rags as he swears even his own prince Christ was once attired. Rags, indeed, for they are pithy bits of moth-chomped wool. Yet the thralls are thick and ployed with his compassion. Hear they not as he scampers after the chiefs who swiftly fill this shore? Or the jingle beneath his pleated tatters where sure is tucked a bag full with this King Tryggvason's hacked bit-silver?

These others surely must be deaf, for they bide more and oft to his high-pitched shrieking: things of Christ's brute strength, of his arms held high and strong upon that cross, of how he came to death and then was risen triumphant after. Most, my mother stands among that crowd mouth-gaped, her face some lit as if with a sun's quick spark. All the while, my mistress Thorbjorg, fair neglected night upon each dawn, merely sits within our shivered, rough-built booth, her head held hard between her palms.

Nay, she will do nothing, while I meek about at petty bond-girl's chores, stoking up the waning coals, and sleeping close upon her spine when they grow chill. Yet, each dawn, I trip away to the feint and fright of these long-hall's conversations, hearing once even my mother's long-now master, Einar, call the priest as he deserves: a foul, defiant liar. Ah, it pleases me as his son, Torvard, spits bile into the priest's own book. But my mother likes it not. She ever trembles in the long-hall's corner. Nor Thorbjorg, oddly, pale and silent, her knuckles chafing at her narwhal cane's rough jewels.

Till, one dawn, as our embers' smoke casts up a noxious dew, I awake to the sound of strokes as a new ship breaks beyond the vapor. There, above its certain, even rhythm, rides an oarsmen's call, somewhat awkward, high, and strained. I raise my head, for the voice is odd familiar, till I remember suddenly the winter past: it must be Torkel Herjolfsson's offspring Gudmund crying out upon those boards.

I roll awake and stroll down to the sea, where the haze is broke by the first raw slice of sun. Drawing closer, Gudmund's gawky pitch trips low, then screeches high—Gudmund, standing there upon the ship's lean keel, posed for looking hard and fierce, grown some two inches taller since the Yule. Ah, it is a first cool sight—he, near comely now, as some softest whiskers catch the fresh, amiable light, his sharp-drawn chin shimmering spring-gold with those tender bristles.

I sense in me a curious quiver—strange that I should feel it so, as I wait upon the beach, my face set cold as ice. Thralls loiter till the sea-boards come to settle on the shore. Then they bear upon the knarr, hauling ropes and rig, bounding out the walking plank, while this young man's eyes slide across the throng.

Sure, I think, he sees me now. Once, twice, three times Gudmund turns about his gazing. Yet his glance trips dully past—straight-blind, without the slightest blink!—as he hurries down the sea-dripped timber, fast over the fjord's rocks. Hard-bent he is, turning not a peek as he trips to his father's beck, sharp upon his heels, then into Brattahlid's dank, smoky hall.

Oh, I am furious on this slight! I follow quickly close behind, hiding beneath the shadowed roof beams while already freemen chew fat-meat and the priest-man shrieks above them all, "King Tryggvason hails ye! Implores ye! Beseeches ye! Follow after and forsake your misbeliefs, your faulty gods and your ways of sin, and step upon the path of the one true Saviour!"

There Gudmund sits beside his very father, looking fair misplaced and ill-at-ease.

Eirik barks, "Will you turn so easily against our gods?"

Gudmund kicks with his boot till dust drifts upon a cloud. Then he bends some low to pluck rot-straw off the earth-wrought bench.

"Our gods?" Mistress Thjoldhilde quips. "Husband, pray indeed! Do you bend yourself before your handy idols? Do you careful tend our homestead hof, making sacrifices up to Thor as Einar does, or Herjolf Bardsson before his death?"

As I watch, Gudmund tears brown bits and tosses them roughly, though he bends his glance and I see his aim: he eyes to strike upon my knees.

"Nay!" cries Thjoldhilde. "I say deceitful faith for you is fine. Yet, for me, I see not much so changed if we are Christians."

Torkel Herjolfsson turns upon this pitch. "My father would have stood with Eirik," he utters firmly. "Ne'er would Herjolf have prayed upon some foreign god."

"No foreign god," yelps the word-thick priest, "but the one true God and Saviour!"

Pressing close, I reach to tug on Gudmund's jerkin. His breath catches quick, broadening his narrow back, his hand hard on mine, as if to stay before a fall.

Just then Gudmund's father raises a heavy eye. Barely has he caught my sight but I slip again into the shadows. Yet Torkel turns and whispers nearly loud and somewhat crossly. I hear not what, only see Gudmund set heavy-footed across the hall. There he sits sullenly beside his foster-father, Thorbjorn Glora. Oh, and then I know full well why Gudmund has ignored me: 'tis consciously and curtly, and on his household's 'count. I feel my raging rise—

"Leif," Eirik growls, "your priest's a swindler. Says he now he'll only borrow one small spit of land—oh! to build his hof—and perhaps a fouled slave girl. . . . Yet see already how his perversion sunders? Even he goads my wife—your very mother—for all her woman's favor. Yet wait! He rides us like a 'mare. Soon he'll steal off all our strength! Vassal of Tryggvason, next he'll beg some bit of ivory for his cross, then some ells of cloth for making robes, and very soon our swords, as I have heard, to 'batter into plowshares. . . .' "

I creep some harsh and quickly among the waiting women and the work-dull thralls. Crouching low, I make my way through the sleeping eaves and slither close to where Gudmund, stooping, broods. Oh, I can see him well enough, dark and hard and well-incensed. Yet, too, my mistress stands some near, listening to this spit and fuss of Christians. And her lips, somehow odd and cracked, a bit of flesh held hard and white beneath her shredding teeth. She eyes me not, yet her hands shake roughly, her knobby fingers red and clutched about her sack of runes.

Of a sudden, she tears her bag of knots and flings them wide across the table-board. The room quick hushes. Even I myself loose my venture's grip and hold quite still. Then the mistress, though she turns not an inch her head, speaks calmly: "Bibrau, come. Study how the truth here lies."

I scuttle fast from out the shadows, quick-consumed by all those freemen's startled stares; most of all by Gudmund's wonder as I bend before those scattered boughs. I lay my hand and feel them, hot and tingling—oh, as they've not felt in all my mistress' days of mock and brood, ever since that Althing meet so many jaunts ago. Strange it seems, and full of bare misgiving. Yet I feel such heat lying still beneath my palms.

Even as I do, sudden the priest-man's mewling, "Nay! Shove her off. Turn against the demon!" His voice, high-pitched and lacking substance, flies sanctimoniously across the hall. "Satan's soothsayer. I warn you, not this child nor this witch is the true prophetess of God!"

Some others wary-laugh, and even I purse my lip corners tight to squelch my scorn. Yet, as I set my hand again, this priest-man bends his fingers and, with a sudden pitch of his dainty, useless weight, tips the hefty balance of the board.

Oh, it falls with a clattered crash from its standing stilts. "No!" my mistress gasps as the rune-twigs spread across the pounded floor.

I stare. The twigs glare up at me, lying split and thrown asunder. Some few have landed in the fire and are quick consumed by the growing flames. There they snap, sizzle, flare, then wisp to white and fly, drifting, wild, dwindling, such as men's true fates, all strewn.

"Foster-daughter, gather them," the mistress Thorbjorg hisses as all their futures shrivel to an ember's spark. So I bend, but cannot stop some strange-demanded trembling in my fingers. As I reach—I cannot help myself—I turn an eye upon the rune-twigs' tenor: there in the twisting lies my own fortune's fate, wrapped and twined among their fall.

There it burns, and I see it crumbling, ashen, blacked. So those others see my fright. Some Christians dare call, "Lord Jesus Christ!" while others mumble one of Odin's names, "Alfather!" "Old One-Eye!" "Hangagod!" "Ganglari!"

I cannot help myself; I turn my terror to Thorbjorg.

Just then, I hear my fylgie howl.

Oh, it turns me cold. I whirl about, but cannot see the imp among the gathering, or find him in the smoke or fire. But I feel him—oh!—fierce and flying. Well, I know he wants me to cry out loud—to shriek and curse him rightly for what he's, taunting, shown them. But I will not do it. No. Not among these watchers. Instead, I turn and hie upon my heel, out into the broody cold.

'Tis near to wasting night, for hours pass far swifter in this early springtime. Already beyond the byre's bleat are bonfires' brightening flames. There my mother's crouched among her Christians, wan and chanting beside the dirt-bit scar where they dig to house their Christian bane. I turn upon my heel and flee them, fair, far, quick, up across the sheep-bit fields and beyond their screeching's reach. Out to where no freeman walks or talks of Christ or God or even Thor or Odin. Not any of them. Out to where the soft-skinned earth turns hard and coarse and hurtful, where the cold is fixed, the fast stones gripped in a godless clutch, where I can pitch my bone-blown screech up to the frost-giants' cold, sharp ears.

Across the mottled sod I lurch, over the ragged carpet of dusk-dull dandelions and gaudy reddish tufts, crushing buttercups beneath the pleasure of my rage, tripping at the willow binds which cling between the earth-nipped frost, till with a fighting hand I stoop and claw my way up the rocky steep and come upon this Greenland's hovered, icy brow.

Oh, it glows and towers in the frigid night. When I've lumbered far enough so no more fools might hear, I pull my bone flute from where it burns inside my apron and, gasping, rasp a panted breath so I might breathe my scream.

But a footfall. Turning, a shadow's black against the fjord's glow. My fylgie, imp! He dares press close—coming slower—reaching—one more reel! Meaning yet to plague me more. Yet I will not let him—not this time, after what he's done—made of me a fool and raging wild there before that piddling crowd—before the Christian foul-man, most of all. Oh, I will catch him up, ply him madly, till I know full well why he played me for his taunt and, too, what dire lore he meant to bend upon the rune-twigs' fall.

So I listen for his footstep, fixed, my bone flute stuck upon my lips, its dryness clinging to my vapor. Too, the shadow stills. Then takes a breath.

"You can make noise. Ah, I had always wondered."

It is not the fylgie. I stuff my bone into my apron's pouch, but the shadow steps now close and tries to draw it from me. I tear away. The shadow struggles well to catch. "Perhaps I should have stayed beside the rocks and waited, quiet, just to know your sort of sound. But, then, Bibrau, I can well guess: your voice would have been a howl."

I whip around. Gudmund stands upon that very rock, with the distant glow of the loathsome campfires lighting up his flaxen hair with a bitter brilliance.

"Bibrau, do not trouble. You do not have to speak. I have read the casting runes well enough myself."

Nay! I glare at him. Such gall!

"Think it takes some sip of Odin's wisdom to read such fate? Or perhaps I cannot help myself. I bear your sense as I hold your scars. See how you have marked me? Not once but twice now. Look upon my lip." 'Tis true, the scar is raised and reddened, ragged with the shape of my small teeth upon his pout. "Such as it is, my father forbids me near you. Yet I will not stay back—not among those purblind idiots and Christian fools."

I look on him. Indeed, some honest ire's in his shaded frown. But on his face, something other, too, as he sits upon the jutting rock and places his hands on his thighs, turned round.

" 'Tis useless," Gudmund mutters. "Says my father the freemen's Christian talk is more of ells of cloth and silver's trade. They say it not before the priest, yet in time they will. Says he, they care more for the price of walrus ivory than for breaking oaths or Old One-Eyed's rage."

I look on him with my heart some pounding—from a chafe, I think, to hear such muddling, feckless faith. Yet, even then, Gudmund changes tack. "Know you"—he bears on me a gazing—"a witching woman lives upon these hills? They say a skogsrå spirit—one sleek and sly and far-most cruel. She lures men off with her wanton taunts and dances, and slowly, here upon the fells, she turns them wild."

His words speak low yet with a boldness, his voice half-changed, no longer sounding like a child's. And his stance, hard-wrought to a sailor's brazen hunger. Such a thought—bare caught, yet there it's trapped and dangles on his wasting breath—that this Gudmund Torkelsson has come upon this slope to ply his want on me.

He, want me? Ha! But the laugh stays silent in my throat, for an unwont taste upon my lips, that I might want him also. Gudmund? Aye! Never have I known such vulgar desiring. Never in my life, and now it comes unwelcome—for this slim man-child with his golden pate and bare-grown whiskers—only a fuzzy rind of wool rising on his lip—want him? Yet it is there, and I cannot hide it—not from myself, though I can hide it well enough from him.

I will not tell it—nay! for fear and wasting. So well have I heard my mistress' heeds, my fylgie's taunts, and my own true jeers. Well I know what a man is made for—how to take and make—how to avoid to give.

Yet Gudmund knows it not as he looks upon me. Oh, he gapes, lips near set upon a drool. Though I show no sign. Only place the narrow hollow of my pipe again between my sharpened teeth. Hard, I bite the long, slim bone as I catch his gaze, feeling strangely chilled by his eyes' low gleam.

Unsure, he moves his hand across the air. He stretches. I feel him shaking—just as I before, in the chieftains' hall, over those fallen runes. I allow his touch. Firm upon the sacred bone. Why? Yet I let his hand stay, clutching harder now, reaching round my back from just behind, his hands spread wide, mating up with mine to fill the holes. I breathe but soft. I cannot help—bare enough to make a gust, yet one small note slips out. His fingers quiver as they feel my wind. No more do I give than that one note, but more than I have ever deigned before to give.

Sudden my heart goes racing. Blind with some confusion, I snatch my tone and startle from the slope. Down, for I know some trouble stays behind me. My fylgie's shrieking. Oh, he skips and giggles, chasing me from the glacier's frigid peak. His dance is sharp and sets my feet tripping over slippery pitches while Gudmund skillful-skips about the heaves and piled stones.

We race all the way to Eirik's byre wall. There we stay our chase, Gudmund's chest quick-heaving. I watch his lips. He wets them soft to get them moist. His eyes grow wide, as white as the ashen color of the moon. From within the byre, we both hear moaning.

"Some bond-thrall and his whore," Gudmund gasps, "plying at the rut." His hands press nearer, clutching sod from between the wall of stones. I watch him, hearing well the sounds within. Then the byre gate flies back. Torvard Einarsson steps out into the nighttime's mist. From the pounded scents and the hanging hay about his shoulders, well we both know who has plied his ache within.

Gudmund spies me awkwardly. "Remember what I'd spoke at Yule? Of the very name and face of the man who made you on your mother? Well, I'll tell it to you, fair and fully—for a price." His eyes are stark, shining in the shadows. All too well I know what that price will be.

I know not why, yet my fingers lift to Gudmund's throat and stroke the scar my stone left there so long ago. "Would," he chokes, "that those sounds were ours. Ah, I see it in your eye, you'd like it well."

Just then my fylgie titters. Well he ought—that I might trip this human trap and lose the path of wily ways. Oh, how clear I see the pit before me—as clear as I feel this longing ache, this hungry, vicious seethe! Yet I catch myself and steady till I regain my step. I know full well just then how to turn this bargain to my pleasure. Yes. Indeed, to know my father's nature, thwart the foul Christians, and kill my mother's joy—all this I might, if I play this bargain rightly. Then my fylgie chimes the secret music of our pact. With him whisper-telling out the treacherous steps, I begin to construct a sturdy ladder down.

First, with a breath, I let my hands fall light and gently on Gudmund's clammy palms, then raise them to my bosom, one on either side. To these new-swollen, bulbous flanks I feel Gudmund's body reaching, feel his feather cheeks pressing down between my flesh. Cold, I shiver as his saliva damps, his head buried there, smelling the crevice deep within the wadmal folds.

Ah! Such a reeling! Such a fragile writhe! All at once, I am wanting more! Yet—no!

Not yet, my fylgie cautions. I push Gudmund aside. There he stands, panting, dripping, his tongue almost lapping up with foam—

naught but a lamb to come into my wolfen teeth. I turn my eye to softness and a mock upon my cheeks to feign a smile, coy.

"Yes," he whispers, " 'tis the first of any gladness I've ever seen upon your face."

He comes at me again. That lip, that breath, that slobber, smelling set of teeth, but I hold him back, leaving him in the dewy dung as I heave around the byre's eave with my song-bone on my lips, daring but the softest tune, swinging my hips just as my fylgie mimic-sways before me.

And well Gudmund follows, half across the hillside's dip and to its rising. There, lit by the moon, is Thjoldhilde's half-built church and, thereabouts in the grasses, some sullen Christians snoring. 'Tis naught but a bare-built hollow—scarce a storage shelter, but three arms' span by four—with nooks clumped up with turf and some driftwood timbers laid about, half trimmed to be a hefty door. Bare enough to squeeze in twelve men standing. Bare but large enough for a master chieftain's bed. Or a fairy maiden's . . . So I think of Gudmund's ancient "changeling" taunt. Knows he not so well, I am all of that and more?

At my fylgie's prompt, I step inside the church—lift my skirts up to my knees and leap right over the wall so as not to use the doorway's entrance; for, though 'tis not yet plaited up, it is well known no sprite half-wise would ever use a door.

Gudmund follows till he stands just beyond the church's edging. "Bibrau!" he begs as if awaiting my command. "I have longed for you . . . dreamt of you!"

Oh, but words a-pity, and such a pity's fool! I set my bone aside upon the sodded wall, knot up my skirts, and squat down low.

Gudmund leaps at me. Fair I welcome him, his body's weight surprising heavy as he pins me. I am none afraid. With my fairy friends and my fylgie's playing, late upon an eve I have known the shape and touch and mix of such a deed. I have seen and smelled it all before. Such is my thought as he plays and dallies me with his fumbling lips and his groping knees. Ah, but such, still he trembles, awkward, hesitating with his fate, until, at last, I lay my hands hard upon his chest and turn him round.

Then I feel him—cast between my deepest thighs—the urgent press and sudden tear! Ah! What precious, joyous bleeding! I sit upon him, work him, grip him, suck him, take all the life from him, and watch him in the dark and madness, listening as he grunts like a beast and groans.

But I am silent, ever still, even as I move with my body's pleasures. Oh, so still, though I long at times to shrill; yet then, instead, I lean down close and bite the tender flesh beneath his eye.

At its most—just when I gasp for breath and faint a bit and falter—oh!—just then comes a rising light, and a sudden, wretched sound. I ope' my eyes to see a flare, a torch, a flame! A crowd of men. A woman shouting, "Stop her!"

I roll as Gudmund pulls up sharp and thrusts away. I see him shaking, bare-cheeked, blanched, and backed against the half-built wall. There I crouch, my own dress spat with blood and stick and semen. Racing up the dew-damped sod is Gudmund's foul birth-mare.

She falls upon him, screaming, "It is as I'd feared, yet worse! As your father warned—this child has bewitched you! Changeling bitch—for all these years—turned my own best son to this taint and twisting!"

Even then, Torkel stands and Chieftain Einar comes. Thorbjorg, too, and Eirik Raude. Before them all storms down the Christian priest, with Ossur bearing high another torch to light his master's contemning gibberish. "A blight upon you! Desire is sin conceived. Demon-child—this girl's possessed. Cast her off! Sin gives birth to death in torment, Hell's everlasting pain! Death to the harlot, as Babylon itself, to bring about the mighty battle at Armageddon!"

Close behind, barely percepted from the rest, brooks my gape-eyed mother. I hear her cloying snot, her muffled stammer, "How could you? Daughter, could you—?"

Upon the edging of the crowd stands Torvard Einarsson.

And from his look, he seems almost proud.

* * *

Once, twice, three times, more, I bear the knife-sharp switch, my new breasts bared to the hardened cuts of walrus hide. Gudmund, too, though his count is fewer—all around believing it was I alone who made this cause. When it is through, Gudmund's whelpish face is thick with bruise and tears, lost of all that hint of manhood I'd admired. I am glad to see it, gladder still to hear, "Never will this girl be let again to Brattahlid. Nor Herjolfsnaes. Nor to set her sight or clutch on Gudmund Torkelsson."

It is sentenced so, with some bit of coin passing from my mistress' coffers and some fair-shook hands and sorry pleadings and invitations next to come this way alone. I am glad of it, of all of it, for I have no want to ever see this place again. Not as more dull freemen gather up to hear the Christian priest-man moaning, " 'Twill ne'er be set aright again—my holy church!—after this loathsome debauchery she's whored."

Sure, but I am pleased. Yet still I look, longing most of all to see my birth-mare's horror. Though she is no place here or anywhere about. Not even in the mistress' skiff as, that very day, we turn back to Tofafjord. Nor will Thorbjorg give me satisfaction, till I know, upon her silence, my mother stays at Brattahlid—there with her foul-man priest and her fool-man Ossur.

So I think some other, petty good has come of this encounter. For, upon this deed, some stranger gain as well: I know at last, with a strong and certain stroke, which among that horrored crowd is my own father.

The Quality of Mercy

KATLA

I STAND at the hill's crest. At my feet the rank corruption, the half-built church once so pure, the perfect vessel which would carry me to my salvation, now made pith and pit, a mocking mirror of my soul.

So my daughter had it of me—had me in her clutch and would have choked me off if well she could—if they'd not stopped her—sent her off with but a scrape and screaming. She and that ill-used boy, Gudmund.

Now they paddle: Torkel Herjolfsson with his battered son, bow-headed, and Thorbjorg after with my daughter at her shoulder, crossing not their wakes as they keenly cut the black fjord. It reminds me of another passing—as once Thorbjorg had carried me so long ago. Yet this time my own daughter, not the freeman, is the foe.

And here she leaves me—Thorbjorg—on this shore. I am cut adrift for the weight of silver pressed from the priest's own palm—sold and left as a bag of woolen or a bundle of useful bone. Well I should be fair relieved—wanting less to follow, surely, than to go. So long I have hungered for this day, praying ever to be apart, first from the witch, then from this errant, rueful daughter. Yet now—yet why?—I feel an empty ache, as if some part of me is set to drifting. I am but a hollow, worthless vessel, abandoned, left swift off, with naught remaining but my daughter's wretched shame.

How am I to be among them? Oddly knowing not my place, sudden here alone while, on all these watchers' faces—nay! even in their wanton hiss: "Ah, she's the one—the one that bore the changeling out. See what ill she's wrought upon us now!"

So they say. Yet none do look on Torvard. There he stands at the bottom of this very slope. His look is feigned and blind toward me, though I know he sees me well enough. There he gazes up. Oh, his glare—just like his daughter's! O'er the skiff's low rail, with her face tucked in beneath Thorbjorg's tender cheek, yet aiming not her bleeding through the wadmal dress to hide it from this crowd. Nay, she turns it round just enough so all can see her torment clearly. And the look upon her face is triumph—as is Torvard's.

The earth beneath me is slick with sweaty dew; the grasses within this church—cut and naked from the scraping of their baleful heels. I must stand without—I dare not enter. No shelter lies within this God's house—not for me—not for me now. But I cannot help—I bend my knees and fall before the church's entrance, upon the very sod, wet and curled, starting some to brown where its roots are severed—as mine are sliced away or having never truly grown down deep. Well I know it—upon my mother's heart—my one strong root, cleaved so long ago.

I roll my brow over, over against the hard, scratched stone, across the bitter sharpness' edging—as if such act should draw fresh blood. Surely pray! Come, blood, if it can purge me of my daughter's cruelty. Of my own pain! Yet it cannot. Nay, I am impure myself. Ever hateful, ever sinful, made this way of a thousand curses bred and nurtured—worst of all, my cursed will.

And pride. What little pride? How my mother prayed against it! Begged me—lo!—accept my fate, give what little good I might, and go upon the heavens in the end to join my long-dead—murdered—father—*My Father, who art in Heaven*— No! Such sins upon my lips. Such words, to taint them even with my breathing. Nay! I cannot. I am undeserving.

"Daughter—"

Come not near me, Father! I am wrecked and reeking, spoiled, filthy, judged unfit. Father, do not lay your hands upon me. Your fingers fouled by my filth—my hair beneath its kerchief . . . Yet your touch so gentle—breath so soft—I feel my aching— "Forgive me, Father, for I have—"

"Woman, come. What could you have done of weight since your last confession but a day ago?"

"Father," I breathe, "that child—that changeling beast—"

"What mean you? Bibrau? The girl? She's but a twisted thrall, the property of a pagan soothsayer—"

"True—all true—yet I myself have served long years within that soothsayer's house. Thorbjorg—always good to me and kind, but— oh!—what I have seen! What I have done! To draw such blood—even with my own two hands. And sacrificed and served such things as Jesus Christ, my mother's Lord, would hail with terror!"

"Hush, woman. Hush and calm. The Lord is your own Heavenly Father. Tell him and me aloud such things as you think you've done."

And I tell him all as he bends before me, pressing his back against the soiled stones of the half-made church—tell what I have seen, the birds and burnings, beasts rotting on their spits, the chants and dances and all the fervid tunes my daughter piped while the mistress sang about the stones.

"What stones are these?"

"A circle of them."

"At the seeress' homestead?"

"Upon a hollow at the bottom of a knoll. Well I know the place— even I found the ring myself—set its very mark as a boundary for the mistress' homestead with a pregnant cow—pregnant"—I break—"so many years ago . . ."

"Woman, what say you? Do not bow your head. Speak," the priest demands, for sudden my voice is hushed. He shakes me gently. "Speak."

"I—bearing up that child—that cursed girl! Now I think perhaps, even as an unborn beast within me, she guided me upon that heinous round!"

"Unborn beast? Calm, and tell me clearly. This beast—"

"Bibrau . . . Bibrau—is my daughter." I gasp, "She is—of my womb." I cannot bear to hear it spoke', even by myself. I bolt my eyes. But there is Ossur, saying naught, yet bent beside.

"Your daughter . . . ?" asks the priest.

"Forced upon me!" I lean and spit, "Torn out from me, and ever, always, even with each breath, she has cursed my life and wrenched it bare and bloody." I am gasping now, and my tears are streaming. "Mine!" I burst. "Hated—mine! And all her sins are mine, for I've done naught to teach her Christ and only thought to hate her well—"

For a time, the priest says nothing. Then he lays his hands, weighty, full on me, "Woman, quiet now, for the trials of Christ are fraught with kindred suffering. Comes this cause but to strengthen Christ within, so he may enter on your soul to forgive you all your sins."

"Forgive?" I mumble, stunned. "Forgive?" I stare in utter, wretched horror.

The priest rises up, towering above me. "Gudrid," he calls, "come. Teach your newfound sister the proper prayers for God's forgiveness. Teach her well the blessed tunes and on which beads to utter. Katla, all your prayers must be to God and Jesus to cast off hatred. Embracing love, relinquish all your enmity, even to your daughter's sinful making. Only there might be the path to true salvation of your own and your daughter's wasted souls."

The priest lays one spare, white hand upon me, first above one shoulder's plight, then about the other's woe. "Now go in peace," light-lingering before my shamed forehead. "Yet, Ossur"—he turns—"come quickly by. Eirik Raude and the other chiefs await."

The priest takes Ossur with an arm entwined with confidences. My soul breaks more as he draws so fast away; but Gudrid holds me close and guides me soon to her father, Thorbjorn's tent. There she cools my face with a smooth white cloth soaked in the fjord's waters. In time she reaches back to soothe my puckered brow and braids my hair up tight again and tucks the wild strands beneath their wadmal folds. Then, with her holy voice, she hushes with sweetest breathing and sings to me all the wealth of her fragrant psalms.

So our days pass with bending fingers around the rosary, her hands on mine, and from Gudrid's lips I learn the sacred-made devotions. My heavy head feels lighter and slow begins to clear as, through these days, I am let to stay within her father's kind protection, and wake and rise among the Christian women, slave and free.

There are but six in all, and fewer still of men, though I sense some soon there will be many others. Every day we are set upon by watchers from the far fjords. Most from Austerbygd, but even now such word has traveled distant—far enough to draw a goodly ship from the reaches of the western settlement, Vesterbygd. Most they come, 'tis true, to stand in mocking, calling, cackling, throwing at us clots and rocks, dangling their pagan idols wretchedly before us. But these our priest invites. When they are laid upon the ground, he casts a furied look and, with a Latin chanting, crushes them to bits beneath his Christian clout. These watchers, stunned, fall back as we sing and ne'er the slightest harm does cease our faithful rhythm. So, in time, they stop their caterwaul and even lend upon our prayers a different sort of ear.

Among us, Eirik's wife, Thjoldhilde, is far-most wise and boldest. Every day, Eirik Raude sits and broody-gestures by his homefield's stony ledge while she and Leif gather up what chiefs and sons and wives will dare to listen. For these, our priest sings out high praise of the Prince of Peace's great warrior's strength, of his fury, which has led so many mighty kings to triumph. And when these captains shout, "Once upon a rock I stood with these very Christians' thigh bones shattered beneath my boot soles!," says our priest, "If true, then those nary were true Christians, but rank and direful souls God smote upon their sins."

More and more each dawn, our ring grows loud with praying. And upon each dusk, more souls have learned the songs for Lauds, Matins, and Nones. And I, among our number, am neither spurned nor cursed for what has been my lot. Nay, even the Christ-made freemen praise me, saying, "Katla, your heart is strong to fight such hatred, having known such bitter brute and shame."

I cannot smile upon such speech. I care no more to hear them, knowing well my heart's still heavy, scarred beneath its loathsome weight. Only sometimes, when my Ossur raises up his voice with the music of my mother's ancient, secret prayers, I cannot help but find some little solace in them, and softly secret-shed some little, grateful tears.

My Ossur—nay. Sometimes he lifts his eyes to mine, but only then as a kind and distant brother. Our priest says we are siblings now, all kindred blessed in Jesus. So, when Ossur kisses me, 'tis a kiss as all these others'—light and cool upon my cheek. So it should ever be, and I try to find some comfort in it. He cannot be my Ossur now.

Each day, he is there beside the priest's own labors. Well he looks, and happy at his task, seeming purposeful and growing wise and fine in state and stature. He spends long days and nights upon the chieftains' meets, arguing the Christian cause, while we others do such work as is our knack and leaning.

Together we women clip bits of cloth to sew for the soon-come altar's garments, while the men cut new green sod and place fresh stones to mend our church's walls where they had been so horribly profaned. With our work comes singing; and with each song, the taint, if not the memory, of my daughter's strife is cautious cleared away. Too, each stitch I ply is as if to knit my heart up somehow better. When the priest, with Ossur by him in his rite, drips holy water to purify my hem, 'tis as if the shower cleanses even me.

In time the church grows firm and fine. Near upon the seeding moon, it is completed. There upon the hill it stands, small and meek above Brattahlid's great hall's darkness; yet of stones made pure and blessed with fairest Christian songs, and hung above with even a small iron bell Leif had brought, blacked by the Norway king's own smithy's flame.

Oh! 'Tis the first true church I have ever witnessed!—though gray beneath with its low sod roof and its meager entrance, bare wide enough to slip between its doorposts sideways. Gudrid mourns there is no glass, for such things she says are often made of color shining. Yet, for me, this small sod hut is a beacon made of light itself, not clumped about with bits of turf and sea-soaked beam.

At last we are becked to press within, with Ossur's hands wrapped strong about the bellpull and some candles set which, lighted, drip and smoke and cast a heavy vapor. Comes then another smoke, this one plied with scent, heady in its fragrance. Then before us all the priest there stands.

I step most timidly within, with Gudrid at my side, her hand in mine. My place is upon that first cold seat made of a bit of whalebone spine. There we kneel and pray, then stand and pray, then pray again with singing. As our priest murmurs out the Bible's tales, I tremor most, till he speaks of Mary Magdalene. Only then I draw small comfort from his speech, knowing not just I but other women, too, have suffered hard upon their fate and been redeemed.

Within the church's dark comes at last that sweetest dawning as our voices rise and our songs quick grow to chimes which ring out bright against the flinty walls. "Holy, holy, holy!" through the scented haze of the priest's fine smoke and the candles flicker-burning. And I can only think, such things as this my mother did so long ago, as I am let to bite a bit of bread taken from the priest's own fingers, then to sip of sweetest honeyed drink, which the priest calls each Jesus' body and his blood.

Then these songs are over, and the taste of drink still clinging to my tongue. But I cannot leave, not until the very last, even as the press of Christians turns without and dwindles. My knees sink soft into the damp, cold sod—so I am near alone with the smoke and scent and the fires burning. Then Ossur comes again before the altar's edging cloth. There he tends to the priest's own holy book, which he sets down gently with a kiss upon his lips before he turns and sees and comes and lifts me from my kneeling.

"Katla"—noticing the tears upon my cheeks—"are you not joyous?"

"Yes," I say, "as never I had hoped or dared to dream. 'Tis ever as my mother would have wished—if she had lived to see this day—"

"Our father-priest would say upon that wish that she is near, listening with the angels."

"Often I had dreamed it so—she watching me ever and above, and with her look lighting some my path, though it has been but dark and murky."

"Dark and murky," echoes Ossur, "yet now and never more."

I sigh and turn my head. "Do not say it, Ossur. Such talk of hope has never brought me more than sorrow. Only say it not at all, but let me have the moment's briefest brightness before I pass again into the cloud and gloom."

"You fear it, but the storm has passed. Now you are in Christ's own shelter," Ossur speaks and then he quiets. In his eye it is strangely calm. "Katla, do you love me still?"

"Ossur, do not pain me now again with talk of love. Speak of peace, of Christ, of angels—brother—yes!—but not of love." I turn my gaze, yet he turns it back with the slightest touch—his thumbs upon my tears.

"Say you love me. Say it once and say it still, and with such words, ever will you live this brightest joy."

I cannot breathe, feeling the tide short-rising behind my weeping. "You are the priest's own bearer—you hold his holy cup. You dare to kiss his book with your own mouth—"

"Katla." Ossur turns to me so I stare upon his face and see it hot with red and earnest. "Have you forgotten all our dreams? Come." He takes my hand.

"Where?"

"Unto the priest."

"Nay!" I beg, knowing naught but I have done something wrong and sinful. Yet I cannot help, as he draws me fast between the church's rows, then out into the sun, following swiftly down the hill, tripping some upon my feet, but Ossur's fingers are firm and strong and steady as they guide me.

There ahead the Lord's-man stands girdled by his congregation. We step but close, I trembling full with weakness. "God be with you," he says to Ossur, "my son." Then to me, "Christ be with you, daughter." His lips are wet and cold as they brush across my cheeks, but his smile is warm and filled with certain sparkling.

"Father," Ossur speaks, as ever heedful, "now the church is finished, pray, make a marriage in it—a Christ-blessed, holy union."

The priest looks on Ossur, then kindly down on me. Upon them both I can but stare in daze and wonder. "Ossur," I pray, "tell me what this holy union means."

"Katla, don't you see?" Ossur whirls to me in glee and giddy. "Now, at last, we can be wed."

"Wed?" I murmur. "I am the priest's own bond-thrall—"

"Katla," says the priest, "I have given silver but to free you."

"Free?" I stammer, looking on him hard. "Silver to the mistress . . . ?"

Ossur proclaims, "You are free—free to wed, free to roam, free as any born upon that fortune. So you've been all these passing days— ever since your daught– . . . You did not know?"

I cannot find my tongue or words to bear upon it. "Free . . ." I feel my eyes well up, some tingling in my limbs and fingers.

"Free"—Ossur bends to me—"to be my wife, if you will have me."

"Wife?" I stut' and stumble back, but Ossur holds me gently by my arms. "And free?" Seems the earth is a whirl of grass and stone and sea and lightning.

Our father offers out his hands. "There are no slaves in Jesus' house. We are all of us true servants to the Son of God."

I gape upon them both—for what could these words be but frantic wishes?—as Ossur leads me off, and I stagger now somehow across the emptied hillside. Befuddled and bemused, I rest upon a boulder's knob, and I look on him and feel at last the earth stop reeling, knowing Ossur's face now shows no jest or even faint-heart dreaming, but an honest plea as never I had hoped to hear—only forever echoed in the yearning of my soul.

THORBJORG

SMOLDERING STILL, those scattered rune-ish embers, smoking harshly up, singeing Eirik Raude's foot-pound floor. All nary and asunder. A bitter jumble. A garbled, wanton cast. Yet the throw was fair. The cast was true. The truest ever I have witnessed.

Ne'er would it have been, had not that Christian set his hand upon the board. How? Yet how? Hard writ, Alfather, as if your stroke itself had laid them down. Odin, such hollow shapes made into heavy meanings—such as I'd not seen in many seasons past, not since that night when first you showed me he would come.

I knew it not, but now I sense it—that cruel quake as I stood before those ashy coals. Was it this, Alfather—for so long you had felt the earth's quick tremble? From it, low, the flow, the molten seep. And then the burning. I scent it still, even as the winds fly off, even now, before my own, feeble flame.

Fight fire with fire. It is the only way. Still I stoke it up, here beneath the sheltering cliffs within the circle's round. The winds blow hard and, time and again, they douse it with their aching, pelting rain. 'Tis an ill-some portent. I cannot raise it up. Such sacrifice I have brought lies here exposed and rotting. Your ravens circle, hungry for your meat. I would set it out and blaze about such conflagration. But I cannot. So I watch your vision fly far off. Your memory abandons me.

Alone upon this hill I stand, though Bibrau stands beside me. Still her wounds run hot and ooze with fury. Every night I tend them tenderly, with balms and salts, oiled rubs and rotting plasters. It does no good. Such wounds are not for healing. Such wounds as hers are deep and old—older than the ancient giant Ymir's wasted bones which formed the circle's stones themselves.

Yet she was made to be our torch's bearer—she, who burns herself with such a vivid blaze. She, who should stand up boldly to raise the fighting fire. Yet now she is but a wild spark, bare enough to flash before she expires. Her deeds are rash, misdirected, crass. To the certain creep of the coming strife, she only feeds their flame.

Their burning, slow and distant, coming closer. Ever close, ill smoke and blistered twigs. Soon they'll catch. Their flames will lap and search about for timber. Though on this Greenland ground there is barely wood. Only bits of drifting logs and thick, mat sod. It is that sod I smell, its acrid taint already on the winds. What would they have of this—such insufficient feeding? Yet, when such fire craves, it will eat whatever it tastes upon its tongues.

KATLA

FOR SOME NEXT DAYS, we are quick with loom and sewing—we Christian free-made women set together in a round. The cloth we weave is a brilliant red, the crimson color I will wear upon my wedding. Oh! Such songs we sing upon our work. Such joy, so unimagined! And the work, not work, but each thread and stitch of our needles' tug is a tendered, precious prayer.

I see not much of Ossur, even through these eager days. He is oft about the nearby farmers' hofs, aiding wreck and reek as the priest dashes and defames them. He says they are but for ignorance and worship of false gods. It is our priest's own task, he says, to splinter every offering pole and burn up every altar, till naught remains but the one to Jesus Christ our Lord. I miss him well, and cherish what I garner: a gentle kiss, some smallish words, and then again he's gone. Too oft, I wonder for our future, for none can tell me even where my Ossur lays his head. Seems his pillow is the priest's own footpad. His threshold and his hearth are charity and poverty, as ever are our priest's own. Am I to sip upon that cup? I think of it as little as I dare. Gudrid says I must trust in God and Christ and the way of providence, as do these other faithfuls all around.

At last, while my own dress is fitted—which is work, they say, I must not do myself—the priest returns to place another stretch of cloth beneath my fingers. This one's shivered white and of a sturdy, sailing thickness. Begs the priest I should cut it to the shape of the blessed cross and sew that cross upon a blood-red Viking sail. When I ask why, Ossur answers, "Our priest must go preaching to the far fjords. His sail must proclaim the coming triumph of the Son of God."

Hearing, Thjoldhilde counters, "Then he must not go upon such work alone. Pagan chiefs—as I have known well enough my husband—are nary quick nor kindly set to change their passions, even for the saving of their souls."

So it is agreed, and all are filled with sudden fervor to stand upon such rocking planks and spread God's glory through all this Greenland.

I stitch it fair through the waning of the seed-time, when Leif's own ship comes, and fixed upon its mast is that very stiff-blown, glorious sail. Oh, it is a joy to see, rippling in the sunlight. We sing out, "Praise to God! *Sancte Domine!*" Then our priest takes our hands and ushers each upon those ice-bit boards—even I, holding close his palm with an almost loving tender, skipping over Leif's own plank to Ossur, who leads me to a prided place beside the priest's own chair.

As our Christian brethren fill the ship, a ring of pagans gathers— mostly rude, low freemen bound to Eirik's duty, bearing up stones and fists, shouting curses, boisterous and crude. Ever I would shudder, though Leif's presence stays their angled hands, but Ossur's own is upon me now, soft and gentle, tucked beneath my kerchief's length. Bare upon my neck, his fingers twine the loosened wisps of my braided hair. He says, "Soon we will be as one before God and Christ and all this bitter world."

"It seems a dream from which I dare not waken."

"My love, you will not have to waken e'er again."

"Tell me"—I turn to him—"of the Norway court, how all this came to be."

Ossur smiles. "It was as you'd warned. I met upon that court with the king's hard eye. Tryggvason quick recalled how I could ne'er right-kill on that Maldon battlefield. He mocked me harshly, even where Leif Eiriksson and all our proud Greenlanders could hear. Yet, for Christ's own good, our priest stood by the king's ear. I heard him whisper, 'Think you not, fair sovereign, to love one's enemies is an honest, Christian desire?' The king nodded slowly and looked upon me keen. 'Twas then, even before the king himself, I bent and begged to take the Christian vow.

"After some long talk with Leif behind a hard-drawn curtain, the king set me to serve this priest, to hunt and fish for him, and do such chores as will free him to ply our faith in Greenland."

"So that is your chore." I sigh. "I had feared perhaps you would take the priest's own vows."

" 'Twas never to be so. Forever, even as I knelt before Tryggvason's feet with the oath of Christ upon my lips, I knew I would only make that vow for my love of you."

I bow my head—'tis enough to bring my eyes to weeping. Still the pagan rabble shouts its curses, but I sudden feel no threat. For all their words, none can daunt me now from the rightness of our purpose—for what joy has come to me in Christ can surely be for all.

None, till among them comes Thorhall Hunter. Standing on the edging of that crowd, he looks strained and woed, his face a shade of malcontent. Never have I seen him such: always bold and gruff, but ever filled with life's own mischief. Now he spies me only with contempt and the slightest irksome glare. I turn my gaze quick off, fearing how his eyes accuse. Yet there, upon a gasp, is Freydis Eiriksdatter—her gestures crass, eyes red as her flaming hair, her voice far harsh and harder than many of the men's. "Nay," I breathe, knowing well my torment cannot linger far behind her. Indeed, soon there is Torvard, too, looking fat and flushed, groping unspent ire at the air. His eyes light first on Ossur, then on me—keen and cold as ever were his hands.

Ossur whispers as he feels me shiver, "He is naught but coarse, Katla, near beyond all Christian hope. Forgive him his ancient trespass. He cannot touch you now, even if he dared."

I hold him close, turning eyes from Torvard toward the mighty, gleaming heavens. At last Leif withdraws the plank with a scraping screech. Gudrid raises up her voice in a grace of Christian singing. As we set off from Eiriksfjord, her rhythms give measure to our oars' hard pull. Over glistening water, our ship heads south along the coast. Soon the cliffs ring with our crystal chorus, "Gloria! Glory!" Somehow, the cold, gray crags, the white of icebergs, even the harsh black stone which shapes hard Greenland's edges, turn warm and soft with this new, brilliant tune. I pray, in Ossur's arms, my hate for Torvard will perhaps some dull and wither, as the voices of Brattahlid fade with the dawn's last dew.

We reach Sandhavn market in time to rest for the prayerful night before casting on toward Herjolfsnaes. Yet, when old Herjolf's homestead peeks through the first light of misty morning, Leif does not call his sail to drop nor his oars to set us toward the harbor. Instead, he heads off from the coast and turns our course toward Tofafjord.

"Why do we turn?" I ask, my heart sudden beating. No one—not even Ossur—answers as the cliffs rise slowly with their spark of feldspar and their rosy rinse of quartz. Yet in time I know. Ossur gently strokes my fingers as we wedge into the curving bay where the five arms of the fjord's entrance marry. We are heading now toward Mistress Thorbjorg's farm.

"Why?" I beg again, yet the priest turns off from where I stand. Perhaps he does not hear my words beneath the rippling slap of our thick red sail with its bold white Christian cross. On our prow, the fierce dragon's head is cleanly cut. Now it bears instead a gold-gleamed crucifix pointing toward Thorbjorg's manor with a hard, sharp aim. There Thorbjorg's house looks pitiful, somehow tamer, with its wisp of smoke rising thin and puny from a soddy mound barely cut from the mountain's soil, while we bound toward it on a dogged Viking wave.

Now the mistress' hillside fills up quickly—first with Arngunn, Kol, then Nattfari dragging out some sort of wretched doll. Then Thorbjorg comes, her cloak a seeming tatter against our priest's new-given, thick black flapping robe. Kol's harsh whistle cuts across the fjord's stretch. Soon Alof, Svan, and Teit are running from the fells. They join the mistress just as our Christ's-ship strides aground. Yet among them all I see not my daughter.

Our ship lurches at the rattled beach stones. There we wait upon our good priest's caution. He steps first ashore. Moving slowly over the mistress' pasture green—odd, how his robe drinks away the dew and marks a path that is dry and dull beside the morning's fecund wetness. I try to catch my former friendships' faces; yet none about the homefield raise their eyes. Kol leads them now, for the mistress seems somehow reluctant. I sense in her no welcome and no trust, only a standing cold, as if her own slim form were turned an icy floe through which Kol extends his quaking, gnarled cane.

"You'll set no foot within this homefield."

"Would you threaten so," begs my priest, "when we have come in peace?"

"Peace?" Kol scoffs. "Upon a Viking blood-sail?"

"Almighty God and Jesus Christ guide us here to rout out evil and foster virtue."

"What evil here stands just before me." Kol coldly plies his stick, hard and deep, into the ground.

"Mistress Thorbjorg," greets my priest then, smiling. He takes one step. Kol raises up his cane as if a spear. From there, my priest surveys all who stand before him. Nearest, foul Nattfari leans against the homefield wall, plucking filthy hairs from her naked limbs. My priest kneels to show her kindness. In turn, Nattfari reaches up and scratches fast his chin. I gasp and strain to help, but Ossur holds me back with all the other Christians. I cling to the ship's rail as my priest jerks back and Nattfari hurdles round, hiss-and-clawing, crouching, cowering behind my mistress' cloak, quivering, her fingers—mimicked—at her jaw.

Thorbjorg pries her off, sending her to Arngunn, then coming down slowly, stepping calm by calm. Her limp is worse than I have ever seen it. "I am sorry," Thorbjorg speaks. "Nattfari is not well."

The priest mops his blood with the edging of his robe. "Mistress Thorbjorg, I am not your foe."

"No? I know your face, sir. I have seen it long before—and often—in a nightmare."

"You trust better in dreams and visions? Yet I offer out my hand. I took my retribution for your own thrall-daughter's deeds with but a coin, which I then passed back to you. All this to show you mercy and Christ's forgiveness. Was that not far more than fair?"

Thorbjorg answers not at first, though her gown whips hotly in the frigid wind. "What do you want here?"

"But to speak of rites and rituals, of sacrifices Katla says are practiced here."

The mistress' eye falls on me finally, in a quickness. "While she served upon this house, Katla kept her thoughts well and wisely to herself."

"Did she?"

"She did. Here we tend but little what one another thinks, so long as all do properly their chores."

"But, lady, is that wise? I ask you, tend ye not your flocks upon the fells?"

"Flocks, yes, of sheep."

"That is true. But people are not so unlike sheep."

"People do," Thorbjorg says, "what people will."

"Surely you must know they must be guided, and slaves the most, for they are best like children—worst, like beasts."

"Think you so?" challenges the mistress. "Then little do you know such slaves. Or even of such simple beasts. Yet, if they be as you say, then I say let fate and the gods direct their paths, just as the wolf is drawn by nature to the straying sheep."

"Surely even your goodly shepherd keeps sharp watch. I know you yourself often give some good direction. I've seen at Eirik Raude's, the people listen close upon your word."

"They are not my words, sir. I have but a little voice to whisper greater wisdom."

"Yet your influence is powerful, as we've seen upon that child."

He looks up. Then I. There my daughter's standing on the fell-slope.

"Tell me of her training," asks my priest. "They say she follows closely on your path."

"I'll not banter with you the method of my teaching or the manner of it either." Thorbjorg turns from him, not in fury but with a rueful, troubled step.

"Lady, what?" my priest—my ardent priest—pursues. "Do you doubt your guidance of the girl? Tell me this—upon the ill-passed tryst—was she guided so by your own teaching?"

"I guide her as the gods do tell. Yet those gods' wisdom had naught to do with the child's actions. She is but a twisted girl, yet I'll untwine her."

"Will you? With your ring of stones and your oblations?"

Thorbjorg eyes him keenly. "What do you know of these?"

"I know much—"

"Nay!" she sputs. "You know naught at all."

Thorbjorg whirls about then, limping, bounding up the hill. "Kol, have this man away, and all who follow. Should they stubbornly remain, tie one Finn's-knot tight to blow their ship off from its moor so they will have to swim to catch it from the tide."

She says some fiercely, yet I know she surely trifles. Ne'er does she speak so lightly of such dark and secret things. Yet Kol winds a cloth about his fist, just as a cloud creeps darkly o'er the sun. Our trespassers shiver quick, all but the priest, who strongly stands his ground.

He says at once a prayer against the Finn's-knot charm. "The Lord is my shepherd. I shall not want." He shouts to us, "Now, what has the Lord taught you? Will you cower before the demon? Take up your mettle and fight for Jesus' cause!" My priest rallies them all, even Leif and Gudrid, singing brightly as they cross the plank, linking arms with mine as I cling first to Ossur, then to the ship's hard rail.

As my feet touch the Tofafjord earth, so my daughter sudden starts quick-running, wild as a mad Viking berserker with her arms raised up, hands balled about clench-clutched bits of stone. These she hurls, and hard they strike, raining first upon the priest's head, then on all who follow, then so close to mine! Until she crosses Thorbjorg's path. There the mistress catches her so that soon they both are tumbling, Thorbjorg lashing back my daughter's arms with vicious strength to stay her throws.

"Katla, which way to reach this profane circle?" yells my priest.

I stand but stunned. "Nay! No!" Still, it is not long until they've found the way themselves.

I watch them go, with Thorbjorg at my daughter's shoulder, standing now, wrinkled, old, yet strong enough to thwart my child's fury, as the Christians march to the sound of Latin rising, "*Per signum crucis de inimicis nostris libera nos, Deus noster*. . . . Deliver us from our enemies, Thou who art our God."

They are almost beyond our sight when Thorbjorg's household moves to follow. Yet my mistress does not. Nor do I. We stand at odds, I low, she high upon that hillside, holding back my daughter's rage until she can no more. Such force! And then the girl is gone in mad-dened thrashing, running toward the stones. Yet the mistress stays be-hind, looking down—beyond me—at the empty ship and the icy fjord and the darkening sky with its flush of threat. Then comes a sigh I hear even above the wind, which has picked up heartily.

Sometime later, there is smoke. And there is snow. Then a certain warmth rides upon this foehn wind's breathing. The Christians do not return, nor those from Thorbjorg's household. In time we move, we both together, slowly, for the wind whips up the thick-laid, frosty spatterings of this early, springtime slush. Wet, it gathers quickly be-neath our walking. We slosh through it, slippery—Thorbjorg, and I. I cannot help myself. I go to her, take her arm, and help her with her heavy steps. Over the hill together—that very hill I traversed so very long ago, when the cow went astray and I, ignorant, followed, wishing it had not been so. But such it was, and for many years: Thorbjorg's home, full of wet and rotting, yet it was rich to grow.

We crest the hill and come upon the circle—what had been a cir-cle, perfect in the old gods' form. Yet now the stones are tumbled, tossed to ruin, cast about by some inhuman strength of will or fear or need. As a supple spine hurled from a height for the savage savor of its meat—carrion dropped by birds—the stones lie broke apart and wasted. A great white falcon wings above. In the falling dust, he is brighter even than the low white clouds. Or this snow.

"No more," proclaims my priest, "will there be pagan sacrifices, beasts or burning. In the name of the Father, the Son, and the Holy Spirit, I purify and sanctify this place with consecrated oil and with thrice-blessed fire. Blessed be the name of Jesus Christ, our Lord."

Thorbjorg and I look down. There the priest holds his own frail arms about my daughter. Thorbjorg sets off toward her as I hold my place. My priest gives Bibrau back with a revolted thrust. Her foot-steps stumble and scrape across the clean white thickness. Beneath—the scorched black earth beside the broken granite, covering slowly now with the heavy snow like a swath of lint-pressed cloth.

BIBRAU

A DEATH TO HER! A death! A death and worse—if such pain be possible, then send it down upon her, upon all Christians. Oh, to see it so! To see it burn.

Had she but a tiny part of wisdom, she would have seen what she would do and shut her mouth—shut it tight, and kept away those Christians. But no! She, my mother of the wistful, of the gentle, ungrateful sort, who can ne'er keep a precious thought locked upon her tongue! With one sputtered breath, she brings this killing wind! And there is nothing I can do, nothing to stop her foul breathing. Even my mistress cannot hold her back. And I, too fresh, too weak, too slow, too late—I must stand and watch the circle burn.

Burn. Burn. Burn! And then I think, *Burn so there is nothing left! Not even chalky ash or a broken stone!* And mean it sorely, for all meaning there is lost. The circle—such as it has been—powerful and holy—yet now, now tainted! I cannot bear to stand upon its rim.

Nor can my ancient ones, my dear, precious invisibles. I watch them scattering as seeds upon an air. Frightened—they who have never been afraid—out from the stones as they crack apart, up upon those fell-slopes, up those icy crags, to squeeze between those narrow crevasses, catching fragile hold of what sore, frigid shelter they can find before such vicious, seething winds. Down those hidden paths where I have followed once—only once—but now I know I will never find those paths myself again.

I cannot follow. I cannot pry from this priest's dull hands. His grip I'd thought so frail, yet it pierces as a falcon's talons. I cannot turn and kill him. No, too late! He holds until the hills are empty and the only sounds are my breath, the foehn winds rising up, the fall of frost into my tangled ash-dulled wisps, and the sizzle-stench as these Christians' fires burn.

And die. Finally they die, and the Christians march to their cacophony. My mother, turning with them, goes upon their ship, squeezing between the fjord's cliffs, and finally is gone.

Thorbjorg comes next to me—only then laying hands again upon me, helpless as I've never seen her. And Kol beside, and all the rest, looking mourned and gray and themselves nearly cindered, as the fires char to smoke and the smoke updrifts but swiftly. I turn my back and flee the mistress' impotent touch—away and back into the empty household where the hollow of our lives is left cast off. There, in the midst of dullness, with the snowfall flitting down the smoke-hole in the hoary light, I scratch some runes into the hearth fire's dampened ashes, and with them know I will yet tender my recoil.

THORBJORG

IT MATTERS NOT. It matters not.

All is transience. Well I know it. Surely it is no one's fault, not even Katla's. Caught upon the briar's thorn, she is not to blame for what has passed. 'Twas ever meant and fair condemned. 'Twas ever my true vision.

My vision—aye!—though much I doubted, dreaded, blamed myself upon its wreck and wreak. Yet, all the while, I could do naught to hamper what I had full and truly seen.

Indeed, for this is just the start. The priest speaks but weakly now, yet more I know is coming. More to strike, and hard and louder. More, while upon his lips the bleat of sympathy, of sacrifice and poverty, of humility and reason twisted. All the while, he is at his wily aim. This priest has lures and charms and baits. Already I have sensed their power: they are worthy.

And yet, though he bares his spit of words, they spit not from his own soft mouth. He reads from off another's hand and sings their claims with a studied rhythm. He knows naught of the darker depths, or the paths which must be crawled to find them out.

Still I sense in him the weaver's fate: all I have woven up, he will unravel. 'Tis the rising breath of the coming day: it bears a darker shadow. And Bibrau? I? Where will we stand in such a shade? This cloud has come and hovers close and bears upon us. The smell of smoke is thick indeed, the tinge of death is hung upon the fells. And the sea—the sea—white with froth upon the coming darkness.

It matters not. It matters—not.

He speaks but weakly now. And soon is gone.

KATLA

WHAT HAVE I DONE? 'Tis a side of the Christians I had never thought! 'Tis naught of what my mother told—only of Christians good, of Christians loving, of Christians patient, wise. What wise, that could do such harm?

What had I sought but my soul's own absolution? Some small comfort from my wretched pain. Yet ever what has Thorbjorg given? Naught but comfort, care, such patience, fair and free. In her household—true! and why not, that each should choose his way?

For the whole of the journey back, my priest hurls curses, vile condemnations, calls the mistress Thorbjorg "Witch!" and turns to me as some shining, bold display. He praises me for my honest chronicle, spitting bile of the seeress' depravity, until I cower far across the surging deck, wishing only to hide my head in anguished shame.

'Twas my own tongue which brought this wrong. The snow still falls and the winds are rough. It is over. Finished. I can do naught to turn it round.

Even Ossur does not come. Perhaps he knows. But the priest, he, in all his glory, dares to place his hand upon my arm. Too near! I stand and bear it, sudden feeling a vicious, rising rage—such a rage as might my daughter even notice. Oh, 'tis all my might not to shove him off, not to turn about and strike him, not to beat his chest, not to press him back into the fjord's frigid waves. Gentleness and mercy! Instead,

I clutch the rail and steady. He shares my glance but for a breath, then wisely leaves.

In my sort of silence, my head is spinning round with plaintive prayers—such prayers of fear, of guilt, of wanting fair acquittal. Yet such prayers all turn to Christian chants—precious tastes turned bitter on my tongue! How can I pray these words when these themselves have caused this damage? Frantic, fumbling, my rosary grinds against my palm, the small round beads wearing smaller with each stroke—yet each stroke's a mock, and so, much more, the sounds I pray.

Till I hear softly a humming: Gudrid standing far across the ship. Her melody quick rises—not a Vespers hymn nor a rhythm of some pagan drone, but a lullaby my mother used to sing. Meaningless of word yet still and slow, so hushed it cannot help but calm. It seems to ease the fluttered flick of flapping sail. High up in the mast it hangs, and even seems to lull the birds. To this tune comes Ossur by me. Slowly he eases me within his arms, wrapping a shawl about my shoulders, for the wind's turned vicious, pelting icy stones.

"You must not regret it, Katla. You must think now only that what you did was right."

"Right?" I beg. "Thorbjorg would never do such vengeance."

But he hushes me. "Soon we will be married. Think on this, not what has gone." He turns me back, wraps his hands about and holds me within their folding; and though his kiss is trying sweet, gentler than it ever was before, beneath my skin I cannot yield. In me I feel but a wretched core of cold.

This cold does not leave me, not for all the days we return to Eiriksfjord, where we drone Christ's hymns and read aloud pronouncements as we kneel within our finished church which already we've outgrown. And through our daily rounds, though I sing the melodies of Nones and morning Matins, still I find my way about is tripped, my steps troubled, my joy now hacked as once it had full grown.

Yet the Christians attend not my falter, preparing me with that cloth of red, that dress cut up and set upon my shoulders. They pin it all with brooches shining glittering bronze and bind my hair in glistened copper braids and a long headscarf of the finest whitened linen. And Ossur holds a stone of red to be worn upon my finger's joint— red, as is the color of the heart, in gold, the costly fire. Rich, I'm told, from the priest's own coffers—his gift upon this Christian joining, the first to be made whole and holy on this Greenland ground.

This bit of trinket sits and waits upon a cloth on this morning of my marriage—a distant dream, it seems, though all the fresh of the springtime's stretched over this Christian, dew-crisped hill, and the light is almost warm. The women come to lead me down to the very fjord's edge, there to hold my arms behind, so I might lean right forward and see my image mirrored in this wedding gown.

I go with them, though my steps aren't light and my heart not rightly beating. It is a heart in pain, in doubt, and a step which walks yet back as it goes forth. Back to a memory of long ago, when I'd seen this face before. Then 'twas thought—fool thought—I had peered upon a goddess—golden, never to be sorrowed, never to be scarred. Yet then came truth in the shape of force, of hate and anger, in longing to be free. And in all these lonely, hopeless years, never have I dared or even tempted so to peer again.

Ah, I cannot go! Cannot look, for those gentle wisps I know have become gray with tarnish, that blameless visage warped with lines and a reddened scar and some missing teeth and a breast and heart yet ever torn asunder. Though these ladies tease me—meaning well, they clap and tune a pleasant-meaning wedding tale. And they hold me forth. I bear their straining—ope' my eyes as I am begged—watching, fearful, knowing well what I might see—

Yet—I take a breath—upon the ripples' flecks is the image marred, imperfect, washed by the ever-constant lapping of the salted sea as is my face, ever washed by tears. So true an image I had never thought—I smile on it—I cannot help!—at that face cold-chilled with fjord's frost and that joy-ish blush turned rightly pallid. Yet the ladies do not know its why. They laugh and dance in Christian glee. They pull me back and lead me onward, up the hill insisting on a skipping step, and all across the dew-slick grasses, as they reap the honeyed gold of buttercups to slide within my palm.

There Ossur waits beside our holy house above the Brattahlid hill crest. He meets my eye, comes to me, holds my hands, kisses at the fingers. "How long we have waited for this day!" I bend my head. He reaches out and lifts my tear-streaked chin. "Say you love me not? Do you want no more to marry?"

"Nay," I whisper. My voice is caught. "Not that—only I had thought—ever thought, when it should come, Thorbjorg and even my daughter would bear witness."

He hushes me and leads me to the church, before the priest and all this Christian company. We kneel. Gudrid stands beside me as a sister, as I've never hoped or known. The altar's set with cups of silver, strewn about with buds gathered from the fells, stolen from secret hollows where the winds cannot bend to touch—ah! the fairest, tiny petals. I turn to Gudrid—her voice, the tune—they seem to brighten up my dank and chill. And even the crowd, all sudden lightening. The scent of heady smoke makes wafts and waves of silty white, as a sail or an iceberg heading toward the sea.

The priest joins our hands and feeds us bits of meal and the fragrant wine. "In the name of the Father and of the Son and of the Holy Spirit." From the same shining cup I sip as Ossur's lips. "Amen." And then it is done.

A feast is served of the gifts these friends have gathered: hard clotted cheese, sweet mead from Thjoldhilde's household store, and a roasted seal—Ossur's wedding gift—with still enough to dry and stow away for winter. And more—gifts of bone and ivory, full-brimmed sacks of rough-ground grain, skins of fine, tanned leather, ells of wool and linen cloth, tools wrought well, and even a pile of fresh-ored iron with a driftwood stack to smelt it, fat for burning and waxy sticks with wicks—such candles as I've seen only burned within this church before.

All of this is ours. Then Ossur takes my hand. He leads me with the rest across the meadow. Music plays. We dance about, trampling the flowers they have strewn beneath our footfalls. I cannot help but smile, and then, at last, to laugh. And then to cry. I cry with joy. I am a wife—like a child again—and free! And Ossur ever blessed upon the holy church and sworn to me.

Later they bear us down to the fjord, where a small ship's rigged to carry off some of this dowry's weight. There I am set within, with cloaks and furs and gifts all wrapped about me, directing the waves as the ship's stern mistress, and returning all the merry Christian shouts. Then the priest gives up his blessings, and the crowd bears round to send us off. The sound of bawdy shouts dims into the hush of stillness. Ossur and I. The silence slips around.

"Where are we going?" I ask after a time.

I watch as he sets the sail and bends the steering oar, then wraps his arm, warm and close, around my back.

"To Siglufjord. The hunting there is good this time of season. Thorbjorn Glora has just turned himself to Christian worship, so we're sent these next warmish months to serve the priest with Glora's tithe."

"Hunting?"

"Well, and you'll go with me. Help me with the gutting chores and keep our camp and heat a kettle to warm my feet."

I cannot help but giggle. I look from him across the bow. This ship is narrow; the draught is low, the waves not yet very choppy. So closely drifts the ice. Ossur leans, and I know he would touch me, but he holds himself away and sets about to trim the sail into the wind.

We are silent through the mist and wave. We round the mouth of Eiriksfjord and turn about. For some long time we ply among the massive hulks of icebergs and sway, awash in the bare black sea. The ship moves steadily. Ossur's gentle with the sheet as we maneuver past Thorbjorn Glora's homestead, astir with cattle, and thick upon the fells with goats and sheep. A call of greeting floats across the bay. Ossur waves his hand but says no answer.

At will, we come at last upon a still-swept island. Such a flattened coast as none I've known anywhere in Greenland. A mist hangs above, dangling heavy over icebergs which ring about the shoals. Ossur pulls the sail. I help him with its sheathing. We ride the oars to catch the gravel shallows, then he bounds over the rail to drag the ship and me from the lapping waves.

The boat is still and rocking slightly. I feel the breeze, soft upon my cheek, as he lifts me up and gently takes me.

"So long have I longed for you," he whispers, "for what seems now longer than my life."

He lets the gravel touch my feet. Dry. The rounded stones seem old, so old no man has ever touched them. No man, it seems, would ever dare.

We gather up what little driftwood twigs are here to find. Then Ossur leads me, step by step, along a shallow ridge. The mounded walk is thick with lichen. Black flakes beneath our steps. We leave a trail, light and gray, behind. The mist seems, too, to follow. When I turn, I see no ship at all but a soft gray twilight, as if we are slipped behind a curtain, alone in all the world.

Ossur takes my hand. Beyond this barren stretch, we rise before a field. It is golden with poppies the size of babies' fists, all draped in dew and faintly wafting. I gasp as if to speak, but Ossur raises his hand to hush my lips and lightly, barely, guides me on.

Now the mist is risen up complete, coming before me as if the earth itself had learned to breathe it: three small puffs beyond the field of gold and green. We reach the edges—steaming springs—three rings all filled, so clear they seem as tear-filled eyes.

"Healing waters," he murmurs. "Sacred, for the priest has blessed and made them holy in the name of Christ." I turn to see his face, and Ossur mine.

We are soft in the mist-dew, soft as a dream, his hands like angels' wings upon my neck and lightly on my shoulders, barely touching the draping of my dress; yet where it once did hang, it once does fall. And I upon him, too, feeling his cloak and then his jerkin slip away. Somewhere, there slips away all time and thought; a warmth seeps at our feet; we slide into the unguent—there to feel the ancient heat, the softened fire of our timeworn, ill-used passion. The healing spring slips between our skins, no longer separate as Ossur masks my body with his own, heals my eternal pain with some gentle, new sensation.

Never, ever had I thought—for the thought of painful memory is finally washed and borne away, as the tainting mud is swept by rain.

Then we lie in stillness. All the earth is quiet breath and subtle flow. We are naked, my ashen skin touched this once by the cast of cloudy hue. The water calms my odd distortions and adds its own, as if to carve a new beast out of tangled flesh. It is neither woman nor man, but some strange, miraculous creation; and the mists above have formed such shapes as if we both bore wings.

There are no words. Not for a long, still twilight, even as we tuck within our hunter's booth and light our fire and eat some meat.

I watch Ossur keenly. His light-blue eyes fade before the fire's glow, though still they spark, the lines about them soft but clear as the shadows dance, and his flaxen hair, dulled with time, dangled down and dripping, and his beard, newly combed and damp about the edge, is slightly flecked with gray.

"We are old," I say.

"We are old, but does it matter really?"

He takes my hands and presses them to his cheeks, and I feel the moist of both our wants joining as a single tear. He smells of sweetness, chamomile, and juniper as I press myself gently against his skin. And I know by the fire's light he has seen my faded flesh, my white-cracked hands, my arms as brown as any sheep's dung, and the scar upon my breast where he laid his lips as if to soothe the ancient, lingered pain.

My Father
(Deceiver)

BIBRAU

FOR A TIME I play the bond-thrall's bluff, with my head bowed low
and my pallid cheek and my hands ever busy at some dullsome chore.
So—even stitching up my own scant share of sheep's wool gathered
from the fell-slopes' boulders. Hard they are on these house-thralls,
battered, broke, and even on the mistress, now lost of all her force and
will.

Oh, such meek restraint will not be my rejoinder. How I long to
hurl my petty slight upon a sharp and pointed wind! Yet for now revenge must wait. So I stitch my portion slowly, till the others stare
and whisper, almost breathless, "Ah, her will—at last—finally, 'tis
quelled!" And then I smile, if only to myself, that such fools should
grow so quickly used to counterfeit and trusting. Yet they watch me
now not much at all, and ne'er again so closely—not even Mistress
Thorbjorg, who knows my ways and should know well my ploys.

Each night, I sit and stitch my tiny darnings—a little rhyme made
out of runes too small to catch the mistress' aging eye. Such, they
mark the way my yarn will ravel: from a shining day and my mother's
perfect, Christian bliss, to a rough-edged ice and a treacherous, deadly
blow. Yet how to twirl this twine? I have no clear direction. Though I
know my craft—my fylgie's taught me fair—still there is no doer for
the deed. Yet one will come, and soon and surely, for every night I make
the proper ritual: just as my fylgie showed me, from the reeking midden, thick with wasting grist' and bone, I watch bugs creep and maggots wriggle, till at last I spot upon a female mouse come scurrying
and starved. She I catch and set her in a bowl with well-turned edges,

press icy water into fire till some dewy steam rises up. Then I watch this niggling mouse who cannot climb along those scrabbling walls, slowly steep till she expires.

With summer, Thorbjorg returns to speaking prophecy. She has no choice, for our stores are low, the grain we've sown not yet full-ripe, and our sheep's flesh needed more for milk than slaughter. Taking Svan and Kol, a boat and me, we sail upon whatever household near will listen. Though they are less about, for that Christian fiend does claim the mistress' good a mock; and says of me far worse: such words are whispered, hushed and cold, wherever I do enter.

Yet such chat, like chilling stones, is hard and crisp and like to echo. Upon this slander, I learn Gudmund Torkelsson has run from Greenland's shore. "Clipped upon the first ship's sail for Tryggvason's court," hisses a sharp-toothed house-thrall, "there to hie and heed among the lords and Christians! And his mother, too, turned soul and heart upon that lot—some say, on that very eve the wretched deed was done, she bore within her hand a worried cross."

Well to hear, as they eye me keenly, hoping I will turn my head, spit a curse, or shed a tear. Yet my own retort is something finer—on my face, a look serene and of a gentle hue. This they spy—far more a-feared than if I'd flung a dagger's cut—while the truth, indeed, they ne'er can fathom: that I care no more for Gudmund's plight. I've had of him already all I ever wanted.

So and such, into each house I walk with my fair-painted guise, there upon the mistress' heels, my head bent low and my eyes calm, cool, reflected. Even so, I am kept apart—even locked up thrice within a byre—there waiting among the goats and dung till some sickness grows too great and the mistress begs for me. I feed upon it, silent-scoffing as those bond-thralls free me and those freemen watch, a-tremble as I lay my hands—they drawing back as I bandage up a stone-slashed wrist or slice a row of runes into a birthing rafter. And when the wrist heals smooth and the child borne bears no changeling marks, reluctantly they set a place upon their board for me.

Nearly comes the month of sun when a call bears my mistress

toward Einarsfjord and the great hall of Gardar. Still a fortnight till the Althing-tide, but a sickness has befallen the master's calves. 'Tis a petty thing, yet so we go, that none should be too pale for market.

We are greeted fair and treated rightly. The chieftain Einar, wise upon the ancient ways, labors not to do the mistress or me wrong. Well fed we are, on beasts' hearts boiled in a goat's curd stew. Still I dull upon the dinner discourse, such of ever blight and Christians. Most is Einar's talk of the priest's own feeble promise: that to ply with Jesus Christ is to escape death, or at least to be risen from the grave. To me such talk sounds nigh and near enough to Hel itself—to be set upon this wretched earth forever? Yet hereabouts all do heave this rough debate, while I, within the shadows, turn my whittle-knife to the same cruel scratches I had knitted in the Tofafjord wool, this time tight and small upon a knotty Gardar roof-post's beam.

Soon the mistress beckons me to gather thistle brush to strew about the sick calves' stalls. Dutifully I go, pleased to scrape and bow, giving an undue show of obsequious demeanor. Yet out among the twilight shadows of the ice clefts I am myself once more, dancing in the rising beam of the half-lit moon with the ebony cush' of sod beneath my feet and the willow binds twined upon themselves as a death-bound lovers' tangle. Ah, I please to hear them crackle as I tear among the briared slope. Yet as I do, comes a jolt upon my vision.

Barely, but I still my dance. I listen through the hollow. Hushed enough to hear the icebergs coughing in the harbor, sounds a snap and then again a jolt. There, caught within the twilight's keen, is the shadowed, sunken visage of Torvard.

He stands as ever, watching me—as he always has, at every gathering, from the Althing to the Yule. At each I can remember he has come to me, e'er like this, a lurking hulk, till someone rushes to break us off. Ever I had wondered why. Yet now I know.

Know why he reached that day when he lay broken on the horse-field, then again that night when I stalked him out among the frost-nipped heaves—even dared to ply me, dared that once to touch my face. Oh, his shaking hand, the cold of it, the dewy press, and the look upon his eyeball—hard beneath and hating—too, in such a curious crave, as if he'd seen some savage strength in me he himself had lost inside.

My father. Yes. My father. 'Tis a haunting. Sickening. How he shies aback even now as the coward he has always fashioned—a crumbled mite who can barely scratch upon a sheep's dry turd. Oh, it is too much! He, who wept that night like a bare, impotent fool—this pitiful, lumbering wastling! Yet, every time he shoulders near my mother, has she not trembled, gripped and tugged but hard upon my hand? And each time aft'—how often has my mother tremored, turning pale or sickly green upon his sight, then churning nights, shouting terrors in her dreams.

. . . All this, I think, as I watch a thistle with its prickly thorns seep blood from out my finger . . .

Just then I know—I see it all—how at last to make my vengeance. If he is my father, then I will please to play him well. And he'll be much inclined, knowing not my thoughts yet full-prone to my intention. Of the certain sort of menace perfect for my plans. Perhaps far better than my cruelest dreams!

It is not long till I find my method also. 'Tis a simple philter, really. Almost at my call, by the brightening of that moon comes again my woman's bleeding. Just so, I stuff myself with rags and, waiting until midnight, when all of Gardar sleeps, I go to the mountains high, right up to the edge of ice, and whisper words—all those words my fylgie ever taught me—and pluck from off the rag the ruddy, stink-soaked beads. Then I build a fire's smoke about them. For three nights, fasting, breathing tunes, casting herbs and bits of blood and thrice times filth from out my buttocks. Above me, mists sweep thick across the moon when I take the dried bits and grind them down into a fine red dust.

Then I go to him. Early—when Torvard's wastrel body and even his witch-wise wife and my own mistress are locked in sleep, in the morning, before the house-thralls waft up the hearth fire's smoke—I go with my powder, and put it—mixed a bit with spittle into a slimy clot—first, bitter on my lips, and then, hard and silent, spit into Torvard's shoes. I leave them then with their toes pointing toward him, so my spirit—my *hug*—might climb into his soul.

That very night, while the others drink—Thorbjorg, too, with a horn within her hand, for the calves are healed and all around are gay and shrilling—Torvard sucks in heavy draughts of silence until, at times, he sleeps, then wakes just enough to drink some more. Meanwhile, I sit, running sticks across the mead-mucked ground, until I see at last only he and I are broad-eyed, watching one another across the snoring hall.

He leans his head upon the bench where his mistress, Freydis, snores, already with drooling lips and her thick legs sprawling. For a time Torvard and I share a daggered glance, until the game grows cold. Then Torvard slaps a draught into his gullet, emptying the mead-horn, then throws it down and hard across the floor.

It rolls until it rests at my feet. Sudden comes an almost tinkling stillness. I know my fylgie plays upon the eaves. As I listen, Torvard twists, ears burning, seeming almost yet to hear, leaning against the very roof-post I have so keenly altered, rolling his cheek against the rough-hewn beam.

Still holding Torvard's drink-swept gaze, I bend. The hearth fire burns between us. Taking up his cast-off horn, I touch it softly on its rigid edge and sip there just a taste of sweet upon my lips—bare enough to tinge them.

KATLA

AFTER SOME FEW DAYS alone and peaceful on this island, Thorbjorn Glora sends us aid: four ripe, healthy boys. They are young and strong and fair-good hunters, who cast wide nets and hurl their death-clubs swift and sharply. So, together, through these many weeks, we all work to gain the priest his tithe. And though my back hard-aches and my hands grow red and raw, never has my heart known such vivid joy. Beside my love, each dawn and dusk and ofttimes in between, we say our prayers as best we might, singing *"Hallelujah!"* when our catch is won, and again on a fine, bright eve after a week of storms.

So I learn to trust in Christ once more. These days I do my best to think little of what has been: the razing of the circle, of Thorbjorg, or my daughter. 'Twas right and needed, as the good priest said again when he came this way just past the moon's full, blessing our fine seal catch and saying the Mass here with us. He is wise and full with fond compassion, counseling me and Ossur to say each night a prayer to guide Thorbjorg's and my daughter's wandered souls.

Upon midsummer's pale, reluctantly we set our sail, waving fair goodbyes to our helpmates safe ashore at Glora's homestead, and head toward the Althing at Gardar. Our hull is filled with the Lord our God's rich bounty—mounds of salt-dried meat enough to keep the priest well fatted through winter; skins, some I've roughly sewn to cloaks or leather jerkins; and many bones sweetly carved by Ossur's patient fingers into crosses and other righteous signs of Christ our Lord. "All these," Ossur says, "we'll ply for sale upon the Althing market. Surely they will bring the church fine gain." He checks me gently while we work the rigging of our smallish craft.

"Nay, to the port," I shout. "Port!" again, over the sea-lapped railing.

"Good!" he cries. "These days you are near as fine at setting course as at sewing up the edging of a tattered sail." I smile, for I am proud of it. We talk as we work upon these icy waters, Ossur most of how he sorely wants to tie some proper silver keys clanking on my housewife's belt. I listen, wistful, longing for someday when the winds will howl loud and fiercely but we, inside our own homestead with our own hearth fire ablaze, will sit close together, safe and still and warm.

Such wishful talk through the balmy dew of this midsummer's dawn bears us quick to Einarsfjord. Soon we sight upon the Gardar plain, all a-bustle with the Althing's cheerful noise. Here are good Christian merchants, tents drawn up and flapping sails and booths run thick with goods for market, the air hung sharp with shouts of price, scents of roasting meats, birds a-flying on a tether.

I truss our sail while Ossur sets the oars into the shallow waters. Still a dozen lengths away, suddenly the stony beach fills up with what seems almost a brimming crowd.

"So many!" I breathe, "As if we bear some silver-laden Viking spoil!" counting friends, yet strangers, too, and also several thralls—some once I would have thought but foes—feeling ill-at-ease as they reach for us and catch our ropes to pull us shoreward, until I note their bond-runes joined with Christian crosses.

We are grinding on the gravel shallows when, through this congregation, comes a shriek. Inga, round and rosy, runs toward me, her headcloth slipping back as she flings her arms and wraps them hard about. She kisses me quick, then, gasping, asks me in a mocking lilt, "Had you guessed all that would pass while you were off upon your wedding venture? Nay! Yet now don't you know but I am a Christian, too!"

"A Christian?"

"Katla, aye!" She nearly lifts me from the craft. "Katla, remember so, how long ago, your mother said I might find comfort on this path? Then I had thought, No, never! Yet look! I am born to Christ! And even to be married, well and rightly, here upon this very Althing field, to my own Snaebjorn, and at the priest's own words!"

Inga seizes me with a strong and honest grip. Up the hill we walk—arm in arm, as two young girls might—Inga telling me with every step each name of every thrall and freeman who has ever borne the thought to turn a Christian.

"So," she trips, "now has Eirik Raude come at last into the church. They say 'twas fair enough, these four long months Thjoldhilde would not bear his sight! True, for she had turned her very household all to work upon the Christian task, till it seemed our mightiest chieftain might go about to beg his meat and lodging. But then, when came these many Christian traders to our shores, Eirik bent before the priest and made the sign of the Christian cross above his bosom. Most whisper 'twas to prime-sign and nothing more, for when he left from Thjoldhilde's church, that very minute he turned as quickly back upon his pagan hof and, some say, true, he swore as ever up to mighty Thor!"

She giggles, pulling at me faster. "But would you think"—she larks, "would you ever guess—even *he* has turned to Jesus?" She points up toward her master's hall at the crest of the Gardar hill.

"Master Einar?"

"Nay," she chides. "But look again, Katla. Look at *him*!"

I see at once: Torvard at the Gardar door, leaning against the house-bound pillars, chewing at his knuckled hands.

"Nay . . ." He seems more like a wild, vicious, entangled dog. "Nay . . ." as I shake away my shiver.

" 'Tis true! Can you believe? Who'd've ever thought? Torvard, turned a Christian! Well, almost—for of late he comes to Mass and mouths the Latin prayers, though I have yet to hear him rightly baptized."

"It cannot . . . I can't believe it."

"Katla, seems you almost do not wish it. I thought you would be well relieved! In gentleness and mercy, says our father-priest, to welcome all into Christ's strong arms."

"Yet, Inga—yes, I know we should. So I do . . . welcome Torvard."

Inga cocks her head and clucks her tongue against her teeth. " 'Twas all so long ago, Katla. Fair and well enough, forget it! You are married now to your own fine Ossur, and free—fully free, with no more talk of anguish or loss of hope. More than any other of us slaves, though the priest vies upon the chiefs to free more of Christ's worthies. Yet you are free already—free as any maid—free as Freydis, Torunn, or Eirik's Thjoldhilde her very self! Such, you should rejoice in Jesus' love and welcome all his mercies—"

"How can you say, Inga, 'forget,' when you, most of all, know what has gone?"

"Calm," she hushes, seeing now my full-most heart is washed with sickness. "Let us talk no more about it. Soon enough you will see yourself who comes upon the church when we are married. Katla, please do not be cross. You will yet come?"

"Of course. When will be the wedding?"

"Upon the morrow and the morning Mass. I begged our priest to have it so—the day after your return."

On that dawn, 'tis true. There upon the hillside is a tent filled wider than our tiny church at Brattahlid would e'er have room to lodge. Within, indeed, is Eirik Raude, standing gruff and awkward beside Thjoldhilde. Next is Leif, Thorstein, Thorvald, then Gudrid with her father, Thorbjorn Vifilsson, then sits Freydis, Eirik's bastard daughter, at his right. Then, beside her, Torvard, sitting, cowered at the very edge of a too-short bench. And there I stand at the edging of the crowd, with Ossur at my side in his new bright cloak of a rich brown cloth bought with the priest's generous duty, and I wrapped in a shawl about my neck of the softest whitened wool. We look as fine and rightly as the proud and free-made couple we have recent been. Yet Torvard's eyes are sharp and quick—too quick and like to glare. I press Ossur to look his way. Yet, when he does, Torvard sudden turns his gaze into a smile.

"Katla, ah! Come, you must sit by me." Gudrid Thorbjornsdatter takes my hands, entwines her thin white fingers between my own. She guides me through the crowd as the priest then ushers Ossur up to do him service. As he goes, there I stumble, feeling strangely frail and torn asunder. Gudrid helps me sit. I try to calm my heart. At the corner of my vision, thighs line up along that bench—and one set, thick and tucked up tight with musky sealskin leggings, jiggering up and down as with some anxious, angry, cruel, un-Christian need.

Still comes my breath, quickly now as a hare caught in a sharp-toothed snare. I am flushed and hot, yet Gudrid grasps me coolly. "Katla, are you not well?" She turns to me with a curious smile to her fair concern. She touches on my cheeks. Her hands are smooth and tender as she brushes back a strand of curl falling from my kerchief.

The priest intones his praises and his blessings. Some cups are passed, then a ring on Inga's hand. Soon the crowd is rising from their places. Inga stands with her Snaebjorn, her face thick-gleamed in a spread of shining tears. Gudrid helps me rise and walks with me to kiss on Inga's cheeks. "And when we are through," she whisp's, "you must come to join us in the Gardar hall."

"The Gardar hall? Upon the chiefs' meet? Know you well, never have I stood within that hall except to serve?"

"Then all the more," Gudrid presses, "for your presence will do our cause much good. You must be wise and helpful to our purpose—to show these pagans what fine and valued worth are such well-thought, freed, and Christian slaves."

Gudrid gathers me and Ossur both and guides us from the wedding service, across the grassy green, then dark and low into the sod-struck Gardar hall. My ancient master Einar greets us. I fright' away, but he bears me kind, peering in that gaze I recall from when I was but a child. Taking my hand, he shows us to a place at the edging of his table-board—true, on a darker corner—true, so far away we can barely see his high-seat at the center of the hall. Yet truer, too, from this far-ish crook, I can see nothing of Torvard.

Ossur's place is at my side, and well, for our own dear priest is at his other. Though already the holy man is up and wandering, whispering something into Einar's hearing, sounding close upon Eirik Raude's, then nearly bent by Thorbjorn Glora's knee. Yet not far, on another dusky seat—I hold my breath—is Mistress Thorbjorg.

Nay, I turn away. All at once the mistress' gnarled fingers reach me. "Katla, you look well and happy—such as you deserve." On her craggy face, a patient, tempered courtesy. "I am pleased for you." She lets my hand go gently. Well I note my daughter is nowhere about. I do not ask, nor does the mistress offer.

Soon enough come food and drink. I lift my knife and take a nibble. Through the smoky haze and noise, Einar calls the time to speak, when oaths are made and promises and boasting.

"Well"—he clears his throat—"I stand before you now, host upon this Althing meeting. Yet this day I find, instead of welcoming you with toasts to our own and ancient Norse god Bragi, I am called upon to bless this feast in the name of Jesus Christ."

All are shocked to hear it. Though his horn's half full, he seems near sober as he raises it before the crowd. Grumbling's about. Some chieftains turn with horrored looks, while others eye upon their half-supped meat. Only my Ossur's face is sparked with still. The priest himself sits with hands but folded, sudden quiet on his long, black frock.

"We are goodly chieftains—fair men who care for all our households and our flocks. As such, we have learned some smallish wisdom in being limber, as when we came in our drifting craft to this Greenland, fifteen years now past, to make our way. Through these seasons, our own gods have favored us, and we have fared some well. Yet lately we have witnessed harder dealings, as, on calling out to Odin, Thor, and all our greatest gods, still our homesteads echo with the hollow loss from plague. True, and our ports would empty-echo louder if Leif Eiriksson had not brought this Christian priest upon our shores. At first, I'd thought it fool' and faulty to listen to his Latin speech. Yet we have all heard rumors of such ports abroad which will bare abide to hear Old One-Eyed's name aloud; and from pagan merchants we have all seen ships bearing rotting goods which could not be sold upon the Christians' ports. So it seems indeed in Iceland, Norway, and all these lands about, where once the name of Christ was never spoke', now 'tis heard quite often.

"So, though I'd not thought or sought to change my way, here I find such ways do change themselves. Fellows, here again is a chance to rise upon a mighty venture, to make our way as best we can and, like all our forebear Viking fathers, conquer and prevail. Yet, unlike the past, not with battle-ax or sword, but today with a word, a single phrasing. So this day I bend myself before all here and Eirik Raude, my ancient friend and counsel, and make this pledge to sanction worship, upon all my landholds, of Jesus Christ and the Christian Lord."

Thus he speaks—my ancient master, who has ever stood but fast to Thor. Yet he takes this promise to his lips. He sips the mead, then passes on the horn. Eirik Raude sips it quick and sends it with a shaking toward the quizzicked looks of all these Greenland masters.

Again Chieftain Einar clears his throat. "Priest, some months ago, you begged a bit of dirt to build your church. Eirik's mistress made some work upon this task, but not of such a size or worth to serve these many Christians. At first hearing, I quick-rebuked such using of my lands. But now I stand before you giving up such dirt and what free hands I may to aid you in your goal."

Our priest stands up. "In the name of the Father, the Son, and Holy Spirit," he intones, "Jesus Christ welcome you and our Lord God bless you for your generous bequeath. Yet," he breathes, "I have one wish—somewhat small and yet much needed."

"Speak it, father," Einar offers, though the word's still awkward to his lips.

"Upon my mission, I will walk about and travel often. Rarely will I tend such flocks as should gather in this new Jesus' house. I would set my helpmate, Ossur Asbjarnarsson—a fine-born freeman, now servant of our Christian Lord—to serve upon such church, to work its lands and bring about its harvests, to tend its flocks of people and of sheep and guide this fond assemblage with his goodly new-made mistress, Katla, to be as tenants of the Lord."

I hear the words, even hear my name spoke' out, knowing not their honest weight, nor daring on their precious meaning. "Ossur—?" I whisp'.

In his hand is the well-drunk horn. "Sip, my love, for you will be a proper mistress, with such keys bound up on your housewife's belt and a homestead of our own."

His eyes are gleaming, bright as daylight's faulty glow before the sinking of the sun. I know I am full stunned and should be wholly pleased! Yet—"Here?"

"Indeed, my love. Upon this very Gardar soil." He kisses me but soft upon my lips. I pull away, feeling rather, then, to ply aback into the long-hall's darkest corner. Made free and loved and landed fair and even Christian—yet, for all of these, to be settled hard beside my greatest foe!

Another hand is set upon my shoulder. It is wide and strong. My heart pounds as it turns me round.

"Katla, are you content?"

"Master Einar—"

" 'Master?' Never 'master' more. Not to me, nor e'er again to any other." Einar nods to turn my gaze on Thorbjorg. "Your priest and I spoke long and hard while you were gone."

"Spoke?"

"Of many things—of gentleness and mercy. Of sorry promise and vain regret. Of much long passed which cannot be unmade, and reparations too long wasted."

"I had not thought . . ." I bow my head, seeing in his sense such worn and lingered anguish. "I should thank you well."

"Yet thank me not. Only drink some little sweetness from my sorrow." So he lifts his hand to brush the air before my cheek, nearly touching there its long-fixed scar. Yet he lets the gesture fall as, from the closest shadows, our priest quick nears and, not far behind— Torvard.

Einar takes his foul son by the wrist, turns him close and dear upon my Ossur. "Asbjarnarsson," he speaks, "too long have you borne but well my son's abuses. Yet now Torvard is set upon the Christian faith. I pray, indeed—and 'tis our good priest's own persuasion—that he make peace so you may guide him in Jesus' way."

"I would like it so," my Ossur answers. "Ever have I wished it."

And the priest: "One day perhaps even friendship may come between you. In Christ, all may be forgiven."

"Indeed," Torvard says, eyeing me not once in all this play at amity, "in Christ"—he grins—"is it not said to love thy neighbor?"

"So it is." Ossur smiles back while the priest there stands, his palm clutched white upon my husband's long brown robe.

Ossur takes up Torvard's proffered hand as men are wont to do when making mighty compacts, while Torvard tenders, showing through his lips a crack of teeth, "Then let it be between us also."

Jaegers'
Meat

BIBRAU

I CUT THE RUNES. I cut them deep. I draw them down then, stroke by stroke. Cut them backward. Twist them inside out. I cut them as my fylgie taught me, each prong and fork turned in upon itself—as Thorbjorg saw them once, yet when she did she shied her hand a-quiver. Though she chided not, but merely reached to straight' the plying of my tool. From such, and several times before, I have marked when Thorbjorg withholds her thought it is her greatest time for fearing. I have learned to listen to the space between her whispers, for there is where the greatest secrets dwell.

So I cut the runes. I cut them as my fylgie watches, his fist between his small, sharp teeth, pressed into his white and bony hand. How it curls about, seeming sometimes like a claw as it reaches ope', then shuts, then ope's again. At the corner of my glancing, in the edging of my eye, I stare not back nor snicker with his own delight, though he is fair and drooling nearly, tiptoe-dancing on the coming of this strike. Yet nay, for this task of mine I can glee at nothing or else foul up my spite. So I set about with concentration. Not even his wicked laughter can shake the measure of my knife.

I cut the runes. I cut them crooked. I ply them with my left hand turned, my blade held back, shining sharp into the deathly moonlight. So, before the dawn-dew parches and the breath of life grows audible and honest, I finish up my cuts, then spark up fire and burn them down to coals. Of this ash, I call a wind to bear them long and far and distant, cast upon a certain plain, a certain pallid face, a certain mockish manner—to draw this Torvard out and ply him to my will—till naught he does can be set apart to answer, nor e'er again be made up straight or right or whole.

KATLA

So we will be neighbors. So it seems. Yet how, to live within one breath of Gardar's shadow when each slight step might come a tripping greeting from Torvard?

We walk along the Gardar pasture—first the priest, then Einar, then all we Christians in a bandy row—plying toward a place which will one day be our Christian manor. And Ossur glows at me and wraps his arm firm and strong about my shoulder. Triumphant fool! His very look does sap my vigor. I try to touch his cheek, to give a meaning glance, a secret, whispered breath. Yet I say naught—how can I say but naught?—as, beneath our feet, the trembled slog of Torvard's gait rocks the earth as a ship upon a swell.

Oh, unsteady as we sail across the Gardar slopes, fair beside these Christ-made chiefs and all their freeborn kindred. All of them and him and me—and Torvard bare a breath apart—nigh so close as to stagger on my hem's fall. Yet he comes not near and barely raises up an eye. Nay, he seems most solemn as he proceeds.

Near enough, yet I do not trust. I cannot. No, I will not—must not—ever! How to turn the other cheek—so wronged, so old, so brute, so wrecked and wretched? Yet all these about—seems even my own Ossur has forgot—nay! He would not forget what has been my pain.

I would but scream: can I press this grit from out my teeth? Return the bloom to my tooth-scarred bosom? Nay! Nor put back what horror issued from my ill-used womb. It cannot be forgiven.

Comes near me now another footstep. "Ossur, see how Katla stumbles?" Gudrid takes me off and sets me well apart to rest, bending to kiss my brow. "By the Mother of our God, hush and breathe and let me speak for you a little cheerful. I know you are, for you will live beside this church—here—upon this very Gardar soil." She strokes my rough hands with hers, soft as the mossy sod. "A finer fate cannot befall a better Christian."

Knowing nothing—she knowing not! I hide away my glance, though I know she means to praise me highly.

She notes it, bearing with the kindest, prodding quizzick—"Are you not well?"—till I gird myself, shaking my head to wash the fright from off my face—nay, for the thought, near worse than terror's dread, that Gudrid, fine, should ever know my past or pains.

Just then, Chieftain Einar gathers all the trailing crowd upon a nearby grassy hill. "Christ's men," he calls, "come and tell how these Gardar acres suit your pious purpose," with his hand flung out in generous dimension. Ossur comes, sweet, yet rushing—even brushing rashly Torvard's forearm—to catch our waddled priest and share some whispered, urgent counsel.

Then our father squeaks, "Chieftains, unto our good Heaven, these lands will suit Christ's fairest needs full well."

"From this day," Einar proclaims, "this stretch of my own farmstead—from the base of this Greenland ice unto the rocky sea—will be made and kept by this priest and his own servants, ever for the Christian Lord."

"Praise be!" some cry. Yet others in the crowd quick murmur, pulling on their beards' long whiskers, wondering well on the prospect of Einar's ample gift, while I, for all my might, gaze upon what lands will be our soon-day homestead. Here. This very earth. And though 'tis light and warm and set upon with the fairest, greenest pastures, 'tis bare an hour's pace between this stretch and the Gardar hall.

Steps Torvard forth, all aglow with a mocking-pious beacon. "Hear, then! Hear me well, I say! I am happy—glad to make of mine own inheritance this welcome Christian premises. To prove, before this winter's dark I myself will aid our priest's own helpmate Ossur build such church upon this land as ought to rise upon our Greenland!"

Then Torvard turns his eye. It is as a hook upon a string: him stretching, not toward me this time but toward my Ossur—my beloved Ossur, slim and good and fine, so buoyed and so naïve. And Torvard reaching up from where he stands—his hands outstretched, his heavy boots lumbering across the lumpy frost-heaves, and Ossur baited by the twisted glimmer of a smile.

Baited, true, as Torvard clutches hard and fast—his hand, thick and hairy, red and damp with sweat, while Ossur's hand is smooth and gold and dry. And then that smile. So well I know that smile—that smile and all the evil things it hides.

BIBRAU

FATHER, SAY I? Father, fair indeed. Father, borne upon a seed gone brute and twisted. Father, for all my blood bound up with yours, though yours be spit and mire. Yet, Father, good, if it be true: your ancient hate will serve my need.

I bid you well and go. Go silently, so none do note you. Veer not upon a straight-drawn thread but knot a tangled path. You are practiced some in this perjurer's art? You veer upon this chance—even welcome it—so I sense in you the old feud awakening as you bow about and make fine moves and even laugh.

Laugh! Just so—for perhaps it is not only I who would ply this vengeance. Perhaps I've found an apt ally to work upon my hate. But I sense in you an anxious thrust, an unschooled rage, which would bear a thoughtless anger. Quell the thought! I ply you soft to carry on our game.

Be patient. Just a little longer—some fair few weeks till you have cast away your air of threat, plying now your hand to my mother's artless lover in helpful, easy things. Ah, yes, you can wait, for so can I. Truly waiting makes sweet vengeance linger longer. So ply on patience, Torvard—father-fate—for I will have my pleasure's mead.

KATLA

LAST DAYS upon the Althing: more feasts and toasts and drinks and boasting, more of men at mighty meets and sweets and other riches set to prize. Yet each dawn some men stride out with our priest's foot-fall to strike such earth to build this church's new foundation, this time wide and long and deep, with a separate bound of stones to be our homestead nigh.

Well I should be joyous as each day a round of thicker sod is cut to lay between those dirt-dug slabs. Yet I cannot help but quiver as Tor-vard joins each morning—lending, true, his heavy hand, this time not for e'er-borne menace but to build such place he boasts will be our "home in Christ." So he says, smiling much with his ruddy, wind-cracked lips, bowing low before our priest and Ossur. Each day he plies my hand in doleful, cloying style, fair and indiscreet with what ill-wrought aim I can but reckon from the past. Meanwhile, our father-priest sustains and praises Torvard, loud and shrilly, seeming bare to note or remember now my confessed injury, and only pleased with each day's rote as his church grows thick and broadly.

Each hour, each drench of sweat Torvard and my Ossur share, each blistered pus of work, each feeble scratch's bleeding is as Torvard slinking closer. Too close as he wraps his arm like a crush about my Ossur's shoulders, drawing fast his feet as Ossur stumbles, made awkward by his force and the dreadful muscle of his pace and stride. Yet Torvard laughs and Ossur plies to welcome such vile, blatant ges-tures, singing fair how changed this Torvard seems. "Cast well upon the air of Christian virtue. Don't you see him, Katla," Ossur dares, "bringing men from the Gardar hall to build our walls up sure and finely?"

"Fine, indeed," I say aloud, noting how such talk is ripe and riled when the priest is nearest; till such eve as at last we are alone within our Althing booth, I can bear no more and speak my care and trial. "Ossur, how can you endure it? How, when you, above all else, know well what Torvard's done upon us both?" I wait for him to speak. Yet for so long he is silent, I am tempted to bare my bosom e'er again, to show such scar as he himself has touched so oft to tender-heal.

Ossur turns to me at last, laying hands about my cheeks and nearly tearful. "Know you well, beloved, the priest but presses on me hard! He says we must make Torvard our fair and keenest ally."

"Torvard?"

"Torvard, indeed. Says he you must know how dear is this alliance. Chieftain Einar is not young. One day he will pass his riches to his eldest son. So we must befriend him now, to bring the church a greater sway—"

"A greater sway and tithers' riches? And all I've borne of damage, all I've yet endured, is naught before the priest's own cause?"

"Says our priest, if we should play but well among the soon-be chieftains, 'twill not be long before their faiths are fully turned and all this ruddy land made true to Jesus." Ossur looks on me and I on him. " 'Tis a fair and worthy mission."

"Worthy . . ." I whisp', then for a breath can say no more. "To build such church upon such worth as has ever been my woe."

"Says our priest, you must stand and bear it, find within your faith such strength as Mother Mary's before the cross. There she stood, even calm to sacrifice the infant from her bosom. Our priest asks far less of you."

I turn and bite my cheek, but Ossur comes and takes my hands. "Says our priest, there is naught much greater than to cede from hatred's clutch—indeed, to love thine enemies. He begs you try, upon the saving of your soul. Says he, too, in Christ you must turn the other cheek, forget all Torvard's once-transgressions, embrace him to your Christian heart, forgive at last your lifelong pain."

"Forget. Forgive," I murmur. "I have heard it so and oft. It is the Christian mode, and perhaps even my mother would have plied it. Yet, Ossur, do not ask it of me—I cannot—will not—ever."

Ossur shakes his head. "So I've told our priest, and lingered long upon your wrought and deserved pain. Yet he says it is your own heart's cruelest beat, born of pagan anger."

"Pagan?" For that phrase I can bare respond—to ply such talk, which cuts me to the heart, even from our father! So oft have I heard it used, this pagan claim, against the mistress Thorbjorg. Now to use it to quell my reasoned anguish? To tame what little pride I dare to guard my lingered dignity?

I say nothing more as these days roll by and each dawn and dusk bring Torvard's comings and his goings. Before our Althing booth he bends to lend Ossur his hand, smiling at me, and even daring once to reach to kiss my fingers. Yet, that time I pulled but fast and cold away.

When they are gone upon the church's work, my days are mostly spent in fretting, there upon the hillside's crest, with Gudrid at my side. True enough, she is my new and close companion. We talk but little of my strife, though her glance would say she understands. With her little smiles, her patient words, her suggestions that we sit a bit and rest, I find in her some comfort for my weight of woe. Yet I would not taint her calm with full confessing. In truth, though her heart is honest in its concern, ever there is space between us. At times when I spy below and note Torvard with his foul, hovered shadow, I long instead for Inga's simple speech, her ruddy, work-lined cheeks, and her black and broken teeth: such face as hers shows well the honest truth of bond-thralls' lives.

Yet Inga, though she's Christian-made and honest-married, cannot join us on our jaunts, for she toils at the Gardar hall. Our priest speaks loud the call to free all Christ-made slaves. Eirik Raude and Chieftain Einar stand behind such act, speaking bright and righteous words upon the Althing mound. But others rumor they'll make such thralls free as tenants to their former masters, paying tax upon such land they're lent to toil without a master's cost or aid. Oh, it is not kind; yet among our church's builders are many balded pates as would claim our Christian faith. Their faith, I fear, is as Torvard's own—all of them turned upon their lips but not upon their leaning. Our priest seems unconcerned, smiling well and nodding as a raven at his feast when the thralls declare, as they take his Latin blessing, to one day pass their pity-coffers' tribute to the church's tithe.

Oh, is there any here afraid, as my mother fearful spoke of Jesus? Any yet awake to such God-bound, fevered bloom? Only Gudrid—kind, fair Gudrid—and my Ossur, true, though his heart is twined around the priest's own turn. For the rest, such faith seems at best a sheer convenience; at worst, a cruel usurer's ploy.

Strange, of all those come, the most frank seem the brash dissenters who crowd each dawn around our Christian walls in bout and protest's stride. Screaming foul rot, they clout each clot our churchmen dig. With a rash-bit curse and a pelt and heaving, they bare hammers about our hall, beating till the ground rumbles, rousing up the old invisibles' certain ire. I shiver at the thought, listening to their cursings: "Fair'y for a chance! Would you tempt Redbeard Thor or Old One-Eyed Odin's temper? Will you veer so quickly from our own true gods?" Then, upon a certain note, I know the loudest speaker's timbre. It is Thorhall Hunter, even there among the crowd.

"I tell you it is bunk—fair ridiculous!—a ship adrift to steer in flout and flunk upon a rugged sea. Upon first sailing before the autumn's crisp, 'twill be quick-told whose gods are full-faulty and whose are fair! Nary then, no Christ will aid you!" His long, brute howl hurling out such certain censure; and his eye, ever aimed but straight and keen, he lingers on the point, then turns his gaze to seize quickly on my Ossur.

"Asbjarnarsson!" Thorhall growls. "Will you remember fast your own lost faith, your own discarded deeds? How oft had we, bent upon the hunting seas of Vesterbygd and far Nordsetur, followed close some beauteous, long-toothed walrus or a spitting crowd of seals? And knowing well we would lose them fast but for our offerings made to Thunder-Hurler Thor? In a fit of flight some seasons past, you yourself made such cuts and clubs to bring such prize over our sea-slopped rail. Too, and sent up bloody praises set in smoke. Ah, I see! You do indeed remember! Remember, then, how you clung upon that jaggy bit of stone—that pebble carved with the mark of the One-Eyed wisdom-god by our own seeress Thorbjorg? You know Thorbjorg—the very mistress of your new-made bride—and boldly she kept you safe, first before such set of walrus teeth, and then again before the sweep of plague.

"Ah, yet look at you," Thorhall jeers, "all of you in your robes and sweet, sodden singing! Tell me, when the storms are 'told or comes the winter's hunger, will you wait upon these Christians as your prayers grow stale and cold? As your hearth fires cake with ice? As your coffers are quick-cleaned from this thiever's tithe? As your larders are bared but for some scat' of bones and mouse's teething? Wait! Soon you'll see what meagerness will come when you call upon this hapless Jesus Christ!"

With this speech, the crowd wells up and begins to shove and mangle. " 'Tis full disgrace!" Thorhall riles loudly. "Fair misfaithful to a deed. What, for a bit of favor from some traders charging higher price for rank and moldy goods? Nay! I say wait a week or wait a season, but to turn against your own true gods will prove but mighty ill."

At his call, hammers smash against our church stones. Our priest assigns some Christian men to guard. I watch from above the wide, muscled round, feeling well the push and heave, the angry hurl and shouting. My arms do quiver and my face feels sudden flushed, as I keen my eye on Ossur among the crowd.

Quick grows the riot as their ire bloats. Gudrid's tugging at my wrist, pulling me away. But I set her off, for too soon my Ossur's nearly cut beneath some pagan's brutal thrust. Fair on my misgiving!

Yet even then 'tis strange—Torvard stands up quick to take the battle's brunt. When I'd thought he would surely let the hammer stray to Ossur's scalp, instead Torvard catches up the fouler and turns the bloody blow away. Indeed—indeed! It cannot be, as Torvard ushers Ossur and our priest to the riot's calmer edges, then strides with all his bulk to bear these pagans' strikes, raising up his voice with strange command, "Let off! This argument is better spent upon the Althing field than about these half-built sod walls. Call your complaints before the speaker of the law. For now, leave my father's lands alone."

Thorhall's voice again bellows above the crowd like thunder:

"Will you listen to this coward's rot? Indeed, some long ago Torvard
was keen—even hungry for such battle. Now he'd rather cling upon
this meekling than a sword!" Torvard's anger simmers deep beneath
his sheen of honor. "Perhaps he is too long under the fettered thumb
of Eirik Raude's own daughter—"

Well, Thorhall has struck upon this knife of words. He twists it
quick, "What you need is proper fight! 'Tis that which ever brought
us to our best, which has seen our kin upon their greatest trespass:
with a Viking's impudence and courage, conquering on the rock-licked
shores of the Angles and the Gauls, seeing these very sort of Christians
shivering, speaking but a quiver-quake, pleading but to give us goods
from trembled fingers before we had yet unsheathed our swords!"

"Thorhall, let him be!" my Ossur cries from where he stands beside our priest. "Such wars are past. Now has come the Prince of
Peace."

Yet Torvard has quick-bit the bait. Already his face is red upon a
seething.

"Ah, I see," Thorhall stabs, "Torvard, such talk does make your
blood run bold. Well you remember when you were just a boy! Men
like you own father—a fair and mighty warrior, he! On those bright,
starry nights I recall him on Eirik Raude's dragon-ship drakkars:
we all daring at the rout and froth, bearing at the wave tops with
naught but our own Norse gods at our lead. Our thick-armed Thor!
Our rune-struck-wisdomed Odin! Our rowdy, rod-ripe Frey! Fear not!
Hard fight should make it right, eh, Torvard? Fight and rally up and
spill some Christian blood. Indeed, even your old rival Ossur Asbjarnarsson once did ply upon that crisper blade!"

That Thorhall dares to bring such ancient rivalry into this ruddy
fray! I hate him for it, yet he will not stop. "Tell him, Ossur. Speak!
'Tis not enough, simply clubbing brainless seals or tripping caribou
from their mindless course-ways, or, worse, making petty bargains
with Christian merchants on a ship's frail plank. Nay, tell him, Ossur,
of your strikes beside King Tryggvason! All else is naught but children's play. We must make these Greenland boys full men. Set them
out upon the battlefield, burn some petty peasants' church, and take

those riches to be flaunted by some comely pagan women. Such it should be and will be again!"

Torvard then is fuming, turning puffed with Thorhall's mock, eyeing Ossur sudden in a most un-Christian pose—such as I have dreaded from the start. Yet I am strangely calm to see it come at last. Indeed, it is as it should be. Things till now were out of sorts, yet all such veils are gone, and there stands Torvard as I have ever known him. Even then our priest steps forth, luring Torvard off from our Christian line. The brutish beast thrusts our father back with a sturdy shove, then sudden stops and pulls himself away.

He charges down to the Einarsfjord bank, to the rock-slick crash and froth and tides, till our priest bends my Ossur off to join him. Torvard at the bitter water. Too close. Too close! I would shout as Ossur dares to sit beside.

For that quick breath I am certain Torvard will break my beloved's skull upon the stony sea. Indeed, Torvard raises up his arms in fury. But sudden, on a breath, his rage is hasty-quelled. It makes no sense. His arms drop down, his head all limp and waggling as if some strings of purpose have been shredded, some thread of thought has been unwound.

They rise together and go again upon the church's mount. I stand fast above, watching the crowd at last dispersing. They have wearied from their scuffle, leaving our church's walls a jarred and mangled mass. Our priest gathers up his flock and soon calls service within its tattered boundary. Gudrid draws me to join, but I fend her off with a weary gesture, saying I would rather contemplate my prayers alone.

From my perch's height, I watch Torvard bend to set athwart his breast a cross, my own good Ossur there beside him. With their leathern knees settled close into the trampled mud, and above them ringing praises from such grateful Christians, even our priest extols Torvard's intervention and restraint. Yet I cannot say: still in me is a rank and festered feeling. I sense no truth in Torvard's mood—only a shallow haze of grace which will burn away with the highest sun. I know him well, for all I've lost—know there must be reason to this feint and temperance. Yet all about him do not—cannot—see, as our priest lays hands on both Torvard's and my husband's shoulders; and I hear, for the wind blows their sounds back shivered-quick, my Ossur murmuring, on our priest's own coax, how fine and certain changed this Torvard seems.

BIBRAU

WELL SET upon a quiver. Aimed fair-wide to hit upon its mark. Such fine and perfect draw, so bent the shaft and arrow. And the archer's touch nary to be seen or blamed.

So, it is nearly perfect for my strike. My fylgie plies me quick to tug upon the bow. Yet I tell him wait! Greater triumphs require greater calm. Patience, fair, and setting proper traps, honing better tools to meet my goal.

In truth, Torvard is keener than I'd thought. Still, a weakened bird is rare a bird of prey. For me, such claws as his are dull and broke, his teeth not fit for tearing. Yet I will whet them. I will make them sharp, raise them high, and set them on their game.

But for now I lower down the bow. The hunt is paused, the prey sent upon its freedom. Wary, it is quick to jaunt, fresh to feel that fate's been kind and good. Ah, such faith! Ever count it from a fool; for, when the winds bear down upon such waft, I should laugh aloud. Instead, I gather breath and blow.

Still calm. Still cool. The breeze awaits but to turn upon my gambol. Hovering about my call and panting for my beck. Soon enough, I say. The game will come when none about will hear the anguish-cries. Fair'y for the snare, my fowl will be caught, tied up, and, oh, but wild flapping! So, and madly writhing, with naught but to squawk and cluck and dangle from a toe. I scent already where the blood will drip from such flap and kick and struggle. And the bait, even her own mate, gone with Torvard, all alone.

So I set the winds apart. I send them off and leave them stinging. 'Tis a comedy of fates on which the winds will rise. I hie them up, heavy yet to carry on my scent, and soon enough they will bear it back some damp and sweeter. For now there is no need for claws or teeth or knives or spears or broken, pointed arrows. Nay, only one small tripping wire set to snap. Just enough to wait! Hold still upon my joy.

KATLA

FOR ALL MY MIGHT and misgiving nature, nothing comes upon this blight, no brutal host, no shattered enmity. Naught but the Althing's final dawn, when the crowds and freemen dwindle quick, making leave with all their ships, their stock and tents, their squawks and sacks and bald-pate thralls. Soon the wake-foam of the ships' oars settles. Gardar grows sleeping-still as the ripples on the fjord calm.

When the last long days of summer's light recede, and the fuller dark of night begins to lengthen, our church is nearly fashioned, though ever another season's work will make it fully sound. These days fewer come to lend their hands. Our priest is lost upon such chieftains' long-halls with his preacher's speech. Even Torvard's spent upon his father's oat-field harvests. So Ossur and I set to tend the church's fields alone.

What's grown upon these barely planted grounds is not enough, we know, to last the frost; but soon Christian folk come with charitable prayers and stock and victuals. In the eves, with our backs full-ached and our limbs shaking from the growing chill, we bide our rest within a small stone shelter—at last, a household of our own.

Our household, nay! So much as we had ever hoped—though within it is but a narrow dark heaped along each wall with thick dirt benches. To make them soft for sleep, we pile them with mats of rough-combed wool stuffed into linen. A ring of stones we set to make our hearth fire's bound—enough to heat and cook, to light our meager meals. There, beside its crack' and smoke, we ply at chores till the coals grow dim. Through our doorway's gape seeps then the night, ever with its hint of winter's chill and the foehn winds' sudden, heavy blows.

"It is not much," says my Ossur when first we lie beside our own hearth's heat.

"I need no more." Yet, saying so, I know my words fall falsely. "We will make it grow full-fair in time."

"Indeed. Yet, Katla, you are not happy. I have seen you so truly only once before—on Thorbjorn Glora's island."

I sigh, "It seems so long ago."

He is full-right. Too oft do I wist' for its cold and restless comfort, for that bleak abode where the mists rose high and hid us in a depth of safety and silence. Only the squawk of birds and our own footsteps rang against that cold rock beach. There I knew none would ever come upon our camp in menace—or come upon our camp at all.

My Ossur knows it well, though he says it not. Of late our days are spent in awkward still, and our nights—chill nights—when too oft I have sent him rushing out, bearing his knife or spear or club upon some unwont clatter. Ever he returns looking pale and goaded, saying only, " 'Twas a harmless goat prowling late about our midden's dregs."

Then, one eve, as a slim-shot moon grows a beam upon the burnished heavens and I am lying on our rough-made bench with my head on my Ossur's knee, comes a long boot's crush before our wafting gate. I startle for a start.

"Darling, hush," Ossur quiets me, accustomed to my recoil.

Then a voice—such voice as I have ever heard in my most fright'ed dreams. "Ossur Asbjarnarsson!" Too well I know the tone.

I raise up sharp and bear about to find some weapon or, at best, some little crack or place to hide. "Nay!" Ossur holds me, wraps me close in his long wool cloak, then leaves me there to open up our door.

"Who comes?" he shouts, knowing that voice as well as I.

"Your neighbor, Asbjarnarsson! Nary have I seen you in what seems a wasted moon's turn! Shared not a whiff of honest work, nor plied at a Christian prayer"—yet this time with no pretense of Christian coy. Torvard staggers up and presses through our doorway. In his fists, two sloshing cups—one half drunk, sticky now with mead; the other he urges into Ossur's hand. "What, with the Althing done and the harvests short and our two homes but a spear's length's distance, could you not come to me? Though my father is your priest's own patron, would you set yourselves apart so long? Ah, perhaps you're shy upon your neighbor's greatness! So I have come to you—long past my due—to bring a draught in praise of your new-made Christian home!"

Ossur lets him pass, though I eye him hard upon raw apprehension. With a slap on Ossur's shoulder, Torvard belches, "What a finer place! Already I can see the thick-made long-hall, the polished board, the twisted, sharp-toothed carvings on the posts and walls. Praise ye, Asbjarnarsson! Well got at last, and fair deserved. And all upon my father's landholds—indeed, my own inheritance is yours!"

Sucking at his mead, Torvard settles on our narrow sleep shelf—his thigh so very near where my cheek some long had laid. He turns about: "You and your own mild mistress—Katla—at last, we will be like cousins!"

"Truly." Ossur nods. "All will be one in Jesus Christ."

"One, indeed—in Christ, all of us as close as kin! Such, you'll sense, but soon, what finer place this Gardar seems, now with all those interlopers from the Althing gone. Is it not a merry place and fair becoming? Or perhaps, good neighbor, you have not had such chance, for I note your fields are rightly plucked down to the chaff and stubble. Ah, for now, as I look about . . . indeed . . . What, with the harvest nearly through? You and your right mistress have much work to stock this house in food before the season's turning."

"We have not much, for the earth here was not planted," says my Ossur. "Only what was ours to save from this summer's hunts. That, and the fine-brought, good, and Christian charity—"

"Charity? To you, a keen and measured hunter! Well, but I can help, for I know these lands as well as any save my chieftain-father. There is more about than harvest to be garnered. Do you know the many hunting haunts not far along a near-ish string of skerries?"

"Indeed?" Ossur nips his bait.

"Aye! Where the finest seals are hid, so fat and dull they but wait upon a strong man's club. All one needs is a proper sail and crew."

"I have no ship. Mine is lent upon our priest's good purpose. And no crew save myself to set the nets or haul such catch aboard."

"Then you must join in mine, for I'll hunt one last before the seas are frozen."

My Ossur nods. "We have much need. It would be a Christian kindness."

"Kindness." Torvard smiles. "It is settled. I'll return in some few days." With a slosh of mead he offers out his hand.

My Ossur takes it. Oh, the sound of it! The plying strokes and striking flesh, Torvard's grin so thin, in places cracked, flaking white, yet within the creases lacking any hue!

He goes. Even as he steps beyond our doorway's gape, I cannot stop but shake at once with chill and grunt and tremble in my fear.

"Beloved . . ." Ossur mumbles out.

"I like it not, Ossur. Nay, I do not like it."

"How can I refuse him, Katla? Indeed—indeed, after all Torvard has done! Has he not shown us well his turn upon a gentle, Christian nature? Has he not even saved my pate from that rough-borne, pagan mob?"

"This is no Christian kindness, Ossur. It is the foulest sort of feigning rot. I have seen it so before. But heed and listen, 'tis the worst of my misgivings!"

"Love, your pain is old, your hatred fairly measured. But perhaps at last, between him and me, this quarrel now is done—"

"It will ne'er be done!" I spit. "Ossur, do not listen!"

He hushes me: "You must be fair. Be gentle and rightly kind, my Katla, darling, as I know you are. In Christ and for your soul's own want, forgive Torvard his youthful trespasses. So I have tried and well I have. I know our priest would say it so and bid me join him."

I cannot speak. Indeed, I cannot hear as Ossur sounds so grounded in his honest Christian vision. Yet for me—for me—oh, I cannot bear it out! I am no Christian now. Nay, I know my heart's as black as any pagan's—black as even Mistress Thorbjorg's own. For she would understand my plight—she, in fair compassion, or, worse, my foul daughter, in her honest hate, who would ne'er stand quiet by to watch such unwont mission. Nay, she would find some brutal force to defend what was her own. Yet I have naught but the meekest murmur—"You must not go!"—pleading with him, feeble as Ossur barely heeds, holding me against his bosom, stroking my trembling back and my head within his calloused palms, hushing me even as I speak again, again, till my words mean less than none.

BIBRAU

Just a while longer—just a breath, a night, a stroke—and then the dawn. Oh, I wait with excitement I can barely master, begging naught of sleep for fear to miss the tender sound.

'Twill come upon the wind: a fair, clean strike like the cracking of the glaciers. I lie awake, listening close beneath the stars, and spying on the circled moon.

Full moon—the only round I have cherished since the stones' burning. Airy well, it is hung this night upon the sky with not a breath of haze. If I but listen soft, I can ply upon the dew and my birth-mare's praying. And with my plea stone-silent, if I've set this trick up right, I can draw at last my invisible ones home.

Come, come out from the dark and silence! Come to do my own misdeed. When 'tis wrought, we will dance again upon such blood at midnight. And for reward, you will guide me e'er again—and e'er forever—at last, into the blue.

KATLA

If that night I sleep, it is only barely, though such breath as his is sound upon a snore. Most I lie awake—at first nettled by the clamor;

then, fearing aught, listening to each rattled inhalation till each rasp becomes a rare and precious treasure I catch and hold as if to store its memory away.

In time, I find I've drifted. Of a sudden, there's a shout. I jump from my slumber, pressing back hard my coverlet. "Get out! Nay, set away!"

Someone is in the blackened shadows. I bear up, striking wild. "Ossur!" I terror-scream.

"I am here, love, here," he, sighing close—so close his voice, yet still I name him—"Ossur? Ossur?"—trembling, reaching as he holds me to his chest, his strong arms wrapped about my heaving bosom.

"Yes, love, yes. There's no one. It was nary but a nightmare," my Ossur whispers.

"Do not leave me!"

"I am always with you. I will always be . . ." till, well and soon, he is snoring at his peace, nuzzling me with his short-cut beard still smelling sweet of Torvard's celebration mead.

Some three days hence does Torvard come to set my husband on the nearby shoals. That very morn, with a moon full-risen and the fall's first frost touching on the dew. It only lasts a breath—then a spark of sun becomes bright and perfect clearing—when Torvard strides over the beach stones, stiff in all his heavy, fur-fringed jerkin, his arms jutting out as if they cannot be pressed down, hands grasping boldly out as if for beams to hurl. There's a boastful jaunt in Torvard's gait, the shadow of some forgotten spirit—"Asbjarnarsson! Ready yet? Saying your last sweet, fond goodbyes?"—mocking cruelly, ever with a grin— some forgotten spirit somehow now reclaimed.

My Ossur turns from me. Across his face is a shade of doubting.

I bid him, "Do not go!" I pull him back, with Torvard bearing swiftly near. "Dear Christ, beloved, do not leave me!"

Yet Ossur's doubt is fleeting. Gently, he pushes me aside. Still I bind myself, wrapping arms about, clinging like a frightened child.

Ossur goads me back: "I will see you on the morrow, beloved.

Katla, cheer. Now set aback and be but calm. Take from Christ your strength."

He eyes me hard, yet I cannot—nay! I clutch upon him. His arms are strong. He pries out from my grip. "No!" I barely brush his lips as Ossur turns from my embrace.

"Katla"—patient-smiles my beloved—"I say, love, cheer. Remember true, and pray to Mother Mary as we'd spoke. It is only but a dawn and dark—one single, precious day!"

Then he sets astride with Torvard. They clatter over beach stones. I watch them go. I watch my dear, dear husband climb the fjord's ice-slick rocks with his best cloak flying out behind him and his sturdy, hard-tanned leather stockings tight about his shins. Oh, that very leather, those bits I stitched until my fingers bled, each drop a nectar sipped as we summered on Thorbjorn Glora's island in our joy! Now I listen to the leather's heavy protest, squeaking loud in echo of my love-made-silent heart, in echo of my crying soul. My soul still shrieks when sound no longer matters, as my husband heaves and hurls a bundle stuffed with hunting goods onto Torvard's hated boards.

Their footsteps boom across the plank. Then a call—Torvard's voice hard-rasping. The ship scrapes over gravel. The bondsmen cast up oars. There's a splash. Another shout. A wave of arms. A sail quick-swelling. Then a ripple in the water's wake—and then there's naught.

My Ossur's gone.

BIBRAU

An altar make I, heaped up high with stones. All glary they are glowing now, these gathered rocks reddened new with neats' fresh blood, spread about with the stench of certain rotting. I've made it so—pure and hot and still. One I make for Torvard Einarsson. And one again for my mother's love, Ossur.

Ah, an altar: borne to ply the feat of fate, to mark the shade passing e'er to early shadow. Come on quick, such mock and making—of such subtle wastes a beauteous strike is born.

Oh, dance upon the moon! Now the moon shines brighter, still and truly. Upon it, shapes unmasked: figures fair and fleet. These I've known and lingered long to lure. *Come here! Come quick!* I beckon, bind them to my pleasure. Then: *Fly off!* For of such subtle might will ever come an evening glow. And in that glow soon will twist up tremors, ancient faults revealing near forgotten paths, channels walked by tiptoe meeklings, footfalls tread on rock and cruelty's blight. There, where blood runs old, I set it up anew with fire! And heat such stones to send my gory rhyme aloft, so the fool will sense at last upon his chance and take what stake there lies about and drive it brutal home.

KATLA

HAIL MARY, full of grace, the Lord is with thee. The Lord is with thee.
"There is naught to fear," the mistress Thorbjorg once had promised. "He will not hurt you—never more." So she'd even seemed to speak aloud when she cast my bond-thrall's stone from that fell-cliff's height. Once upon a time perhaps, but even she could not have seen this terror. Even she, with all her seeress' vision, could not have known this fright.

Too, our father-priest, speaking oft upon confession's prudence, "My child, Torvard's repented—nay! turned unto the Lord. So you should, too. In faith, outstretch your arms. Embrace and welcome him into our church fold. Full and well, for you'll be given God's good grace if you but trust the patient wisdom of the risen Lord."

I try. I try, waiting on the spindle and the thread's quick turning, trembling alone within our rough-born shelter, tangling up my smoothest thread. The sun full rises. Such light filters down upon our hearth's smoke. It is a single, angled shaft, yet it does not warm me. I am ever colder as such flames we lit together at the dawn are dwindled down to hopeless coals.

Hail Mary, full of grace, the Lord is with thee. The Lord is with thee.

The day is nearly gone. My eyes fix dull upon the faintest corner's shadow. A footstep falls. I leap in hope. Yet there before our threshold stands, not my beloved, but old Einar's mistress, Grima. By her side, her widowed daughter, Torunn.

"You should not bear this night alone," Grima sputs. "Says my husband you should bide before our Gardar fire." Though she looks not kind or rightly pleased as she sets her invitation out. Strange, these two: Grima, ever to me cold, ever hateful as she was to my own mother, and Torunn, once my guileless charge, bearing now no shade of the sweet young girl I had sometimes coddled. Her eyes are bitter, biting for her loss, near as cold as Grima's own. Well I know it is only Einar's prod which bears them by me. Still I cannot face the night, so thank them well, bidding them but wait a little as I gather up my spinning goods to go.

Hail Mary, full of grace, the Lord is with thee. The Lord is with thee.

Now I sit among them, here within the dim of Gardar's spacious hall, enduring such condescending mocks from those who once did call me thrall. Thrall, indeed. Though when Einar bears some close about the long-hall's fire, Mistress Grima turns full-cloying in her courtesy—"Katla, see how fair and graced is Greenland for your Christian priest!"—speaking well and hopefully of our father's imminent return. But when Einar's gone, to Torunn she quickly whispers: "Even at our hearthside! Do you see how she eats her food? And wears her dress—in such a slavish manner!"

"She lacks good grace." Torunn buoys her mother's scorn. "Yet what should we expect? Once a thrall, then ever after." Both of them laughing, clearly thinking I, still like a thrall, should act as though I cannot hear.

Yet worst is Torvard's bolder mistress, Freydis Eiriksdatter, striding among the long-hall's beams, biting at her nails and spitting bits into the fire. On me she barely casts a glance. Indeed, she has ever heeded on me rarely. She simply mutters to herself as she paces up

and down: "E'er to go upon a Viking shore! Never mine, for my hapless brothers—Thorvald! Leif! Men ever wrought and let to make the
greater claim. Yet my husband . . . Oh, my husband . . . ne'er do well,
that lout!" Till, of a breath, she gruffs: "By Freya's favor, this night let
Torvard's ship not return at all!"

My spindle's sudden dizzy, spinning on its whorl. I am almost
sick with fright at her savage, pagan praying, till I note from the shadows' murk comes Inga. She brushes soft my elbow as she passes
toward the dying hearth. There she stoops to take the coal stick
from the fire, daring but a glance—her honest, emerald comfort—
as she stirs the embers, then quickly sets upon herself a cross and
goes.

Oh, do not! Do not go! I long to beg her. Yet I am left again alone
with such freeborn witches as they spin their vicious snares.

"Heard you not, Katla, of your good friend Gudrid Thorbjornsdatter?" Torunn ventures. "She's to marry Thorstein Eiriksson—
already bent upon the task at Brattahlid's far shore."

"Nay," I answer calmly, "indeed, I had not heard."

"And then to Vesterbygd to ply their luck on colder waters." To
learn of Gudrid's leaving when all I seek is a Christian soul to share
my prayers! Torunn smiles as if she savors well my anguish.

"Indeed," Grima turns, "why do they not stay at Stokkanes,
which Eirik's lent to Gudrid's father? 'Tis a fine, good piece, a healthy
shelf for growing grain. At Vesterbygd, 'tis said hay barely grows, oats
ill and weak, and wheat buds not at all."

"And sheep turn wild," Torunn adds, "with such woolly fleece as if
grown upon the foehn winds' bluster."

"She'll not have the strength—not to card the wool and spin and
weave."

"Not by herself, for I hear she'll keep no slaves—nay, be they pagan or full Christian. But, Katla—ah!—perhaps you should go and
help her—you and your sturdy man, Ossur?"

I make no note of Torunn's cut. "It is said, in Vesterbygd, the hunt
brings the greatest bounty."

"A bounty bound with blood, or so I hear, unless a man is some-what wise with net and club."

"But Thorstein!" Grima cries. "He's not like his bolder brothers. Gudrid will soon be widowed, or fall upon the blight herself, for she is frail, much used to softer means."

Oh, such talk! Far worse than even bond-thralls' cruelest taunt-ings. Bear they not the slightest bit of kindness, even for one freeborn as themselves? Yet they seem to laugh, though their faces cool as they work upon their stitches. They are witches all, worse by far than ever was Thorbjorg unfairly claimed.

Nay, I cannot listen to their spit and spite, knowing well they watch but to see me quake and yield. In truth, I would yearn again to be full-bonded, forced to leave their hearth's quick warmth to crouch upon some cold stone sill. I rise, making poor excuse to be in need of some small thimble I've left behind, making my way across the long-hall, nearly tripping through the dim, when Inga's by me, blocking off the door.

"Mistress Katla," she says loudly, "I will run and fetch you any-thing you need." Then she quiet-chides, "Katla, get back quickly."

"I will not—"

"You must. I will bear you some excuse, but stay. You must bear yourself as an equal in their sight."

'Tis true, I know! For all such thralls who strive for Christian freedom, I must remain. So I turn, on danger of my Christian heart, and sit again among these un-Christian crones. Inga follows with a quick-thought, fair excuse. Then I see her gone while I set again about my fruitless whorl.

Hail Mary, full of grace, the Lord is with thee. The Lord is with thee.

Through the hours of the dark, I spin and wait. Wait and spin. Ever does my thread but fray or, when it holds, it clumps. I feel their eyes, re-proachful as I fumble. I am ever slow about my task. With each twisted tie, I pass each hour in tangled yearning, knowing well they watch, all the while, in cruelest denigration, as if I make for them my wool.

BIBRAU

SUCH, upon a river island as in days of old, where men are ever drawn to fight their foes, come two. One is built tall and thick and hefty. The other's thin and frail as grass rough-frayed and tangled by the tides. They come, these two, while I work upon the bellows, sending out such rich and purple mist to mask what cruelish fates I've spun and blown.

So the winds roil up. Soon, soon the sea and sail are flapping. And their shouts come up. The herds all set astray. Follow! Follow fast behind!

Now the fog is closing in upon the shore, fair'y fine, growing thicker as a mantle. Soon the sky's crude black as pitch or tar. So, the crack of stones beneath their steps. I breathe upon their bitter breaths, come hard and hot like steam or smoke or fire.

Fire.

Fire. Who might follow now? There and then, none about can see the distance. None but I, calling fire turned to blood. I pleasure in that murk and meaning. Calling up the slap! Is it cracked upon the skull? Fast a shriek. A turning. Thump. Fall. Drag. Then the blade, made to nick and cut and furrow. Furrows. Rivulets seeping out across that rocky shoal where meat is often plucked and so much blood has ever fallen.

Ever so. And now who might note it where the waves roll up so often as the tides? Now they come again to wash the weak, dull red off, and sweep away such common pulp and bones.

KATLA

THAT ONE NIGHT PASSES—longer than my life. Upon the dawn, I am full awake and rising faster than the morning's chill or the Matins call or even the fjord's sleepless watchman. Up upon the Gardar beach to peer across the gray-green light of Einarsfjord harbor—as Ossur said—upon a day—a single morning's pause.

Through the misty rise, then beyond the daylight's breaking, there is no ship or spout or froth beyond the fjord's gaping maw.

The watchman comes. "Mistress, your lips are chilled and turning blue-ish. Go back within. I will call you if your master rises."

"Rises . . ." feeling my lips between my teeth, the chill upon them numbing with my tremble. I turn upon his hand. "If he rises," I say again. I turn and nod and move aside.

By the sign of the cross deliver us from our enemies.

Another day. Another. The witch-crones say no word—not of any comfort. Only more of gossip's pique, and Freydis even dares to scoff some praise to her goddess Freya's pointed strike. Oh, well met upon such strain! No vain remorse. No proper trepidation. Then the priest returns, bearing only a patronizing smile, speaking loudly of Torvard's better Christian kind. And I, looking to them all for companionship and comfort! And every time Inga comes upon the hearth, her eyes say, "Wait! Hold off!" as I grope about for solace or try to stay my shaking hands.

Another morning dawns. I try to spin, to no avail. I try to weave, but my hands drop down, too weak to hold the shuttle or the bar. Now Inga does not scold me when I come out from the darkness—into the kitchen hall to beg a turn at churning, or even aiding on the dunging of Einar's cows.

"It is not far—these islands." Inga tries to smile weakly. "So I've heard. Perhaps their hunt is good—Katla—very fair—"

Such hopeful sounds tune now but ill.

Upon the fifth-fall evening, I cannot sleep at all. Comes chill the dark, yet still I sit on the fjord's edging, till Inga bids me sleep among the thralls. There, in the familiar dark and cold; there, with the stench so thick to choke all proper breathing; there, where there's no air for thoughts—there I gasp my strangled sobs. *Sancta Maria, Mater Dei— Holy Mary, Mother of God, pray for us sinners, now, and in the hour of our death.*

So, and then the sixth day dawns.

First a grayish light. Then brisk wind. Then a sail.

"Gloria Patri!"—bounding toward the beach, nearly tripping on my steps over byre's filth and sod and grass and stone. "They've come! They've come!"—shouting even before the fjord's watchman.

Yet there's an odd flapping in the sail. 'Tis wrapped about and tattered as if caught upon a shard.

"Nay, come and see it!" calls the watch. "Well, it's been upon a storm. Yet fair enough. Someone's on the mast and waving!"

For now upon that yard-split spar—grace and leaning—I reach out: "Ossur!"

The watchman hushes, "It is but that young one come from Thorbjorn Glora's house—that Evald Thorbjornsson, whom Torvard lately fosters. Praise be, for Glora will be grateful."

Nay . . . I feel my face. It is wet with tears. "Grateful, yes. Praise be. Praise be." It is Evald. It must be. I can see him better now—some like Ossur—looking like my Ossur once—so long ago—when first we were turned Greenland-bound.

Comes the ship ashore. It is bare and creaking. All its crew look stunned, a-fright and weary, weaving through the waves.

"We were set upon by storm," calls one, "a freak—a purple willied billow. Strange and swift it came upon the sea, where before 'twas ope' and bright as ever it be morning."

"A billowed purple"—comes another close—"moving swift over the sunny draught. The seals saw't quick and shunted, seeking harbor, so we followed farther up the coast. 'Twas there—fair upon a middling shoal along the Mellombygd—the unclaimed ground—"

I, fighting through the crowd, over the crust and crackle of the beach stones, and then my feet sopped up and chilled, my hand upon the splintered railing: "Where is my husband?" crying as Torvard stumbles from the plank.

I rush upon him. I am wont to strike him—my fists upon his soiled leather jerkin—as he looks on me, stunned and bruised and seeming worn.

"Katla." Torvard pauses. "Ossur set upon some rocks—slick they were, hiding many beasts. I was far behind along the edging of the beach, and, well, we'd planned to chase them into nets we'd laid through the shallow water, but Ossur slipped. He stumbled. 'Twas there and then the beasts did charge—"

Charge. I hear his word.

"I tried to fend them off—three great males of broadest strength and ire. 'Twas how I got these bruises and cuts"—showing me his arms—

"Nay," I cough.

"We found him ripped—"

"—Nay."

"Shred on shred."

I cannot listen.

"Ossur is dead."

Torvard's words.

"Ossur is dead." Speaking out this fate in hated timbre.

"Woman, hush!"

I do not know I've screamed.

Einar comes, his face washed white with the waste of speaking. He tries to hold me—my fist within my teeth, bunched up and clawing, holding to my palm, and my face already breaking—broke as it was never broke before—"You've killed my husband! Killed him! Killed him! Nay!"—not with pain or stun but with wild, whirling fury.

Einar begs me, "Katla, fair, be calm. Be calm. Be calm."

"Fair ye? Calm ye? Murderous beast!" I scream, then growl, "He killed my husband. Killed my Ossur! So he's wanted—such he's plotted—planned for all his days!"

Torvard fast-defends, "I tried. I fair'y tried to save him! Even for the storm I went quick after. It was too late." His face red-hid, head shaking, eyes bowed down as if afraid of sight, "Father, nay! Ask any man among them—ask any of my crew. They will tell ye truly, if truth you want, in grisly detail."

Huddled across the sod is Evald, still young enough, and perhaps some turned in his father's Christ's compassion. I point to him and quick-demand, "Say it out—what this boy has seen!"

"Nay," Torvard's foster-son answers, "I was on the boat. Only Torvard went ashore. Then Asbjarnarsson. I saw not much. The fog was thick. Then, as quick, the storm did dwindle. It was strange, as the sky sharp cleared, 'twas as if the blight had never been."

There's something in his tone. I know he does but lie. "It did not happen so!" I tremor.

Torvard turns an eye on me—the first as ever old—hotly, straight and bold and numbly, his daggered glance looking clear into my face—such an eye I remember well as a brutal blow of the keenest nature. Yet to his father his gaze is meek. "Never have I wanted but to make this friendship honest"—and to our priest—"in the name of the Father and the Son, God's holy Jesus."

Does he dare such blasphemy? And no one speaks to name it! Even our own father leans and breathes such words to him, even by my hearing, "I know it is true, my son. I have heard your full confession, seen your penance. I know the nature of your soul. Yet you must bear some patience. Katla's pain does bring her freshest grief. In Christ, she will return to calm once Ossur's soul is laid to rest and we have buried what remains in hallowed ground."

"Remains?"

"His corpse."

"His body?" Torvard is speechless. " 'Twas bare but bits, all caught among the rubble."

"It is true," offers Evald. "We could not bring him home."

"You left him?"—like vomit from my lips—"Left him—left . . . !" My heart is double-breaking. "To be eaten by the jaegers and the gulls? Ne'er enough to bear even to dig a grave?"

" 'Tis truly ill"—our father rocks his head—"that so fair a Christian servant should fall and waste on unconsecrated soil. He must be sought and something found to set aground with proper Christian rites."

"I say it is a waste"—no more remorse tarnishing Torvard's cold expression—"to search that salt-rock beach even once more. The storm billowed quick again as we departed. We had no choice but to set upon what sail was left. By now, what once remained is washed or pecked away." Stammering somewhat, with ne'er but a feigned tear upon his cheek—surely anyone can see!

They say naught. Not Einar nor Freydis nor Grima nor Torunn nor even Inga, coming down, holding fast upon my arm. Nor even the somber priest.

"*Hail Mary, full of grace,*" I whisper. "Ne'er to be returned . . . !"

So there is no hole dug for Ossur in our fair new church's grave-yard. There are no proper rites or recollections. Only some small, speaking hollow pities, some half-felt words, and our father's ill-spent prayers as he presses Torvard to sail again to set a stone upon some nameless shallow—there where it will ever bear this lie: "Ossur Asbjarnarsson died here."

Resurrection

THORBJORG

I GO TO HER, not because I am her mistress—was her mistress—nor because I was ever right nor because I was even called, but because I always knew I would. As I went to her upon the first—that bitter day so very long ago.

Her place was never there among them. Nor here in this place either. She is caught between, nary one nor of the other, wanting both, fitting into none. Nary slave nor free. Nary Christian-made nor of the older, brutish creed. But of some other fiber. Malleable, yes; fragile also; if roughly handled, cruelly frayed, but, upon a certain, gentle spinning, become some strange, uncertain fineness I would preserve.

I go to her, though she shake me off at first. In the end, she will fall into my arms, hard upon my breast and still there, trying not to fracture.

"It is her grief," I will say. "Let her be."

Her cries will rustle through me, harsh as the bitterest wind, cutting as the claws that scratch. Well I know their pitch and timbre; well I know their sharpness; well I know the angle of their gash and the volume of their howl. So well I know, for I have sung these fair laments some oft myself. With so much singing, the mournful rasp grows to a somewhat lovely tune.

Then, in some time, she will still. Upon the mourning's passing, when all is lost, in some small time the emptiness will fill. Through the dark, though one cannot see, will come shapes and space and the winding of a way. So it will be for her. Drawn upon the dark and moon which linger of her young man's vision. Dead and hollow those eyes are now. Yet they will live again.

Within her.

At least for a little breath.

For a time.

KATLA

HE IS GONE. Gone! Ne'er to be returned, except upon my mind and soul and ever in my dreaming. How brief is happy joy! How quick to fall to sorrow. For dreams are naught—only wisps quick cast away, to leave me ever cold.

And lonely. The only binding I had ever sought in all my life was to be beside my Ossur—my one true love. Oh, my cold one. My fate-accursed one! My ever almost—never truly sound! Nay, the Norns did not like him much. They wound against him as never was a free-man coiled, and spun upon him death—ever death—and sewed in tragedy—

Somewhat like unto Jesus was my Ossur.

I bend my head and fall to weeping. I am set adrift; this grief is thick; I have no bearing dial. Yet then, a glimmer's crack. A door is opened. Through the howling wind and light comes Thorbjorg—standing at the door.

Thorbjorg as a strange-built, sullen angel ringed around with the fading autumn light. She comes slowly, slowly. I find I screech some louder, falling for full fear. Thorbjorg—speaker for her gods—I cannot hear! I do not want her! I am hopeless, spitting gall as would crack the skull of night. Yet she does not stop. She bends close by me. For some breath, I set my fists against her chest, but she takes my flailing arms, holds them still, and wraps them hard around, heavy within her own, laying my cheek against her bosom.

Then she whispers, "Katla, hush now. Hush. You must cry."

Cry.

Cry.

For some long time there is no sound within my head but my own sobbing. I know not even if those others stay about by Einar's fire. Only I know Thorbjorg, tall as a tree and warm as my own mother, and her voice—such a voice, like a balm against knowing pain.

The others there—whoe'er they are—pagan, Christian—it matters not, for they cannot help me. Not even our father-priest, who stands so close I smell his frankincense perfume. "Leave her," I hear him say. "Seeress, give her up—in the name of Jesus—"

Too well Thorbjorg knows me—far better than these others here. "It is her grief." She holds him off. "Let her be."

Let her be. It is her grief. As if I have some right upon it, as never I have known such right before. Sudden slow then, Gudrid comes, taking off our priest gently with a Christian whisper. In time Thorbjorg turns me round and helps me stand and leads me from the hearth fire's heat. Toward the harbor, toward her waiting skiff and Kol's old, crumpled smile, awash in tenderness and the spatter-spray of the rising tide, and Svan's strong hands guiding my stumbled steps over the rocking rail.

From behind, somewhere, the voice of the priest, a screeching raven's: "Hand her back. She will not venture with you. Katla is a Christian. Witch! Lord Jesus, preserve us from our enemies!"

Thorbjorg is beside me, standing in that skiff, as Svan holds the oars and Kol twines loose the cord to hoist the rippled sail—Thorbjorg beside me as a willow in the wind, bending softly. "Katla, would you stay? Or return home?"

Home. Never had I thought to find it. Lost upon my mother's speech, my father's fate, and distant Irish shores and bloodshed. Lost again with Ossur, left on some unnamed shoal. Yet here it is even before me, ever damaged by my own stray stroke, and lacking trust and love—yet Thorbjorg somehow forgiving all and waiting for me, arms reaching tender round and soft, finally somehow found.

Upon Thorbjorg's footpath, in the witch's steps, where never would

I have wandered. Where for so long I was afraid to step. Yet here she sets the path before me. It is strange and dark, but no darker than my own. It is true, she never begged me step within, but just beside.

Now it does not matter if I be pagan, Christian. To walk beside her, yet still in my own path—what a simple thing it seems—so hard to do. My priest—he cannot do it, as he spits his Christian fire from the hill. His aim's too great to damage, his sighting honed but to condemn. Just as my own, all these years sharp'ed to cut the cords which bound me. Yet now those cords are severed. Now I am fully free. It was all but foolish, wasted. Now I know.

"Christ be with you, Katla"—Gudrid's voice ringing out as Inga's cheeks flow red and hard with tears. Now only the priest is left still railing in the name of Jesus, and Torvard standing gray and close, his evil somehow shaded in a strangeish blue. I turn away to gaze into the distance, sitting low within the skiff, feeling Thorbjorg's arms, warm and weighty as a heavy skin about me. Then the cool and haze. Then but fog and mist as Svan pries up oars and, with their round and splash, slowly takes us home.

BIBRAU

THE MAN IS DEAD and it does please me. For once I have my way in everything. And none suspect my hand in it. Not even Thorbjorg, come upon the Tofafjord house with my mother draped so, wasted, wanting, in her arms.

"Come and aid me," she begs, nearly dragging in my mother from out the cold. And my mother, stumbling, stunned beyond her sense, far past any recognition of even where her footsteps falter.

"Bibrau, stop your stare. Come at once and give your mother kindness." There she lays her out upon the mossy bench, looking thick and bloated, much like death—like glorious death, as ever she had wished on me.

I step some close to see her quiver, gape, and writhing. Her sob—

oh, I hear it—lovely! This, so much better than I had ever planned! So much better than when, long ago, I set Nattfari on the mountain path. That was but a budding start, a meager practice. Here's the truer art— my mother so firm along that wanton ramble, no words the mistress speaks can ease her back. And I to blame for it—for such glorious fate, for such certain madness. And, best of all, no one yet blames me!

I almost glee upon my triumph, but instead I think some wise to stand full-meek beside my mother's bed. "Foster-daughter, that's a gentle touch. You've grown quite skilled to give your mother tending"—Thorbjorg questioning me not as I kneel to play my mother's sick-nurse, holding gently on her hand.

Cold and stiff as death's own fingers—these tortured digits, clenched then sudden springing out with the twisted convolutions of her mind. Yet these I suffer, staying patient, waiting through the long, dull hours with her claws wrapped, tense and riveted about my own. Getting free only to help concoct some wisdom-potent, twist some trinket, spit some tones from my frigid pipes, and bear such skins and scents as my mistress says will ripe' my mother's grieving.

Ripe indeed. It grows in time to fits of wailing, and sighs so deep they set such fingers trembling, teeth bit into knuckles, raw. And then to struggles—even once—oh, joy!—she bounding out from my own small hold, reeling across the household's dirt, then dragging through the homefield frost, where my mother shatters its fine-wrought silence, striding her bumble-walk to cast herself into the fjord.

There she stands upon the ledge with her arms flung wide as if to flop from off its boulders. At most, the sea is hard that day, frozen crisp as the winter's breathing. Fine, sharp, and piercing—well I could let her drop and pleasure at the frigid clatter. Or I could shove her, slippery, off; but instead I step behind. I prefer to wait, prepared to catch her. To watch my birth-mare enfeebled, languishing—I prefer to let her live, remembering ever all her woe.

Just a subtle breath, and the wind hard-blowing as her arms raise up, near about to jump. Then, with my little might, I snatch her back from her want-death's brink and hold her firmly. She is fighting now, but only slightly, with her head bent low, tears quick-falling on her breast, her mouth hard on her fists, and yelping cries, till she takes one breath.

"Daughter"—my mother sputters, looking into my eyes.

Then Kol, then Svan come rushing. They bear her wasted weight between, weary-marking a stumble-path up from the fjord's edge, I following just behind as we stagger toward the homefield gate and the open door where the mistress stands watching.

When they have set my mother back beside the fire, the mistress listens soft to Kol's and Svan's surprise, whispering out their strained praise, marking me with wonder. Thorbjorg still keeps some way off, her aging gaze withheld, only bidding me with a careless toss to feed my mother well. So I do, bringing broth too rich and meat too slick and tender, playing pleased to wipe my mother's chin as she gags upon those bitty mouths of fatty foods.

KATLA

FROM THEN I do not remember much. My grief, but a waft and wave, sometimes gleaming, then quick-caught again upon a haze. Dark days and coldish feelings, my throat some sore from a sort of shriek, though I cannot hear. Then a breath. Then again I'm drowning, the current's tow is a maelstrom's drag and drift. Somehow I am wanting to be falling, ice-stones beneath my feet, a cutting wind tearing about the hemming of my dress. Whipping at my sleeves. Then some arms about me. Strange arms, small, yet oddly sturdy.

Not much. Not much at all . . .

Bibrau.

Until—

A sudden kick. A glimmer. Bare a movement—more a feeling, almost trembled, almost light. Yet it is there—I know he is—alive in me. . . . Still deep within—that sweet, small part of him. Slowly growing in me now. Alive!

This strangeness is a wonder. Nay, a miracle come from God! Oh, his child—Ossur's child—my child! That part of us which cannot be unjoined, which cannot be separated even unto death, which will lie upon the fragrant fields and rise up—ever one—even unto Heaven!

When I'd known this state before, it was twisted, hated. I'd pulled and clenched and cursed my fate. Now it seems a dance, a breath, a sudden longing to be fresh and fat and full and round as never I have been before.

Borne on me—though I be naught but sinful. Yet, suddenly, all I see is set aglow—not from without but from some deeper wellspring. He is growing in me as a winter seed lifts its stem up from the ground with the first warm sun. Oh, such warmth! I am that earth into which that seed is planted. I am that holy, blessed ground.

BIBRAU

FOR SOME LONG WEEKS, I tend upon this grieving. My mother's shrieks do split the night. They destroy my peaceful dreams. Ah, but it does please me well. So very much it pleases me—until, suddenly, something's changed.

All at once, a stillness veils about her grief, then the strangest sort of smile. Though she says naught, only takes up once again some interest in the spindle. Her hands slow, her spinning rough, oft a finger resting briefly on her bosom and her whorl cast out, hapless, rolling across the floor. When I stoop to pick it up, in her glance—though she tries to hide it—I note a sort of hopeful glow.

Nay, too well I've know such sparks. I've seen them oft enough before. She has deceived me. Somehow, she and Ossur—dead, yet even still. Tricked me! Three months since the murderous act, yet in all that time . . . Now I count the waning moons: three since my mother returned, and not once bent upon her knees to rinse the monthly blood from off her cloth. Not once! Then, out upon a dawn's chill start, I remember how she rushed away and I found her retching by the byre. I thought it then to be full grief. But no! 'Twas some growing bit, some

filthy tumor—some dross of his they hid within my mother's womb—
alive.

Alive! And well I know the mistress knows it, too. Yet she must
have slyly hid its portents from me. Well and wisely, for I would have
found some sip or suck to make this malignance drop away. I would
have done it! Yea, I will do it still!

No, I will not have it so. . . . I had seen a way to kill my mother's
joy. Yet now the rose wash blooms daily higher on her cheeks. No
more is there the painted rouge of sorrow. Now she is full singing!
"*Gloria Maria . . . Filius Patris . . . Sancte Domine! Gloria in excelsis
Deo!*"

Even she dares to claim its sex—that he will be a man-child. A
man, indeed—when did she ever have such care or joy for me? What
thought had she ever but for herself—for her Ossur—for her Christians? *Her* Christians. What thought has she ever but for what she
longs to love? Not for me nor for any she could have—should have—
given. Am I not already and forever of her blood? Yet better that she
hates me, ignores me, counts me nothing other than some estranged
part of her own dull self—as a bit of hangnail or a strand of half-split
hair to be plucked, to be torn apart and thrust away, noting not even
where it falls and crushes into the dust.

No, she will not outplay me. No simple vengeance will strike
down this deceit. I will find another way. Yet slowly . . . slowly . . . So I
watch upon her eye, and her eye on me. Then, even slower still, I begin to see—

Oh, such a path! My mother blithely tripping in her own dull
footsteps. That she dares to claim upon her Christian coax, yet I can
play upon that ploy. Bend and twist it, trip and skip along her stumble.
Follow? Follow her! Such a path I will please to tread as never was
that path so tread before.

Ah, what a lark! I will work to play the mimic to my mother's
faith till she thinks to make a Christian of me, too. Then, once that
faith and love are mine, I will give her back something so long owed
her, something more to hate and more to writhe, something more to

anguish and more to retch. Then, for sure, I will make her finally re-member which child of hers was first born.

Already I have made a cunning start, plying hands to heal and ease her love-lost sorrow. Now I add some small and truly simple things: holding back the gate when she comes, apron full, from gath-ering frost-touched berries; bearing up her goat's-milk bucket when her stomach grows too broad to hold it well. Ah, not much. Though somewhat more when, at night, I take to sleeping again beside her, hearing her say aloud that the baby in her womb makes her bones throb. So I attend her nightly groanings, though she thinks it some-how strange. Yet, in the morning, blinking slightly from her sleep, my drum-dull mother thanks me. "Daughter, you are good to me. Better, truly, than I'd ever thought," at which I bend my lips into a sort of simper.

I watch, amused at how quickly her lifelong hate dissolves, first into confusion, then into a sort of trial trust. She begins to speak some, not to me but with me near: "See," with her voice nervous-rising, "how loving Christ comes with all his comfort's good? Rest your head in Jesus' palm. All soul's remorse will be forgiven. All sins redressed. All pain forgot. All that's taken off will be but given back. All love that's lost will be replaced with joy." She eyes me some and hums again a bit of strident tune, *"Ave Maria, gratia plena. . . ."* I want so then to bare my teeth, to snarl, bite, to slash away the shape and sound of her Christian breathing; but instead I nod, thinking to myself I yet steel my soul to do some greater harm.

Indeed, such feigning mock has much effect. Even the mistress Thorbjorg watches me but keenly. Blinded by such wonder, she notes not the guile behind my gest', so that slowly, slowly, even Thorbjorg errs to trust my winsome demeanor, leaving me ever more alone upon my mother's tend.

It is easy then to grind my pit, following as my mother daily climbs up to the fell-slopes. I nearly laugh as she struggles to her knees, clutching her awkward growth beneath her prayerful palms. Yet, wise, I keep some back, where I know she sees me standing barely at the corner of her vision. There I wait, two days, three, then four, until, finally, I plot to bend my knees.

Ah! Falling on some soggy bit of sod, there I press my own hands above my cheating breast in imitation of her foul Christ-beseeching. My mother watches. Indeed, I wait just until I see her notice me. Then I awkward rise and wipe my wadmal of its filth, and hiss beneath my breath a rune-bit prayer of my own devising.

That night, as she sits beside me by the fire, she peers across her sanguine cheeks and her seal meat stew, bearing eyes welled up with newfound triumph and lips full-fat with awe and glee. "Daughter, how well and worthy is our Jesus"—she catches on my glance and gives it her own meaning—"so much better than your idols there, for those are all but sticks and stones, nary worth the weight you've ever given."

It twists my gut to hear her Christian condescension. Yet I hold quite still and swallow down my bile as my mother takes my hand and clutches it to her heart. I feel it beat, a strangeish sort of flutter. And her hand—so odd to be held by that cold, dead thing.

In months, my mother grows much rounder, so much that the bench we share is bare enough to sleep us both. Through the days, my mother's work to me is preaching, teaching all she thinks she's learned—all she's gleaned upon Brattahlid's sprout-grasses and those rigid hymns and psalms and prayers she's sucked from the woman Gudrid's lips or from the mouth of her dead lover—what foolish, twisted, half-right things. And on each I smile. On each I bob my head in rhythm, but whisp' no word and never will. In my heart I spit and hiss upon her witless strains.

Yet once—only once—she dares reach out to coax me make some music—"Here, 'tis worthy of accompaniment, daughter. Pray, consecrate your pagan fife with a holy tune."

I look on her—I cannot help myself, for the rage within me nearly spews and scratches. All my power holds me back as her hand hovers— there—above—oh, my sacred speaking! Yet I stop myself, for sudden she does also—of some sense perhaps of impending doom. Strange, her glimmered fright, as if awakened from a madness: still, then drawing nearly back, "Nay," she pipes, "perhaps you're right. 'Tis best if sung alone."

Perhaps.

Perhaps.

Perhaps she has some slightest, wiser sense, for I see just then my fylgie, slung up in the rafter, hanging low.

KATLA

MY DAUGHTER. Oh, my daughter! At first I did but spit, I so despised. . . . But then I sudden saw as never I had seen before—a look upon her eye some kind—and remembered slowly now those hands which wrapped about me. Remembered they had dragged me from the brink—when I could well—*would* well—have set myself and all this last of my love upon the fjord's ragged stones. Oh, it was a Christian act. And sudden then I knew that even this—this beast, as I have ever named her—is something other than her father's bane, but some sort of gift—strange, tender gift indeed.

For here she is and beside me she does linger, helping me in gentle, simple ways. And seeming wanting naught. So strange I had not noticed. How long has this been? I do not know. Yet then I think: before I could not see. Before I was so thick with despairing hate. Now perhaps I have found a clearer vision. Here, indeed, God's grace—his mercy on me—to turn my eye and there to find that other part of me which cannot be unjoined, there, where it has ever, always been.

It seems now suddenly so clear! To turn Bibrau's conception toward a truer purpose. To undo the terrored act of which she was first made. It was not, at last or ever, of her fault. Perhaps it was more my own in some small fashion: to be battered so and made to know such anguish, to bear such pain as perhaps our own Lord Christ had known before his death. Was all of this made for one strange cause: that my woe would be as a crucible to teach me? To teach her. To bring Bibrau, my own half-flesh, to know our God.

So it must be. My sorry, sullen daughter—never loved or ever wanted. I see I must, for she is only as I've made her—of twist and taint and hatred—yet I can make her up again of sweet and polished gold! So I set myself to do—to thank the Lord for what he has begot— this chance at last to repent my sins—to bring this child of my flesh into our Christian fold.

So I begin to sing but soft. Then louder some. I begin to teach her well: slowly the notes at first, and then with careful Latin phrasing, for, though Bibrau never will speak aloud, she can well hear and seems to like their sounds.

And slowly, as these lessons come, I sense she hears me better, and listens with a will to know, and even sometimes nearly joins along. Yet she's fair afraid to breach what has for so long been her stronghold. I must be patient. I must not push. I must let her keep her pipe strained upon a pagan note if it should comfort. I must allow her error when the curves she carves are tainted with impure font. But slowly, slowly, I do teach, and I think Bibrau does learn.

Sounds As Happy Children Make

THORBJORG

IT CANNOT BE in truth. Bibrau feeds upon her mother's hunger. Here she bows and sways, pressing hands in mimic of her mother's prayers. And Katla—fragile hope upon her ravaged visage—sees her daughter's feigning offered up as if some honeyed, fragrant meal. No. 'Tis ne'er of worth. It is too sweet and seeming fair. I do not know what game she plays. Well it is of mock and making, yet my foster-daughter plays so fine, I cannot see the flaws upon her truss. She stitches it but close and seamly, till I find even I myself am near inclined to turn a casual cheek and almost cast upon that pair a nod.

Nay, unwise! All the world is rank and twisted. Yet perhaps my sight itself is false, and only now my vision honest, seeing even Bibrau cannot press against this pulling tide. So strong it drags the wasting stones beneath our steps. Alfather, I hear their clatter, watch the seeping foam. I do not know what I can trust. So much my vision's blurred. My tongue is addled. Even now my thoughts grow jumbled. All is muck and murk. No words I speak will stop the certain weaving of the Norns.

The Norns. The Norns. Ever they have woven toward an end. Now 'tis come: the last fine knot, the fraying ends nearly clipped and tied. We can only wait and watch. Listen, Alfather, to their stitch and tremble. The fire's light is growing dim. The sky is heavy with the coming storm. It is still some off, the lightning faint, but the rumble's there beneath my feet. Steps coming soft and crisp with anticipation. So hard to wait, breathing in such brutal calm.

* * *

It is said the wind presages pestilence, famine, fire.

Yet here, within my shelter, it is still and dark, silent as the falling snows. Upon the empty fell-slopes, the mist rises up before the ever-watching moon. I heed our breaths: Katla's there, and then my own, my foster-daughter's, Kol's and Arngunn's, even poor Nattfari's set against the crumbled, sod-soft wall, bearing at her scabs and sores with fingers thick and hard and sooted. No, it is not warm or pleasing, but it is full-like, all of us together as we've done before. It is a household of a kind.

A knock upon my door.

Thorhall Hunter. I hear him almost before his footsteps crush the certain fall of still-pure snow, his shape full-bent upon the wind's hard press, climbing my homefield hill on a night when none with any sense should be out about or riding. Yet he lumbers, rests there, pauses one small breath, lifts his thick, gloved fist before it falls.

"Thorbjorg!" I hear him as an echo. "Thorbjorg, it is Thorhall! Let me in from out the cold!"

I nod to Kol to open the door and let him through. Then I wait. My hand, still upon a simple stitch—women's work—I am not apart from my own household's choring. Simple is the task: to be silent, to stitch, to weave, to sew. Yet, as keenly as I pluck the needle, draw the thread, guide the narrow hem—the thin, straight line—the Norns gnaw with yellow teeth upon these ill-spun fibers.

I wait upon the two men's slap of backs and the sparkled light of frost from dangled fur in tatters, rising up and falling down into the mud where the warmth of fire has met the breath of ice.

Thorhall stands in the hallway's gaping. "Old friend!" he gruffs, blocking off the wind.

"Old friend," I whisper in return.

His shape shows dark against the midnight's glow, his long beard gray now where it was once ebon, wired now more than it is curled. But that is not what strikes me: only his glance, full-gaunt, his lips parched white, his whiskers bound up with a breathing frost. His breath rises up as clouds hovering to shade our view.

"Mistress Thorbjorg," he gasps, "good of you to let me in, for it is cold without, and hungry also. Well if, fair, have ye any food?"

"Food, Thorhall?" I try to smile. "Ever enough for you, old comfort."

Slowly I rise from the tremor of the fire and set him down and call to Arngunn, "Warm the pot from which we had our stew."

"Stew?" Thorhall blusters. "Well, then, say it not so loud! If it be true, then half of Austerbygd will bear upon your step before the morrow's morning."

"Say it so?" I feign a laugh. "It is hard upon that icy road."

"Aye, I say it so! Did you not hear? There is famine in these parts."

My hand's upon an empty bowl. "Indeed?" So I know one coal of why my heart is weighty.

"First," Thorhall continues, "all the crops from Vesterbygd to Austerbygd were cut down quick by an early frost. Then the seed and grain we'd saved were blighted by a sudden thaw setting flood into the storage stalls. For meat, what caribou we followed on the autumn fells were scant and skittish to our strikes. And now such dried-up seal meat from last summer's hunts is mostly eaten up or, still more foolish, sold away for bits of profit none can eat or void. Naught but sheep and goats remain—and none of these we dare to slaughter, or have no milk or wool for cloth or even curdled cheese."

"Nay, I see it so. Even at Brattahlid?" I glance away.

"I tell you there's bare a bit of fat or sip of ale. This Yule— on which you were full-missed, Thorbjorg—there was naught. Not enough even to fill the chieftains' horns. It made for fair chagrin, with Eirik mighty mournful for treating so ill his new-come comrades— mostly Thorbjorn Vifilsson and Gudrid Thorbjornsdatter, who ne'er were yet received at a proper Greenland Yule. Full of ire Eirik was, faulting me for not buying up more grain upon the Althing markets, for not caulking well the chinks and gashes in the stalls, for every sort of blame and injury. All this, while his Christian mistress went about at every turn to pray upon the priest. And he!—blowhard!—scenting up the air! That priest with sickly smoke as from unruly bowels, dripping such candles of stickly wax, chanting as you may—"

"Dominus Christus—Sancte Domine—"

Thorhall pauses. "Thorbjorg, what's that Christian sound?"

He turns quick around, flailing his cloak's snow-soaked tails of rabbits near the fire. Thorhall rises up, plodding to tower over Katla. "It is you. You! After all, I would have thought—nay—that your love for Christ had died with your most pitiable husband!"

I see Katla gasp. "Thorhall, leave the woman be."

"I might have some compassion," he turns. "Yet, Thorbjorg, hush her up! You must, for one more breath of that Christian stuff will be my killing. And yours! Nay, I tell you—her or me—for I will not stand, nor stay and have it out. Nor should you, I swear, after all this Christ has done—"

"Come, Thorhall, hush." I pull him off.

"Nay, I'll not, or go the way of all these Christian traitors—down upon the slippery ice, upon their fault and lie—smiling well to have their trade, yet along the way to have forgot their e'er embattled gods. Such—but you have been so long apart, Thorbjorg—don't you see it? Don't you know such songs as hers have blocked our own gods' ears? Stuffed them up with jabber till they cannot listen even when such cries go loud to feed this raging hunger!

"So it is, Thorbjorg, for I myself set about to make it better— sent a prayer to Odin—well, to Thor—to any who might hear! One night myself I made sacrifice upon a simple beast—a goat—not much, but all I could slip from out the byre when none about would notice. Yea, I gave it up—brought it high upon the frosty fells, and myself slit its throat and plucked its parts and set them up on stakes in a ring around a fire, as I've seen so often you have done. Then, from the skull, I drank the blood, as you once and thrice have shared with me. Yet, of a sudden, the smoke from my fire turned black—coal-black against a moonless vault of winter. I thought at first 'twas a fair'y omen, for I heard an almost rumbling and a sudden crack! Quick I chewed my lips upon your chants, but then a sickly screech set my voice full-still. 'Twas the foul Christian priest, and close behind Eirik's mistress, Thjoldhilde, both their steps falling hard upon the crackling ice, and their torches rippling wild in the foehn wind's howl, coming toward me as if a thunderbolt from Thor.

"But none did our gods do much to stop them. Nay, not while they found me out and dragged me back even as I held the fair, thick drinking cup to my sipping lips! This they dashed hard off, spilling it across the filth-caked mud floor. Wasted! All that blood along with my proper, god-bound feast. Wasted—even such food which might be better served at least to feed some starve-struck children. But no! ' 'Tis taint!' they shrieked. 'A pagan profanation!' Shouted, 'Say a Christian prayer for Thorhall Hunter. This is all he's known from his lifelong friendship with the witch Thorbjorg!' "

"Such they said, and then some Latin mumblings. Then—full-worst!—they took my carving blade and threw it off into the snow. Threw it off! A fine blade, too! Well made and proper, of a strong, quick-sharp'ing metal—thrown so it should rust and rot and ne'er be of use or likely found." He takes another sip and spits. "Such waste. Such waste, when I had plied only to keep us all from dying. I shouted, 'Fair, but know ye now, Alfather with his one eye watches! If I were you, I would quick pray upon our fate, for, as I've seen, no Christ of yours has ever found us yet proper meal!' So I said, then left them all there, gathered round at Herjolfsnaes—"

"Herjolfsnaes?"

"Aye, there, where all this farce did happen—for only there, among the bigger farms, is there some bitty meal. True, 'twas scraped from the corners of the stalls at Sandhavn market. Bare it was enough, for all of Eirik's house and guests and thralls had gone, and most the other chieftains, fast about to Herjolfsnaes to ring in counsel what to do. For some days they prayed, ever spitting 'Christ!' upon their lips; but none from me—no, never will you hear it! For all their prayers, came the hunger only quicker, and some rattling of bones about our guts, and little children's shrieks, until, at last, no longer could I hold my tongue with your name upon my tippy teeth.

" 'Thorbjorg! Thorbjorg,' I said upon a roar. 'Well you'll do to call her out, to beg her see beyond this hungry piece to what will sooner be. 'Nay,' they shouted, 'witch!' Swore, 'Seeress!'—swallowed even 'Little

Sibyl!' with a hiss. So I said, 'Say whate'er you might, but I would call her out, for she has seen us through such bitter blight before.'

"Well, don't you know, there were whisp's and mumblings, till the priest rose up and howled, 'Stop such talk or—fate!—you'll bring us back beneath the heathen shadow.' I scoffed at this, though I quick heard no other men were cackling. They were seeming thinking, pulling on their beards, until, at last, Torkel Herjolfsson—who is near as wise as was his now-cold father—uttered, 'Thorhall Hunter, go upon it. Bring the mistress Thorbjorg here.' "

Thorhall munches on a bone. "So I have come." He swallows back a hefty sip of mead. Through all this I have but held his hand, somewhat red, as if burning still from bitter winter. Held it in my own some time, and even now, listening as he slurps the last thickened scoops of stew—as my husband long ago—his name was Knut—was used to do—then licks the drippings off his whiskers.

I breathe but slowly, "What am I to answer?"

Thorhall throws his spoon into his bowl. "Answer? Woman, come! Come! For they have begged ye utter!"

"Nay. Not begged. Only broken from their fear." I turn back to my stitch.

"So—broke! Call it what you may, but I have told—I would have thought . . . I've promised . . . thought you'd welcome such a chance to ply upon their reason. To bear some hope of less of Latin spitting and more of our own proper cants and sacrificial prayers. Such, to turn their ways aback upon the proper leaning. Well, but come, for I tell you, all would change should you but breathe a wisdom-word."

"So you think, Thorhall?" I feel an aching as I try to smile. "You are kind, old friend, and good to me. Faithful as old Kol." I pat his hand and rub it gently, then turn upon my needle.

"What say you, woman?" Thorhall batters. "Come upon it!"

"Nay, old friend. Such time is past. The priest speaks loudly now. I can barely hear. There is no room within that din to breathe my feeble musings."

"Feeble musings? Lady, too late to raise a voice and lift your arms upon the arch of Ymir's brow?"

"I am old, Thorhall. I am full-tired. I have no such wiles left, nor much of power now."

"Come upon it, Seeress! For you'll win some back of what you never should have lost—"

I hold my stitch and watch my hands a-quiver. "Nay. Not lost. 'Twas only taken from me—slowly, as the strength of youth is minusculely shed." I set my hands down, feeling sudden weight as embers crumble-falling from a fire. "Nay, it is not for me to press upon them. If they gain some solace from such Christian prayers, then let them pray."

Thorhall nearly sets upon me. "You must come, Thorbjorg. The hunger's spread! It must be stopped—"

"If e'er it truly could . . ." I sigh.

"What means all this?"

"Nothing, Thorhall. Naught." Though I long indeed to spit the truth upon the fire, to cry out loud at last that I have ever given naught—ever plied blindly on my craft, and if I harmed or helped, did so in chance and wanting. I see it now—having naught but speaking as 'twas pressed upon my tongue, feeling ever Odin's callused fingers. Even now I feel their scratch, but the grip is weak and the force is sloughed. No, I have not even that—not even you, Alfather—now.

So I would say, yet I say nothing as Thorhall looks on me: on his lips, a wind-chapped scar, and in his eyes, such faith as ever I have seen. There—as if my tongue can shape the very runes, as if my pouch of herbs is truly useful. Can he not see my palms are dry? The corners of my lips are cracked and bleeding! The taste of blood—my wounds long-deep and festered, ne'er to fully mend. But I say naught. Only turn and gaze upon my stitching. There the narrow thread, so fine and fleet upon its path. Bound into the cloth, it comes but strong and sure and binding; but, set alone, so frail, so quick to fray.

I murmur, "Ask me not, old friend. I beg you, go. Come not to me like this again. Come only to see me as your ancient, loved companion. Now and ever, for there is naught that I can do. Indeed, I've spent time enough chilled upon the frost of Christians."

"So you say," Thorhall grumbles, "yet you bear one still within your house," his gaze on Katla sharp and biting.

I near-to laugh. "Thorhall, nay, and calm. Know you well, Katla was ever of my Greenland household."

"It is not right, after all that's been. . . ."

"I will not turn her out, Thorhall. You know I would not, for soon she'll bear upon her labor. I will not leave her to try such brutal fate alone."

"Mistress Thorbjorg—"

I catch upon a turn: from out the shadows, Katla is rising, gripping hard for aid the roofing beam, then my foster-daughter's sturdy arm. "I will not be alone," she pants. "Bibrau can help me bear."

"Nay, it is not wise—"

"Not wise," Katla begs, "when Bibrau's skill is near a mirror of your own? When her touch itself does ply against my grieving? Well you know, for all these months, she herself did bring me up from the still of loss, and shows me even now to such fair and gentle dreaming. 'Tis true, and her remedy tempered now with calm and Christian touch—"

"Christian?" Thorhall gapes.

"Indeed, for I've been teaching her the Holy Book and the ways of Jesus."

Thorhall turns a shade of pallid white and presses hands down hard upon the table-board. He looks on me, some ripe; then on Bibrau, keen.

"So you see all will be well, my mistress. I pray you, go. 'Tis righteous, fair, to bring them comfort as you may—as you ever have. Now more than ever, for they have wronged you. Forsaken you. Indeed, they do not trust, yet they turn to you because they are full a-feared. So you must go to give them patient comfort, as a mother, even in her pain and sorrow, should ever love her child."

As Katla speaks, her eyes fall long on Bibrau. And Bibrau's gaze turns to her mother's own—as near to docile as I have ever seen. It is a strange and twisted apparition. Indeed, all about my household sense the tinge. There's a hush, so still I can hear their breathing. Only Nattfari scrapes her tattered nails across a sooted beam.

"Indeed!" Thorhall coughs, knowing well the strangeness, yet setting better for his purpose. "Perhaps, then, for a Christian, Katla is some different. Lady, see? Katla is well pleased to stay behind. And our foster-daughter—there she is—the finest midwife save yourself in all this Greenland! 'Tis true. 'Tis true. Where is our rebel creature now? You hear, Thorbjorg? I pray you, come, and quick! You have naught to stop you now."

We pack my things.

Bibrau brings my dark-blue cloak, the lighter shade of midnight dragging now with its stones sewn down to the very hem. After all these years, I have grown used to its great weight, though we must hold it on my shoulders with wide leathern straps, then hide them as best we can with a string of thick glass beads. For my brass-tipped cane, I am full grateful; it holds me steady even as such baubles weigh me heavy down. And my sturdy touchwood belt, which Gizur—long grown cold but ne'er forgotten—once carved upon a summer's eve. "Sturdy," he had said, "so all your magics packed in their pouch will not pull upon your waist." Yet now I feel their sudden heft as more— yet ever more—is set upon me.

I look about, fearing near at once to choke. It is more than fright of speaking empty words; that I've known and felt some often. It is some- thing other gripped about my bones—some hollow in my gullet, hard to swallow as a strangled pit, knowing well I must not leave, not go upon this journey, feeling full the weight of desolation—a certain cry of fate. More than Bibrau, Katla—now I feel at last the shape of it—at first a doubtful mass, now it sets about to slow congeal. Yet they look on me, seeing naught, seeming almost glee'd upon my passing. And the sound of it is a haunting, distant scream. Can they hear it not? It is not the wind nor a precipice for birds, but a slow, dull rotting, cold and dire, alone upon the rocks—'tis death, as inescapable as a bitter breeze.

Still my household hies about, mustering all that I can wear of warmth, for the cold is ripe and beating. From Bibrau, the lambskin hat she stitched so long ago in anguish; from Kol, such thick, hairy calfskin boots which once he wore upon his falcon hunts. These he ties himself, up tight against the seeping in of frost, with thick, dangled laces and clanking buttons made of tin. And on my fingers, from Katla's tender hands, catskin gloves with soft white fur she stitched upon her freedom. With these and such other needs as I require, they tend me, then send me out, daughter, mother, one upon each corner of my cloak, then both hands about me, and Kol helping push me up as Thorhall eases me into his waiting sledge. Then he lifts the reins and, in an instant, we are fast away.

We are gone. Being dragged along that stiff, ever-fragile surface. Listening to the ice's dull creak, to the rattle of the wisp and wind. Cold within my heaving breath—Thorbjorg Seeress, Little Sibyl—in all my wretched keeping, out upon that night which will lead upon the dawn which—now I know—must never be.

It comes, the dawn, which is no dawn at all but a shifting of the spray of stars and a barely purpled prospect. We come upon the flame of torches set to mark the harbor at the edge of Tofafjord: Herjolfsnaes. Such, there's none about but bare-head slaves, who raise us up from the sledge without a whisper. They bear us gravely toward the longhouse where the others wait—where once, not long ago, old Herjolf died.

I stand. I listen to the wind. Its choked refrain, strained as the last small breaths before the still of dying. From the distance, quick and sharp upon the fragile night, break laughs and chatter from Herjolf's old hall.

We take some steps. There—just before we go much farther—half upon the harbor's rocky slope, I pause, holding Thorhall by the arm. I turn, slowly, slowly, listening to the strange, soft silence beneath this cliff, so open to the sea. In that quiet, snow begins to fall, shining on the air like moonlit crystals. I still, sudden sensing something in the shadows. It is the first strong sense I have felt in many years.

"Mistress?" Thorhall coaxes me to take his hand, pressing me to step upon the climbing rise.

"Here." I shake, pointing with my narwhal staff.

Thorhall bends into the snow, searching blindly for some quarry, until at last I stoop myself and feel about. In a breath, I lay his cast-off knife into his hand.

Thorhall looks on me, his face gone flush, then brusques a gruff and helps me stand.

He ushers me on toward Herjolfsnaes' fire. There is smoke within.

Indeed, there is a crowd. Thjoldhilde, Eirik, and their sons, Thorstein, Thorvald, and Leif—ever tall beside his father. There Torkel Herjolfsson, acting master of this hall now in his father's stead, and there Torgerd, Herjolf Bardsson's widow. There the younger brother Bjarne and even Torkel's own son, Gudmund, back again from Norway—Gudmund, whom my foster-daughter had but crudely, cruelly known. All within this hall, even these other chiefs I know, whose faces have welcomed me since they were somewhat smooth: Thorbjorn Glora, Arnlaug, Ketil, Einar with his goodwife, Grima, and their fool-foul son, Torvard. Torvard, whose brutish work has often bent upon my fortune. 'Tis true, for his seed did bring to me both Katla and Bibrau.

Yet there are others, the stranger-Christians: Gudrid; her father, Thorbjorn Vifilsson; and, beside them, the rank, sanctimonious priest. I take some steps, feeling a taste upon my tongue, bitter, burning as some hard, cold metal, feeling words foaming up that I would spit or shout—*Dare you call me to this hall with him within?*

It is not hard to see already how the Christian blight has spread full wide and draping, this heavy veil of fear, as the priest whispers, "*Sancte Domine . . . Sancte Christe . . . Sancte Spiritus . . . ,*" his eyes tight shut—so tight, he must not wish to see.

Sensing my rage, Torkel plies a tremored hand upon the black-robed fraud. He nearly shakes him—kind of him, that. The priest opens up his eyes then, turning off from Torkel's glancing, sets his crosier and beads away.

"Seeress, welcome," finally Torkel greets me. "You are ever welcome to my house, even as you were so oft beneath my late father's wood beams. All of us are grateful, say in truth, to see you've come."

I hear in Torkel's voice his father's tone and words, so like Herjolf's, ever calm and warm and earnest. But these others—these chieftains even—as they nod accord, do wary glance, their lips a-wonder-trembling. Indeed, some strange—'tis bare distrust from such as would not long ago have turned to me in greatest gasping. From such as would have begged me once to comfort them toward life's last breath. Yet this—yet now—such disdain painted on their eyes in such empty hues, as again comes the priest beneath his breath, "Lead us not into temptation, but deliver us from evil . . . ," chanting phrase as the rest shift and dip about me, as if meeting now should be a bane.

Torkel sets his arm beneath my own and guides me slowly out among them.

"Mistress Thorbjorg!" Arnlaug smiles. "Aye, but you look well."

I judge him harshly. "So I should, Arnlaug. When life is hard, all the best to temper mettle. Yet you, I see, still fat and full. I had heard a blight had fallen on your farm. Yet round your midriff not a bitty bit of slack! Fair, for you must trade on faith for grain upon the Christians' stores." I sense him quake and see he turns quick from me, with his hand some stiff and his forebrow furrowed.

"And you, Ketil?" I speak, for he's come fast behind. "This famine travels far. More's the pity when, just springtime last, you had calves enough to make a mighty feast. Yet, I remember, did you share one piece—one piece even—upon a stake for the One-Eyed god?"

True, I am biting, paining, cutting each as their distrustful looks wound me. Pity to their hurt and worry! Pity to their wonder quake! For what of theirs was ever not of my own? What suffering have they endured that I've not felt in threefold plenty? What, for have they ever, always, come to me in need? And I have ever borne it, stood among their sweat and spit, their puke and gall and bile, ever breathed their prayers up high and bold toward Old One-Eye's hearing. Yet, when I myself was hurt or harmed, maligned, mistrusted, first upon the Norway fells, then upon old Iceland's soil, then even here—this Greenland—my circle burned, and I abandoned, hated, terrored, made to suffer Christians—never once did one here bend an arm or leg or proffer up a palm in aid of me.

Never. And only come upon me now—again. So now, at last, I let my mouth spit out these words—clipped, harsh, twisted as the music of a scraped, dull sword, its edge not quite sharp, not enough to kill, but well to maim, to pierce, to mangle.

Such—for I can bear but that. I cannot hurt them more.

Torkel takes me up and leads me through them, places me on his very father's seat, upon a cushion stuffed with the just-plucked plumes of hens. Then he says, "Lady, well and look about you. All our very best is yours, all within this house which still remains. Yet I tell you—here is suffering and confusion. I beg you, cast your eye about, over each one, small and great and barely born. Over all our households, homes, and herds, Little Sibyl, speak. Tell us what your vision knows."

I look on them a bit. Strange to view from here, from so much angry sorrow. Anger I'd not thought I'd known, yet here among them all it sputters. A soggy leak in a well-sewn bladder. I hold it up. I try to knit it tight, but it spills in silence, a brutal, perverse mute. "I see not much at all among you now."

And what I mean—what I mean to say is so much better—mean that, all about, all have lost their souls, their hollow hearts, their scabby legs—crusts which will yet flake and fall to dust. Yet—what? I dare say nothing and act upon my stubborn pride? Even Thorhall—there, old friend—looking on me in somewhat shame and wonder.

"Mistress"—Torkel tries to quick-appease me—"Seeress—you are full-tired now. And well you should be, for your journey's long and rough, frigid on the bounding beast over rattled ice. Quick—all about, we will set tables out and make for her our finest feast!"

Feast—I think—upon a famine.

Yet I sit still and watch them scurry, setting tables first, then clanking cooking pots. Slow comes the smell of gruel—some bitty grain scraped up from the dusty storage corners. Then, in time, as the grain is cooked, comes a bleat, a bellow, bray, a moan, a lower. Here a proper, prayerful feast, as Odin, Frey, and Thor ought well recall. I smell the beating of their hearts—of goat and sheep and cow and dog and pig and cat set hard to boil against the kettle's iron mantle. Soon they serve me up this broth. I savor it, taking my bright brass spoon and my walrus-handled knife to cut. I hear now pounding stakes into the frost—some small part upon this feast sent up to the hungry gods.

So I witness, eyeing on my blade, bound up in its tarnished copper fastenings. Where comes that nick? Well—I don't remember. . . . Now I think—upon the hearth fire's light—the perfect tip was chipped by Bibrau long ago.

They eat upon their feast, pass some bitty bit around. Not much, yet enough to sate, a smallish remedy. There the eldest thrall gets help to crack the stubborn marrow. There the wasted bones and the unfit parts are gnawed by Torkel's leanest dogs.

Then Torkel says, after watching long and eating little, "Mistress Thorbjorg, are you pleased upon my house? Have you had your fill? Are you ready yet to speak?"

I look about. I cannot help but snap, "I must rest. I will speak upon the morrow." Why do I trifle when I see yet all and then much more? But I hiss only, "I must sleep one night within this house," then hie myself to bed without another word.

There I toss and turn and hear such voices coming to me, all about. I know, I sense—Old Odin—your quick spirit rests beside, though you are nowhere near, still and cold and snoring on your throne Hlidskialf. Yet close enough, and others, too—others some long dead: Herjolf, like and well; my dear old Gyde, my fair, kind servant-sister. And Gizur—shy but with such a laugh as sounds like a hoarse guffaw. And Orm, Vidur, even Arngunn's bare-born twins. Too, even the Christians, James and John. And Katla's Ossur. These I do not question. All are gone such way as they are meant but I.

Only I and Kol are left—Kol, who will rest beside me even in my dying. So I know. I hear—his breathing near enough, though he sleeps but still and sound far off within the Tofafjord house. Yet I hear. 'Twill not be long. His gentle rumble. I feel his flesh: his rough, wide palm brushes about my brow, growing dry and cracked as soon to dust 'twill crumble.

I listen to the swell and droop of all their breaths. Even better, I hear distant murmurs. So, my ancient husband comes! Knut—stay back!—long dead. Long brittle. And my children born, then burned beneath the hateful fires—hateful, but for me. Before that, too, long ashes, dance my nine dead sisters.

I hear them all. All the voices of the dead and near-to-dying. All of them, and also me, for I hear my dwindled breath. I see it rising in the mist. I bend to whisp' on the ebbing coals of the weary fire, but my breath is chill. Red brightens once, then the coals burn out.

I rest again. I cannot sleep. I must not—willing not to. Nay, for I know the sort of speaking which must come. As ever, it comes from me. No more from the depth of passion—lost, the honest words of the ancient gods. Lost. All of them—lost from me. I am hollow. Empty. I am as dull ash from a well-used log—the fine white flake before the door is ope'd and wind strips away the char.

Upon the dawn, I rise. I drape my cloak about my back and stand and wait until the others waken. Then, though they are weary, wiping their eyes from the goo of sleep, quick I call them out: "Does any here about yet know the kvads?"

I see a shiver, enough to rouse them even from their dreary dreaming. "Nay," I say again, "does any here yet know the ancient singing? I must have it, with all my potents, my stones and sticks and all my reasonable magics. Any yet? Come. Thjoldhilde, come—for, once before, upon your husband's want, you sang fair well enough for all."

"I cannot!" Eirik's wife shrinks back and cowers in her priest's own garment.

His vestments reel and he quivers out, "You'll tempt this woman not with your wiles! Out upon it! Thjoldhilde, come. All good Christians, come away!"

So they leave us, and Thorbjorn Vifilsson and Grima and several others with them—all beyond the hall and out of my clouded sight. Soon enough, the room then somewhat clears.

I look about me. "Does any here yet know the ancient music?"

"I know it," comes a tone—a pretty, gentle timbre. "I know it." It is Gudrid Thorbjornsdatter. "From my foster-mother, Halldis. She sang such lullabies long ago to me—her voice and singing ever lovely of their pagan speech, and she, full beloved to me, so that I remember even now every word and how she sang them well."

"Gudrid," Torkel Herjolfsson counters, "you are Christian—you, most of all these turned. Do not sing if you have no wish to."

"Yet I have some wish. I am Christian, yet, if there is good need upon our fate, I will be well pleased to sing the songs out loud."

Somewhat amused and full-content, I bid her take her place upon the platform well beside me. Then, calling all the other women to the center of the hall, I settle back into old Herjolf's chair, deep down upon the feather cushion, setting wrists heavy-bound upon the high-seat's arms, my breasts lifted up, my chin held back above my nose, my head let to fall, my both eyes fully closed.

Gudrid sings. Such notes as never I have heard them—all the music in them sounding rightly, all the strain of pitch rounding up and flowing, sinuous and slow, as ever they should be, as ever I have yearned, even on my greatest flights and longest, lingered fancies, such music coming light yet stronger than the birds.

She sings and I lose myself upon the thread, the fragile strand. I lift and writhe, feel my body fall away. Fall and stay behind, and I am rising, drifting off from place and time upon a fiber.

The famine is over.

Other deaths have come and gone.

Greenland's tides rise up, quick-crash, fall down.

Such people as are here alive still live or die as ever well they might. Other comings, goings pass there quickly, before my eyes.

There is no more circle. There are no more stones. Such promises to Thor and Odin, to Frigga, Freya, Frey—all lost upon the snows. Such, they are still—ever dreaming—not to be forgot precisely, yet never to be sung so sweet again.

Ne'er so sweet. So the music sways and I follow lightly on its wind—back upon a ship's sail. Iceland. Such a lonely place as I have ever been. Yet not for all. Nay! There, ancient Gudrid: aged, black in robes, white the Christian cross draped around her throat, cut across a withered bosom. About her, women, men, bounds of children—the finest family. In this woman's face, shriveled peace as ever I should hope to see.

Then it is gone. The last notes dying. Drifting off. I wake to faces, others wanting, hovered round. I raise my head again upon my neck. Stiff it is, with cricks and creaks and straining. I sit some up. I bend over my knees. Quivered, I take the horn from someone's shaking hand and swallow down the mead.

Gudrid kneels beside me. I see in her the wrinkles are all gone; her face is plain and pleasant as it was ever. Too, I see, as my eyes dip down on my own reflection in firelight and the ruddy cup, a rippled look as scoured rock in the frozen sea.

"Thank you, Gudrid. That was lovely."

All acquiesce about it, saying, "Fine. 'Twas the fairest singing ever we have heard."

"Now," I call them, "hush! Many spirits now are listening. Many who were not here before, and many things revealed. I say to you, soon this famine will be over. All such sicknesses and miseries will go quicker than is thought. By spring, with such sun and warmth, strength will return among you."

Then I pause, for so much else I cannot tell them. So much more which I had not thought to know before.

"Yet one more thing I tell—one last—to Gudrid, a gift in kindness for your aid, for I have seen your future, a destiny which slightly slipped before my eyes. I have seen you make a marriage, sailing far again away to Iceland. There you will grow old and make a fair and august progeny, surrounded by the brightest light. Fare you well upon it, Gudrid Thorbjornsdatter."

I say it, in simple, casual tones—tones which lie from the truth I truly tell, which is: in Christ, the world will come to prosper, and in Gudrid's host, her future will soon flourish, while in my own world my battle has been lost, and Christ's is won.

Yet no longer am I angry, for I have seen such fate as true and clear as ever there was need. I have tasted of it, sad and earnest on my tongue, and the taste was sweet and warm as the last brief brush of autumn sun before it drifts beneath the mountains' crests and fades.

Then and there, all about are crowding round in triumph, holding hands—mine both—quick clasped and shaking merrily. Drink is passed—some berried juice, for there is not much left of mead—and some cold, hard bits are scraped from the bottom of the kettle to be made for bitty morning's food.

So. And as they come to me, they ask me petty things, such as how their crops will fare and if their daughters will also marry. I tell them everything I know, for little will they ask the harder questions. I see how much it pleases them. How grateful are their thanks. I smile at them, an earnest, open smile, for I know these things they ask and these I answer are the last true things the ancient gods will ever put upon my lips to tell.

BIBRAU

WE ARE ALONE. Only me and my own mother. Just she and I as the fell-slopes drip and slip to sudden gurgled springs.

Day after day, just where I want her—beside me smiling, happy by the homefield wall, humming some, then saying sweetly, "Daughter, you think it strange this spring should come so soon?" Then, when I say naught, she sighing, "Strange indeed, but it would be mostly pleasant—a pleasant morning to be born." Then sighing more, dreaming, "Bibrau, think you not the child will come soon?"

And I—nodding back, holding out my hands, and she taking them, gathering them close beside her heart—"You are good to me, my daughter, better than I would have thought"—smoothing them against her swollen belly's bloom so I might feel the lively kick! But—ah . . .

Just where I want her, while I help her at her narrow walk: awkward, ever slower, pausing some, putting one hand on a widened hip while her breath comes sudden high and shallow. "Hear? Hear?" she gasps a-miss. "Listen! Bibrau, can you hear the meltwaters singing?" And she, silent last, clutching close my fingers. "Such sweet sounds as these will my child make," she hushes aloud, and slightly shakes me. "Any day now. Any day! All joyfulness and happy. Such are sounds as happy children make, I'm sure."

I'm sure. For never did I make such sounds. Not me. Oh, no. Never sound indeed. Never peep. Never babble. Never "Mama! Papa!" me. Oh, no. Not once, not in all their hearing. Yet there my mother sighs and smiles—not at me precise, but just beyond—as she squeezes, trembles, her hand caught up within my palm.

So we go, she and I. Every day, so pleasant. Ever we together all these thrice times seven dawns—nearly one full changing of the moon. Nearly a month since the mistress' recent parting; and on each day, together in the household's shadow we sit—alone—me and my mother—to weave, to spin, to sew.

Alone, as the ice does melt, as the fjord cracks with brutal echoes, as the fells but drip and the winds are quick to whine; as day after day grows warmer with the sun and glowing; and each thrall in turn heads off toward the fell-slopes, to the fjord's banks, to the byre, storehouse, or to pluck some just-shed wool from off the jagged rocks set high and low. They go each day, at first with an eye on me of ill-suspicion; but then, when, upon the dark, each quick returns to find some meal of mine set upon the table and my mother growing fat as a sow upon the slop, they grow more trusting, each day more fully fools, leaving me and my mother here together—she and I, so soft and gentle—to do about what well we can and will.

Just so, I watch as slowly the household empties, until there is not one foul thrall, but only mad Nattfari lingering with us. Mad Nattfari, and she does not matter much, staying there within her corner eating lice from off her hairs. Nay, she does not matter much at all.

So the time does pass till half the moon has fallen dark and the nights are growing slowly full with stars. Such stars, so bright, and the milky road Bifröst is gathered up, bounding out across the fading colors of the aurora's winter draping.

Soon.

Not yet. I sense in me some waiting. Not yet. But soon . . . while my mother stitches distractedly, her hand dropping down more often than it pulls the thread. Then she, sighing some, or singing out a bit of song—another Christian, tuneless ditty. So oft she sings, I find their hateful melodies ringing in my ears. Oh, even my precious silence tainted! I long to wrench them from my hearing, yet I will not force them out. Oh, no—nor, at nights, slip away to hear the cackled black birds crow. Where once I would have strode to make my bitty rounds, now I choose to linger close, to stay, all meek compassion. All gentle touch. I will suffer such to make my ruse complete.

Ah, and such a ruse! Oh, I suffer greatly, pressed on with a constant vex. Yet I steel my mind to it—each note a barb whet' sharp to spur me better. I ply upon my plan, ever stirring at the cauldron's heat: the boiled meats there bobbing against the blackened metal in rhythm with my mother's sounds.

KATLA

IT WILL NOT BE LONG. I can sense the subtle movement: the groping hand there reaching out—the cramp and darkness longing yet for breadth and room and breathing. The ache of him slowly growing, the writhe of him ever more within, the twist and hungry turning, soon to have him out, soon to see that flesh, that visage—to hold him soon again within my arms!

Oh, I cannot wait for wanting. Each day seems ripe and ready, yet the sun moves slow. The horizon brightens, then grows quickly dark, and naught comes but some bit of stitch or weaving from my jittered, busy fingers. Yet—upon the power of the Christ—God give me patience. Patience, come!

For Christ's own miracle, that the dead should rise once more. The dead to live—yet not upon the gates of Heaven, but here. Now. Soon. This very day! Oh, the longing sets me unto song! I cannot hold my joyous notes. They quiver, triumph, rise that they should never fall! Heaven and earth are mixed upon my hymns; yet those final notes fly off and fade away, and I am left yet—still—alone.

Almost. Bibrau's here beside me. Bibrau, my strangest work, my daughter some, yet no. Most not. Mostly other. Yet how can I think it so, after all she has become? In these long days past, my helpmate and companion. My constant comfort, my stronger second arm. Transformed from vicious rage to precious benediction. So, as all Christ's miracles are turned to good—set the blind to see, the deaf to hear, and perhaps, one day, even the ever-mute to speak. To speak aloud with a lovely voice—Bibrau—to speak—a holy consecration! Yet she is ever still. She is ever silent. Child—

Mea culpa, mea culpa, mea maxima culpa.

My daughter, Bibrau, her face ever as the moon—fixed with steely distance, though calm and placid as a frost lake's crust. I would like, with my gentle, loving finger, to break that chilly surface, to shatter it to warmth. I feel in me a rising, even as this weight within me presses me back down, to kneel before her—before this, my loving daughter—betwixt me and our own fire, with the others long departed for the fells. I should take her fingers up—Bibrau's fingers—cold as ever they are—freezing—yet I would warm them. Between my own, bending over my own gross belly, and say—oh! what I would say to her!—while my daughter stares, so plain, so still, so calm.

Mea culpa, mea culpa, mea maxima culpa.

"Bibrau . . ." I start, but my words aren't nimble. "For all you've changed . . . you've grown . . . Bibrau, I am grateful—"

Yet the look on her, just then, before the fire—the very shadow—Torvard there, staring back at me but hard. That face of hers, and eyes, so light as to seem but staring out from crystal pools, as the glow toward dark of the icebergs' frigid luster. Chilling. Furtive.

No!

I gasp and turn away, for there's a kick in me. Just then my child kicks—such a life in me, to sense already his mother's lifelong anguish! Still Bibrau is staring, waiting. The shadows are all gone. But the words just on my lips are slipped away, the loving thoughts stolen off my tongue—swept from me—gripped and torn asunder. Nay, I cannot speak it out. I rise, my stomach crumpled up, brushing off small bits of dirt and straw. Yet, under my breath, I cannot help, "Would you were more unlike your father."

She does not hear. Nay, for when I turn she's smiling. An angel's glow, such a perfect kindness. She sets aside her own crochet to help me sit again and start my thread.

I stitch. Still my hands do shake. I feel my fright and know I need protection. So I sing. My tune is "Holy, Holy, Holy!"—my voice raised up, feeling fear, upon each note, abate and fall away.

Yet, even as such calm begins, there's a sudden rush and flow of seeping wet between my thighs. I take a breath. "Bibrau"—holding hard to my own belly—"Bibrau, the baby's come."

So Bibrau lays her stitch aside. She drops down on her knees and puts her hand upon my belly and between my limbs, groping yet, as keen and sure as if she were the very wisdom-mistress. Thorbjorg herself could not have been so kind.

In spurts, the waters drain between my legs. "It is he? It is my Ossur?"—trembling first for hope, accompanied now by terror. Yet in my daughter's face there is Heaven's calm; her hands about my belly, tender. "You will help me, daughter? With the mistress gone and all the rest about and we alone? Naught could the others do but bring us water or prepare a bed where the baby soon will lie. All must be done, and soon enough, yet, fair and well, you will do better. Better yet alone. You and I—just like this—a daughter and her mother. This is but a time for us alone."

My daughter smiles. I reach to touch her hand. There's a sound— I think it is a beast there scratching. Beyond the hearth fire's ledge, upon the floor, Nattfari's bent, her fingers in the muck, handing up to catch the fire's glaze upon my belly's wasted waters. She turns to see it slowly in the air as she's squatted down, her dress pulled up above her knees.

"Nattfari!" I cry, but cannot rise for my belly's pulling. Bibrau sets me back with a firm-pressed hand, then rushes round to gaze upon the woman's madness.

"Now!" Nattfari bellows. " 'Tis mine!" Her words are grogged and hard to fathom. Bibrau grasps but Nattfari pulls away, scrambling to the darkest corner, cowering, hissing like a fevered cat when Bibrau steps but near.

"It is all right. She'll calm." But Bibrau shifts beyond my touch, easing toward the hearth-fire pit for a stick of flame, which she wafts across the corner where Nattfari's screaming.

"Nay! Think you some fire'll keep me off?" When she ventures close, Bibrau waves it fast so the flames ripple. Nattfari clutches low and crumples down against the stones.

"There she'll stay," I say, "she'll stay"—begging Bibrau but to lay the fire back into the hearth. "There, now, child, tend me, for your brother begs to come. Bibrau, help me. Guide my Ossur back into the day!"

So slight, yet she nearly lifts me, setting me on the mistress' bedding moss, kept thick and soft and with the cleanest cloth for all these weeks, prepared for me. Bibrau presses a rag to cool my fevered brow. She plies me with caresses—chill white hands and smooth, strong strokes—easing off the growing labor. Then she mixes up a draught of soothing herbs from out the mistress' stores. When, in time, the pains grow sharp so no strong draught can ease them, Bibrau untangles from her waist the mistress' keys.

They clank with all their heavy silver freedom. She hands them to me, and I know they are an honest gift—a token to ease my pain, just as once, so long ago, Thorbjorg herself untied them to ease the wrench and rend of my first labor.

I take them, reaching up to touch my Bibrau's face, still cold and calm as stone, yet her eyes a'sudden twinkled, her cheeks full flushed with a sort of twilight's brilliance, as when, before the dark, icebergs glow blue.

At once I feel another pain—a wrenching horror. The keys fall sudden from my hands. "Bibrau!" I scream, "Sweet Mary bore without such woe!" Stretching down nearly, I am desperate for them, but Nattfari races out from the corner's gloom.

"I'll have them off. . . . I'll have them to me!" muttering just as Bibrau snatches them back.

"Daughter, pray—sweet Jesus!" She ties them to my wrist so they will not fall again. "Daughter—*benedicta tu*. You are good to me—good as I never would have dreamed! In Christ—'tis true—in Christ, all tender mercies. Though none do see it in you, I see upon your face, there is goodness seeping. *Benedicta tu!* What good our Jesus Christ can do!"

And Nattfari, mumbling, "Well I know what you're about. I see him there—dangling in the corners, in the rafters, in the eaves!"

Bibrau folds the keys down within my fingers. I know they are blessed, for their metal's weight already draws away the sharpest suffering.

The pains do come, and the pains do go, one upon another. Each time, the keys within my hand grow cold, then hot as I squeeze them mightily. But the torment's greatly lessened—pain as slight as Mary's, perhaps no; yet enough, for the draughts Bibrau gives are ripe and potent and ease my soul.

As I lie and rest some breaths, with Bibrau's face above me, I think behind somewhere I see another face. Soft and dim, yet the eyes I know—they are Ossur's eyes. Now he watches with me, even as I cry and clutch the keys. "Ossur, love! Not gone, but only lost. Not forever dead—so I knew 'twas true! Knew you would return to me, for you ever have and always will. Now here again beside me even as our child—Bibrau, come! Look upon him! See!"

And my daughter smiles. It is then I know 'tis true! And Nattfari mumbling, her muddy fingers tearing at her lips.

"Ossur, here—our child will be born a freeman. He will rise upon this hillside and carry the cross which has joined our hands. He will bear your name, Ossur Ossursson, and will be of grace and Christ's own goodness. And none about our house will ever be slaves again!"

Then I push harder than I thought I ever could, for I long for him to see his child. In so long coming, now it will not wait. At last, the burning press comes between my thighs.

And there before me—turned cold and hard and dark—I see on my daughter's face again her father's grimace.

"No!" I scream. "Not here. Torvard—no. He cannot—must not come! Bibrau, stop! Bibrau! Pray—*per signum crucis*—deliver us from our enemies. An evil is upon us—the beast himself—Torvard! Satan—oh, my Lord! Hail Mary, full of grace—for the Lord God's fallen angel. Let not my child be born within his sight—"

Bibrau lifts up the burnished body. The bleeding child squirms within her clasp. I see now—my daughter's smile—I see it all at last.

BIBRAU

WHITE AND WET and dripping from my fingers. I hold him now. He cannot escape me. He, who breathes not air and yet has briefly seen the light.

Daylight.

Naught but my mother's fingers, reaching. Frightened, frantic, yet not perceiving still what I will do.

And why I'll do it. Indeed. Because I must. Because I can. Because I have ever meant to. All my life, waiting just to steal that bit which was kept from me, withheld from me, resented most of me, in all my life since my own birthing.

To steal that love which should ever have been mine.

I cannot see much now. Not much but the squirming body. The film about his face is blue and scragged with clots and drenched with womb's dross fluid. Still alive. Almost alive, yet not. Still tied upon his life's blood-cord. I could cut it sharp, but I will not. Never. So he will never fully be. Ever an almost birth, an almost—ended. Almost, yet not quite. Not quite. Not. No.

Yet for this—he is good enough to die. Good enough for sacrifice upon the stones and circle. Upon the sacred altar. Good enough—not for Thor, nor Odin—no! For who of them would want this measly little piece? His meat's not much, but, for my purpose, his meaning's better.

Better, indeed. I'll have him well, out to the once-perfect circle, now marred to ash and made a taint by those Christian bawds. It matters not. Upon this death, I will make it again perfect. Again my sacred place. My sanctuary. Sanctity. Now my invisibles will smell the scent of this small burnt flesh and they will all come back. They will take me home.

To that secret place. That hole within the ice—to that riotous brilliance. Inside the stunning blue. I smile. My fylgie's here beside me; I feel him breathing. And I know my mother sees him, too. Amusing, truly, that now, finally, she sees, yet knows not what she sees; thinks at first it is beloved, then sees it hated, then sees it ill. Evil. Ha! What is evil? What is good? What is within her sight? Only all that's true.

Now listen to my mother. Listen to her! Mock! What tripe! What weary lamentations! Now she begs me—she looks on me as if I ever were a Christian. Fool with her jibbered chants and useless words. Me, a Christian, as foolish, wanton, useless as herself. She looks upon me now, wide with want of comfort—smiling almost—reaching out to me as if my hands were not the clutch that held back death. Her eyes wide ope'd but body pale and, between her legs, the afterbirth almost exposed.

I turn away. There is naught about me, only the fire and crazed Nattfari rising from the corner there, flashing a fluttering flame before my eyes. I think I feel some warmth of it, but more, the failing warmth of the body in my fingers. I look down upon the birth-mare–whore. She is nearly still, but trembling slightly. I take the child, this newborn brother whom my mother begs to let her hold.

Take him high upon my hands while the cord wraps once, then twice, then three times round his tiny shoulders, stretching tighter. I feel him slipping, squirming from my hold, but he cannot free himself. There is no freedom from this menace. This fate—I hold it in my hands alone.

Slowly the breath which will never come slips from him. Slowly his mincing movements surely still. I hear nothing, though my mother must be screaming. I hear nothing but a ringing rush within my ears, then a high-pitched shriek, as if the wind were racing by me. Haggard, wrenching, rough with sound. Even my fylgie drops his pipes to listen. Still it comes. Still the sound, so harsh I would hold my hands against the shrill.

But I watch my fylgie's face—it is twisted up with laughter. Oh! Such laughter as he knows I love—to hear him laugh that way, all menacing and lowly! That laugh, yet why? When all I hear is horrid tone.

Yet then I know. Somehow I know it. That sound's a scream, and I know that scream's my own.

The Girl Who Sits in the Blue

THORBJORG

In the end, there was little trouble for it. My foster-daughter was a slave, though none would have thought it so from the power she had learned to wield. Yet power, in the end, is a brittle, fragile thing—when used for ill, as is most oft. Hers, in its last, was cruel beyond all cruelty's reason.

The talk about the Althing come that summer was how much she had used such skill to cozen me, and well to punish hard her mother. Both were true. Yet, most, such talk was only thick among the thralls. The freemen, fraught with other fair attentions, scorned such smallish gossip and trifling woes. First there was the death of King Tryggvason, killed upon a battleground against the Dane and Swedish kings. Yet talk of Christ still lingered, in some small part because of my own last prophecy's result: upon the spring, Gudrid returned from Vesterbygd a widow of some haunting sickness, and now was courted well again by an Icelander just come on Greenland's shores. The man to be her mate was called Karlsefni.

As closer drew that second chime of the Christian bells, the Althing there grew thick with wedding preparations, but some did think to remember other, lesser things, and came to see my foster-daughter tried.

Upon the Gardar plain, Thorbjorn Glora stood as the Althing's Lawspeaker—there upon the earthy mound, calling swift the trial's course, as Bibrau struggled between strong men's arms. "Thorbjorg Seeress," he uttered out, "claim you this mute girl to be your bond-thrall?"

Bibrau's head held high, her feet planted wide upon the muddy, trampled earth. I stated, "Yes. I claim her."

"Claim her who's tried and nearly killed the infant Ossur Ossursson?"

" 'Tis true the infant was born within my house. True, as well, that he still lives. Yet I was not there, and when I returned found only a troubled babe, ill with heat, thick of air, and much convulsing."

"Yet the woman Katla, your once–bond-thrall, some one year passing freed and a baptized Christian, claims that he was not born so—that this harm and sickness were wrought by her own daughter."

I nodded to it.

"Too, this boy, now living in your house, is also free and even Christian-born?"

"So he is." I nodded once again.

Slowly Glora pulled upon his dusky beard. Slowly came his voice, dark as winter, though the summer sun fell bright upon the Althing field. "Far more ill is this foul act than mere exposure's crime. If she had not been stopped, 'twould be fullest murder, condemned by both the Christian and our ancient laws. Say you, Thorbjorg, some word in her defense?"

"I have none," came my answer. "There is none, for what she's done—if she's done—is far beyond my ken."

What little crowd stood near was stiff and hushed with whispers. Yet a bellow came from the rigid throng. "None, good mistress? No defense for your own small girl?"

The crier pressing through their midst was Thorhall Hunter. He thrashed hard to cut the watchers back. "None, when she's healed already half this Greenland? None, that these settlements are rife with gain from her wisdom's skill? None, that she's birthed so many hearty babes even before your very watchful eye? None, that this, her skill, was given by your own hand?"

"I have none," I said again.

"Then why? Think you not, perhaps the child should have died but rightly, being sickly born, ensnared in the Norns' cruel threads?

Why should the girl wish to kill her own blood brother when she had learned to heal and birth so well?"

I said, "Thorhall, know, the child was bruised where 'twas set on him to strangle, the very cord stretched and nearly torn where it had twined about his throat. Too, certain marks on him to be as sacrifice before the very stones still standing. Well you know it—you have set such flames yourself—no ill-wrought beast will suit upon the holy fire."

"And for this you condemn her? For this, when all her world is lost? And yours? And mine? Lost upon this talk of Christians! For this—but a tiny piece of cold, dead flesh—to bring back our own true gods?"

"Enough!" called the Lawspeaker. "Enough of pagans' speech! What of it, Thorbjorg Seeress?"

"I have no more to speak than what I've said."

"Then stand back, for there is a proper witness. The thrall Nattfari."

"Nattfari?" shouted Thorhall. "But a witless fool! So she's ever been since her babe was blighted—since—"

"Nattfari," I said, to keep him from his cause, "has stood by me since a well-built, tolerable girl."

The Lawspeaker countered, "It is for Thorbjorg to disavow, for, though Nattfari be wise or dull, she is bonded and must speak upon her mistress' favor. Will we hear this witness?"

I answered, "Yes."

"And can we trust her truth?"

I sighed. "It is speech against me and my own. Yet she'll bear no punishment except for lying. Well you can trust her. She will speak but true, for, though she's weak of reason, 'twas her hand which kept him living. She speaks of naught, day and night, since the deed was done."

"Bring her in, then. Let her speak yet sanely."

They brought her, wrangled up with a thrall as usher: Nattfari, limping, groping, thrusting off the slave's thick palms, then rushing, falling before the Speaker's knees.

"Yea, I saw her! Saw this girl, this demon. Changeling! Evil from the start. Evil. Well I knew it! Fooled us. Fooled us all! Would have had the child dead—my own sweet girl—"

"You see?" Thorhall shouted. "How she speaks? But of ancient happenings! A daughter? Nay! She speaks of her own blood—born and dead some seven years ago. She speaks from her own madness!"

The Lawspeaker turned. "Nattfari, tell us calmly. What child? A boy born, or a girl?"

"A boy! A boy! I saw between his legs! Tiny it was—smaller than a finger. And red—red was in her eyes! Alight and striking out! Dragon's tongues, burning out with screeching flames!"

"Then?"

"I cast her out—cast her with a fire's stick. Never trust her! Took the babe. I took him, and she flew upon my flames. Flew! Never touch him—never. Not my child!" Nattfari fell then into a fit of tears. In her arms, stroking air, rocking hardily as if upon a child, until her keeper touched her—gently, yet she flailed at him, writhing, hissing hard with menace, till he grabbed her back and took her fast away.

All the while, Glora twined his fist inside his beard, waiting so long, the crowd mumbled some and mustered. At last, he cleared his throat.

"Are there no more? None to stand beside this bond-thrall or against her?"

"There is one," came a voice. All turned upon its timbre. Katla stood by the edging of the Althing ground.

"Come, then," Glora summoned, and though no one had thought she would, slowly she came, bearing forth her child.

Such as was born to her: raw and ragged, nary but an ill-bent beast. In truth, before their Christ did come, he would have set full well upon the fell-slopes. Such, his death would have been a mercy. But now his soul would be preserved, as I had heard her priest say upon my own hearth fire, *"In nomine Patris, et Filii, et Spiritus Sancti. Amen."*

"Katla Christian, is this babe your child?"

"He is, or what is left of him, now this deed is done."

THE GIRL WHO SITS IN THE BLUE 🌸 435

"What do you recall?"

"Not very much. The flames were thick, and smoke, and my head full-hot and groggy. Yet enough to say there were flames and shrieks. Then a flurry and my child raised and the cord still pulling from my innards—that I do remember well."

"Then what came?"

"The scent of searing flesh. Our men's footfalls from the fells. Their hammer-fists upon the door. It took some long till the hinges broke—so it seemed—till they fell upon her and dragged her off. And Bibrau screaming."

At this, she took a breath, then held the infant higher. "This is what is left of him. He is dull and mangled, but as he lives I will love him for it. Yet, for her, with this wretched act I bear no hope for healing. Though, in truth, till now—upon good Christ—I have wished and prayed and tried."

At this, the baby set to crying. Such a pitiable bawl, bare a breath and nar' a sound. Yet she held him to her breast and bore him forth, and he started sucking. Sucking, while I sensed full well he would live, though ever he would suffer long.

Now the crowd grew coarse upon its edges, for there were other fights and bargains near of a grander, greater cause. Yet Thorbjorn Glora held them with his fists raised up. "All hear! Hear all and bear full witness! This bond-thrall Bibrau—on testimony of this slave Nattfari and her mistress Thorbjorg and on such speech as her own freed and honored mother bore—is full-convicted of trying murder, of nearly casting off this newborn infant and this honest Christian soul. Her treachery, though the child lives, will be sentenced as full murder, and all such charge and punishment as if the boy had died."

The crowd then groaned, for it was a hearty strike, even for such gruesome business. Yet Glora raised up hands. "Just so, first her mistress. Say our laws, Thorbjorg, that you must bear accounting. You must yield some fault for your own thrall's acts, though I know too well already you bear the pain. So it will be that you will forfeit all such good as your thrall might yet deliver. To you this girl will be as cattle lost or gold yet stole away. You will take no profit from her loss, for this is as the wergeld—the blood payment—to a freeman for a killing by a thrall.

"Yet there is more. This girl, en-thralled, can make no rightful restitution for herself. Still, she must be made to pay for her trans-gression. Bibrau will suffer the law of this Greenland itself—hard as the law will hold, and the law upon this frigid land is harsh indeed. So this child, nearly yet a woman, will be set upon and banished from our midst. From this place she'll hie, and none about will give her lawful aiding. She'll have none to protect, none to feed, none to clothe her, none to shelter, nor to lend her warmth. No retribution will come if she is wrongly used or rightly killed. She'll be shunned from the com-pany of others. She'll trespass not upon another's lands except to cross beyond our settlements' bounds to find some place where she might live awhile. And there, if she finds some living among these shores of rock and ice, she will bear alone until she dies."

For a time, that was the final word. No one spoke. Not even Thorhall. He stood silent, reddened, fierce with rage, then turned, looking on me with a tainted eye, as if to blame that I should dare to let this statement lie.

Yet what would I say but that I ever knew it would? Knew the truth. Knew it long before it ever came to pass. It was clearly written—not upon some stick or stone all scratched about with runes, but in the blood borne so very long ago, e'er upon my foster-daughter's first beginning.

As quick, the next case came upon the Althing field. Yet my foster-daughter—Bibrau would not have it. Nay, she flailed and fled from her captors' grasp and flew before the Lawspeaker's mound. There, be-fore his feet, she begged some silent witness, some wordless want, some charity of kind. But the Lawspeaker, looking down upon her frantic eyes, sensing now full well her wily tricks and that strange, be-guiling visage, struck down sharply. "Piteous girl, would you beg upon me now? It is too late to pray upon our mercy."

Bibrau writhed and reeled away, looking e'er beseeching. The crowd fell back as she hurled herself and crawled and scraped across the edging of the Althing ground.

Now Bibrau could barely stand, her face set hard into the dirt, her shoulders bearing up her weight, her knees tripping on her dress, which was tearing into tatters. So she crept, yet came upon a stop, for she saw at once before whose boots she'd crawled.

Torvard stood full-still, towering over as she turned up from the soil, her face flushed sudden white and pure as a chunk of quartz upturned upon a new-plowed field. Torvard did not move. He did not speak or slip away, but only stared against these watchers' murmurs. Few remained who remembered now how their fates were bound. Yet, for a breath, all felt her cold, steel eyes upon him. And Torvard—his face grew white with terror.

While I watched. I stood aback and watched. Too late. Too late it was to claim or e'er accuse. Too late to turn back upon the trail hard-pounded. I knew what must be done. I went myself. With a tug, I heaved and hied Bibrau off from Torvard's shoes. She fought me with a wild fury. She tore my cloak and nearly knocked the staff from out my fingers. So I threw her off. "Child, what? You would turn so quick to blame another? Ne'er before were you ashamed for your own fault. Do not play your coy tricks now, my foster-daughter. I'd thought you would take this punishment but proudly. Proud as you have suffered all. Proud as you beguiled. Proud as you had won my love. Proud as you twisted all that was ever good and spat it back upon our lot as pit and curse and offal."

She turned but more to me, shaking, pleading, crawling, raising up her eyes. I pressed her back. "Daughter, indeed, I thought I'd taught you better. But now I think again, perhaps I should have taught you more of better things." I shoved her off. "Bibrau, go. Be off and banished. The time for you is no longer. Our time here has passed away."

That day, my foster-daughter left me. Such a startle on the cold stone face, yet not a whimper. None, as I expected. Not a subtle gasp or a healthy tear. Few I think even watched her go but I and her own mother; and Thorhall, who let her hang upon his arm some time, pleading silent with her gaping eyes as he talked with other men who would go again to Vinland. But they would never speak their plans while she lingered there beside. Anyway, he was forbidden now to take her off, though I think he would have if he could, at least to spite the Christians.

But no one else, in all the glee of Christian weddings and the hope of rise and might.

None, except perhaps Torvard.

So it was, that night, while the sun set not upon the far horizon but hovered low and shed bare warmth, the fires burned in the Althing booths, but my foster-daughter stood above. From an unnamed cleft, she watched. I knew because I felt her eyes, as I almost always have; for, anywhere they lit, they burned. Burned with a kind of passion. I had not thought, but now I knew for certain: it was hate. Hate that I did feed with whims and skills for something greater. Yet she took them from my hands and churned them with her hunger, then spat them back with but a fiery rage.

Bibrau watched from where she stood. I did my best to turn away—my best, but most, I sensed my eyes kept slipping up to where she lingered.

She was my heart's own daughter, even after all that had come to pass. Perhaps it was foolish to rest upon this child, to lay on her this vain, false hope, on her to cling when the rocks were already all but wasting. For, in the end, I could not hold—could not resist—all is swept by the raging sea. So she was destroyed—every twist and grain worn down to but a tracing. Bare, and then this last swept upon the reckless waves.

KATLA

THAT WAS ALL some years ago. Yet still I hear my daughter's screaming. Most at nights upon the spring, when I wake to dark and think I hear the sound.

Such a sound, so low and scratched and fearful, that sound of a wrenching pain, stretched and strained to force its burden out. Such a sound not meant for human ears.

Yet again, I listen harder, and in time I know it is but the silence of my fear. Sometimes now I have learned that, when I still my cringe and pry my hands away, that sound is not her voice at all, but the shrilling of the whistled wind.

Too, sometimes I think I hear a baby's whimper—not some frail refrain, as my child Ossur's ever was, but a hale and certain cry, as it should have been. At that, more hard, I hide my head and hold my tears against his mounded shoulder. Even now, though nearly grown a man, my Ossur rests by me.

Still sometimes the tears do fall, even after all these passing seasons. Then my son awakes and gazes, soft and frightened through a child's eyes which will never grow much old, till, slowly, I have learned to tell him that this brutish fright is but the faintest flying off, the bounding note of a jaeger or a gull heading up to sky from hill, then slipping low, far down the slope, to below the sea. To this he sleeps contented, while I lie cold, hard, long, listening to that darkened keening, till I hear at last only the surf lapping up its frothy foam.

Sometimes, as I go about my chores on such dawns after such forbidding wakenings, I remember yet again how we came upon that hill that morning after: I and my once-mistress, together but we two, to see what had become of our once-own girl.

We went, though we knew it was neither right nor needed nor well-wise. Yet how could we not, after half the night staying far from sleep and watching up from our cold Althing booth? That steady little flicker, just a speck of flame upon that hill. Then, with the morn', but a puff of smoke, a lingering tendril. Then, even as we watched, 'twas gone.

We watched it, both, and spoke not much. Yet both, upon the other's untoned turning, found our footsteps mete to travel toward that slope. I, leaving my child in Arngunn's arms, hearing Thorbjorg from behind, pausing to await her proud yet aching stumble, then reaching out to grasp her arm in mine, entwined.

There was little sign of Bibrau. Just a pile of ash snatched up and dancing on the wind. From there I turned away, looking out across the Gardar meadow, there seeing what she must have seen that dawn: all our booths about, and the paths our feet made, a riot of muddy, twining snakes between our civil market-stands; the muck-wracked field where the horses and the strong men countered; the longhouse, Einar's roof stacks smoking up in puffs of gray against the frigid sky; and, beyond, upon the sea, the specks of bergs which floated of their own beguiling, themselves the mighty power shifted on the breath of summer winds while all our great ships drifted, so tiny there beside.

I looked down once more. On the ground before my feet were some odd pressed footsteps in the moss and campion matting. Beyond, my mistress' knees, my mistress' hands: in them, a few clipped branches from a willow's limb. She bent over one of them, mulling it slowly, turning it but once and then again.

The mistress Thorbjorg sighed.

I knelt beside her, catching at her hands. There, touching suddenly on the bough, were the certain, lucid etchings.

"Runes," she answered, without my even wondering, "just as I had taught them. Fine and ordered, neater than she's done before." Then she turned the bough again. "Here. My hand on hers, I remember etching with the sharpened blade. The secret runes—the shapes of prophecy." Then she turned the stick once more. There, but a sweep of strokes. She did not speak or draw from me as I fingered at them slowly.

"What does it read?" I asked upon the pause.

She uttered, without a lingered breathing, " 'In the blue, the blue, awaiting the invisibles—Bibrau is the name of the girl who sits in the blue.' "

After that, ne'er about did ever see her. Perhaps, and well, she was lost to this Greenland's cold. Yet some have said, when a calf's gone missing, 'tis she who's trailing blood from the byre stall. And others, too, when a firebrand's found doused before a glacier's tongue, or when strange footprints mar the springtime's mud, or oft when a child's gone sick with fever overnight, that Bibrau must have set her evil hand or foot or her evil eye upon them.

She's become as a haugbo or a draug, haunting the shadowed corners of these rocky fells. But never seen with open eyes. Ne'er again. Not even on the distant shores where these settlements grow thinly. Ne'er even beyond, in far Nordsetur, where only men go hunting and are long for lust. But none about has ever boasted of a lone, strange, silent girl.

Within our own house, no one ever spoke of her. We went about as if she herself had never been. 'Twas like a wretched dream from which we'd sudden waked to find our mistress ailing. It took not long before she withered before our eyes.

At the end, Thorbjorg was but a brittle bone, yet her gaze grew ever wider. With each day, her body wasted as I and Kol and all the others served upon her hand. In the end, barely could she part her cracking lips, yet, on her last few breaths, I heard her pagan praying. Come and going. Though never once did she heed my plea to take the Christian oath. Yet I would swear what she must have seen upon her final vision: 'twas sure divine as the light of our Saviour Jesus Christ himself.

Before her death, Thorbjorg scratched the runes to give all her thralls their freedom, and to Kol this land which we had worked together for so long. We stayed there for some time. Svan and Alof dug the earth, and Kol made the rite to lay Thorbjorg proper in it. Heavy were the stones laid down upon her feet and around her, set to draw the ship to sail her to her nether world. Kol slew a fine filly, recent-born, and burned in sacrifice its meat. And though I ate none of it, and was still through all the ritual, it was ever right to have Thorbjorg praised and buried so. She had been but a faithful thrall to the old Norse gods. To send her off to the Christian Hell would have done her wrongly. Surely Jesus himself would not have had it so.

That season, our household grew quite still. Last I'd heard, Torvard followed off to Vinland, but on his Freydis' sly command, came again to treachery and murder. Too, Thorhall left for Vinland's shores, and never were we to ever see him more. There were tales of how he died, beaten, enslaved upon the Irish shore, blown off his course after calling up to Old Redbeard Thor from a mountain crag in a fit of tremendous hunger. So he, too, was near the last who never took the Christian vow; and his end came swift and sadly and forever.

We went about at the Tofafjord house as if the mistress were only gone to do her prophesying rounds, I tending to my child, the others to their usual chores. But with the winter's winds and the cold and drip and howl, I found I could not bear to stay much more. Too much, too long within that house hearing those sounds, those creaks, those shrieks of memory. With the breaking of the frost and the first small skiff set on our fjord's turning, I waved about and begged that I and my child be taken off to the only other place I knew we might yet go.

Now, though I no longer am a slave, I am servant to the risen God. It is much the same at this Gardar church: I cook, I clean, I glean, I weave, I sew the master's clothing. My son does what he can, yet so stooped and dull of wit, at most he can but sweep the church's pounded floor. Meanwhile, the priest intones, his ragged hand outstretching toward my child, "Take care and tend but well upon the pitiable, as Jesus Christ would heal all wounds!"

Still we are as bond-thralls, but now of my own making. Who is to blame for the lot that has been my own?

It is best, I think. It is all but right to pay fully for my sins. So I bear with patience such pain that's due to all who are flesh-born. Yet there are times, long times, when the wind does blow and I hear upon it all my ancient hatreds. On such nights, I often dream I stand above those circle stones, now wrecked and overgrown and bound with weeds. Still I see it well enough: the scar on the earth's green bosom. I think on mine, long healed but ever marked with madness, and I wonder well if, after all, I will ever sit by my mother's side at the table of the Lord.

THORBJORG

SO YOU TOLD ME. So you showed me. And I did think, Alfather, I had listened well, but now I know I could not hear. Not all of it. Not for Bibrau nor myself nor any which would happen. Only some small whisperings of your wisdom-warnings, and these themselves too often misperceived.

Now I see to the endless reaches. Though ever I have known nary would last upon this earth. Ever chaos. Ever dissolution. Still, I had not believed. So I sought to fight when 'twas a fruitless battle. Now I see: even these Greenland settlements will fade.

So you tried to speak that night with the rune-twigs thrown from out my fingers. Scattered by the Christian priest before those many chieftains' eyes, they burned. I thought in this would come our ending: yours and mine, destroyed upon this Church's passion. Surely Bibrau saw it, too. She was frightened—that I do remember. Not long aft, her vile acts upon those Christians' sacred grounds.

Yet, even then, neither she nor I did fully understand. That cast had borne an even longer shadow. Some years beyond, but a blink in the greater stretch of time, the seas grow cold. The settlements at first forgot' amidst such wiles and whims on distant Europe's shores. Wars and peaces, plagues and changed prosperities. Years will pass. When, at last, the settlements recalled, one ship will dare to break this Greenland's ice, and here find silence. Mists above a weedy field. The settlers' fates unknown. No final word. But a scattering of empty stalls in crumbled byres. In their vacant houses, not even wasted bones.

So, this fate will come. The invisibles will quick reclaim. Made from the rime of Ymir's sweat, this Greenland ever was the dark ones' refuge. Cold and bleak and full indifferent. We were but trespassers here, blithe indeed to think we could hold this place for long.

Still, in it I sense somehow Bibrau's touch and leaning, as if she herself had twisted up those runes to change the shape of the Norns' thick threads. 'Twas nothing I had taught her. Perhaps such things are ever taught upon themselves. Or, more like, by something darker, barely named, and better left unknown.

In the blue. In the blue. Awaiting the invisibles . . . As if she were one of them. As if she could e'er and join them. Perhaps she has, and still abides. Her bitter retribution lingers.

So it will be, though it matters little. Old Graybeard, it is nearly finished. And then—all your offspring, your poetry, your wise prediction—soon there will be no trace. None but of rumor, scoff, and scorn. Soon enough, even your great son Thor—his thunder will be silenced. When the clouds do tower up and roll, they'll say it is this new god's might, or perhaps some other, distance force we can barely yet discern.

So it is. And will be. Still, I can regret it. Will there be no Ragnarok? No death of all the gods? No mighty battle where the metal's clash will crash to end this earth, only then to be reborn? Where is this final anguish? Long have I waited for it, this last rising, this new rebirth. Here I sit before your table, but the feast is bare, the mead-horns half full, and little do the warriors cheer for fight. Now their sounds are faded, Alfather, overwhelmed by hymn and Latin cure. There is no lightning, no thunder, and no blood—a bloodless combat—that ever-dull straw death, shunned by warriors, even as it was my own.

Though now straw death, upon this Christ, is no longer thought a weakness. It is mighty-praised, met with solemn rites and no more reprehension. Still, lying there, those dried straw spines did spike; they broke my skin and riddled me with torment.

Now I am survived it. I, who departed beneath that bitter shade and expected well to be full-shunned before Valhalla's gates. Yet I found you here, before your very threshold. Waiting. Found you telling Heimdall to let me through your door. And you, even you yourself, reaching out to me, taking up my withered fingers. Though no blood ever spilled upon them, not in mighty battles cut about with ax or sword—yet well you know, have known it all along, that all my battles fought with rune and twig and herb and breath and fire were waged and weighty-managed for your cause.

Still I am your warrior, as I have ever been. I hungered for this place beside you, and now I am here, my hands upon your table-board. I look about me—the stones of great Valhalla—growing thick with moss. Your roof is fallen, and none about do set up quick to mend it rightly. Still we eat, we drink, we rally, waiting yet for time—though now I know they'll call the battle not Ragnarok but Armageddon, and what gods they'll call upon that fight are named Lord and Jesus Christ.

It matters not. The old gods pass, and others, new ones, take their places. It matters not—not what they are named, so long as they are called.

Still I mourn. I cannot help—what will come upon that day? What force will raise up armies? Will meet upon that barren plain? Will fight against those blackish beasts? Will wrap Fenris' jaw about Thor's great wrist while he strangles yet the Midgard snake?

None. E'er none. For this siege will take another shape. So you, Almighty Asa, you who bear so many shapes and forms and names, now you take another. Yet still I know you. You cannot fool me. I know your face, for you have shown it to me often. I know your lips, for you have given me my breath and shaped my very tongue upon your speaking.

I am here, Alfather. Ever your servant, even as our one world dies. Yet it transforms into another. All of us, Old One-Eye, who were ever truly warriors, will be here and needed, there and then and when, as we ever were before.

Until that time, I wait beside you. True, my vision now is weak and all my wisdom faulty; yet, also true, all my words and sight are yours. I will speak for you as ever I have done. True, if fewer listen now, it is not for me to blame. Yet do not forsake them, Alfather. Have pity on them, Asa—on all of us who spoke your name—as now we watch our old world fade away.

What—that? No, 'tis not the graying haze of the fire's smoke. No. It is something more. I see it, too, though my eyes are weary. Weary, yet I'll look again. For you. For your One Eye, all-seeing, I will look with my imperfect two. Yes, I see the shroud. Falling. Softly, slowly, gently, firmly. Yes, I am beside you. Here, let me near. Let me lay your head upon my lap and I will stroke your brow. There. And sing for you all those songs which were known before the tree Yggdrasil ever set its roots. I will sing you off to sleep, beloved, and with that song I will fill up both our dreams.

HISTORICAL NOTES

The main characters of *The Thrall's Tale* are at most a footnote in the well-recorded history of the Norse. Known more familiarly as the Vikings, these warriors, farmers, adventurers, and pastoralists spread their influence east as far as Russia and west all the way to Greenland and the New World.

The Norse and particularly the Icelanders were among the most literate European cultures of their day, inscribing their oral history and genealogy in the form of eddas—poetry and prose chronicling their mythological and heroic heritage—and sagas, semihistoric tales of feuds and families, kingships, and battles lost and won. As is often the case, such grand themes generally overlook the mundane details of ordinary people's lives. For this grittier flavor, I turned to archaeological evidence of conditions in Greenland and elsewhere in the Viking world in the late tenth and early eleventh centuries.

Both *Eirik's Saga* and *Graenlendinga Saga*, collectively known as the *Vinland Sagas*, relate the journey of twenty-five ships and four hundred settlers from Breidafjord ("Broad Fjord"), Iceland, to Greenland in A.D. 985/6. Eirik the Red (here Eirik Raude) led this precarious venture to the distant, unclaimed territory he'd discovered three years earlier, while outlawed from Iceland for several killings over an argument about some house timbers. As both sagas note, Eirik gave the country its appealing name to make it more attractive to those he could coax to follow.

Only one of the principal characters in *The Thrall's Tale*, Thorbjorg the Seeress, appears in *Eirik's Saga*—and there only briefly—

foretelling the destiny of Gudrid Thorbjornsdatter, who journeyed from Iceland to Greenland, then to Vinland, and eventually returned to Iceland to become the matriarch of an eminent Icelandic family.

Katla was named for "the fire burning beneath the mountain's ice"—the glacier-capped Icelandic volcano that, along with volcanic Mount Hekla and several craters in Oraefi, were said to be the mouths of both the Old Norse and Christian underworlds.

The name Bibrau was carved on a runestick much like that described in the final chapter of the novel. Discovered at Narssaq, Greenland, not far from where Eirik the Red's homestead, Brattahlid, once stood, it bears Swedish-Norwegian *futhark*, or short-twig, runes, like those used for chapter numbering in this volume. Since short-twig runes became obsolete at the start of the eleventh century, the artifact can be dated to the earliest settlement period. The runestick now resides at the Danmarks Nationalmuseet, Copenhagen.

Ossur Asbjarnarsson also derives from an archaeological source. His name was inscribed on a grave marker discovered on an island off Ivigtut in Greenland, an area known as Mellombygd (the "Middle Settlement") during the Norse settlement period.

Torvard Einarsson evolved from a composite of several minor mentions in the *Vinland Sagas*: first, that Einarsfjord was originally settled by a chieftain named Einar; second, that Einarsfjord is the location of the farm Gardar; and, third, that Freydis Eiriksdatter, Eirik the Red's illegitimate daughter, married a man called Torvard, primarily to inherit the vast, prosperous homestead Gardar. Considering time frame and various laws of inheritance, I combined these disparate facts to assume that Torvard was Einar's firstborn son.

Freydis Eiriksdatter is a powerful figure in both *Vinland Sagas*. In one, she is a vicious manipulator who coerces her husband, Torvard, into committing numerous murders, then commits several more herself. In another, she is seen in Vinland, pregnant, terrifying hostile "skraelings" (the Old Norse term for the native North Americans they encountered—probably either the Micmac or Beothuk Indians) by bearing her breast and slapping it with a sword.

Who first discovered North America is contradicted in the sagas.

Graenlendinga Saga states that Bjarne Herjolfsson first spotted the continent, but in his rush to meet his father in Greenland, neglected to investigate; whereby Leif Eiriksson purchased his ship and set sail to explore properly what he would eventually call Vinland. *Eirik's Saga* flatly states that Leif was the first to discover Vinland, and also credits him with bringing Christianity to Greenland at King Olaf Tryggvason's request, as well as with saving some shipwrecked Christians, including Gudrid Thorbjornsdatter. In 1960, evidence of an Old Norse settlement dating from around A.D. 1000 was found at L'Anse aux Meadows in Newfoundland, Canada, giving historicity to the Viking sagas' claims.

Leif's mother, Thjoldhilde, built the first Christian church in Greenland, also around A.D. 1000, and, according to *Eirik's Saga*, refused to live with her husband until he became a Christian, too. The outline of Thjoldhilde's church is still visible today in the raised grasses on a hill overlooking Brattahlid's ruined longhouse in Qagssiarssuk, Greenland.

Thorhall the Hunter appears in *Eirik's Saga* as a foul-mouthed troublemaker who never gives up his faith in his patron god, Thor. He persists in his beliefs, bringing illness and misery to the Christians around him, and pays for his devotion with eventual enslavement and death in Ireland.

The Norse Greenlandic settlements persisted for almost five hundred years, providing walrus-ivory tusks from the distant northern hunting grounds, high-quality wadmal cloth, and pure-white falcons and polar bears shipped alive to Europe's kings. But economics and nature itself turned against the settlers. With the onset of the Little Ice Age in the early fourteenth century, temperatures declined only a couple of degrees, but the deteriorating climate put the already marginal settlements at risk. Demand for Greenlandic trade goods waned, and an increase in sea-ice made the difficult ocean voyage even less profitable.

In the mid-fourteenth century, Norwegian priest Ivar Bardarsson attempted to visit his long-neglected Christian flock in Greenland. He arrived in Vesterbygd to find "nobody, either Christians or heathens, only some wild cattle and sheep." Settlement at Austerbygd languished soon after. Last word of Austerbygd was an announcement in the *King's Mirror* from September 1408 of the marriage of Thorstein Olafsson and Sigrid Bjørnsdatter at Hvalsey Church. The wedding was well attended, with two priests officiating and guests from Greenland and abroad. But the ship that, a few years later, carried the couple to Iceland was the last ever known to touch Norse Greenland's shores.

Judith Lindbergh
2006

ACKNOWLEDGMENTS

My appreciation goes to Drs. Thomas McGovern and Christian Keller, and a host of other Norse archaeologists and scholars whose work informed many aspects of this novel. I am also indebted to Dr. William Fitzhugh and Elisabeth Ward of the Smithsonian Institution's National Museum of Natural History, for their enthusiastic support.

To my writers group, I owe incalculable gratitude: Stephanie Cowell, Peggy Harrington, Elsa Rael, Katherine Kirkpatrick, Casey Kelly, Ruth Henderson, the late Isabelle Holland; and to Madeleine L'Engle, for bringing us together and inspiring us all.

My warmest thanks belongs to Ada Brown Mather, for teaching me to "stay on the thread of the scene"; to Dorothy and William Berinstein, for many dusty texts scoured from forgotten shelves of used bookstores; to Albie Collins, Jr., Sarah Reid, and Gloria Malter, for support in both substance and spirit; to Penny Stoodley, Holley Bishop, Leslie Nelson, and the many other beloved friends who buoyed my early efforts; and to those few who shared this manuscript in its developing stages.

Finally, to my agent, Emma Sweeney, and my editor, Carole DeSanti, I am deeply grateful.

Da 164-165

<u>Xerox</u> for 20

(2pdv)

daught/mother/
Thorbjorg's ——→ Katla's
page   Xe

Bribau

①

Sun 20 March 2016

Begn w/ Patty Crane's story

Then read ⊕ dd/poem —

Then Fulton, Swedish, Crane of Cyne"

② Intro Thrall's Tale   pdv
164-165   3

Close w/ birth of baby

to dd →crane/death